WHAT THE PRESS SAYS A
AND HIS JACK SHE

"Asia's most stylish and atmospheric writer of crime fiction. In between the lines of his plot, Needham's provocative views about Asian culture jump at you from almost every page." — *The Straits Times* Singapore

"One of the distinctive strengths of Needham's novels is that he has the urban landscape of Asia down absolutely cold. He sketches it in sharp, sure strokes using language that is razor-edged with a touch of melancholy, at times even richly poetic. In his raw power to bring the street-level flavor of contemporary Asian cities to life, Needham is Michael Connelly with steamed rice." — *The Bangkok Post*

"Jake Needham has a knack for bringing intricate plots to life. His stories blur the line between fact and fiction and have a ripped-from-the-headlines feel." — *CNNgo*

"What you will not get is pseudo-intellectual new-wave Asian literature, sappy relationship writing, or Bangkok bargirl sensationalism. This is top-class fiction that happens to be set in an Asian context. As you turn the pages and follow Jack Shepherd in his quest for the truth, you can smell the roadside food stalls and hear the long-tail boats roar up and down the Chao Praya River." — Singapore Airlines *SilverKris* Magazine

"Needham certainly knows where a few bodies are buried." — *Asia Inc.*

"Thrillers written with a wry sense of irony in the mean-streets, fast-car, tough-talk tradition of Elmore Leonard. Needham has found acclaim as one of the best-selling English-language writers in Asia."
— *The Edge* Singapore

A WORLD OF TROUBLE

BOOKS BY JAKE NEEDHAM

The Jack Shepherd Crime Novels
LAUNDRY MAN
KILLING PLATO
A WORLD OF TROUBLE

Other Novels
THE BIG MANGO
THE AMBASSADOR'S WIFE

A WORLD OF TROUBLE

JAKE NEEDHAM

Text copyright © 2012 Jake Raymond Needham

Cover art by OpalWorks Co Ltd

Published in 2012 by Marshall Cavendish Editions
An imprint of Marshall Cavendish International
1 New Industrial Road, Singapore 536196

All rights reserved

No part of this publication may be reproduced, stored in a retrieval system or transmitted, in any form or by any means, electronic, mechanical, photocopying, recording or otherwise, without the prior permission of the copyright owner. Requests for permission should be addressed to the Publisher, Marshall Cavendish International (Asia) Private Limited, 1 New Industrial Road, Singapore 536196. Tel: (65) 6213 9300, Fax: (65) 6285 4871. E-mail: genref@sg.marshallcavendish.com

The publisher makes no representation or warranties with respect to the contents of this book, and specifically disclaims any implied warranties or merchantability or fitness for any particular purpose, and shall in no events be liable for any loss of profit or any other commercial damage, including but not limited to special, incidental, consequential, or other damages.

Other Marshall Cavendish Offices: Marshall Cavendish International. PO Box 65829, London EC1P 1NY, UK • Marshall Cavendish Corporation. 99 White Plains Road, Tarrytown NY 10591-9001, USA • Marshall Cavendish International (Thailand) Co Ltd. 253 Asoke, 12th Flr, Sukhumvit 21 Road, Klongtoey Nua, Wattana, Bangkok 10110, Thailand • Marshall Cavendish (Malaysia) Sdn Bhd, Times Subang, Lot 46, Subang Hi-Tech Industrial Park, Batu Tiga, 40000 Shah Alam, Selangor Darul Ehsan, Malaysia.

Marshall Cavendish is a trademark of Times Publishing Limited

National Library Board, Singapore Cataloguing-in-Publication Data
Needham, Jake.
A world of trouble / Jake Needham. –
Singapore : Marshall Cavendish Editions, 2012.
p. cm.
ISBN : 978-981-4361-51-4 (pbk.)
1. Conspiracies – Fiction. 2. Thailand – Fiction. I. Title.

PS3564.E228
813.6 — dc22   OCN775714254

Printed in Singapore by KWF Printing Pte Ltd

In memory of John Lewis

*CNN's first correspondent in Asia
and my last best friend.*

Author's Note

THIS IS A novel. It's not journalism. That's why I got into the fiction business in the first place, folks. I make this stuff up.

Yes, I hear you say, but you've been around Asia a long time. You've seen a lot of things. You know a lot of people. Isn't this book, at least to some degree, based on people who are real and events that are true?

This is what Mario Vargas Llosa, the Peruvian writer who won the 2010 Nobel Prize in Literature, had to say on the subject of whether his novels were true:

"Novels lie—they can't help doing so—but that's only one part of the story. The other is that, through lying, they express a curious truth, which can only be expressed in a veiled and concealed fashion, masquerading as what it is not."

I think he's right about that. But I'll leave it to you to decide how it applies to this book. If it applies at all.

One other thing.

I have a friend who was a senior intelligence officer in Asia during most of his career. On a night not long ago in Macau, we were smoking a couple of good cigars and talking about my books. He asked me how I had found out the truth about an event around which I had built the plot of one of them. I didn't find out about anything, I told him. I just made it up.

"That's the thing about Asia," he chuckled. "You really *can't* make anything up. No matter how outrageous what you have written might seem, one day somebody will come up to you and tell you it really happened, or that it is about to happen."

Let me repeat this: I made up the events, the characters, and most of the politics in this novel.

But more than once while writing it, I remembered what my friend said that night in Macau. He usually turns out to be right when he makes an observation like that about Asia.

Just this once, however, I really do hope he's wrong.

A WORLD OF TROUBLE

Prologue

I HAVE THE right to remain silent and mostly I have exercised that right. Anything I say can and will be used against me in a court of law. I have the right to an attorney. If I cannot afford an attorney, one will be appointed for me.

That's what they told me.

Of course, I figure it's mostly crap. If I don't start talking pretty soon, telling them what they want to hear, they'll haul me out to a little room somewhere in the back and beat the shit out of me.

So let's get one thing straight right now. Before they come back.

I am not who they say I am. I am not a criminal, not a spy, certainly not an assassin. I am not any of those things.

Maybe I cut a few corners here and there. I would admit to that. But at every turn I tried to do what seemed to me to be right. When you come down to it, that is my only real defense. I did what seemed to me to be right.

There is a pathetic air to that claim. I understand that. And it is something that embarrasses me. But nevertheless it is the truth, so I say it whenever they ask why I did what I did. At least, I think it is the truth. I am not absolutely certain I know what the truth actually is anymore.

Five years ago I was a high-flying lawyer in Washington, D.C., well enough connected to the masters of the universe to occasionally lunch at the White House mess. Three years ago, for reasons I will skip over now,

I left the United States to become a professor of international business at Bangkok's Chulalongkorn University. It was not long before I had a beautiful Italian-born girlfriend, a woman who would later become my wife, and together Anita and I moved into one of Bangkok's toniest apartment buildings.

That was when I really hit my stride. Half the companies in Asia seemed to want an American academic on their board of directors. Particularly one with connections in Washington who had been publicly hailed as an expert in international finance and money laundering. There was money and there was prestige. There were private jets and there were suites at famous hotels. There was, let's face it, ego stroking on an international scale. It was like a blow job that never stopped. It was a great time. The best.

Today, on the other hand, is not a great time. Not the best.

I am no longer a professor of anything. I am no longer on anyone's board of directors or taking meetings with those good corporate citizens who were lined up outside my office door just a few months ago. I was a reluctant player in a little drama with an international fugitive just slightly less notorious than O.J. Simpson, one who thought I was his ticket to a White House pardon, and I attracted a lot of attention. All of it bad.

And that, as they say, was that.

Goodbye Chulalongkorn University. Goodbye corporate directorships. Goodbye private jets. Goodbye suites in famous hotels. Goodbye blow job.

I earn my living these days practicing law again. Or at least that is what I say when someone asks me what I am doing since I have no better answer. I work by myself in a one-room office in Hong Kong that is above a noodle shop. I live alone in a borrowed apartment. And I have absolutely no idea where, or with who, Anita may be anymore. There's a pattern there, but it's one I try not to dwell on.

In order to convince myself I was really a lawyer again, I had to have at least one client, of course. I had known Charlie for a while and he offered to become my first client and I took him on gratefully, without a second thought. It was just that simple. It never once occurred to me back then that having Charlie for a client would lead me straight to where I am today, sitting here in this chair, waiting for the FBI goons to come back and say what is to become of me.

Perhaps if I can explain to you what really happened, if I can convince you this is all just a terrible mistake, I can convince them, too. Perhaps I can even convince myself.

The problem is where to start. This is a story with a lot of beginnings. Sadly, it still has only one ending. All the same, I must begin somewhere, so I will do so here.

On a gloomy day in January in, of all places, Dubai, a tiny city-state in the United Arab Emirates perched on the edge of the Persian Gulf.

Just before dawn that morning a brief but furious storm had rolled in from the desert and left the whole city smelling like a roll of aluminum foil.

Oh wait, I almost forgot.

My name is Jack Shepherd.

And that may be the last thing I tell you of which I am completely and absolutely certain.

Part One

DUBAI

In Italy, for thirty years under the Borgias, they had warfare, terror, murder, and bloodshed, but they produced Michelangelo, Leonardo da Vinci and the Renaissance.

In Switzerland, they had brotherly love, they had five hundred years of democracy and peace. And what did that produce? The cuckoo clock.

— Graham Greene,
The Third Man

One

THE BLACK MERCEDES S500 pulled to the curb and stopped. Shepherd opened his eyes. He didn't much like what he saw when he did.

"I thought we were going to your office," he said.

"We are," the man in the backseat with him replied.

"This isn't your office."

"I need to stop here first."

"What for?"

General Chalerm 'Charlie' Kitnarok didn't answer. He just opened the rear door and got out, and his driver and security man jumped out right behind him. Charlie bent back down and beckoned. Shepherd was the only person left in the car, so he sighed and got out, too.

Shepherd stretched and yawned and he damn well took his time doing it. It was only mid-morning in Dubai but he hadn't slept more than a couple of hours on the overnight flight from Hong Kong and he was dog-tired and grumpy. He rolled his shoulders and looked around. They weren't anywhere near Charlie's office. They were parked on Baniyas Road a little west of the St. George Hotel, just outside the souk.

"CNN wants some local color for their piece," Charlie said as if he could see exactly what Shepherd was thinking. "You and I are going to take a walk through the souk and let them shoot a little film for background."

Shepherd glanced at the white Jeep Cherokee that had stopped right behind them. A cameraman and a soundman were unloading their gear while they ignored a young female producer who was barking instructions. The two men looked like world-weary old hands who had earned their chops covering the Vietnam War. The producer looked like she had graduated from Bryn Mawr the day before and didn't have any idea what the Vietnam War was.

"You think this is a bad idea, don't you?" Charlie asked.

"What?"

Charlie jerked his thumb at the CNN crew.

"It's none of my business," Shepherd said. "I'm a lawyer, not a media consultant. I don't give public relations advice, I give legal advice."

"Then give me legal advice."

"Sure. My legal advice is that there's nothing illegal about letting CNN hang around with you to do a story about an unimaginably wealthy former prime minister of Thailand now living in splendid exile in Dubai and devoting his life to helping the poor and wretched of this earth."

"That's what I thought," Charlie said. "So let's take a little walk and get this over with."

Charlie pressed his hand lightly against Shepherd's back, ushering him toward a murky passageway that led into the souk.

DUBAI SHOWS THE world a face that is gaudy and futuristic, but the souk is what Dubai is really about. Dark and primeval, its twisting maze of alleyways is clogged with so many burlap bags, cardboard boxes, and wooden crates that there is seldom room enough for more than two people to walk abreast. The pervasive gloom drains everything of color and renders the world in murky shades of gray. Only the souk's smells give it the illusion of depth and dimension. The cloying sweetness of the air, the spicy scents of cayenne and red pepper, the heady musk of wet burlap bags, the sour odor of garbage baking on hot concrete, the rich waft of bitter coffee, and the acrid aroma of strong tobacco smoked by men you cannot see.

Shepherd hated the souk. Every time he entered its cramped tangle of tiny passageways, some so narrow they were more like cracks between buildings than places to walk, he felt like a guy in a horror movie, the one who never figures out the axe murderer is standing right behind him until it's too late. Shepherd was certain that a malevolent beast lived somewhere deep inside the souk. The place made his skin crawl.

Charlie didn't seem to feel any of that. He strolled the souk as if he owned it, and maybe he did. He certainly could afford it. According to Forbes, Charlie Kitnarok was the world's ninety-eighth richest man. And that was just counting the stuff they knew about.

Shepherd was Charlie's lawyer. He knew about the other stuff.

At least he knew about a lot of the other stuff. Maybe even he didn't know about everything. Charlie was a man who took pleasure in secrets and he had a great many of them. Shepherd doubted there was anybody alive who knew all of the things Charlie was involved in.

Possibly not even Charlie.

CHARLIE LED THE way with Shepherd walking next to him. The CNN camera crew took up a position about thirty feet behind them and the driver and the security man brought up the rear. They entered the souk and the gloom closed in. Split and pitted concrete walls rose up on both sides of them. Iron pipes and black rubber electrical cables snaked haphazardly back and forth over their heads and air conditioners buzzed and dripped from somewhere above. Metal handcarts piled with bulging burlap sacks and heavily taped brown cartons rattled past them in both directions.

Fifty feet inside the souk the alleyway made a sharp turn to the left and they passed a narrow shop with mounds of car batteries piled head-high behind a stained and dusty window. In front of the shop two men dressed in *dishdashas*, the long white shirt-dress that is the preferred attire of locals in Dubai, sat on upturned wooded boxes smoking cigarettes. Their dark eyes tracked Charlie and Shepherd as the little procession passed.

"Where are we going, Charlie?"

"Nowhere. Just walking."

It didn't feel to Shepherd like they were just walking. It felt more like they were going somewhere, but he had no idea where. Still, Charlie was his client, his only client if he were being completely honest, and no matter how tired he was, that was a boat Shepherd had absolutely no intention of rocking. So he nodded and said nothing.

Charlie took a heavy-framed pair of tortoiseshell sunglasses from his jacket pocket and slipped them on. The lenses were so dark they were almost black. Shepherd wondered why Charlie was putting on sunglasses when the light around them was already so dim he felt like he was walking under water.

A few minutes later they rounded a sharp bend, slipped past a tall stack of odd smelling burlap bags, and emerged into a rectangular courtyard. The courtyard didn't have much to recommend it as a destination, but something about it made Shepherd wonder if it was the place they had been heading all along.

It was about eighty feet long and twenty-five feet wide with narrow shophouses walling off all four sides. There was some kind of merchandise stacked in front of most of them. Brightly-colored spices sealed in clear plastic cylinders the size of barrels; concrete packed in heavy red-and-blue striped paper bags; hundreds of pairs of slippers arranged by color on aluminum racks; wooden cases the size of refrigerators lettered in red Korean characters; and tan cardboard cartoons tightly bound with white plastic straps. The only exit was another narrow passageway at the opposite end.

Two men brushed by them walking in the direction from which they had just come. The first man was Iranian-looking, clean-shaven and wearing a dark suit with a white shirt buttoned at the neck. The other man wore a *dishdasha* and a blue Yankees baseball cap. Both men were talking on mobile telephones and Shepherd wondered briefly if they were talking to each other.

Charlie was a half step ahead of Shepherd, walking just in front of his right shoulder. They were almost exactly in the center of the rectangular space when Charlie turned his head as if he was about to say something. Whatever he was going to say, he never got the chance.

The shots came from behind them.

In the confined space of the courtyard, they sounded like mortar fire.

Two

SHEPHERD REACTED BY instinct. He pushed Charlie behind two pallets piled high with burlap-wrapped bales and dived on top of him. The bales were stacked about four feet high and looked pretty solid. Shepherd had no idea what was in them, but he hoped to hell whatever it was would stop bullets.

Shepherd scrambled to his knees and took a quick glance over the bales.

The Iranian-looking man who had brushed past them was standing in front of an open-fronted shop with a sign in English over the door: SALEM ALI BAKERY. He was holding a .45 in his left hand with his right hand wrapped over the bottom of the grip. His feet were planted shoulder-width apart, his knees bent, and his shoulders back. He looked like a model demonstrating the Weaver stance for a handgunner's manual.

"What the fuck you doing, Jack?" Charlie bellowed.

The gunman shifted the muzzle toward the sound of Charlie's voice and fired twice. Shepherd ducked back unharmed, but he didn't hear the shots thumping into the bags or ricocheting off the concrete behind them and he wondered about that for a moment.

That guy must be the world's worst shot, he thought. But even lousy shots get lucky, so Shepherd stayed as low as he could.

"Any more questions, Charlie?"

"Yeah. Why would anyone want to kill *you*, Jack?"

"Very fucking funny."

Shepherd glanced over his shoulder. They were near the center of the courtyard and there was very little behind them but a narrow walkway disappearing into the gloom between a mobile phone dealer and a warehouse.

"What's going on here, Charlie?"

"How should I know?"

"Somebody's trying to kill you and you have no idea *why*? What are you into that I don't know about?"

"Nothing, Jack. Nothing at all."

Bullshit, Shepherd thought.

Charlie may have once been a military man, but the Thai army didn't do much fighting so Shepherd doubted Charlie was any more comfortable under fire than he was. Still, Charlie looked calm enough to him. More annoyed than frightened really.

What the hell is happening here? Shepherd asked himself. *And why isn't Charlie more disturbed about it?*

Shepherd took another glance over the bales and this time he didn't draw fire. The Iranian-looking gunman's full attention had shifted to the opposite end of the courtyard where Charlie's driver and security man had suddenly appeared with the CNN crew right behind them. It looked to Shepherd like they were all about to be famous, although whether their fame would be posthumous was still an open question.

The security man didn't hesitate. His weapon was out in front of him in a two-handed grip and he charged straight at the shooter, firing as he ran. The driver pulled a handgun, too, and slid to his left, blasting away. The gunman took two steps back, firing at first one man then the other as he retreated. Then all at once, he dropped straight down like a puppet whose strings had been cut.

The security man took a few more strides, kicked the gunman's gun out of his hand, and dived behind a pile of cardboard cartons. Across the courtyard, the driver flattened himself against the wooden crates with the Korean writing.

For a moment, everything stopped.

No more than twenty feet beyond where the gunman sprawled in the courtyard, the CNN cameraman had his camera up and his eye pressed to the viewfinder. All Shepherd could see of the man behind the camera was a blue baseball cap with CNN in red letters above the bill, a denim jacket, wrinkled blue jeans, and a pair of blue-and-white athletic shoes. The soundman was just to the cameraman's right, arms straight out in front of him, a black microphone dangling from a short aluminum pole gripped in both hands. Slightly behind the cameraman and to his left hovered the producer. She was wearing a khaki safari jacket and khaki pants tucked into the tops of brown work boots. She had short blond hair, a rosy complexion, and eyes the color of jade.

As Shepherd watched, the woman sank slowly to her knees and pressed her hands together in front of her face. She looked as if she was so emotionally overcome by the sight of a man shot to death right in front of her that she had been moved to prayer. Then Shepherd spotted the dark stain on the woman's safari jacket, right in the center of her chest.

She tilted her head down and examined the stain. Her mouth opened and closed, but no sound came out. Gradually she slumped forward, twisted slightly to her right, and laid her cheek gently against the dirty concrete of the courtyard. A bubble of red formed on her lips, popped, and slid onto the ground. She didn't move again.

Three

SHEPHERD GOT HIS feet underneath him and grabbed Charlie by the arm.

"What are you doing?" Charlie asked.

"We're getting the hell out of here!"

"Just stay put, Jack."

"We don't know how many gunmen there are, Charlie. They may be others, and they may have automatic weapons or even grenades. Your guys don't have anything but handguns."

"You think too much." Charlie got his own feet under him and started to stand up. "Just stay where you are and—"

A fresh volley of shots cut Charlie off. Shepherd grabbed him and jerked him back down, but Charlie's feet slid out from under him and he went head first into the bales. Shepherd heard the hollow sound of Charlie's head bouncing off the wooden pallet. His sunglasses flew off and caromed away across the courtyard. Charlie sat up grunting in pain and lifted both hands to his face. A thick line of blood appeared across his forehead.

It was the blood that made up Shepherd's mind.

Dragging Charlie behind him, he duck-walked behind the bales until they made it to the nearest shophouse. Inside was a single, large room filled almost to the ceiling with more burlap-wrapped bales just like the ones outside. Shepherd pulled Charlie toward the back.

There was a door. He grabbed the handle.
Locked, damn it.

Shepherd pushed hard on the door with his free hand. It gave slightly but didn't open. He stepped back, lifted his foot, and slammed it into the wood beside the lock. The door popped open as smoothly as if he had opened it with a key. Shepherd gave Charlie a quick glance. He seemed dazed and the bleeding had gotten worse. Keeping a tight grip on his arm, Shepherd pulled him into the alley behind the shophouse. He had no idea where they were going, but he had to keep them moving.

A right and two lefts brought them into another courtyard. It looked a lot like the one in which they had just been ambushed, but it wasn't. There was a shadowy passageway at the opposite end right next to a windowless stucco building exactly the color of sand. Shepherd headed straight for it. The gloom of the souk was now their friend. If Shepherd could lose them in it, they would probably be safe. He tightened his grip on Charlie and pulled him along.

THEY WENT ON like that through the twisting passageways of the souk, making random turns every so often. Shepherd thought they were moving further and further away from the place where they had been attacked, but he wasn't absolutely certain. What he was certain of was that he would know the right way to get them out of this when he saw it.

And then he did see it.

Shepherd and Charlie emerged suddenly onto a wide boulevard. Just on the other side of the boulevard were the aqua waters of Dubai Creek. Dubai Creek isn't really a creek at all, but rather a narrow inlet from the Persian Gulf that for centuries has been a port of call for small traders and a refuge for smugglers. The Creek was cluttered as it always was with its usual traffic of broad-beamed *dhows* while, between them, tiny *abras* darted like water bugs ferrying small groups of people from one side to the other.

Shepherd didn't hesitate. Dragging Charlie behind him, he broke into a lope across the road and headed straight for the Creek.

There was a line of *abras* tied up at the bank right in front of them and Shepherd made straight for the nearest one. He jumped down into the boat, steadied himself for a moment as the little craft rocked from his weight, and helped Charlie to climb down behind him. The boatman was a dark-skinned fellow in blue shorts and a dirty white shirt. He was sitting in the stern of the boat methodically peeling and eating an orange. He regarded the new arrivals with curiosity.

"Go!" Shepherd shouted at the boatman. He pushed Charlie down onto the hard wooden bench in the center of the little boat. "Go, for Christ's sake!"

The boatman didn't move. He just sat there and stared at the crazy white guy screaming at him.

Everyone in Dubai might not speak English, but Shepherd spoke another language he was sure would be understood. He pulled a wad of currency out of his pocket and waved it at the boatman. The man responded immediately. Dropping his orange, he shoved the boat off the wharf with one hand and fired the engine with the other. They sputtered into the Creek and the boatman turned downriver toward the wharf on the opposite bank where *abras* usually put in.

Shepherd shook his head and pointed upriver. He could see the Sheraton Hotel in the distance and right now an American hotel looked pretty damn good to him. The boatman just stared at him, so Shepherd did the thing with the money again and pointed to the Sheraton. The man quickly swung the bow toward it.

Shepherd sat down on the wooden bench next to Charlie. "Are you okay?" he called over the throbbing of the boat's engine. "Were you hit?"

When Charlie didn't answer, Shepherd ran his hands over Charlie's chest and neck looking for gunshot wounds. He was sure Charlie hadn't taken a direct hit, but maybe a ricochet had caught him. The cut on his forehead wasn't serious, Shepherd could see that now, just bleeding like a son of a bitch the way head cuts do.

"Are you okay?" he shouted again.

Charlie grunted, shook off Shepherd's hands, and straightened up a little. He wiped a hand over his forehead and it came away covered with blood. Charlie held up his hand and looked at it for a moment.

"Stop screaming," he said. "I'm bleeding. I haven't gone fucking deaf."

"I thought maybe you'd been—"

"I'm fine except for this shit," he said and wiggled his bloody hand.

Charlie fished in his pocket with his other hand and came out with a white handkerchief. He used it to wipe some of the blood away and then he folded the handkerchief lengthwise and pressed it against the cut on his forehead to stop the bleeding. As the boat wallowed up Dubai Creek toward the Sheraton, Charlie shifted himself into a more comfortable position on the hard wooden seat.

"Fuck," he muttered, "I would have been better off letting those guys shoot me than getting rescued by you."

Shepherd didn't know what to say to that, so he said nothing at all.

Four

ALONE IN HIS hotel room later that afternoon, Shepherd watched CNN as they ran the story over and over. It was spectacular, of course, all the more so because the really dramatic parts were in slow motion. Shepherd saw everything he had seen only a few hours ago all over again, but now he saw it from the point of view of the cameraman who had been at the other end of the courtyard. It was an odd feeling watching himself from the opposite direction. There was a sense of unreality to it, like he was part of a video game.

The footage started with an innocuous view of the narrow passageway through which they had entered the courtyard. There was a slight motion at the bottom of the frame and the camera panned down. A brown and white cat, scrawny and mean looking, snarled at the camera and moved away at a deliberate pace.

Exactly at the moment the cat disappeared from the frame there were several loud noises. Although the sounds weren't recognizable on the film as gunshots, that's what they were. The camera jerked slightly in reaction to the first shot or two, then the image started to bounce as the cameraman ran toward the sound. He rounded the bend in the passageway and entered the courtyard, and his lens went straight to the Iranian-looking shooter with the .45.

When the bullets are flying, it's the gun that makes the impression, not the man behind it, but now that Shepherd was safely tucked up in his hotel room it was the man who held his attention. Each time the shooter's face turned toward the camera, Shepherd leaned forward and studied it.

The man looked younger than Shepherd recalled and the expression on his face was puzzling. Shepherd wasn't sure what he expected. Rage, fanaticism, triumph perhaps. But it was none of those things. The man looked amused. That was the only word for it. Amused.

The security man was on the left side of the courtyard charging directly at the gunman, firing as he ran, but the shooter never moved. The muzzle of his .45 stayed where it was, pointing directly into the camera lens. It was like a scene from a movie. The big, black handgun pointed straight at the camera; the muzzle opening looked as big as the Lincoln Tunnel; and the eyes of every viewer were drawn straight into it. The gunman held that pose, not firing. He looked more like a man posing for the camera than he did a killer.

The driver was on the opposite side of the courtyard from the security man, running and firing across his body at the same time. He was spraying bullets everywhere. Shepherd saw at least three shots go high, catch the concrete façade of one of the shophouses, and ricochet away.

That's how the producer got hit, he thought. *The shooter didn't target her. One of Charlie's bodyguards shot her by accident.*

When the shooter jerked, lurched a couple of steps away from the camera, and crumpled to the ground, it was impossible to tell whether the security man or the driver had hit him. He just went down. That's all there was to see. After that, the security man sprinted straight at the gunman and kicked the .45 out of his hand. Then he dived behind a pile of cardboard boxes and crouched down while the driver flattened himself against the crates on the opposite side of the courtyard.

That was when the silence fell, the one that Shepherd remembered so well, and it was a full minute before the security man broke it. Rising up from behind the cover of the stack of boxes, he lifted his weapon and fired methodically into the motionless body of the gunman sprawled on the concrete. He kept firing until his gun was empty and the slide locked open, and then he dropped the clip and used the heel of his hand to slap in a fresh one.

Right after that, in the background beyond where the gunman lay dying, Shepherd could see something bobbing along just above a wall of burlap-wrapped bales. If he hadn't already known what it was, he might not have been able to guess, but of course he knew very well. It was the top of two heads, his and Charlie's, as they scuttled away to safety.

Everything that happened after that was new to Shepherd so he watched the rest with particular care every time the film was broadcast. But each time he did, he understood what he was seeing even less than he had before.

HE AND CHARLIE had been gone no more than a few seconds when there was a sudden flash of white just beyond the security man. A *dishdasha*-clad man wearing a blue Yankee's cap had suddenly appeared from somewhere and was running across the courtyard. It was the same man Shepherd had seen with the Iranian-looking shooter when they entered the courtyard. Was he looking for a new angle from which to attack, or was he trying to escape? It was impossible to tell.

From the white folds of his *dishdasha*, Yankee Cap produced what Shepherd could see was an Ingram MAC-10. He held it high as he ran, out away from his body with the muzzle up. The MAC-10 isn't a particularly accurate weapon, but it's cheap and it's reliable and it lays down a thousand rounds a minute. Fire a thousand rounds a minute in a confined space and you don't have to worry a hell of a lot about accuracy.

About halfway across the courtyard Yankee Cap twisted toward the camera and began to lower the muzzle of the Ingram. Charlie's security man pulled back behind his cover, but the cameraman held firm, his lens never wavering. He was either the bravest man Shepherd had ever seen, or the dumbest.

Yankee Cap started shooting. His gun was firing so fast that the individual reports merged into a single continuous noise. The sound of it was deafening. The muzzle of the MAC-10 tracked inexorably downward. Moving lower and lower, it swung toward the cameraman. Then, abruptly, the noise stopped.

Yankee Cap stopped running, turned the MAC-10 slightly to one side, and stared at it with a confused expression on his face. That was when the driver stepped out from behind the crates with the Korean writing and fired six evenly spaced shots. All six appeared to hit Yankee Cap in the chest and the man jerked from left to right like he was trying out a new dance step. Big stains blossomed his stark white *dishdasha*. They made the garment looked like a choir robe printed with red flowers.

Charlie's security man rose up and targeted his own volley. He fired four shots that punched Yankee Cap straight back into a pile of white canvas rice bags. The cap fell off his head and he sat slowly down right on top of it. Leaning back against the rice bags, his legs out in front of him, Yankee Cap jerked a few more times and a thin line of blood appeared between his lips.

Then, as if resigned to his fate, perhaps even a little embarrassed by the way it had come upon him, the man turned his head discreetly away from the camera, pulled his knees to his chest, and died.

CNN AIRED THE story over and over. It must have been seen by hundreds of millions of people around the world. Journalists are never more tireless than when they cover each other so the death of the network's producer in the attack gave it real legs. Every television news broadcast in the world led with the story and it stayed at the top of the news cycle hour after hour.

Until then, most of the world had never heard of Charlie Kitnarok, the former prime minister of Thailand now living in exile in Dubai. Maybe a good part of the world had never heard of Thailand either. But everyone certainly knew about Thailand now, and they knew exactly who Charlie Kitnarok was.

Charlie was the man who had stood up to the killers sent by his political opponents to prevent him from restoring democracy to Thailand. Charlie was the man who had bravely faced down a hail of gunfire. Charlie was the man who had risked his own life to pull an unidentified assistant to safety. Shepherd shook his head every time he heard that last part. The unidentified assistant, of course, would be him.

The CNN story included a few words from Charlie. They didn't amount to much, just a quick sound bite. CNN was good at that, reducing everything to a sound bite. All they used was Charlie responding to a question about the bandage on his forehead. He had just been grazed, he said, nothing worth talking about. Charlie gazed steadily into the camera when he said it, clear-eyed and square-jawed, looking every bit the old soldier. Trust Charlie to turn an assassination attempt into self-serving publicity, Shepherd thought. And trust CNN to merchandise Charlie's bullshit without even blushing.

"THE MOST EXHILARATING thing in life," Winston Churchill is supposed to have said, "is to be shot at without effect." Shepherd had just been shot at without effect, but he didn't feel particularly exhilarated. He just felt tired, more tired than he could ever remember feeling before.

The sky began to darken and the afternoon turned into evening.

Shepherd remembered he hadn't eaten anything in a long time. He started to work out how long it had actually been, but he decided it didn't really matter and ordered a grilled cheese sandwich and a beer from room service. They asked him what kind of beer he wanted and he told them he didn't care. The room service guy sounded like he didn't believe him.

When the food came, Shepherd ate the sandwich and drank half the beer. Then he got undressed, left his clothes on the floor, and got into bed. It was not long before jet lag and exhaustion overwhelmed him and he fell asleep. It was a restless, uneven sleep and he woke repeatedly through the night. Each time he did, he felt even more ragged and exhausted than he had before.

Five

THE NEXT MORNING Shepherd showered and shaved while he waited for room service to deliver breakfast, then he watched CNN some more while he ate. There was really nothing new about the attack on Charlie and no information at all about the identity of the gunmen, which seemed odd. He wondered if the information was being withheld for some reason and, if so, by whom, and why. That was something he would have to ask Charlie.

Along with a whole hell of a lot of other things, of course.

Shepherd got dressed. Then he went downstairs and hired a hotel car to take him out to Charlie's villa on Palm Jumeirah.

PALM JUMEIRAH IS a palm-shaped projection into the Persian Gulf which, like much of Dubai, is entirely artificial. In a spectacular demonstration of either inspiration or hubris, Shepherd could never decide which, tens of millions of tons of sand had been dredged up from the sea bottom, compacted into a series of graceful arcs resembling palm fronds, and then connected to the mainland by a slightly wider spit of sand representing the trunk.

The trunk of the tree is filled with cheesy apartment buildings, but the arcs of land representing the fronds of the palm tree are given over exclusively to private houses expansively referred to as villas, more because of their outrageous cost than any grandness of design. The houses are laid out on each palm frond in two lines along opposite sides of a single roadway. Most of them undistinguished, even tacky.

Charlie owned both houses at the very end of Frond G, where he had created a small compound by building a high wall and placing a security gate across the end of the road. With the wall forming one side of the compound and the Persian Gulf surrounding the other three sides, the place was as secure as any private home in Dubai could be. Shepherd sometimes wondered what it had cost Charlie in gratuities to local government functionaries to pull that off, but he had never asked.

When the hotel car pulled up at Charlie's security gate, Shepherd got out and a brown-uniformed guard directed the driver where to park. The guard gestured for Shepherd to raise his arms and ran a wand over his body. Then he asked for Shepherd's passport and inspected it carefully. Eventually the guard handed it back, tilted his head, and murmured something in Arabic into a shoulder mike. The gate slid open just far enough for Shepherd to walk through.

The two houses in the compound were very similar. Two stories, high-pitched red-tiled roofs, tan stucco siding, a great many arched windows, double front doors of polished wood, and a few fake pillars and gables stuck here and there for decoration. The house on the left where Charlie lived with his wife Sally looked to be the more hospitable of the two since it had a long terrace paved in dark brown ceramic tile that ran the length of the second floor. The house on the right that had been converted into an office had nothing to recommend it. It was as plain as a self-storage warehouse.

Shepherd rang the bell at the house where Charlie lived and a maid who appeared to be Filipino opened the door and showed him into Charlie's study. After a few minutes she returned with a pot of coffee and two china cups on a silver tray, then she closed the door behind her and disappeared. Shepherd poured himself some coffee, sat down one of the two facing love seats upholstered in yellow silk, and waited.

CHARLIE CAME THROUGH the door talking on a cell phone. He said *uh-huh* a couple of times while he poured himself some coffee with his free hand, then he said *uh-huh* once more, hung up, and put the phone in his pocket. He settled himself on the other love seat, took a sip of coffee, and looked at Shepherd over the rim of the cup.

"You okay?"

"I'm fine."

Charlie nodded absentmindedly, his mind apparently on things more important than the current state of Shepherd's health.

"How's your head?" Shepherd asked.

Charlie looked puzzled. "What are you talking about?"

"Your head," Shepherd said, tapping his own with his finger just in case the word was unfamiliar to Charlie. "The cut you got when I pulled you down."

Shepherd didn't mention hearing Charlie say on CNN that his injury came from being grazed by a bullet.

Charlie shrugged and looked away, but he didn't say anything. Shepherd would have liked to think he was embarrassed, but he doubted it. Charlie had just been a politician milking the moment and politicians were hard to embarrass.

"There was a lot of coverage," Charlie said after a moment. "CNN, Fox, BBC, ITN, even Al Jazeera."

"It was entertaining television."

"Great stuff!" Charlie said. "Great!"

Maybe Churchill had been right after all. Charlie, at least, seemed to lend support to his theory.

"Have they identified the gunmen yet?" Shepherd asked.

Charlie shook his head.

"Nobody's taken credit?"

"You think credit is the right word to use here, Jack?"

"Sorry. You know what I mean."

Charlie sipped at his coffee again. He didn't say anything else, but Shepherd wasn't ready to give up. Lawyers ask questions. It's what they do.

"Were the gunmen locals?"

Charlie shrugged.

"You have no idea where they came from?"

"Probably imported. Iraqis maybe."

"If somebody was going to bring in a couple of hitters to go after you, why would they hire two boobs like that?"

"What do you mean?"

"Come on, Charlie. Those had to be the world's lousiest assassins. The attack was stupidly planned and badly executed. Those idiots didn't even hit anybody."

"They killed the woman. That news producer."

"No, they didn't. Your bodyguards killed her. They weren't much better shots than the guys who came after you."

"It's hard to get good help these days."

"Maybe that's it," Shepherd said.

But he didn't think it was.

"Anyway, that's not really the point, is it," Charlie said, looking genuinely annoyed.

"No? Then what *is* the point?"

"The point is who hired those guys."

"Okay, so who hired them?"

Charlie shot Shepherd a hard look. "You know who it was as well as I do."

"No," he said. "I don't."

"Oh, come on, Jack. You of all people ought to know exactly

who it was. You understand what's happening in Thailand now."

"Pretend I don't. Explain it to me."

Charlie smiled slightly at that. He put his cup down on the table between them, leaned back, and folded his arms.

Shepherd nodded encouragingly. Not that Charlie really needed any encouraging.

"It's a mess. It's been a fucking mess ever since I left."

Shepherd said nothing.

"A lot of people want me to become prime minister again. But there are other people who would kill me to prevent something like that from happening, to stop me from coming back."

"I didn't know you were thinking of going back."

"I was just speaking hypothetically. As long as I'm alive, I *could* go back to Thailand. If I did, I'd be prime minister again in a week. You know how many people want me to do that?"

"How many exactly?" Shepherd asked. "Not counting the army."

Charlie gave him a half smile. "I thought you were on my side, Jack."

"I am on your side, Charlie. You pay me a lot of money to be on your side."

"Would you be on the other side if *they* paid you a lot of money?"

"It depends on how much it is. I'm a lawyer. I'm always paid to be on somebody's side."

Charlie laughed, but Shepherd could also see him wondering if he was serious about that. That was understandable. He was wondering, too.

Charlie's cell phone rang and he pulled it from his pocket and glanced at the screen.

"I've got to take this, Jack. Would you excuse me?"

Shepherd stood up. When he left the study, he closed the door behind him. He noticed Charlie remained silent until after he did.

Six

SHEPHERD WAITED IN the hallway outside Charlie's study until he began feeling foolish just standing there doing nothing, then he walked to the end of the hall and out onto the big terrace behind the house. The terrace was paved in glazed tiles the color of Hershey Bars and dotted with outdoor furniture, all of which looked uncomfortable. Shepherd chose a high-back rattan chair that seemed slightly better than the rest, dragged it around until it faced the sea, and propped his feet up on a glass-topped coffee table with an iron base.

It was a nice day by Dubai standards. The air was warm without being hot and there was a light breeze off the sea. Just beyond the breakwater, two black rubber boats filled with UAE commandos drifted on the glassy smooth surface of the Persian Gulf. Each of the boats carried four men dressed in black, automatic weapons slung over their chests. One of the men peered at him through a pair of field glasses. Shepherd gave him a friendly wave, but the man didn't wave back.

After about ten minutes Charlie walked out and sat down next to Shepherd. He had put on a pair of sunglasses with gold metal frames, which caused Shepherd think of the tortoise shell sunglasses Charlie had worn in the souk, the ones that had fallen off when he went down behind the burlap-wrapped bales and hit his head. Shepherd had no doubt those damned glasses would turn up on eBay someday.

"There's obviously something on your mind, Jack. What is it?"

Shepherd couldn't see Charlie's eyes through the sunglasses, but his face looked earnest enough and the question seemed to be entirely serious. Shepherd stood up and walked to the edge of the terrace. He doubted there were any lip readers among the commandos in the rubber boats but, if there were, it certainly wouldn't have been the weirdest thing he had ever encountered in Dubai. Just in case, he turned his back to them before he spoke to Charlie again.

"What did you mean inside when you said people were willing to kill you to keep you from going back to Thailand?" he asked.

Charlie glanced over Shepherd's shoulder at the two rubber boats full of UAE commandos.

"This is neither the time nor the place to talk about that," he said.

"Are you going back into politics?"

"This is neither the time nor the place to talk about that."

"I don't do politics."

"I'm not asking you to."

"I'm a lawyer. I shuffle papers. I organize corporations. I argue with banks. That's all I do."

"I understand that."

Shepherd could feel in his bones that something was about to happen here that he wasn't going to like. He thought about telling Charlie right then he didn't want any part of whatever it was. He thought about it, but he didn't tell Charlie that. Later, looking back, he would always wonder how differently things might have turned out if he had.

Charlie stood up and moved to a different chair, one that put his back to the watching commandos. He swung his feet up onto the glass and iron table and took off his sunglasses.

"Sit down, Jack. There's something we need to talk about."

Charlie pointed to a chair that would put Shepherd's back to the commandos as well and Shepherd walked over and sat down.

"Some guys are trying to fuck me," Charlie said.

"Some guys are trying to kill you," Shepherd said. "In my book, that's a lot worse than fucking you."

"That's not what I'm talking about," Charlie said, waving away Shepherd's wisecrack. "I mean those pricks at the Ministry of Finance in Thailand. They're trying to grab my money."

"I didn't know you had any money in Thailand."

"It goes back to before we started working together. There are some accounts at Bangkok Bank and some more at SCB. I need for you to sort them out for me."

Bangkok Bank was Thailand's largest bank and SCB was Siam Commercial Bank, the second or third largest. They were both good places to have money in Thailand, if you had to have money in Thailand at all.

"Sort it out how?" Shepherd asked.

"Get it out of the country. All of it."

"How much are we talking about?"

"Maybe in all, say, five or six hundred million."

Six hundred million Thai baht was a little less than twenty million US dollars. Not an insignificant sum, of course, but less than Shepherd was often called on to handle for Charlie.

"Five or six hundred million baht shouldn't be any problem," Shepherd said.

Then he noticed that Charlie was looking at him like he had suddenly begun speaking in tongues.

"Not baht, Jack. I wouldn't care if it was just baht. Dollars. US dollars. Five or six hundred million US dollars."

Oh, right, US dollars. Five or six hundred million US dollars. Of course.

"I want you to get your ass to Bangkok. I'll get everything gathered up in Bangkok Bank for you. I've got a contact there. You talk to him and get everything shifted to Hong Kong, then you can bury it in some nominee companies."

"Look, Charlie, I don't—"

"Leave tonight. Those pricks are really trying to fuck me."

"I don't want to go to Thailand."

"I know you don't."

"I told you I wasn't going back there again."

"I wouldn't ask you to go if it weren't important. You're the only person I can trust with something like this."

"Look, Charlie, even if I went to Thailand, I'm not sure how much good I could do you."

"You know more about moving money than anyone I ever met, Jack. You're a goddamned wizard when it comes to stuff like that."

"I appreciate your confidence, Charlie, but—"

"But nothing. When the Asian Bank of Commerce collapsed, how much was in the wind? Five hundred million? And it was all CIA black money, wasn't it?"

Shepherd said nothing.

"Your old pals back in Washington were running around shrieking like a bunch of little girls. Somebody had fucked them, too."

Shepherd said nothing.

"But you worked out the scam, didn't you? Then you tracked down the money all by yourself and you got it back. And I'll bet to this day there're not more than five people in the whole world who even know it was you who figured the whole thing out."

"Is that the way you think it happened?"

"That's the way it *did* happen."

Shepherd shrugged. "A penny saved is a penny earned."

"What the fuck does that mean?"

"I'm a big fan of clichés. They say so much and require so little effort."

Nothing useful could come of telling Charlie what really happened to the money from the Asian Bank of Commerce. A lot of people had died trying to grab that money. Some of them were good people and some of them were not so good. But in the end everything had turned to crap and the good and the bad alike had both shared exactly the same fate. They had all ended up losers. Shepherd didn't want to talk about it. He *wasn't* going to talk about it.

So Shepherd cleared his throat and changed the subject back to the money Charlie wanted to get out of Thailand.

"You know as well as I do that we would have to get permission from the Bank of Thailand to move that much money out of the country."

"I know."

"And I really don't think—"

"When you get there, go to Bangkok Bank. See a guy named Tanit Chaiya who's an Executive Vice President in the head office on Silom Road."

"I didn't say I'd go, Charlie."

"All Tanit needs from you is a structure he can use to make it all look okay. Some kind of overseas corporate acquisition will do it. Tell him we're buying the Eiffel Tower or some goddamn sports team in the United States. Just make it look good."

"If that's all there is to it, why can't I just draft something after I get back to Hong Kong and email it to this guy?"

"Because the Bank of Thailand wouldn't approve the transfer if that was all you did. They're not going to approve it at all without a little persuasion."

Shepherd nodded, but he didn't say anything. He could see now where this was going.

"You with me here?" Charlie asked.

"How much persuasion?"

"I'd say a couple of million would probably get the job done.

Maybe a little less or a little more. Use your own judgment. I don't know exactly how they're going to play it when we try to move the money, but I know what the bottom line is going to be. That's why I need somebody there to look them in the eye and make sure this gets done. Buying people is easy. Making sure they stay bought is a lot harder."

"You're making me uncomfortable here, Charlie."

"Yeah, I know."

"I'm not going to get involved in bribing the Bank of Thailand. The US government takes a dim view of that sort of thing. Americans go to jail for bribery."

"This isn't a bribe."

"Then what would you call it?"

"It's like ransoming a kidnapped child. Americans don't put people in jail for paying ransoms, do they?"

"I doubt the Department of Justice would look at this quite that way."

"I'm not going to sit here and let them steal my money, Jack. That's not right."

"No, it isn't," Shepherd admitted.

"I've got to pay a few people if I want my money back. That's the way business works in Thailand. You know that."

"Yes, I know that, but still—"

"So I'm asking you to take care of this for me, Jack. If I can't do something myself, you're my guy."

"I'm flattered."

"I'm just looking after my own interests here. You're the best. You know everything there is to know about international corporate structures and banking operations. You're Mozart with money. You can make chicken salad out of chicken shit."

"Far be it from me to sound modest, but—"

"And I trust you," Charlie interrupted. "You're smart, you're tough, you're connected. And you're an honest man. That's why I hired you."

A silence fell and they both sat back for a while and just watched those black rubber boats drifting on the Persian Gulf. It was a companionable silence. Shepherd liked Charlie no matter what some people said about him. He even liked all the outrageous bullshit Charlie got involved in. Charlie was good for more outrageous bullshit in a day than most men were in their entire lifetimes.

The truth of the matter, Shepherd knew full well, was that managing outrageous bullshit was what he was good at. Managing outrageous bullshit was what he did for a living. Sometimes he even wondered if he could do anything else.

After a moment Charlie started talking again. "I've asked Adnan to pull together the documentation on the Thai accounts for you. You can start with that. If you need anything else, just ask him and he'll get it for you."

"Is Adnan here?" Shepherd asked.

"He's over in the office," Charlie said, gesturing vaguely in the direction of the other house across the compound.

Adnan was Charlie's personal assistant. He was in his forties, slight with slicked-back hair and pale skin, and he claimed to be Lebanese. Shepherd didn't think Adnan really was Lebanese, but he had never challenged him on the point. After Charlie fled Thailand two steps in front of a flood of corruption charges and settled in Dubai, Adnan had taken on the vague title of personal assistant. Shepherd didn't know for certain what Adnan actually did for Charlie, but what he did know for certain was that he really didn't like Adnan. Adnan clearly didn't like him either, so Shepherd figured they were square all around.

"What's really going on here, Charlie? I need to know."

"I thought you didn't do politics, Jack."

"Assassination attempts and bribing central banks isn't politics."

"It is in Thailand."

Shepherd said nothing. Charlie did have a point there.

"You can't have it both ways, Jack." Charlie leaned forward and rested his forearms on his knees. "Either you're part of everything here or you're a lawyer who just looks after financial matters for me. We can do this either way, but you need to decide which way it's going to be."

Shepherd didn't say anything for a moment. He just sat and looked at Charlie, and Charlie just sat and looked back.

"I don't do politics," Shepherd repeated after a minute or two had passed like that.

"Fine." Charlie stood up and rubbed his hands together. "So you're my lawyer and you look after financial matters. Then go to Bangkok and rescue my money. Go right now. You want to take one of the planes? Use the G-4."

"No thanks," Shepherd said. "I like flying commercial."

Charlie chuckled and shook his head. "You're really a piece of work, Jack. Here I put a thirty million dollar jet at your disposal and you tell me you'd rather drag your ass out to the airport, stand in the security line, and take a commercial flight. What the *hell* am I going to do with you?"

What was Charlie going to do with him? It was a question Shepherd had asked himself from time to time, although he suspected in a somewhat different context. He had never come up with a particularly satisfactory answer either.

"So are you going to do this for me, Jack?" Charlie asked. "There's no one else I trust."

"It's only money, Charlie."

"Yeah, but it's a *lot* of money."

Shepherd sighed and pulled a small notebook and a pen out of his pocket.

"What was the name of that guy at Bangkok Bank again?"

Seven

SHEPHERD WALKED ACROSS to the villa Charlie called the office and went in through the kitchen door. A large room with a faux-beamed ceiling that overlooked the sea at the back of the house had been turned into a conference room, and that was where Shepherd found Adnan.

Adnan was leaning over a big oak table that filled the center of the room examining what looked like a large map. Shepherd couldn't see what the map depicted, partly because the angle was wrong and partly because Robert Darling was standing at the table next to Adnan blocking his view.

Shepherd had met Darling a half dozen times. They were both trustees of Charlie's charitable foundation and had run into each other at trustees meetings but not on any other occasion. Darling had said little about himself other than something professionally vague about being in the private investment business. Shepherd hadn't pressed. He figured it was none of his business what the man did for a living. He had met a lot of people who introduced themselves in exactly the same way and he wouldn't *want* to know what most of them did for a living.

"I didn't know you were here, Robert," Shepherd said.

Darling turned his head very slowly.

"Hello, Shepherd. You look tired. Up late last night?"

"No. Must be all the excitement. It's a shame you missed it."

Shepherd knew he sounded testy and frankly he didn't give a fig. *What was with the you-look-tired shit?* Darling was just the kind of guy who always had to take a shot, even when there was nothing to shoot at.

Adnan quickly rolled up whatever it was they had been examining. He blocked Shepherd's view of it with his body until he was done, then turned around holding it in his hands.

"I wasn't expecting you," he said.

"So I see."

Adnan had a stiff smile that bared his teeth far more than was really desirable. Sometimes Shepherd thought he looked downright reptilian. Today was one of those times.

"What do you want?" he asked.

Darling seemed quite amused at Adnan's belligerence. He folded his arms and waited, a half smile on his face.

"Charlie said you have some documents for me," Shepherd said.

"They're in my office."

"Fine."

Adnan just stood and looked at Shepherd and said nothing else.

"May I have them?" Shepherd prompted.

"I would have sent them to you if you had telephoned."

"I'm sure you would. But I'm here, so I'll take them with me."

Adnan still looked irritated and Darling still looked amused. Shepherd couldn't work out what the hell was going on.

"Look, guys, I'm sorry I interrupted whatever you were doing," he said. "If somebody will just give me the stuff I came for, I'll be on my way and leave you to it."

Darling glanced at Adnan and gave a little jerk of his head and Adnan scurried off. He carried his rolled up map or whatever it was with him when he left.

That was interesting, Shepherd thought. He didn't even realize Adnan knew Darling. Now here they were huddled together looking as if they were plotting something and Darling was running whatever it was. Shepherd filed the observation away with the large stockpile of other curiosities he had already collected in his wanderings around the royal court of Charlie Kitnarok. You could never tell when little things like that might turn out to be useful.

After Adnan had gone, Darling took a blue and white box of Gitanes Brunes out of his inside jacket pocket, the non-filter kind, and held them out.

"No thanks," Shepherd said.

Darling grunted, shook one out, and lit it with a gold lighter. He was a small man with a large head. On each occasion Darling and Shepherd had met, Darling had worn a well-cut dark suit, a white shirt, and a bow tie. His clothing gave him an air of primness. He looked like a man constantly smelling something unpleasant and suspecting it might be you.

"I keep trying to quit," Darling said, sliding the box of Gitanes back into his pocket. "I've even done hypnosis and acupuncture. Nothing works."

Darling loosed a world-class shrug, one any genuine Frenchman would have been proud to author.

"I just like the fucking things too much," he said.

Shepherd nodded but he didn't say anything.

Darling took a long pull on his cigarette. "What are you up to these days, Shepherd?" he asked.

"Same as always. Just practicing law. Trying to get by."

"I hear you're living in Hong Kong now."

"That's right."

"You like Hong Kong better than Bangkok?"

"Yeah. You meet a better class of bar trash there."

Darling nodded slowly, almost as if Shepherd had made an interesting observation worthy of reflection, and drew on his cigarette again.

"You've really been up and down these last few years, haven't you, Shepherd?"

Shepherd wasn't sure what to say to that. Actually, he *was* sure since Darling was absolutely right. He just wasn't about to give the bastard the satisfaction of agreeing with him.

"You should have tried Paris," Darling nodded as if he knew exactly what Shepherd was thinking. "There's a long tradition of Americans running away to Paris when they are unhappy."

"Is that why you're there?"

"Don't be cranky, Shepherd. It doesn't become you."

"No? Most people think it does."

Darling puffed on his cigarette and watched Shepherd without expression. Either he didn't have much of a sense of humor or he didn't think Shepherd did.

"Anyway," Shepherd went on when Darling didn't say anything else, "I wasn't unhappy and I didn't run away. I just decided it was time for a change and Hong Kong seemed like a place to start a law practice."

He tossed out his own shrug, not nearly as good as Darling's, but then he didn't have so many role models.

"Do you ever miss Bangkok?" Darling asked.

"No."

"Dealing with Thais gets old pretty quickly, doesn't it?"

"It does."

"And yet," Darling said, taking another puff of his cigarette, "here you are today."

"And yet," Shepherd nodded, "here I am today."

"You are a walking contradiction, Shepherd. A living conundrum."

Shepherd had the feeling this conversation was about something. He just couldn't figure out what it was.

Adnan came back into the room carrying a thick manila envelope.

"These are the documents I was asked to collect for you," he said.

Adnan walked over and shoved the envelope at him. Shepherd took it and nodded. He made a point of not thanking Adnan.

"There are copies of the statements for all the accounts at Bangkok Bank and Siam Commercial Bank," Adnan added. "Both the corporate ones and the personal ones."

Shepherd nodded, but he didn't say anything.

The expression on Adnan's face was transparent. He wanted to know why he had been told to give those statements to Shepherd. Shepherd said nothing at all and Adnan was left with no alternative but either to come right out and ask or to let the matter go.

He came right out and asked.

"What are you going to do with them?"

"These are copies, aren't they? They're not the originals?"

Adnan nodded. "Yes, they're copies."

"Then I'll destroy them when I'm done."

Adnan's eyes shifted quickly to Darling, then back to Shepherd.

"Done with what?" he asked.

"I'm sure if Charlie wanted you to know, he would have told you."

Adnan blinked at that and in the silence that followed Shepherd heard Darling snort softly.

"Well, gentlemen, I'll leave you to it," Shepherd went on quickly. "I'm sorry to have bothered you."

"No bother at all, Shepherd," Darling said. "You and I ought to have lunch while we're both in town. Perhaps get to know each other a little better."

"Sure," Shepherd nodded. "Give me a call."

"Maybe I'll do that," Darling said.

Adnan, Shepherd noticed, said nothing at all.

DARLING WATCHED thoughtfully as the door closed behind Shepherd. He took a last pull on his cigarette and stubbed it out in a heavy glass ashtray.

"What do you think?" Adnan asked.

Darling glanced back at the door through which Shepherd had just left.

"About him?" he asked.

Adnan nodded.

Darling cocked his head. "I'm not sure."

"I am," Adnan said. "He's just another one of the general's whims. He doesn't matter."

Darling pondered that for a while. He pursed his lips and let his eyes wander the room.

"I don't know about that," he said eventually. "I have a feeling he just might matter more than you think."

Eight

OUTSIDE THE OFFICE was a ceramic-tiled terrace similar to the one outside the villa where Charlie lived. Shepherd settled into a green cushioned chair, swung his feet onto an ottoman, and pulled back the flap of the envelope Adnan had given him. Before he could take anything out of it, Sally Kitnarok sat down in the chair next to him.

"Hello, Jack," she said. "Over yesterday's excitement yet?"

"Still in recovery."

"They say you weren't hurt."

"They're right, whoever they are."

Sally had been married to Charlie for something like twenty years. Shepherd liked Sally. She was British-born, but had grown up in Indonesia and Thailand where her father had done something or another with Save the Children. To the surprise of many, her foreign birth had never weighed on Charlie politically nearly as much as some of his allies thought it might when he began his rise to prominence.

Normally Thais don't much like other Thais marrying foreigners. Most of the hostility is normally directed at Thai women who marry foreign men, and there are a great many of them. They range from the much-maligned mail order brides to the daughters of the most prominent families in the country. Sometimes it seemed to Shepherd that women and rice were Thailand's only exports of any value.

For a Thai man to marry a foreign woman, on the other hand, is something else again. It's rare, but not unheard of, and it doesn't seem to bother Thais nearly as much. The arrangement even has a whiff of revenge about it, a humiliation of the foreigners who have carried off Thai women for generations. And there are few things that make the average Thai happier than seeing foreigners humiliated, even when that humiliation is just a figment of their imagination.

"How much longer are you here for?" Sally asked.

"I'm leaving soon. Probably tonight."

"For where?"

Shepherd hesitated. Telling Sally that he was going to Bangkok didn't seem the right thing to do for some reason. So he didn't.

"Home," he said instead.

Sally sighed. "I wish I could say that."

"You don't like Dubai?"

"You've heard that old expression, haven't you, Jack? When your life is in the toilet, it's Shanghai, Mumbai, Dubai, or goodbye."

"I've heard it. I'm just not sure it means very much."

"Maybe not," Sally sighed again. "But Dubai just isn't home. Oh, what am I saying? I haven't got a bloody clue where home is anymore."

"That's a pretty common problem in the twenty-first century," Shepherd said.

"Do you miss America?"

Shepherd had never known how to answer that question. If he said yes, the next question would be why he didn't just go back. If he said no, he would be asked why he disliked his own country. Shepherd had always made ducking the question altogether something of a personal policy so he turned Sally's inquiry back on her.

"Do I gather from that," he asked, "that you miss the UK? Or is it Thailand you miss?"

"I don't know," she said "but I miss somewhere. All I really want is a little peace and stability. Sometimes I wonder if I'll ever have that again."

Shepherd knew that was his cue to say something comforting, but he didn't know what it ought to be. Sally was married to a political figure beloved by roughly half of Thailand and reviled by the other half. No matter what Charlie did in the future, he would always be a saint to about thirty million people and a devil to thirty million more. Sally was probably right. Security and stability were unlikely to be part of her future.

They sat for a few minutes in companionable silence. Although Shepherd wanted to ask Sally if she knew anything about Charlie's plans for the future, he wasn't sure he should. Trying to pry information out of a wife about her husband felt unseemly, and there were issues of client confidentiality to consider, too. On the other hand, if Charlie really was going back into politics and was being less than honest with him about that, maybe that excused him from being entirely honest himself.

An old lawyer joke popped into Shepherd's mind. *What I really want is a one-armed lawyer, so he can't say on one hand but then on the other hand.* Sometimes he had no problem at all understanding why people loved lawyer jokes so much.

Shepherd stopped trying to decide if he should ask and just asked Sally what he wanted to know.

"Is Charlie preparing for a triumphal return to Thailand?"

"What do you mean?"

"Is he going back into politics? Does he want to be prime minister of Thailand again?"

"I don't know. What's he telling you?"

"He thinks that was what the attack was all about. He thinks someone was trying to stop him from going back."

"Maybe," Sally said, "but then again maybe it was just an angry husband."

Shepherd looked away. It made him uncomfortable when married people joked about each other's presumed infidelities. He had taken that tour and it still hurt far too much for him to joke along with them.

"It's not what Charlie's saying that bothers me," Shepherd said, going back to where they had been before Sally's little lurch into the inner workings of her marital life. "It's the things he's doing. They're things that make me wonder if he's not preparing for a political comeback."

"What things?"

Shepherd paused. He felt awkward and Sally obviously saw it.

"Never mind, Jack. I shouldn't have asked."

Shepherd thought for a moment. If the funds in Thailand were really family funds as Charlie had claimed, then they were Sally's funds, too, weren't they? So he composed an answer for Sally that he could at least tell himself skirted the edge of violating client confidence.

"Charlie asked me to reorganize the funds you have in Thailand." He tapped his palm against the brown envelope on his lap. "To get it all out of the country immediately."

Shepherd knew he shouldn't have said even that much, but he wanted to see Sally's reaction. He was disappointed when she didn't give him one.

"I don't know anything about that, Jack. That kind of thing is way over my head."

He doubted that, but there seemed to be no reason to say so.

"Does Charlie think something is about to happen in Thailand?" he asked instead.

"I really don't know. Charlie hasn't said anything specific to me."

Sally's eyes shifted slightly down and to the left. It was a classic tell. There was more, but she wasn't going to say what it was. Still, that was fair enough, Shepherd thought. What a man tells his wife should remain between them.

"I'm sorry," he said to Sally. "I shouldn't have asked."

Sally leaned across and put her hand on his arm.

"You're our friend, Jack. You can ask anything you like. If I knew, I'd tell you."

Shepherd just nodded at that. It wasn't true, of course. He knew it and he was sure Sally knew he knew it, but it would have been churlish of him to say that so he just let it go.

"Are you finally over that ex-wife of yours?"

The change of subject was so naked that Shepherd wondered briefly how Sally had managed it without laughing out loud.

"Yeah," he said. "Absolutely."

Sally gave him a look brimming with sympathy, the sort of look people gave to beggars in wheelchairs.

"Charlie and I care about you, Jack. You're our friend and we want you to be happy. You don't deserve what happened to you. You need to meet somebody new. You have to open your heart to someone else."

Suddenly the conversation was turning into a visit with Oprah.

"Do you keep in touch with Anita?" Sally asked before Shepherd could leap to his feet and flee.

"Anita and I were married," he said. "She found somebody she liked better, she left me, we got divorced. End of story. What do we have to keep in touch about?"

"Charlie and I keep thinking that maybe you'll get back together. You and Anita were a wonderful couple."

"Apparently not."

"Yes, you were. And surely Anita knows that, too."

"It must have slipped her mind there for a few minutes."

"Give her a chance, Jack. Things change, you know."

"Not this thing."

"Never give up, Jack. Never."

Shepherd really didn't want to talk about Anita any longer. Love never comes to anyone logically and there is certainly nothing logical about the way it vanishes. He'd had that discussion before with too many other people already and it had never taken him any place he wanted to go.

Shepherd found a way to excuse himself as quickly as possible after that, gave Sally a goodbye kiss on the cheek, and walked out to where the hotel driver was waiting for him beyond the security gate. He got into the car, leaned his head against the thick cushions of the back seat, and closed his eyes.

It felt good to be alone again.

Nine

ON THE WAY back to the hotel Shepherd got out his phone and checked the flights to Bangkok. There were no seats until the next day and he thought for a moment of calling Charlie and telling him he had changed his mind about using one of his jets. But, he knew Charlie would give him a lot of crap and he didn't want to hear it, so he just let it go and booked himself on an Emirates Airways flight that left the next morning. The major problem there was that then he had the rest of the afternoon and the evening to kill in Dubai, which as far as Shepherd was concerned was like unexpectedly scoring free time in Dallas. It was a windfall he could live a long time without.

Shepherd didn't really feel like going back to the hotel, but he didn't know what else to do. That was when it occurred to him he hadn't had a decent meal since he left Hong Kong. The idea of getting a little comfort food suddenly seemed pretty appealing, so he told the driver to take him to the Dubai Mall.

The Dubai Mall has millions of square feet of space, maybe tens of millions; several hundred stores; miles of marble-floored corridors; an Olympic-sized ice rink; and even the world's largest aquarium, one three stories high, fifty yards long, and filled with sharks. Shepherd wondered if anyone else in Dubai saw the sharks as ironic. Probably not. He doubted Dubai was a place where irony played particularly well.

He entered the mall through an entrance called the Waterfall, which actually *was* a waterfall, and rode an escalator that rose hundreds of feet up behind the tumbling water. He strolled past Bloomingdales, Banana Republic, Armani, Fendi, Ralph Lauren, Jimmy Choo, and even a Dean & Deluca market. Anyone who doubts the power of globalization has never been to a shopping mall in Dubai.

THE MAN PICKED up Shepherd when the hotel car turned onto the main road at Palm Jumeirah. He stayed well back as Shepherd's car headed north on Sheikh Zayed Road, but easily kept it in sight.

The man didn't think Shepherd would be expecting surveillance. He was certain the possibility of it had never even crossed Shepherd's mind, but he didn't want to take any chances. It was almost time to move, he might even move today, but if Shepherd suspected he was being watched he would have to back off. And he didn't want to back off.

It surprised the man when the car dropped Shepherd at the Dubai Mall, and he was not a man who liked surprises. He had assumed Shepherd was going back to his hotel. So what the hell was he doing at a shopping mall? Was he meeting someone there? That might prove to be a problem. Fortunately, there was a valet parking station at the entrance where Shepherd got out of the hotel car, so the man dumped his car with the valet and followed Shepherd inside.

SHEPHERD TOOK AN escalator to the mall's next level and walked until he spotted the familiar red and yellow sign.

FAT BURGER

THE LAST GREAT HAMBURGER STAND

When Shepherd had stumbled upon the place for the first time he could hardly believe it. A Fat Burger in Dubai? He hadn't had a Fat Burger since the last time he was in L.A. That was several years back, but he had never waivered in his conviction that Fat Burgers were the greatest hamburgers ever sold anywhere. The name was pretty unappetizing, of course—downright disgusting if he were to be completely honest about it—but he could live with almost anything they wanted to call themselves since the burgers tasted so good.

Shepherd went in and looked around. The place was absolutely identical to the Fat Burgers in L.A. and appeared to be about half full of what seemed a mix of locals and tourists. He was damn near starving to death by then, so he ordered a double Fat Burger, fries, and a Coke from the cheerful Filipino girl behind the counter and sat down to wait for it.

THE MAN WAS a Caucasian dressed in khaki trousers and a plain, white short-sleeved shirt. Neither tall nor short, neither heavy nor skinny, neither young nor old, he looked ordinary in every respect. His appearance was completely forgettable, which was why he was so good at surveillance.

At first he was afraid he might have been spotted and Shepherd was about to launch himself on a cleaning route. A shopping mall was a textbook location for it. But soon it became obvious that Shepherd wasn't doing anything of the sort. He had no idea anyone was on him. The man could have been driving a float from the Rose Parade and Shepherd wouldn't have spotted him.

The crowds were thinner in the part of the mall where Shepherd was walking now and the man started thinking about making his move. Somewhere public, but not too public. He was just wondering if this might not be the best chance he was likely to get when Shepherd suddenly started walking very fast and darted into a storefront about thirty yards ahead.

For a moment the man panicked. Shepherd must have spotted him after all and had just been lulling him into a sense of false confidence. Now Shepherd was moving and he had been caught flat-footed. Walking as fast as he dared without calling attention to himself, he headed for the same storefront into which Shepherd had vanished. He glanced at the sign as he got closer. *Fat Burger.* What the hell was *that?*

When the man walked in, he almost fell over Shepherd. He was sitting on a molded yellow plastic chair at a small black Formica table. His back was to the door, and he was watching the opposite end of the room where half a dozen red-and-yellow uniformed girls worked behind a counter.

The man suddenly understood he hadn't been spotted at all. This was some kind of fast food place and Shepherd had just gone in to eat. He kept walking toward the counter and ordered a Coke. He paid for it, turned around as if he were looking for something, and glanced in Shepherd's direction. One of the red-and-yellow uniformed girls had just delivered his order to him on a red plastic tray and Shepherd was so involved in digging into it that he wasn't paying the slightest attention to anything else.

The man went to a table by the wall and took a chair that faced Shepherd's direction. He sipped at his Coke and watched for a while. There was no one else seated in the area around Shepherd and he appeared totally absorbed in his food. After watching for five minutes, the man decided this was the best chance he was going to get. He knocked back the rest of his Coke, stood up, and walked toward Shepherd.

SHEPHERD FELT RATHER than saw the man approaching. He didn't look up. He still had a few bites of his Fat Burger left and they were far more interesting to him than some guy walking by his table. But the man didn't walk by his table. He stopped, stood right next to it, and cleared his throat.

"How did a guy like you end up working for somebody like General Kitnarok?" the man asked.

Now Shepherd looked up. He wasn't sure he had heard right.

"A man like you, Mr. Shepherd? With your background and reputation? How did you get mixed up with General Kitnarok?"

The guy was a middle-aged Caucasian with a completely forgettable face. Shepherd was certain he had never seen him before.

"No, Mr. Shepherd," the man said as if he were reading his mind. "We've never met."

Shepherd picked up a paper napkin, folded it over once, and wiped his mouth. Then he just sat and looked at the guy and waited to see what was coming next.

"I'm Special Agent Leonard Keur of the FBI."

"You've got to be kidding."

"Do I look like somebody who's kidding?"

"Can I see some ID?"

The man took a dark brown leather folder out of his right rear trouser pocket. The folder looked beaten up, like it had a lot of mileage on it. Without being invited, he sat down in the plastic chair across from Shepherd and laid the folder on the table between them. He slid his forefinger inside and flipped it open.

Clipped to one side of the folder was a gold badge that said Department of Justice at the top and Federal Bureau of Investigation at the bottom. On the other side was an identification card with the FBI seal and FBI printed in big blue letters. Shepherd bent forward and looked at the card. He popped the last bite of his Fat Burger in his mouth and chewed thoughtfully while he examined it.

The card said the bearer's name was Leonard Keur. Shepherd looked up and compared the face sitting across from him with the color photograph laminated to the card. It was the same guy. No doubt about it. The ID looked genuine enough, too, but since Shepherd had no idea what genuine FBI identification looked like, his opinion in the matter was probably of limited value.

"What is this about?" he asked.

"How long has General Kitnarok been your client?"

"I don't talk about my clients."

"Clients? Shouldn't that be *client*? Isn't General Kitnarok your only client, Jack?"

In Shepherd's experience, when cops went from calling him Mr. Shepherd to calling him Jack, it never meant anything good. So he wiped his mouth again, pushed his tray away, and awaited developments.

"What is your personal relationship with General Kitnarok?"

"Good."

"That's not what I meant."

"Then what *did* you mean?"

"Is the general just a client or do you consider him a friend?"

"Who are you really?"

Keur was starting to look annoyed, which Shepherd rather liked.

"I showed you my identification," he snapped.

"Maybe you bought that badge on the internet."

"Call Washington if you have any doubts. Call the field office there. Or call the Director for all I care." The man pulled a Blackberry out of a front trouser pocket and laid it on the table. "There you go. Knock yourself out."

Shepherd didn't pick it up.

"Who is Pete Logan and what does he look like?" he asked instead.

"Pete is the legat in Bangkok," Keur replied without hesitation. "He's about five foot nine, forty-five years old, has a clean-shaved head, and drinks more scotch than he should. By the way, he speaks very highly of you."

Legat is State Department slang for the resident FBI agent in an American embassy abroad. It's a contraction of the title Legal Attaché, abbreviations and acronyms being much beloved by government types. Pete Logan was the agent posted at the American embassy in Bangkok and Shepherd had hung around with him a little during his ill-fated tour there teaching business at Chulalongkorn University. If this guy knew Logan well enough to describe him that way, he was probably for real.

"Okay, let's say for the sake of argument I'm convinced you're actually an FBI agent named Leonard Keur. What do you want?"

"I want to talk to you."

"About what?"

Keur stood up. "Let's take a walk."

"I don't want to take a walk."

"Yes, you do, Jack. You want to take a walk, and you want to take a walk with me."

Shepherd sat looking at Keur and thought about how to play this. His first instinct was to be a hard ass, but then that was always his first instinct and he knew that sometimes it really wasn't the best way to go.

"Just one thing," Keur said.

"Yeah? What's that?"

Keur reached down, plucked an unused napkin off Shepherd's tray, and handed to him.

"Wipe your mouth. You've got mustard on your top lip."

Ten

THEY RODE THE escalator up two levels in silence and strolled down a wide corridor lined with women's clothing stores. They passed Guess, Shanghai Tang, Miss Selfridge, and something with the unlikely and, Shepherd thought, remarkably unattractive name of S*uce. They got all the way to Bloomingdales before Keur spoke again.

"You going to answer my question, Jack?"

"I didn't hear a question."

"The one I asked you back in the burger place. Why is a man like you working for General Kitnarok?"

"I don't work for him. He's my client."

"You have a client or you work for the guy. It's a distinction without a difference."

"A distinction without a difference? That's a familiar phrase. Where did you go to law school, Agent Keur?"

"I went to Fordham."

"Why? Couldn't you get into Yale?"

It was a snide thing to say and Shepherd felt lousy almost as soon as the words were out of his mouth. He was letting Keur get under his skin.

They passed through an enormous round atrium that rose in gold-trimmed tiers to a glass dome. Through it Shepherd could see a cloudless, cobalt-blue sky.

"What do you want from me, Keur?"

"Look, Jack, we need your help. There's an investigation underway on which we want your advice."

"Are you serious? The Bureau wants to hire me?"

"Not exactly hire. We can't pay you."

"That doesn't make you a very attractive client."

"We thought you might be willing to help us anyway. Money's not everything. There could be other rewards."

"Such as what?"

"Having the FBI owe you a favor is pretty valuable, don't you think?"

Shepherd wasn't so sure of that, but he was curious where this was going so he tried to look impressed. It wasn't easy.

"What are you investigating?" he asked.

"I can't tell you that."

"So you want my help investigating something, you don't want to pay me for my help, and you won't tell me what you're investigating. Do you guys ever stop and think how stupid you sound sometimes?"

"Look, Jack, we need to know what's going on in General Kitnarok's inner circle. We need to understand who the players are and how they relate to each other. We thought you might be in a good position to give us some guidance on that kind of thing."

"Why do you need to know that?"

"I've already told you too much."

"You told me exactly nothing."

"I've gone as far as I can go. Can you help me?"

"Look, Agent Keur, in my line of work you don't talk to people about your clients, not unless the subpoena is nicely typed and has your name spelled right. And most of the time not even then."

"We're not asking you for anything confidential, Counselor, just some general observations about how General Kitnarok's inner circle works."

"I don't know how Charlie's inner circle works. I couldn't help you even if I wanted to. I live in Hong Kong. I mostly deal with Charlie by telephone and email. I hardly ever see him. I don't know who he talks to or about what."

"Then how about this? From now on, find a way to watch the comings and going of the people around General Kitnarok for me. Just keep me in the picture as to who's got his ear, that sort of thing."

They walked on in silence until Shepherd realized they had reached the colossal aquarium that was the centerpiece of the mall. It held, so the mall claimed, five hundred sharks. They stopped and watched a huge school of fish swim by right at eye level. There looked to be hundreds of them, their red and gold bands shimmering as if they were wrapped in Christmas foil. Immediately behind the school of fish came three big sharks, swimming very slowly with such economy of motion that tiny motors might have been propelling them. The sharks swam with their mouths half open as they shadowed the red and gold fish and the sharp-pointed triangular teeth lining their jagged jaws were clearly visible. The message was so clear that Shepherd wondered if Keur had been leading him there all along.

"Let me make certain I understand exactly what you mean," Shepherd said when the sharks had passed. "Are you asking me to *spy* on Charlie for you?"

"Well, not exactly spy on him. More like… well, like—"

"You're asking me to spy on Charlie for you."

"Yeah," Keur sighed. "When you cut through all the bullshit, I guess that about sums it up."

"Why would it ever cross your mind I might do something like that?"

"I talked to some people in Washington. A lot of people remember you. They thought you might be my guy."

"You're saying you asked around Washington and everyone told you I'd make a dandy snitch?"

"No, people told me you're discreet. And that you care about what's right."

"Yes, I am, and yes I do. So let me just say one thing to you, Agent Keur. Go to hell. We're all done here."

"Slow down, Jack. I think maybe we've gotten off on the wrong foot."

"We don't require any feet. We're not going anywhere together."

"Has anyone ever told you that your wisecracks get old fast?"

"Frequently. And yet I persist. Isn't that amazing?"

They passed the end of the aquarium and took an escalator up to the next level. They walked through another huge atrium, this one with a full-size ice hockey rink at the bottom, and passed a Starbucks with ranks of sofas and easy chairs facing into the atrium.

"I'm asking nicely for your help, Jack. Please just hear me out. I'll put all my cards on the table. I'll tell you everything."

Shepherd said nothing.

"Okay, here's the truth of the matter," Keur said. "The target of our investigation isn't General Kitnarok. It's Robert Darling."

Shepherd glanced at Keur, but he said nothing.

"Surprised?"

He was and he wasn't, but he didn't see any need to tell Keur that.

"Why are you investigating Darling?" Shepherd asked instead.

"Darling is a trustee of the Kitnarok Foundation," Keur said.

"Yes, and I am, too. So what?"

"And Darling is also a director of Blossom Trading."

Shepherd shrugged.

"Do you know what Blossom Trading does?"

"I assume it trades."

"Do you know what it trades, and with whom?"

"No idea."

"You never asked anybody?"

"I never had any reason to ask anybody. I've got nothing to do with Blossom Trading."

"Sure you do. You've been there at least a half dozen times that I know of."

That caught Shepherd off guard as he gathered Keur must have intended. He stopped walking and stood for a moment examining the titles in the window of a huge bookstore named Kinokuniya. What was an English-language bookstore with a Japanese name doing in a Middle Eastern country? Shepherd couldn't even imagine.

"Is the FBI following me, Keur?"

"Don't be ridiculous, Jack. You're not nearly that important."

"Then why do you think I've ever been to Blossom Trading?"

"Come on, Jack. We're the FBI. We're not completely stupid."

"You could have fooled me."

Keur mimed a laugh, but he didn't say anything.

"I've never been to Blossom Trading," Shepherd said. "The Kitnarok Foundation has its offices at the same address as Blossom Trading so I've been in the building, but that's it. Are you people watching that building for some reason?"

Keur ignored the question. "I assume you know General Kitnarok owns part of Blossom Trading," he said instead.

"Of course, I do. Charlie owns a lot of companies I have nothing to do with."

"You want me to tell you what Blossom Trading does?" Keur asked me.

"Is there any way for me to stop you?"

"Blossom Trading trades with Iran. Iran buys arms through them to evade the arms embargo."

Shepherd suddenly wished he *had* thought of a way to stop Keur.

"You're telling me Charlie is running guns to Iran?"

"Blossom Trading is running guns to Iran. We're not sure how deeply General Kitnarok is involved. That's what we need your help to find out."

"But you think Darling is involved."

"Darling is an American citizen and a director of Blossom Trading. If he were involved in a violation of the arms embargo on Iran, the FBI would be interested." Keur spread his hands, palms up. "Draw your own conclusions."

Shepherd nodded and thought that over.

"You've met with Darling several times recently, haven't you?" Keur asked.

Shepherd nodded again.

"What did you talk about?"

"Nothing in particular."

"I find that hard to believe, Jack."

"Why?"

"Talking about nothing in particular just doesn't sound like you."

"Wait a minute. Are you saying you think *I'm* involved in selling arms to Iran?"

"Are you?"

"You can't be serious, Keur."

"Then just put me in the picture here. What did you and Darling talk about?"

"I already told you. I barely know Darling. We sit in trustee meetings together. I bump into him occasionally. That's it."

Keur didn't look to Shepherd like he believed him and suddenly Shepherd went from feeling mildly irritated to completely pissed off.

"I can't believe this shit, Keur. Do you honestly think that I'm going to rattle off a report of conversations I've had with Darling just because you suddenly drop out of the sky, tell me he's an arms smuggler, and ask me what we've been talking about?"

"Let's not quarrel, Jack."

"Why not? You're no fun when you're all serious. Actually, come to think of it, I'll bet you're no fun under any circumstances."

They walked into the bookstore with the Japanese name that was so big Shepherd couldn't even see the other end of it. As they slowly strolled the aisles, he wondered how the place stayed in business. He had never seen a single person in Dubai reading a book.

"I need to know if General Kitnarok is involved in Blossom Trading's arms deals, Jack. The only way I can find out for sure is through you."

"Then I'd say you're pretty well screwed. Got a Plan B?"

"Think about it. It's to your advantage as well as General Kitnarok's."

"You can say anything you want, Keur, but I'm not spying on my client for the FBI."

Abruptly, Keur changed the subject. "You handled yourself well out there yesterday, Jack. Cool as a cucumber, you were. Both shooters dead and you and General Kitnarok walk away without a scratch."

"We were lucky. The CNN woman wasn't."

"From where I sat, luck had nothing to do with it."

"And where were you sitting?"

"In front of a TV set watching CNN like everybody else. What did you think I meant?"

"I thought you meant you were there."

Keur snorted, a sound Shepherd could have lived a long time without hearing. "You think the FBI tried to kill General Kitnarok yesterday?"

"I don't know who it was. Do you?"

"It wasn't us."

"But you know who it was, don't you?"

"No idea. None at all."

Shepherd looked at Keur. He decided he didn't believe him.

"Anyway, forget all that, Jack. Here's what you really need to know about yesterday. We don't think it was a genuine attempt to kill General Kitnarok."

"No?" Shepherd said. "Well, darn, it sure looked genuine to me, and I had a hell of a lot better view of it than you did."

"That's not what I meant. It was a real hit, all right. But killing General Kitnarok wasn't the objective."

Shepherd must have look puzzled, which would have been easy enough since he had no idea at all what Keur was talking about.

"You don't see where I going with this, do you, Jack?"

Shepherd said nothing.

"Killing General Kitnarok would have served no purpose," Keur said. "Quite on the contrary, it would have turned him into a martyr, which would have hurt his political opponents, not helped them."

"You're telling me those guys weren't trying to kill Charlie?"

"No, they were trying to disrupt his comeback by crippling his financial resources."

"I don't understand. How would an attack on Charlie cripple his financial resources?"

"It wouldn't. That's what I'm telling you. General Kitnarok wasn't the target of the attack."

Keur's face took on an expression that was almost but not quite a smile.

"You were, Jack. They were trying to kill you."

Shepherd stopped walking and stood and stared at Keur.

"Be careful, Jack. Stay cool and keep your head down. I'll be in touch."

Keur turned and walked away. He left the bookstore and was almost immediately swallowed up by the crowds in the mall. Shepherd was too dumbfounded to do anything but stand and watch him go.

Eleven

SHEPHERD WENT BACK to his hotel, but he couldn't concentrate enough to read and watching television was way too depressing to think about. He took out a legal pad and started making notes on corporate structures he might be able to use to get Charlie's money out of Thailand, but that didn't hold his attention for very long either. Soon he gave up even pretending to do anything productive and just sat, doing nothing, looking out the window at the sunlight glinting off the blue and cream panels of the Burj Khalifa.

The Burj Khalifa is the world's tallest building. It's a few feet short of half a mile high, almost the same height as two Empire State Buildings stacked one on top of another. Up close you lose perspective and the Burj looks pretty much like any other office building, just a lot bigger. But when you see it from a distance, reaching for the heavens out of the featureless monotony of the desert, the one-hundred-sixty story Burj looks like a giant rocket ship about to roar into deep space carrying samples of all the earth's living creatures. If Noah were to come back today and build an ark, Shepherd figured it would look exactly like the Burj Khalifa.

He swung his feet up on a coffee table, laced his fingers together behind his head, and thought about the events of the last couple of days. Twenty-four hours ago two guys had done their best to kill somebody, even if their best hadn't been very much. It never occurred to him that their target could have been anybody other than Charlie Kitnarok and that didn't seem to have crossed anyone else's mind either. Certainly not Charlie's.

However hard it might be for Shepherd to believe that someone had hired two gunmen to kill *him*, it was even harder for him to understand what had happened since the attack, whoever the real target might have been. Because *nothing* had happened since the attack. It was almost as if it had never occurred at all. He hadn't been questioned by the Dubai police or anybody else who was investigating the incident. Adnan and Robert Darling hadn't mentioned it when he saw them. Sally Kitnarok seemed to be about as worried as if her husband had slipped on a loose rug. And Charlie himself was absolutely exhilarated.

What in the hell was really going on here?

All at once, an impulse came over Shepherd that at first seemed silly. But the more he thought about it, the more reasonable it began to feel. Besides, he had absolutely nothing else to do.

He went downstairs, got into a taxi, and told the driver to take him to the souk. Although he wasn't absolutely certain where the ambush had taken place, he remembered more or less where he had hijacked the *abra* in which he and Charlie had made their escape. If he started there, he could probably work his way back along their escape route and find the place where they had been ambushed.

He wanted to see it again. He wanted to look at where the attacked had happened. He didn't know what good that would do him or anyone else, but nevertheless that was what he wanted.

REVERSE ENGINEERING THEIR escape route turned out to be harder than Shepherd expected.

Once he left Dubai Creek, crossed over Baniyas Road, and entered the souk, he quickly became confused. The tangled warren of narrow passageways would have robbed a bloodhound of its sense of direction and Shepherd was no bloodhound. He stumbled around for nearly an hour, doubling back and turning around so many times he figured he had to be going in circles. He was about to give up on the whole idea and find a taxi to take him back to the hotel when a sign over a shophouse caught his eye.

SALEM ALI BAKERY

At first he couldn't work out why the sign seemed so familiar, but then all in a rush it came back to him. He was poking his head above the wall of bales where he and Charlie had taken cover. The first shooter was holding the big handgun in front of him in a perfect Weaver stance. The shooter was lifting the gun's muzzle and swinging it toward him. And just as Shepherd ducked back behind the bags, he caught sight of that sign on a building behind the shooter.

Shepherd looked around. He was standing in an open courtyard formed by two rows of shophouses and now he realized it was the same one in which the ambush had taken place yesterday. He hadn't recognized it at first because nothing about it looked the same. The two pallets of burlap bales behind which he and Charlie had taken cover were gone, leaving the front of the building through which they had made their escape appearing curiously denuded. Everything else was different as well.

There had been several big wooden crates where Charlie's driver had taken cover, and Shepherd clearly remembered seeing on CNN a pile of red and blue cement bags against which the second gunman had died. Neither of those things there anymore either. Instead, one side of the courtyard was now littered with haphazard piles of yellow, red, and blue plastic crates, most of which appeared to be filled with women's clothing. The other side of the courtyard was empty.

Near the place where the CNN cameraman must have stood,

several dozen long bolts of dark-colored cloth were propped on end against the wall and six or eight small metal chairs with black vinyl seats were pushed into a tight clump. They were the kind of chairs people used to call stenographers' chairs back when there were still such things as stenographers. A man dressed in a white *dishdasha* and wearing a red and white checked *ghutra* wrapped around his head was sitting quietly in one of the chairs at the front of the clump. Shepherd couldn't see the man's face clearly at that distance, but he was old and weathered and his jaw was working as if he were chewing something.

This did not look like the place where a political assassination attempt had occurred only twenty-four hours earlier, a place where two men and a woman had died.

And yet, it was.

Shepherd walked over to the building through which he and Charlie had escaped. A metal shutter was pulled down over the front window and the door was locked. He ran his eyes slowly over the pitted concrete surface of the building's facade, but saw no signs of bullet marks. The shots the gunman fired in their direction must have gone into the bales, and someone had taken the bales away.

He turned and walked slowly toward the old man sitting in the stenographer's chair. The surface of the courtyard was paved with concrete stones mortared into neat rows, and his eyes scanned back and forth over them as he walked. He saw no shell casings, but no doubt those would have all been picked up by now anyway. He saw no bloodstains either, and yet three people had bled to death right here.

When he reached the place where the old man was, he rolled out one of the stenographer's chairs and sat down. The man remained silent, not even turning his head. If he cared one way or another that Shepherd was there, he gave no sign. Looking up the courtyard, Shepherd saw he was viewing the area at roughly the same angle from which the CNN cameraman had been filming. The perspective was right. The facades of the buildings were right. Only the goods stored in front of the buildings were different.

Still, there was no sign at all this was a crime scene or that an investigation had been conducted here. No tape, no chalk marks, no litter. Something else felt wrong, too, but it took him a few minutes before it finally occurred to him what it was. The whole courtyard was unnaturally clean, certainly far cleaner than any other part of the souk he had seen. Were the Dubai police that efficient? Had they swept down in force, measured and photographed everything, and then scrubbed and cleaned the whole scene, all in less than twenty-four hours? He supposed it was possible. Obviously more than possible, since that was exactly what had happened.

What am I really looking at here?

It was the scene of a political assassination attempt, every trace of which had been erased in less than twenty-four hours. Could it be that the Dubai authorities, embarrassed that something like this could happen in their country, were trying to wrap it up quickly? Or was somebody else altogether behind the clean up, somebody connected somehow to Charlie?

But how did that make any sense?

Shepherd had no idea. No idea at all.

After ten minutes of thinking about it, he gave up. He stood up, wished his still silent companion a good afternoon, and walked off in search of a road big enough for him to find a taxi.

SHEPHERD HAD DINNER alone at the Manhattan Grill at the Grand Hyatt. For what a steak cost there he could have bought a small car in some countries, but he figured Charlie could afford it. It was certainly one hell of a lot cheaper than flying him to Bangkok in a G-4.

After dinner, he went back to his hotel and sat on the balcony just staring out into the blackness of the Persian Gulf. Shepherd hadn't smoked a cigar in a week or two, but all at once a cigar was exactly what he wanted. He went back inside, got a Montecristo out of his briefcase, cut it, and lit it. He was in a non-smoking room and there weren't any ashtrays so he went into the bathroom and drafted a drinking glass to play the role. It didn't seem to mind. Back out onto the balcony, he put his makeshift ashtray on the table, then leaned against the railing on his forearms and smoked quietly for a while. The air was moist and thick and there was an odor of ocean salt on the hot night wind.

Those guys had been trying to kill somebody, Shepherd reminded himself. Whether it was Charlie or it was him, it was sure as hell one of them, and they were both still alive. The gunmen might be dead, but they were only hired hands. Whoever hired them wasn't dead, at least not as far as he knew, so it seemed possible, even likely, that there would be another attempt. And if necessary, another one after that. The more he thought about it, the more it seemed to him that the attempts would probably continue until somebody tracked down whoever was behind this, or until they eventually succeeded.

If he was right, if that was the way it was, then Shepherd figured there wasn't much he could do about it. He sure as hell wasn't equipped to track down the plotters, whoever they were. And, other than ducking at every possible opportunity, he had no control that he could think of over whether or not they were successful.

Then there was the matter of Agent Keur. Clearly Keur wasn't just going to disappear any more than the shooters were. That wasn't the way the Feds worked when they wanted something, which caused Shepherd to ask himself just what it was that Keur really *did* want. Asking him to keep tabs on who Charlie saw was ridiculous. If that was all Keur wanted to know, there were better and less risky ways to find out. No, there had to be more to Keur's approach than that, even if Shepherd didn't have the slightest idea what it might be.

Whatever Keur was really after, Shepherd figured Keur would keep cranking up the pressure until Shepherd either did it or Keur didn't want it anymore. If that was what Keur was going to do, Shepherd decided there wasn't much he could do about that either.

Perhaps it was Shepherd's growing sense that he was losing control over nearly everything that was the source of it, but suddenly he thought about Anita. It had been a while since he had last thought about Anita, several days perhaps, but he thought about her now, and with the thought came the old terror of wondering where she was, who she was with, and what she was doing right at that moment.

Like an alcoholic pushing away a glass of whiskey, Shepherd took a deep breath, expelled all such thoughts from his consciousness, and chalked up another entry on the ever-expanding list of things he couldn't do anything about.

Part Two

BANGKOK

"But I don't want to go among mad people," Alice responded.
"Oh, you can't help that," said the Cat. "We're all mad here. I'm mad. You're mad."
"How do you know I'm mad?" said Alice.
"You must be," said the Cat. "Or you wouldn't have come here."

— Lewis Carroll,
Alice in Wonderland

Twelve

THAILAND IS THE Italy of Asia. Great food, beautiful women, joyously corrupt, and totally dysfunctional. Sometimes Shepherd wondered if maybe it might not be the right place for him after all. He liked food. He liked women. He was a true connoisseur of corruption. And for the last six months he had been even more dysfunctional than Thailand.

It had been raining on and off ever since Shepherd got in from Dubai. He had checked into the hotel, made a couple of calls, and gone for a quick run in Lumpini Park to shake off the funk of the long flight. Now he was doing very little but sitting by himself at a window table at a pub in Bangkok's financial district called the Duke of Wellington. He was drinking coffee, watching the rain, and pretending to read the *International Herald Tribune.* Outside the window the wind kicked up a notch and the rain swirled like smoke through the hard neon light of the big multicolored signs along the street.

He had gotten used to the rain in Bangkok. It rains a lot in the evenings. It rains a lot in the mornings, too, and the afternoons, and at night. It just didn't matter very much to anyone that it did. Bangkok is a twenty-four hour town and a little rain does nothing to hold it back. Ten million people, more or less; a city no worse than a lot of others, but no better either.

Some people say that Bangkok attracts a miserable bunch of foreigners: drifters, losers, loners, people on the run from broken lives. They claim the place is a magnet for the lost, the lonely, and the misbegotten. Shepherd knew some people even thought that was why he had once taken up residence there. It wasn't true, of course. At least not altogether.

Shepherd wasn't bothered much over what people said about him. He figured that what people said about anything depended mostly on where they sat. As for him, he was sitting at a table at the Duke of Wellington drinking coffee. And he didn't really care what anyone thought about why he had moved to Bangkok once upon a time, because he didn't live in Bangkok anymore.

Shepherd finished his coffee, pushed back from the table, and went to look for the toilet.

WHEN HE CAME out, Pete Logan was sitting at the bar drinking something brown. Shepherd walked over and took the stool next to him.

"Thanks for coming," he said.

Pete examined Shepherd with curiosity.

"What?" Shepherd asked.

"I don't hear from you for three months, you don't call, you don't write, then suddenly you ring up and ask me to come out on a rainy night to meet you here and I do. Right about now I'm asking myself: why am I doing this?"

"Because you think I'm a really cool guy and you've missed me?"

"No, that's not it."

Pete had been the FBI's resident agent in Bangkok for a little over three years. Back when Shepherd lived there, too, they had discovered that they were two guys from similar backgrounds stranded in a culture that didn't much care for either one of them.

They occasionally had meals together and even ran together in Lumpini Park a few times. What Shepherd always remembered most clearly, however, was that when Anita left him, Pete had been a pal. He bought drinks and told some stories, but he never offered a word of advice. Shepherd thought that was a pretty good definition of a real friend: somebody who's there when you need him and understands how to help without being told. Shepherd didn't have all that many real friends, but from that time on Pete Logan was one of them.

The bartender brought Shepherd another cup of coffee and Pete stared at it in disbelief.

Shepherd shrugged. "Jet lag."

"When did you get in?"

"A few hours ago."

"Where from?"

"Dubai."

"Don't tell me you were in Dubai to see—"

"Yeah."

"Were you there when those guys—"

"Yeah."

"Did it really go down the way CNN said it did?" Pete asked.

Shepherd bobbed his head around in a gesture that could have meant practically anything. Then he took another sip of coffee and changed the subject.

"I need a favor, Pete."

"Of course you do. When have you ever called me that you didn't need a favor?"

Shepherd told Pete about Agent Keur and his tale about the investigation of Robert Darling and Blossom Trading. Then he told Pete that Keur had asked him to feed the Bureau information about what was happening around Charlie.

"Did you agree to that?" Pete asked.

"Of course not."

Pete nodded, but he didn't say anything.

"So what about Robert Darling and Blossom Trading?" Shepherd prompted.

"Got me," Pete said. "I never heard of either one."

"What do you know about Keur?"

"Nothing. I never heard of him either."

"That's funny. I asked Keur if he knew you and he described you perfectly."

Pete spread his hands slightly, but he didn't say anything.

"He even said you spoke highly of me," Shepherd added.

"So there you are. Right off the bat we've established that the man is a pathological liar."

"Can you find out?"

"About Keur?"

"No, about the Bureau's investigation of Darling and Blossom Trading."

Pete pushed back slightly from the bar and cleared his throat.

"Information like that would be pretty closely restricted, Jack."

"I don't want anything heavy duty. Just when the investigation started, what it's about, who else has been targeted. Stuff like that."

"Right. Nothing heavy duty. Just pretty much everything the Bureau knows."

"Well… whatever you feel comfortable telling me, at least."

Pete swirled the whiskey in his glass and then threw back the rest of it. Shepherd signaled to the bartender to bring him another and they sat quietly until Pete had it in front of him.

"I suppose now you think I'll give it up just because you've bought me a drink."

"Yeah, I do."

Pete shrugged and gave his glass a couple of turns.

"I'll make some calls," he said. "But no promises. Let me see what turns up and I'll decide then what I can tell you."

They talked for a little longer about this and that. Then Pete finished his whiskey and left. Shepherd walked to the door with him to see if it was still raining. Of course it was still raining. He went back to the bar, picked up the *Herald Tribune* again, and ordered another cup of coffee.

Up on one of the flat screen televisions hanging above the bar a satellite channel was broadcasting a game between the Dallas Cowboys and the New York Giants. Shepherd glanced at his watch and did the math. The game couldn't have been coming in live, but he supposed it could have been a rebroadcast of a game played earlier in the day. On the other hand, for all he knew it was a re-broadcast of a game played several seasons back. He had pretty much lost track of American sports during the last few years. Occasionally he wished he hadn't, but not all that often.

The picture shifted to the Cowboys cheerleaders and that naturally got Shepherd's full attention. He sat for a minute with his arms folded over his chest and just watched. The star-spangled silver-and-blue uniforms, the tiny white shorts molded to perfect bottoms, the bubbling energy, and the face-splitting smiles all mesmerized him. America was the only culture in the history of mankind to have spawned cheerleaders. He wasn't sure what that meant, but he was absolutely certain it couldn't be anything good.

WHEN THE RAIN eventually stopped, Shepherd paid his tab and headed back to his hotel. It was a nice night for walking and Bangkok didn't give up many of those. The air, cleansed by the rain, had turned almost cool, at least cool for a place where the locals hauled out parkas and mukluks anytime the temperature dropped below eighty degrees.

Shepherd liked walking in Bangkok. That was a good thing, since walking was the most practical way to get around. Cars, motorcycles, buses, bicycles, vans, and even tuk-tuks, little three-wheeled vehicles that roared like pissed-off lawnmowers, choked the city's narrow streets day and night with traffic so snarled it had become a tourist attraction.

A lot of the city's life was lived right out there on its streets. People ate their meals on the streets, got their hair cut on the streets, had their shoes repaired on the streets, and did their shopping on the streets. On every walk through the city, he passed through an endless succession of vignettes of people living their lives. It all somehow fused together into an exotic brew of adventure and romance that still held a lot of attraction for him, whatever else he might think about Bangkok now.

He walked west on Silom Road, then turned left at the old Christian cemetery and followed its concrete wall south. Up ahead he could see the radio masts rising from behind the high, ocher wall topped with razor wire that surround the Russian Embassy. Just in front of that wall was the Grand Hotel.

The Grand Hotel wasn't really all that grand. To be absolutely truthful, it was slightly shabby. Some of the great hotels of the world were in Bangkok: hotels like the Mandarin Oriental, the Four Seasons, and the Peninsula. Charlie was paying the bill so naturally Shepherd could have stayed anywhere he wanted, but he stayed at the Grand regardless. It was clean, it was comfortable, it was a ten-minute walk from the business district, and it had soul.

There was something else, too, of course. He had lived at the Grand for nearly six months after Anita left, so there was also an element of loyalty involved in returning there. The Grand had been his sanctuary when he needed one, his safe house while he was trying to decide what was to become of him. The small suite where he lived back then had been agreeable. He ate most of his meals at the Duke of Wellington, and he didn't do any entertaining. What else had he needed but a bedroom, a bathroom, and a little sitting room where he could lie on the sofa and watch television? The Grand had been a steadfast friend when he needed one. He felt now like he owed it the same allegiance and fidelity in return.

The atmosphere of the place was just right for him as well. The Grand was almost a private club, one dedicated to the preservation of a particular species of foreigner: the slightly off-kilter refugees from reality who usually washed up on the great dirty beach of Bangkok. That was Shepherd back then all right. Off-kilter and washed up. He had fit right in at the Grand.

IT WAS LATE when he got to the Grand and no one was in the lobby but a dozing security guard. He was an elderly man in a wrinkled khaki uniform and he sat on a stool next to the front desk, his head pitched forward on his folded arms. He snored gently as Shepherd walked by. Since he had dropped his bag off before going to the Duke, he bypassed the elevator and took the stairs. He was on the third floor, which wasn't much of a climb, and the elevator was so slow that he had long ago developed the habit of walking whenever it was practical.

In his room Shepherd quickly shed his clothes, depositing them on the nearest available piece of floor, climbed into the shower, and turned the hot water up all the way. After a pleasant enough few minutes soaking in the scalding spray, the water began to go cold, so he shut off the shower, toweled himself dry, and climbed into bed.

Lying under the sheet, his hands clasped across his chest, he listened to the humming of the air-conditioner and thought about the last time he had been in Bangkok. Anita had come back to him from everywhere then. Perhaps this time would be different.

It wasn't different.

Soon enough the memories came, padding quietly on little cat feet through the grey half-darkness of his room. He surrendered without a struggle and drifted with Anita for a long while in the borderlands of consciousness, visiting and being visited by images he thought he had long forgotten. It was far too long before sleep took him, but eventually it did. The Technicolor memories faded, folding seamlessly into black and white dreams.

Thirteen

WHEN SHEPHERD WOKE the next morning, his first thought was of how hungry he was. After taking a quick shower and getting dressed, he slipped his telephone into a side pocket of his trousers and shoved his wallet into one back pocket and his passport into the other.

Almost as an afterthought, Shepherd grabbed the envelope of documents he had gotten from Adnan about Charlie's Thai bank accounts. He had drafted a set of transfer instructions on the flight into Bangkok that included what he thought was a fairly imaginative explanation as to how the money was going to be used. He figured he had better check through everything one more time over breakfast just to make absolutely certain the instructions were all ready to go. He wanted to go see this guy at Bangkok Bank right away, make sure the money was moved, and get the hell out of there as quickly as he could.

Shutting the door behind him and jiggling the handle to be sure it was locked, Shepherd headed out to get himself a lot of caffeine and a big-time sugar rush. He had the feeling he was going to need both.

Downstairs in the lobby, Mr. Tang, the elderly Thai-Chinese who ran the Grand, was at his customary post behind the front desk, while Hamster was sprawled on a couch reading the *Bangkok Post*.

Shepherd had no idea what Hamster's real name was. He was a wiry little Brit with the nervous habit of wiggling his nose whenever he talked and Shepherd had always assumed that unfortunate affliction was the source of his nickname. Hamster had been living at the Grand since before anyone Shepherd knew could remember, and Hamster was what everyone, even Mr. Tang, called him. Maybe Hamster didn't have any other name or, if he did, even he had forgotten what it was.

Hamster peeked over the top of the *Post* when he heard Shepherd coming down the stairs.

"Tang said you were back in the house, Jacko. You staying long?"

Shepherd smiled and shook his head.

"You finally get yourself a new apartment?"

"Yeah."

"Where?"

"In Hong Kong."

That got Hamster's attention. He lowered his paper and stared at Shepherd as if he had just mutated into a camel.

"You're shittin' me, mate. You're living in Honkers now?"

Shepherd nodded.

"What the fuck you doing up there?"

"You know. Building up a law practice again. Just trying to find a way to earn a living."

Hamster shook his head sadly and returned his attention to the *Post*. "Hell, Jacko, I'm disappointed in you, man. I thought you'd given up the straight world and dedicated yourself to a lifetime of exotic adventure in the magical Kingdom of Siam."

If Hamster only knew, Shepherd thought to himself.

The press had never publicly linked him with Charlie Kitnarok, so not many people in Thailand had any idea about the sort of adventure he was really living. That was altogether a good thing as far as Shepherd was concerned since it allowed him to operate under the radar. But he wasn't at all sure how long his state of grace was going to last. At least a few people at the American embassy knew about his connection to Charlie; and if a few knew then pretty soon all the rest would know, too. After that it would be just a matter of time, probably very little time, before the press started poking around and asking questions. Exactly what would happen to his life when his intimate involvement with Charlie's finances became public knowledge he wasn't entirely certain. All he knew was that it wasn't going to be pretty.

Hamster yawned hugely and folded up the paper.

"So you're off to join the demonstration, are you?" he asked.

"What demonstration?"

"It's the red shirts today, I think. Or maybe it's the yellow shirts. Shit, it might even be purple striped shirts for all I care."

Thailand was generally in the throes of some sort of political upheaval, but the results were usually pretty benign. Nothing much in Thailand ever really changed. Recently, however, the locals had taken to exhibiting their political sentiments somewhat more belligerently than they had in the past. They had adopted what amounted to team colors for each of the two primary movements. The yellow shirts were the supporters of the current government, whatever that might mean on any particular day, and the red shirts were the people who wanted to throw the government out and return Charlie Kitnarok to power.

Bands of red- and yellow-shirted demonstrators now roved the streets of Bangkok almost daily, proclaiming their support for whichever causes they had been told to love this week by the guys who were really running things. The whole business would have been mostly comic if the color-coded armies hadn't started bashing each other occasionally. Although the weaponry had so far remained primitive and the conflict limited, a feeling of unease was inexorably sliding over the city. Would that be the extent of the street violence, or was something worse, perhaps much worse, out there just over the horizon?

"The reds and the yellows are both marching on Silom Road this morning, it says here." Hamster lifted the *Post* and gave it a shake just in case Shepherd was uncertain of the source of his information. "I'd keep my head down if I were you, Jacko."

"Hey, Hamster, see this face?" Shepherd framed his Caucasian features with his open palms. "It's my personal free pass."

Hamster cocked one eyebrow. "You mean ugly old farts are exempt from the hostilities?"

Shepherd flipped him the finger and headed out to get some breakfast.

THE GRAND WAS in one of the few pockets of the old city the real estate developers had somehow overlooked. Wedged into a few blocks between the embassy compounds on Sathorn Road and Bangkok Christian College, the neighborhood was marked by narrow streets overhung with willow trees and high walls that concealed crumbling villas a decade or two overdue for a paint job. It was a modest reminder of how life had been in Bangkok back in an age now largely forgotten by almost everyone.

In less than a generation Bangkok had been transformed from a lazy village crisscrossed by canals into a sprawling forest of glass and steel. Now almost none of the old city was left. The canals had been paved over to become roads gridlocked with traffic and the gentle swish of frangipani trees had turned into the throb of air-conditioning compressors. Shepherd knew the developers would eventually get to the Grand and its neighborhood, too, but for the moment at least an older, more tranquil way of life still survived there, and he hoped it could hold out just a little bit longer.

It was a good four hundred yards from the Grand up to Silom

Road, but as soon as Shepherd stepped outside he heard in the distance the tinny screech of loudspeakers and the deeper rumble of a rhythmically chanting crowd. He stood for a moment and listened, wondering if perhaps he would be better off walking in another direction.

It was the general conceit among foreigners in Bangkok that none of this had anything to do with them, which is what Shepherd had meant when he told Hamster that his Caucasian face was his free pass. Yet sometimes he wondered if that was true anymore. Even in the best of times, foreigners were more tolerated by Thais than liked. They spent money, which was good; but they were big and loud, smelled funny, and screwed around with the women, which was not.

The innate shyness and natural deference of most Thais had shielded foreigners from the ups and downs of the kingdom almost from the time the first white men had sailed up the Chao Phraya River and demanded trade concessions from the puzzled and no doubt slightly bemused rulers of ancient Siam. In the last few months, however, shyness had inexorably turned into truculence and deference into confrontation. It was true that, for the moment at least, Thais were primarily taunting and confronting each other, but it seemed to Shepherd that it might be only a matter of time before foreigners might be tarred as the real enemy and the warring camps stopped bashing each other and joined together to bash foreigners instead.

It had gone pretty much that way almost everywhere else on the planet. Why should Thailand be any different?

Fourteen

WHEN SHEPHERD GOT to Silom Road he stood on the sidewalk and watched the masses of yellow-shirted marchers surge by. There were a lot more of them than he expected. Was the government really that popular? Maybe, but then again, maybe not. He understood the basic principle of the color-coding and knew it was government supporters who wore yellow, but he was a little vague on all the nuances involved in the concept. And this being Thailand, he suspected they were many and largely unfathomable to foreigners.

Of course, most of the demonstrators were no doubt a little vague on the nuances as well. Many of them were not believers in any cause, but merely hired hands paid on a daily basis to carry the colors of one side or the other. Well behind them, deep in the shadows, stood the men who paid the poor to battle it out in the streets in the name of platitudes about which not one of them gave a damn. The goal, of course, was to control the government so the men in the shadows could line their own pockets and those of their friends. If one group had that power then the other side didn't. It was that simple really. And that was why the battle went on and on, gaining almost daily in ferocity, with no end in sight.

Elizabeth Corbin slipped through the crowd and pushed in next to Shepherd.

"Where's your shirt, Jack?"

She was a rail-thin blond, although whether natural or not Shepherd had no idea, and very tall, even slightly taller than he was.

"Gotta have a shirt," she said. "Red or yellow, don't make no never mind. But you gotta have a shirt to play."

"Hello, Liz. Doing a story about the demonstration?"

"Nope. This stuff was cute for a while, but it got old fast. I won't get another line into the paper until they kill a few people."

Liz was the Bangkok bureau chief for *The New York Times* and her casual cynicism was a standard part of the kit carried by every foreign reporter Shepherd had ever met in Thailand.

"Then I hope you don't get another line about it into the paper," Shepherd said.

"I will sooner or later. You can take that to the bank."

Shepherd nodded but said nothing.

"So where've you been, big boy? Lose my number?"

Liz flirted casually with Shepherd every time he saw her. It generally made him slightly uncomfortable, which Liz naturally realized and that just caused her to step it up. He often wondered if she handled every man she knew the same way or if he had been designated for special treatment.

"Not in the market, Liz. But if I were—"

"Yeah, I know. I'd be your first stop. You've said that before and I'm still waiting."

"I'm flattered at your patience."

"And I'm amazed at yours. Anita's been gone how long now?"

It was Shepherd's policy not to talk to *The New York Times* about his personal humiliations, so he said nothing.

"Okay, I get the message. Never mind. When you get over Anita, give me a ring. I may or may not be waiting."

The last of the yellow shirts passed by and automobile traffic reclaimed Silom again. So much for politics. There was money to be made.

"You had breakfast yet?" Liz asked. "I think the *Times* can still afford to treat you at Coffee World, if only barely."

"Sold," Shepherd said. "It'll make my whole day to know the *Times* is paying for my coffee and muffins."

"Who said anything about muffins?" Liz asked.

COFFEE WORLD WASN'T very crowded and it didn't take them very long to collect two lattes and a couple of bran muffins and settle in at a table by the window. Shepherd put the brown envelope with Charlie's banking documents on the table, pulled his cell phone out of his pocket, and laid it on top.

Liz tapped the envelope with one perfectly manicured forefinger.

"What's that?" she asked.

If she only knew, Shepherd thought. But that was not what he said.

"Just some corporate organization documents I'm reviewing for a client."

Liz quickly lost interest in the envelope just as Shepherd thought she would. "I hear the prime minister's going to resign," she said. "What do you hear?"

Shepherd took a long hit on his coffee and pinched off a chunk of his bran muffin. "I'm not the guy you need to ask about that, Liz. I don't know a thing about Thai politics."

"Bullshit. You used to be big pals with General Kitnarok. Word around is that you still are."

Shepherd gave Liz what he hoped was an appropriately enigmatic smile and said nothing.

"And how about your girlfriend, Jack? She's right in the middle of everything that happens in this country. What does she say about it?"

Kathleeya Srisophon was the woman Liz always referred to as Shepherd's girlfriend, no matter how often he told her how wrong she was. It was true that Kate was the Director General of the NIA, Thailand's National Intelligence Agency, the local version of the CIA, and it was also true that Kate and Shepherd were acquaintances. It would probably even have been fair to call them friends. But calling Kate his girlfriend was stretching a modest acquaintanceship beyond all recognition.

"I guess there's no point in my saying again—"

"Absolutely none, Jack. You can't bullshit me. You and Kate have been an item ever since that mess you got into with Plato Karsarkis. I hear she saved your life."

Shepherd knew better than to argue with Liz. He had already tried that. So he said nothing.

"What is NIA saying about the prime minister?" Liz pressed. "Is there going to be civil war?"

"Now look, Liz, just because there are a bunch of kids strutting around in colored shirts, don't—"

"I'll bet that's exactly what the Jews in Germany said about the Brownshirts in 1936."

Shepherd just shook his head and tore another chunk out of his muffin.

"I've heard something about Kate," Liz started up again when she realized Shepherd wasn't going to take the bait. "I know you're going to say you don't know anything, but at least tell me if you think I'm way off base here. Will you do that?"

Shepherd chewed silently, but Liz apparently took that as a yes. He wasn't surprised. Liz took almost everything as a yes. Even an outright no.

"My sources tell me the prime minister will resign within a week," she said. "And the ruling coalition is going to pick Kate to replace him."

Shepherd almost choked on his muffin.

"You can't be serious."

Kate wasn't a politician and Shepherd was certain she had no interest in becoming one. She was an administrator who ran Thailand's intelligence apparatus, one that was both more extensive and more effective than most people knew. She wasn't anything like the ignorant, corrupt farmers with bad haircuts who had controlled the Thai political system since the overthrow of the absolute monarchy in 1932. Kathleeya Srisophon as Prime Minister of Thailand? There was no way in the world that was going to happen.

"Then she hasn't told you anything about it?" Liz prodded.

"I haven't talked to Kate in a while," Shepherd said.

It was true, but as an answer to Liz's question it sounded pretty lame, even to him.

"Uh-huh," Liz said. "Sure."

"Look, Liz, I really don't think—"

"She'd be the perfect choice, Jack. Think about it. Her great-grandfather was some mucky-muck in the court of King Rama VI. Her grandfather went to Oxford and led the Free Thai movement that fought the Japanese in World War II. And her father was a Nobel Prize winning economist who became president of the Asian Development Bank."

"There is no way Kate is going to become Prime Minister of Thailand, Liz." Shepherd shook his head again. "Absolutely no way."

"Why the hell not? She's spent nine years at the NIA and was Director General by the age of thirty-five. She has degrees from both the University of Massachusetts and Oxford University. She's as qualified to run a country as Barack Obama was when he was elected President of the United States."

"It's not that, Liz. Kate's not going to be Prime Minister of Thailand because—"

When Shepherd realized what he was about to say, he abruptly stopped talking.

"What?" Liz snapped. "A woman? Is that what you were going

to say, Jack? That Kate Srisophon will never be Prime Minister of Thailand because she's a woman?"

Shepherd did his best to look offended, but of course that was exactly what he was going to say.

No woman had ever been prime minister of Thailand, a country whose social order is as nearly feudal as anyplace left on earth. Those few women who have achieved national office in Thailand had all been stuck away in places like the health ministry from which they could smile nicely for the cabinet photographs and then get the hell out of the way while the men got on with running the country. Shepherd had always assumed Kate had been appointed Director General of NIA only because the politicians had her marked down as a wealthy aristocrat with neither the need nor the stomach to demand a place around the open feeding trough that was government in Thailand. Kate probably seemed like a safe choice for an office out of which none of the real politicians could figure out a way to make any money.

Shepherd was about to say that to Liz when his cell phone rang. He glanced at the display. It was Pete Logan.

"I'm just finishing breakfast," he answered. "Can I call you back in ten minutes?"

Shepherd could have sworn he actually saw Liz's ears rotate toward him like two little satellite dishes.

"Who's that?" she asked.

"Ten minutes," he said into the phone. Then he hung up and put it back on the table.

"It was Kate, wasn't it?" Liz said.

"It was a client," Shepherd said.

"You're lying."

"I'm a lawyer, Liz. That's what I do."

"Look, Jack, I can tell you know something, something important, and—"

"Damn," Shepherd interrupted, looking at his watch. "I had no idea it was almost eleven. I've got an appointment. Got to run, Liz."

He shoved the rest of the bran muffin into his mouth and stood up.

"Thanks for breakfast. I'll call you."

"Look here, you slick bastard, if you even think of leaving this table before you tell me what you know about all this, I'll—"

Shepherd was certain Liz's threats would be both inventive and terrifying but, before she could work up a decent head of steam, he snatched his telephone and Charlie's documents off the table and bolted for the door.

Fifteen

SHEPHERD DODGED ACROSS Silom Road through the traffic and walked up a quiet side street overhung with a dense canopy of willow trees. He stopped, pulled out his telephone, and called Pete.

"So you got lucky last night," Pete said immediately.

"I was just having breakfast."

"Bullshit. I could hear that broad from the *Times*. I know she was with you."

When Frank Sinatra died, Pete became the last man on earth to use the word broad in connection with the identification of a woman.

"I went out for breakfast. I just bumped into Liz by accident."

"Bullshit. I'm a trained law enforcement officer. I know when people are lying to me."

"You're with the FBI. Everyone lies to you."

"Just admit it, Jack. Give an old man a thrill. You got lucky."

"You're younger than I am."

"Hell, almost *everybody* is younger than you are."

Shepherd dodged a helmeted motorcyclist who for some reason apparently preferred riding on the sidewalk to riding in the street. When the whine of the bike died away, he tried nudging Pete toward a more productive topic.

"Did you find out anything about Robert Darling and Blossom Trading?"

"You're changing the subject."

"Can't get anything past you. You really are a trained law enforcement officer, aren't you?"

"Okay, be a prick. I got nothing for you."

"You mean if I don't tell you some smutty stories, you won't give me any information?"

"I meant that I got nothing for you. Zip. Nada. The Bureau has no interest in either Robert Darling or any company named Blossom Trading."

"They've dropped the investigation already?"

"There is no investigation. Never has been."

"But Keur told me—"

"I understand that, Jack. But there is no investigation. Period."

"Are you shining me on here, Pete?"

"I could be." Shepherd could hear the grin in Pete's voice. "But I'm not."

"Did you check out Keur?" Shepherd asked.

"Yeah. Leonard Keur is a senior agent working out of the D.C. field office. Is that what he told you?"

"That's what he told me."

"So there you go."

"But then why would he—"

"Keur was just pulling your chain for some reason. I wouldn't worry about it. Hey, I'd be the first to admit that we do that kind of shit every now and then, but don't quote me, huh?"

"I don't see why—"

"Got to go, Jack. You owe me one."

Then Pete hung up without saying goodbye.

SHEPHERD WALKED BACK to the Grand thinking about what Pete had just told him and not seeing how it made any sense. When he got there Hamster had disappeared from his perch on the couch in the lobby, but Mr. Tang was still sitting behind the front desk just like he had been when Shepherd left for breakfast. He was sucking energetically on a pencil while he studied a computer monitor so old Bill Gates' initials might well have been scratched on the bottom. The thing with the pencil was something Mr. Tang did when he was worried and Shepherd had noticed that it always seemed to soothe him. Sometimes he wondered if the taste of lead had a tranquilizing quality that might work for him, too. Maybe he ought to try it and find out.

"Business very bad," Mr. Tang said, glancing up. "Very bad."

"Then maybe I should ask for a discount."

Mr. Tang gave Shepherd a hard look, then quickly dismissed the comment as a joke, a poor one from his point of view, and went back to studying his computer screen.

"I'm serious," Shepherd said.

Mr. Tang didn't even bother to look up again, not believing for a moment such a thing was possible.

"Your friends tired of waiting and go," he said instead, his eyes still on the screen.

"What friends?"

"Your friends," Mr. Tang repeated. "They come about ten, wait a while, but you no come back. So they leave."

"What are you talking about, Mr. Tang?"

"Said you give them key so they wait in room." Mr. Tang gave Shepherd a hard look. "Don't do that no more. Don't give nobody key to my rooms."

Shepherd was accustomed to conversations with Mr. Tang being uninformative, but this time he understood exactly what the old guy was trying to say and he didn't like the sound of it one bit. He headed straight for the steps and took them two at a time.

Shepherd half expected to find the door to his room hanging off its hinges or something equally dramatic, but the door looked just like it always did. It was closed and still firmly attached to the wall. Gingerly, he tried the knob. Locked. Just as he had left it.

Could he have misunderstood Mr. Tang? It certainly wouldn't be the first time.

He took out his key, fitted it into the handle, and turned. Released from its bolt, the door gently drifted open of its own weight. He stepped inside.

No, he hadn't misunderstood Mr. Tang.

His room had been tossed, although it looked like no real damage had been done in the process. The stuffing wasn't torn out of the sofa, the lamps weren't smashed on the floor, and the mattress hadn't been ripped open. Still, somebody had searched the room, somebody who either wanted him to know it, or at the very least, didn't mind. The sofa and chair cushions were piled on the floor, the television set was turned sideways on its table, and one of the drawers in the desk had been left standing open. Some of the mess was probably his own fault, he hadn't exactly tidied up before he left for breakfast, but then again he hadn't taken all his socks and underwear out of the dresser drawers and dumped them on the floor either.

He stepped into the bathroom. His shaving bag was upside down on the floor and a bottle of Tylenol had been dumped out in the sink.

He closed the toilet lid and sat down on it to think. Had he been hit by burglars while he was out having breakfast? Who was he kidding? He knew the answer to that one without wasting time thinking about it. Nobody robs hotel rooms at ten in the morning. Too big a chance at that hour the occupant is either still there or could suddenly return.

The sound of soft footfalls from the living room cut short Shepherd's reverie and he looked around quickly for a weapon of some sort. He remembered reading once about an assassin using a toothbrush to dispatch his target, but he wasn't quite sure of the precise technique required and it was probably too late to work it out right then. He was contemplating the toilet brush as a possible alternative when Mr. Tang's head popped into the bathroom.

"What they do?" he asked.

"Don't sneak up on people like that, Mr. Tang," Shepherd snapped. "It could get you in real trouble some day."

"They search room, huh?"

Shepherd waved his hands and Mr. Tang backed out of the doorway and released Shepherd from the bathroom.

"They really mess up room," Mr. Tang said, looking around.

Shepherd didn't have the heart to tell him that some of the mess was exactly the way he had left it.

"How many men did you see, Mr. Tang?"

"Three," he answered immediately and nodded his head vigorously. "Or four."

"So was it three, or four?"

"Yes," Mr. Tang said. "Maybe."

Shepherd knew Mr. Tang well enough to see that line of inquiry had already hit a dead end so he tried a different tack.

"Were they foreigners?"

"Not think foreigners," Mr. Tang shook his head. "Spoke Thai, look Thai. I think all Thai."

That was interesting, although of course it didn't prove anything. Maybe representatives of Charlie's opposition had come calling, but then again Thais could be rented relatively cheaply for all sorts of heavy lifting and anybody could have hired a few mugs to toss his room. Knowing his visitors were Thai didn't help him to figure out what they wanted or, more importantly, who sent them.

"Did you give them a key?"

"You not listen to me?" Mr. Tang barked indignantly. "They say they have key so they come upstairs. I tell you not give anybody key to room."

Then Mr. Tang put Shepherd's question together with his answer and a cautious note crept into his voice.

"You not give them key?" he asked.

Shepherd shook his head.

Mr. Tang made a hissing noise as he drew air in between his clinched teeth.

"How long were they here?" Shepherd asked.

"Not long. Half hour maybe. They come down and say they not wait any longer. Then leave."

"Were they carrying anything?"

Mr. Tang's brow wrinkled in puzzlement.

"Did you see them take anything with them?" Shepherd clarified. "When they left."

"No," Mr. Tang shook his head firmly. "Not see anything."

Shepherd nodded. He began ushering Mr. Tang toward the door while he continued to look the room over for any suggestion as to what his callers had been searching for.

"You gonna call police?" Mr. Tang asked.

Shepherd hadn't thought about that yet, but now that the subject had come up, it didn't seem to him to be a very good idea. The kind of Thai cops who would answer a call about a break in at a foreigner's hotel room were more likely to be looking for a contribution to their personal benevolent fund than to have any genuine interest in locating the culprits. Besides, he was already getting more attention than he wanted and calling the cops to report a break-in could go nowhere good.

"No need, huh?" Mr. Tang nudged. "No problem. No police. Police bad for business and business bad now."

"Okay," Shepherd said. "No police."

"No police." Mr. Tang actually rubbed his palms together in delight. "I get maid."

Shepherd shook his head.

"No, I'll take care of it," I said. "No maid."

Mr. Tang looked doubtful.

"Thank you for coming up, Mr. Tang, but everything is fine. I'm going to straighten up and I'll see to it that everything is put back exactly like it was. No problem. No police. No maid."

"Yes. No problem. No police. No maid."

Mr. Tang was still nodding as Shepherd closed the door on him.

He put the cushions back on the couch and sat down, but he didn't bother to look around to see if anything was stolen. It hadn't been. There wasn't anything in that room worth stealing. No money, no jewelry, not even a laptop since he had decided he didn't feel like carrying one around this trip and had left it back home in Hong Kong. His passport, wallet, and telephone were all in his trouser pockets.

Even if there *had* been something worth stealing in the room, Shepherd would have bet it would still be there. Boosting a few odd items clearly wasn't why his visitors had come to call.

He looked at the envelope Adnan had given him, the one with Charlie's Thai banking records in it. He had put both it and his phone on the desk when he came through the door and now both were sitting there looking profoundly conspicuous.

The more Shepherd thought about it, the more it seemed obvious that his visitors had been looking for what was in that envelope, or something very much like it. Something that would tell them what he was doing in Bangkok and how it might be connected to Charlie Kitnarok. They were looking for Shepherd's notes and files, or at least a calendar or an address book, but they had found none of those things. The only documents he had with him were in that brown envelope, and his calendar and address book were on his cell phone.

Shepherd got up and turned the television set back around, then he closed the desk drawers and started picking stuff up off the floor. Not that he was much of a housekeeper, but there was something about knowing that somebody's hands had been pawing through his underwear and socks that gave him the creeps. Better to clean up the place a little so he wouldn't have to think about it. Putting things back where they had been wouldn't change anything, of course. What had happened had happened. But something about the process made him feel better anyway. At the very least, his hands now were the last to have touched his things, not some rented thug's.

Regardless of how much better it might make him feel, Shepherd didn't intend to waste a whole lot of time cleaning up his room. He needed to get moving. Because the sooner he got Charlie's money moving, too, the sooner he could get the hell out of Thailand and go home to Hong Kong.

And right now, going home to anywhere sounded pretty good to him.

Sixteen

IT WASN'T A very long walk from the Grand to the head office of Bangkok Bank up on Silom Road. Shepherd covered the distance in fifteen minutes, the envelope with his notes for the wire instructions and the documents Adnan had given him tucked safely under his arm.

Ten minutes more and he was sitting in a visitor's chair staring across a cluttered desk at a nervous-looking man who said he was Tanit Chaiya. Shepherd figured there was a reasonable chance the man actually *was* Tanit Chaiya since there was a black nameplate on the desk in front of him that said: TANIT CHAIYA, EXECUTIVE VICE-PRESIDENT, BANGKOK BANK.

Shepherd could have called first, of course, but he hadn't. He had learned a long time ago that sometimes you found out things about people when you turn up unannounced. Sometimes they were even things you wanted to know.

Tanit was wearing a blue suit, white shirt, and a nondescript blue tie. He looked like he had stepped straight out of a Wal-Mart ad. Tall and skinny with heavy black glasses, he bore an uncanny resemblance to Woody Allen, except for being a lot taller. In Shepherd's experience, it was unusual for a Thai to be tall and look like Woody Allen, but Tanit actually was and he actually did. It was even more unusual for a Thai to get straight to the point, but Tanit actually did that, too.

"I have received a valid power of attorney from our account holder authorizing me to accept your instructions on his behalf," Tanit said.

Shepherd wondered why he was being so careful not to mention Charlie by name. Maybe somebody was listening.

"Do you have instructions for me?" Tanit concluded with what he probably thought of as a smile on his face.

"Yes, I do. The funds you hold in the accounts in question are required for a major corporate transaction and we need for you to wire them to Citibank in New York."

"I am required by Thai banking regulations to inquire as to the nature of this transaction."

"My client is purchasing an interest in the Los Angeles Lakers."

Shepherd kept a straight face. Tanit kept a straight face. In fact, Tanit's face was so straight it didn't move at all, which was when it occurred to Shepherd that Tanit had no idea what the Los Angeles Lakers were.

"That's a basketball team," he added.

Shepherd watched Tanit think about that.

"You client is buying a basketball team?" he asked.

"Yes."

"In Los Angeles?"

"Yes."

Tanit examined Shepherd carefully for any hint that he was being made the butt of some obscure joke, possibly one with dubious cultural connotations in which he would end up looking like an idiot. Shepherd smiled blandly at him. If somebody was listening, it would be interesting to see what Tanit did next. Shepherd's guess was that Tanit would just get on with the script rather than run any risk of rocking the boat, and after a moment that was exactly what Tanit did.

"You are asking on behalf of the account holder to remit funds abroad?"

"Yes."

"In what amount?"

"We require remittance of the total balance of all the accounts that you are holding in his name or the names of companies controlled by him. The remittance should be made in United States dollars, of course."

They were talking about nearly half a billion dollars, but Tanit didn't even blink.

"Of course," he said. "And do you have the details of how these funds should be remitted?"

Shepherd opened the flap of the envelope on his lap and handed Tanit the instructions he had prepared.

"A complete list of the accounts to which the funds should be wired and the amounts to be wired to each account is included in these instructions."

"Naturally I must also ask for appropriate identification," Tanit said, "to confirm formally that you may exercise authority over the accounts listed in the power of attorney and instruct me to execute the transfers."

Shepherd pulled his passport out of his pocket and handed it across his desk. Tanit accepted it, nodded gravely, and carefully copied down the particulars on some kind of form he had in front of him.

"As to the purpose of this remittance," he said, "I have recorded that the account holder will purchase the Los Angeles Lackers."

"It's Lakers," Shepherd said. "L-A-K-E-R-S."

"Ah," Tanit said, then bent back to the form and wrote some more.

When he was done, he returned Shepherd's passport, stapled the instructions he had been given to the form, and pushed it across the desk for Shepherd's signature. The form was entirely in Thai, a language that in its written form is as incomprehensible to westerners as Sanskrit, which is more or less what it actually is. Shepherd signed the form anyway. Signing documents you couldn't read might not be the approved way to conduct business in New York, but in Thailand it was an everyday occurrence. Shepherd returned the form and the instructions to Tanit, then he handed him the brown envelope filled with the documents he had been carrying around.

"Could I ask that you shred these for me?" Shepherd said. "They are only copies of the original documents and I would prefer that they be destroyed now that they are no longer needed."

Tanit nodded and accepted the envelope. He smiled. Shepherd smiled. They were getting along just famously. Shepherd figured the grand climax of their little duet was drawing near, and just then it arrived.

"Have you completed the other formalities necessary for me to execute the remittance?" Tanit asked, his eyes sliding away from Shepherd.

"What other formalities are you referring to?"

"Because of the amount involved, you must obtain a certificate of approval from the Bank of Thailand to send the funds out of the country."

"I assumed you would obtain that for us."

"I cannot."

Tanit still wasn't making eye contact and Shepherd just sat and waited for what he knew was coming.

"I can suggest someone at the Bank of Thailand who might assist you," Tanit said after a moment.

"I would appreciate that."

"Her name is Khun Sumalee Suchinda. She is one of the deputy governors."

"Can you suggest how I could best approach her?"

"Khun Sumalee has two daughters in school in England," Tanit said.

To most people, Tanit's response would have seemed like a non sequitur, but after living in Thailand for two years Shepherd had no doubt at all what it meant.

"Do you know the amount of their school fees?" he asked.

Tanit tilted his head back and studied a spot on the ceiling.

"I would say about thirty million Thai baht would cover them," he mumbled after a few moments of suitable contemplation.

Shepherd did the math in his head. Thirty million Thai baht was about one million United States dollars. He briefly considered reminding Woody Allen that it wasn't necessary to buy the school in England in order for the deputy governor's daughters to attend it, but decided not to bother. Besides, what did he care? It was Charlie's money and he was just following his instructions. Anyway, Charlie thought it might cost him as much as two million dollars to get his money out of Thailand and here he was getting it done for the bargain price of one million. He was a heck of a negotiator, wasn't he? Just imagine how much money he might have saved Charlie if he had actually said something.

Tanit slid a piece of paper across his desk. "Here are the names of Khun Sumalee's daughters, their London banks, and their account numbers."

Shepherd picked up the paper and glanced at it. There was nothing on it but two names that naturally meant nothing to him, each accompanied by an account number at the National Westminster Bank. He wondered how much of the million dollars would eventually be kicked back to Tanit for negotiating the deal. Thailand was indeed an amazing place. You paid bribes to facilitate the payment of bribes.

"There is one other thing I would like to ask then, Khun Tanit," Shepherd said.

"Yes?"

"Could you arrange two more wire transfers for me?" Shepherd slid the same piece of paper he had just been given back across his desk. "Five hundred thousand US dollars to each of these two accounts at NatWest, please."

Tanit nodded gravely. He carefully transcribed the bank account information he had just given Shepherd onto two forms that had conveniently appeared on his desktop. When he was done, Shepherd signed them as well.

Only one step of the process remained. The final movement in a Thai art form that was as precise as a Bach cantata.

"In order to complete the transfer of my client's funds, I understand that a certificate of approval from the Bank of Thailand will be required," Shepherd said, playing his part to the hilt.

"That is true."

"Would it be possible for you to obtain it for us, Khun Tanit?"

"Of course," Tanit said. "It would be my pleasure entirely."

Shepherd thought it probably would be.

Seventeen

WHEN SHEPHERD LEFT the Bangkok Bank building, he walked out onto Silom Road and straight into the biggest crowd he had ever seen on the streets of Bangkok.

Shepherd knew the sidewalks in that part of town were always a mess. Gangs of street vendors selling everything from pirated DVDs to fried grasshoppers took up most of the available space. Since they paid off the police to let them do business there, the vendors acted as if they owned the sidewalks, which in a way he supposed they did. The locals who had their offices around there and the mobs of tourists drawn to the neighborhood by the cheap goods were left to compete for whatever tiny bit of public space the cops hadn't rented out.

Still, it seemed to Shepherd that things were even more of a shambles than usual and he wondered what was going on. He slipped behind a metal cart from which an elderly woman was hawking Chinese-made Rolexes and Cambodian-made Patek Phillipes, and took a couple of steps out into Silom Road.

About two hundred yards away on his left, a band of marchers was trooping slowly toward the spot where he was standing. There were a lot of them. They completely blocked the roadway from one side to the other and Shepherd couldn't even begin to guess how far back they stretched. The marchers were led by a pickup truck with a huge loudspeaker on top through which somebody was shouting unintelligible slogans. The demonstration didn't seem very threatening. It was more or less like the one he had stood and watched with Liz Corbin earlier in the day. The only differences he could see was that this march was going in the opposite direction, and the people in it were wearing yellow shirts instead of red ones.

Then Shepherd looked the other way and all at once he saw the real problem.

A couple of hundred yards to his right, an even larger band of red shirts had taken up a position completely blocking the roadway on which the yellow shirts were marching. Perhaps it was the same group of red shirts he had seen earlier. Perhaps it was a different group altogether. But either way, the yellow shirts were heading directly for them.

It seemed inconceivable to Shepherd that a street battle would take place right there in the middle of the financial district. Thais famously avoided face-to-face confrontations and nothing like that had happened yet in spite of the political turmoil that had gripped Bangkok for months. It wasn't that Thais were shy about attacking their enemies, it was just the face-to-face part they didn't get. The locals had never been able to understand the Western obsession for duking it out toe-to-toe with your adversaries. To Thais, it seemed silly to square off against anyone. That was why Thais generally nursed their anger, waited patiently until their enemy's back was turned, and then brought everything they had.

"Excuse me, sir?"

Shepherd glanced at the two women standing next to him. They were what in less politically correct times people might have called hippie chicks. Long greasy hair, shapeless grey clothing, open-toed leather sandals, and huge, top-heavy backpacks. Shepherd wondered what the proper term was these days for people like that.

"Do you speak English?" the taller of the two girls asked him.

"If I have to," Shepherd said.

The woman looked puzzled. "So… then you *do* speak English?"

This time Shepherd just nodded.

"Can you tell us what's going on here?" the other girl asked, pointing toward the yellow shirts matching toward them.

Shepherd thought of telling the two women the real truth, which was that nobody ever really understood what was going on in Thailand, but in his experience irony seldom played in conversations with strangers. Instead he settled for giving the girl the simplest answer he could think of.

"A political demonstration," he said.

"You mean like against global warming?" the tall girl asked.

"No," Shepherd said, "like against each other."

The yellow shirts were now within fifty yards of them. The old green pickup truck leading them was dusty and dented and, as it rolled slowly down Silom Road, the Thai national anthem began to blare out of the metal bullhorn mounted on top of the cab. Behind the bullhorn there were at least a dozen men standing in the bed of the pickup, one of whom had his arms uplifted and was exhorting the yellow-shirted ranks behind the truck.

Some of the marchers carried large Thai flags on tall poles and others waved homemade posters written in Thai. Most of the rest of the marchers Shepherd could see had the palms of their hands pressed together in front of them in a graceful gesture of humility and respect that Thais called a *wai*. The flags flapped in unison and the posters bobbed in time with the music. The whole effect was anything but threatening. It was more like the cheering squad from a poorly funded local college taking the field for halftime at a football game.

The two women just stood patiently and waited for Shepherd to go on. He doubted any good would come of it, but he continued anyway.

"The yellow shirts support the present government," he told

the two women. "They include a lot of people of Thai-Chinese background who see the government's embrace of China as the best course for Thailand."

Then he pointed in the opposite direction toward where the red shirts had now begun moving as well.

"The red shirts support General Kitnarok, who has always had the support of the United States and Europe," Shepherd continued. "He was defeated in the last election and left the country when the new government charged him with corruption and tried sending him to prison. The red shirts say the election was stolen by pro-China Thais and that General Kitnarok is the victim of political persecution. They're demanding that the government resign so the general can return and form a new government."

"Was this general really corrupt?" one of the girls asked.

"Almost everyone in government is corrupt to some degree. Government in Thailand is a just another business you go into to make some money."

"But then what happens to the people?"

A good question, Shepherd thought to himself. A *damned* good question actually. He didn't even try to answer the girl. He just shrugged.

The reds shirts had their pickup trucks too. Two of them were now cruising slowly side-by-side, leading their marchers. Not surprisingly, both of the trucks were red, but other than that they were pretty much like the truck leading the yellows: old and dented and with loud speakers mounted on top of their cabs. Men stood in the beds of both trucks and waved their followers forward while martial music blared out of the loudspeakers at an ear-splitting volume.

Many of the red shirts, at least the ones Shepherd could see in the front ranks just behind the pickup trucks, were wearing long strips of white cloth tied around their heads like the headbands worn by Indian extras in old cowboy-and-Indian movies. There was something written in red on the headbands, but it was in Thai characters and Shepherd couldn't read Thai characters. Still, he very much doubted the headbands said *Have a Nice Day*.

Some of the marchers carried flags and Thai-language signs like the yellow shirts did, but the reds also had huge posters with smiling images of General Kitnarok and even a giant banner that stretched from one side of the road to the other. It said, in English no less, *The People Will Bring Back Democracy!* Apparently the red shirts were more concerned about their appeal to the international media than the yellows were, or at least they had enough money to hire Western political consultants.

"Is there going to be a riot?" one of the women asked.

"No," Shepherd said. "Thais don't riot."

"Cool," she nodded.

The yellows were now no more than thirty yards to their left and the reds were a little less than thirty yards to their right. The racket from the competing loudspeakers had melded into a single formless din and the sound of the contending groups of marchers became nothing more than an incoherent, angry-sounding rumbling. The two groups were moving slowly but steadily toward each other.

Shepherd saw that he and the two girls were standing very near to the point at which the reds and the yellows would most likely converge. He glanced around for the police and was anything but surprised not to see the slightest sign of them. All the local cops would no doubt be at the station, probably knocking back a few cold drinks and pretending that nothing at all was going on. There was simply no money to be made out of getting between two angry mobs.

In another two or three minutes the pickup trucks would be bumper to bumper. Shepherd could not imagine what would happen when that occurred, but he was still certain it could not possibly be what one might expect to happen under similar circumstances in almost any other country anywhere in the world.

He was wrong.

Later, when Shepherd thought of the moment in which the reds and the yellows came together, it would be the sound of the screams he remembered most clearly.

Eighteen

EVERYWHERE SHEPHERD LOOKED, reds and yellows were flailing at each other with crude weapons. And, as more and more people joined in, the carnage grew.

Along the roadside, vendors carts had been pushed onto their sides and shoved together into makeshift barricades. What a few moments before had been merchandise for tourists—T-shirts, copy watches, pirated CDs, and fake Louie Vuitton bags—was now just debris under the feet of the battlers.

Shepherd knew he and the two women had to get out of the way, but he couldn't see exactly how they were going to do that. They had no chance to get back onto the sidewalk or into the buildings that lined Silom since some of the demonstrators were already slugging it out behind them. The pickup trucks leading both marches had stopped nose-to-nose right in front of them and the only safety seemed to lie in moving further into the street, toward the trucks. Shepherd put his hands on the two women's backs and herded them forward.

At that moment, the main mass of the red shirts gave a terrifying roar, broke ranks, and swarmed toward the yellows. Both groups had now armed themselves. Metal bars, paving stones, wooden planks, and homemade clubs were everywhere. One man even swung a golf club overhead. Shepherd thought it was a four iron.

At the front of the attacking reds was a man hefting a wide, flat board a little longer than a baseball bat. The yellow-shirted woman closest to him carried a Thai flag on a long staff. Neither the man nor the woman was young and they were ordinary enough looking people. Later, what Shepherd remembered most about both of them was the rage that contorted their faces as they charged toward each other.

The woman attempted to bring the flag down and use its staff as a lance to spear the onrushing man, but she was too slow. The man caught the flagpole on his upper arm and swatted it aside. Then he lifted the board above his shoulders and swung from the hips, putting all of his weight behind it.

The flat of the board smashed into the side of the woman's head and Shepherd saw her skull buckle. Her face bulged on one side like a rubber ball pounded by a mallet. It contorted into something that looked more like a Halloween mask than a human head and a spray of blood burst in the air like red fireworks. The woman dropped to the pavement; then the two mobs surged together and she disappeared under a hundred pairs of feet.

That was when the screams started in earnest. The two girls were beginning to panic so Shepherd kept them moving. He slipped his arms around them and hauled them toward the green pickup truck that had stopped directly in front of them. By the time they got to it, they were directly in the eye of a full-scale battle.

"Crawl under!" he shouted at the women.

They stood there motionless, too frightened to move.

"Get under the goddamned truck!" he shouted again and shoved them both toward it.

The taller girl suddenly snapped to her senses. She dropped her pack, went down on her belly, and tugged the other girl after her. Both of them squirmed underneath the pickup.

Shepherd crouched down and pressed his back to the truck. He watched the battle as it swirled around him.

A yellow-shirted man to his left was scything a golf club back and forth, whipping it through the air like he was clearing brush with a machete. A red-shirted man ducked under the golf club and drove his shoulder into the yellow shirt's stomach. Yellow shirt lost his balance and went down, then red shirt jerked the golf club away and kicked him in the head.

Shepherd still wasn't particularly worried. This was a Thai fight and foreigners had nothing to do with it. Still, Thais didn't really like foreigners all that much and he knew that having a free shot at one who happened to be in the wrong place at the wrong time might be appealing to some of them. Just to be on the safe side, he stayed low and tried not to look too white.

For a while, that worked fine and the combatants ignored Shepherd. Then one didn't.

Out of the corner of his eye Shepherd caught a glimpse of an iron bar coming straight at his head. He ducked and the bar whistled by just above him. It came so close he felt the breeze from its passage ruffle his hair. When the bar crunched into the truck cab with a sickening thud, he thought about what it would have done to his skull if it had connected.

But Shepherd only thought about it for an instant. Then he jumped to his feet and grabbed the bar with both hands. He jerked it down and to the side and tried to twist it away. When his head came up, Shepherd looked directly into the eyes of his assailant.

He was just a boy, one no more than fourteen years old, Shepherd judged. But the boy was strong and seemed desperate to do Shepherd serious bodily harm. He couldn't imagine why, but there didn't seem to be any point in asking right then.

Because of the boy's strength, Shepherd gave up trying to twist the bar away from him and instead gave it a sudden jerk directly toward his midsection. The boy stumbled forward, momentarily off balance, and Shepherd swung his right foot upward like a field goal kicker going for a sixty-yarder. When his toe connected with the boy's crotch, he felt a soft, squishing sensation and the boy lifted completely off the ground. Screaming in agony, he lurched away. Then he fell to his knees and started to vomit.

Shepherd scooped up the iron bar and pushed his back against the truck again. He had just kicked a teenage kid in the balls as hard as he could and the truth was that he damn well hoped he had hurt him. The little shit was trying to take his head off with that iron bar. Shepherd wasn't a bit sorry for what he had done. Not really.

But he was thinking about it anyway. And that was why he didn't see the woman coming.

She was small and middle-aged and she didn't look very strong. She held a folding chair by its legs, one that she had probably liberated from a trashed street vendor's stand. Still, she was young enough and strong enough to swing it, and that was exactly what she did.

Because of her height she had to swing the chair in an upward trajectory to get a shot at Shepherd's head and that took most of the momentum out of her swing. Even then, the blow glanced off his ear and rocked him to his knees. He went down, breaking his fall with his hands. He had the presence of mind to pull up his knees and twist his body to ward off what he assumed would be another blow, but when he looked up from where he lay on the pavement, the woman was gone.

The green pickup was right next to him and he tried desperately to pull himself underneath it. He clawed at the roadway with his hands like a swimmer doing the breaststroke. His palms scraped over the concrete and they hurt like hell, but he kept stroking. Shepherd's head throbbed and nausea hit him in waves. Bright lights began to spin behind his eyes. He closed them, which really didn't help much, and kept swimming.

He was starting to black out, he knew. That didn't seem all that bad really, since at least then the pain would stop, but he had to get underneath the truck before it happened or he would be trampled. His right hand came down on something soft and a dozen unpleasant possibilities as to what it might be passed through his mind all at once. Then he opened his eyes and saw his hand had only landed on a woman's shoe. He kept going.

Somehow Shepherd made it to the truck and pulled himself underneath. The two hippie chicks were gone and he wondered briefly what had happened to them.

Then all at once the pain stopped, and he was gone, too.

Nineteen

"JACK, CAN YOU hear me?"

It was a man's voice. Shepherd was pretty sure of that much at least.

"Are you okay, Jack?"

Slowly Shepherd opened his eyes. He struggled to make sense out of the flashing colors and flickering shapes that were all he could see.

"How many fingers?" the voice asked.

What the hell is this guy talking about?

Shepherd closed his eyes and then opened them again. That helped a little, but not much.

Finally a man's face swam into focus. He was bending over and holding three fingers about a foot in front of Shepherd's eyes. It took another moment or two, but then Shepherd worked out who the man was. He was a Canadian doctor who drank at the Duke. At least he said he was a doctor. In Bangkok, you could never be absolutely certain about claims like that. Still, to give the guy the benefit of the doubt, everybody called him Dr. Mike.

"How may fingers?" Dr. Mike repeated.

"Three."

"What day is it?"

"Tuesday."

"What city are you in?"

"Bangkok."

"What were those people outside rioting about?"

"I don't have any idea."

Dr. Mike snapped his fingers and gave Shepherd a thumbs-up.

"Not a fucking thing wrong with you, boy," he grinned.

Shepherd sat up gingerly. Looking around, he realized he was sitting on the floor at the Duke of Wellington.

"How did I get here?"

"Two cops carried you in," Dr. Mike said. "I guess they figured the logical place to take a white guy in Bangkok is to the nearest bar."

Shepherd would have nodded in agreement, but he couldn't even imagine moving his head.

"You were lucky," Dr. Mike added. "I just happened to be here."

"That's not luck. Where else would you be?"

Dr. Mike squatted back down and took a closer look at Shepherd.

"The skin's not broken," he said. He gently probed at the edges of the swelling. "But you're going to look like you've got an egg stuck to your head for a few weeks."

Dr. Mike methodically worked his way over the rest of Shepherd's body checking for other damage. He didn't find any until he came to Shepherd's hands. He examined his scraped and battered palms carefully, twisting them first one way and then the other to catch the light.

"What the hell is this?" Dr. Mike asked.

"A swimming injury."

Dr. Mike just nodded as if that made complete sense to him.

"I could put you in for a neurological work up," he said, "but the local quacks would drive you crazy doing it and it probably wouldn't be of much use anyway. Instead, I prescribe two large whiskeys and an hour at Titty Twister A-Go-Go and you'll be right as rain."

"Good enough, doc," Shepherd said. "Help me up, huh?"

Mike stood up and Shepherd took his hands and pulled himself to his feet. A wave of dizziness briefly swept over him, but then the room resumed its customary place beneath his feet and he decided he was going to survive. A waitress rushed out from behind the bar, pushed a chair under him, and held out a large glass filled with what appeared to be whiskey. Shepherd accepted both the chair and the glass. He sat down. The chair was fine, but the glass turned out to be filled with ginger ale. He drank it anyway.

"How bad?" he asked Dr. Mike.

"Scrapes, bruises, and a minor concussion," Mike said.

That was disappointing to Shepherd. As lousy as he felt, he figured he at least deserved a major concussion. Finding out it was only a minor concussion somehow diminished the worth of his suffering. Still, that wasn't what he had been asking Mike about.

"I didn't mean me," he said and pointed toward Silom Road. "I meant out there. How bad is it out there?"

"Bad," Dr. Mike said. "Really bad."

"Casualties?"

"Some. It will be worse next time."

Shepherd knew Mike was right. He had seen their faces as they tore into each other.

Dr. Mike went to the bar and came back with his own glass filled with amber-colored liquid. Shepherd was pretty certain it wasn't ginger ale. Mike pulled up a chair and sat down beside him.

"What do you think is going to happen to this place, Jack?"

This time Shepherd did shake his head, although he did it carefully.

"Do you think foreigners are in any danger?"

Shepherd reached up slowly with one hand and pointed to the lump on his head.

"Good point," Mike nodded. "You think the army will come in?"

"The army *is* in," Shepherd said. "They're just letting the red shirts do their fighting for them. It looks better that way."

"The army's killing Muslims in the south. Why not just kill the yellow shirts in Bangkok, too?"

"Because nobody in the whole world gives a shit about the Muslims in the south of Thailand. The army's been burning and butchering them for years and nobody anywhere has noticed or cared. But if the Thai army starts shooting people in the shopping malls of Bangkok, all of a sudden they're going to be the lead on CNN and the tourists will get scared and go someplace else."

Mike nodded and Shepherd could see him thinking about what that might mean to him. He was right in the midst of an upheaval that was beginning to look very much like a civil war, and he wasn't weighing the great principles of human rights and self-government that the talking heads on TV went on about. Instead, Shepherd figured Mike probably had a bag packed and a route to the airport mapped out, and he was thinking about how much longer he would risk getting his ass shot off before he decided to run.

"I've got to get to the hospital," Dr. Mike said after a while and slugged back the rest of whatever was in his glass. For the sake of his patients, Shepherd really *hoped* it was ginger ale, but he still doubted it.

"Don't worry about me, Mike. I'm fine."

"If the dizziness continues or if you have any feeling of nausea, I want you to call me right away. You hear? You got that?"

Automatically Shepherd started to nod, but he stopped when a wave of pain swept over him.

"Got it," he murmured instead, keeping his head as still as he could. "Thanks, doc."

Shepherd stayed in that chair for quite a while after Dr. Mike left, sipping his ginger ale and wondering what it was like out on Silom Road right then. As soon as he was certain he could walk to the door without falling down, he got up and went outside to find out.

In front of the Duke everything looked pretty much like it always looked in front of the Duke. It was as if Shepherd had dreamed everything. Silom Road was open and snarled with traffic as always. The street vendors were back clogging the sidewalks, too, and pedestrians were walking in the street to get around the vendors just as they always did.

The red- and yellow-shirted people were gone. Only a short time before, they had been beating on each other with metal poles, boards, folding chairs, golf clubs and anything else at hand that could be turned into a weapon. Now they had all simply vanished. In their place, office girls hurried back to work from their shopping breaks, tourists squinted at the fake antiques in shop windows, and the first wave of bar trash headed for the go-go bars of Patpong.

For a moment Shepherd felt dizzy again. There *had* been a riot right here, hadn't there? It *had* really happened just like he remembered, hadn't it? He pushed at the bump on his head and flinched as the pain shot through his scalp. Yes, of course it had.

If the mass of the Thai people has a genius for anything, and that is certainly a fit subject for spirited debate, it is a talent for living day to day no matter what happens around them. It isn't a show of resilience exactly—at least not in the sense that the Israelis standing up to a barrage of Hezbollah rockets is resilience—it's more like the repeated invocation of a widespread collective unconsciousness. Thais can turn a blind eye to even the unhappiest of events. The Thais are a people who, after all, mostly managed to ignore World War II. They probably looked at the invading Japanese army as only the latest wave of sex tourists to arrive on their shores, just a bunch of horny guys with money to spend, all of whom happened to be wearing identical outfits.

Shepherd thought back to the faces he had watched not very long ago right on this very street. Thai faces contorted with rage and twisted in hatred. And he wondered if this time it might be different, if this time all the collective unconsciousness in the world might not be enough. But now, standing there and looking at Silom Road and seeing how quickly it had returned to what passed locally for normal, he was starting to believe again that everything would be all right.

Nothing in Thailand ever really changed. *Mai pen rai*, loosely translated as 'never mind,' was practically the Thai national motto. Nothing dented the somnolence of Thais for very long.

SHEPHERD WALKED SLOWLY back to the Grand and took a shower. Then he turned on the television and sat on the bed naked and stared at it. There was a replay of a Knicks game on ESPN and he watched that for a while, then he switched over to CNN and let the collected anguish of the day slide past his eyes in an uninterrupted parade of miseries.

The Silom Road riot hadn't even made the international news. Thailand seldom did, not unless another American pedophile on the lam had been caught there or an elephant polo match was filling out a slow news day. Charlie had been briefly turned into a media star by CNN, of course, but that was because he was a billionaire attacked by terrorists in Dubai, not because he had once been the prime minister of a country most Americans couldn't find on a map.

At about 9:00 P.M. Shepherd swallowed three aspirin, turned off the TV and the lights, and pulled the sheet up to his chin. At least now Charlie's money was winging its way out of the country and the job he had come to Thailand to do was finished. Tomorrow he could go home to Hong Kong and leave the damned Thais to beat each other senseless if they really wanted to. Whether they did or not, it didn't have a thing to do with him.

He told himself that over and over until it became a mantra as rhythmic and repetitious as the counting of sheep in a dreamland meadow. It wasn't true, of course, and no matter how many times he said it he didn't really believe it, but repeating it over and over did serve at least one beneficial purpose. It put him right to sleep.

Twenty

THE TELEPHONE RANG. Shepherd cleared his throat, shifted his body, and propped himself up on one elbow. The hands of the clock on the bedside table glowed in a green tint that was probably meant to be restful but which was mostly irritating.

4:37 A.M.

Shit.

Shepherd fumbled around until he found his cell phone and managed a successful stab at the answer button.

"This better be damn good," he snapped.

"It is, my friend."

"Jello?" Shepherd cleared his throat again. "Is that you, Jello?"

"Yeah. Did I wake you?"

"No, I had to get up to answer the phone anyway."

"That's a very old joke."

"I only know very old jokes."

Jello's real name was Chatawan Pianaskool, but Shepherd had never heard anyone call him anything but Jello. Shepherd had no idea at all what the origin of his nickname was, but Thais often called each other by names that seemed bizarre to Westerners, so he had never asked.

When Jello and Shepherd first met, Jello was a Thai police captain assigned to the Economic Crime Investigation Division.

About a year later he was suddenly promoted to colonel and assigned to the Department of Special Investigations, usually referred to as Special Branch. Shepherd understood enough about the way things worked in Thailand to know that wasn't a real promotion. Jello had apparently stepped on some powerful toes and made some big players nervous. Special Branch was where all the really nasty cases went, the ones nobody else wanted to touch for fear that they would leave a stain on a promising career that could never be wiped clean. He had no doubt a fair few of Jello's superiors were probably waiting for one of those kind of cases to mark the end of Jello's career, but Jello was an uncommonly savvy and nimble fellow. Shepherd's guess was that they would be waiting for one hell of a long time.

"I'll pick you up in twenty minutes," Jello said.

"What are you talking about?"

"I need for you to look at something."

"It's the middle of the goddamned night, Jello. Can't this wait for a few hours?"

"No," Jello said, "it can't. Twenty minutes. Outside."

"Wait a minute."

Shepherd shook his head and fought his way through the cobwebs.

"How do you know where I am? How do you even know I'm in Bangkok?"

"I guess all Thais aren't as stupid as you think, huh, white boy?"

"That's not what I meant, man. All I'm saying is—"

"What are you doing in a shithole like the Grand?" Jello interrupted.

"The Oriental is all booked up."

"No, it isn't."

"Okay, you got me. I like shitholes. I'm just a shithole kind of guy."

"Downstairs. Twenty minutes," Jello repeated.

Then he hung up without another word.

SHEPHERD WAS DOWNSTAIRS in fifteen. Unwashed, carrying nothing but a bad attitude, and willing to kill for coffee. Five minutes after that Jello drove up in a Bangkok cop's version of a white Crown Victoria, an unmarked tan Toyota, so plain it was downright conspicuous.

"What the fuck is going on?" Shepherd asked as he wrenched open the passenger door.

"Nice to see you, too, man," Jello said.

Jello was wearing a blue Hawaiian shirt printed with yellow pineapples. It was stretched so tightly across his paunch that it could have passed for a wetsuit. Shepherd got in and sat down. Jello lifted a white Styrofoam cup out of the Toyota's cup holder and handed it to him. Thumbing off the lid, Shepherd took a hit. It was the worst coffee he had ever tasted. He was still trying to decide whether to swallow it or spit it out when Jello pulled away from the curb and headed toward Silom Road.

"We found a body," Jello said. "We think it's someone you know."

Shepherd not only swallowed the coffee, he took another couple of quick gulps.

"Why do you think I know him?" Shepherd asked.

"I didn't say it was a man."

"A woman?"

"I didn't say that either."

"Hey," Shepherd spread his hands, "I know this is Thailand, but chances are still pretty good it's one or the other."

Jello turned left on Silom Road, caught a red light at the next intersection, and stopped. It was not yet 5:00 A.M. and there wasn't another car in sight. But Jello stopped for the light.

"Bold move, man," Shepherd said. "Real guts ball."

Jello reached into his shirt pocket and handed Shepherd an old model Motorola flip-phone that was plain black.

"This was on the body," he said. "Have a look."

The light changed and Jello drove through the empty intersection as carefully as if it were choked with traffic.

Shepherd took the phone and looked at Jello.

"Start with the address book," Jello said.

It took a minute, but Shepherd finally located the right menu and opened the address book. There were about a dozen numbers, but no names were paired with any of them. The numbers looked local. At least the codes looked like a mixture of Thai landlines and cell phones, but Shepherd supposed they might have been something else entirely. He didn't recognize any of the numbers. Except one.

His.

"Aw crap," Shepherd said.

Jello took Silom Road past the Holiday Inn, then turned left on Charoen Krung Road toward the Taksin Bridge. The Taksin Bridge over the Chao Phraya River is one of Bangkok's main arteries and links Sathorn Road, where many of the largest foreign embassies are located, with the city's western districts.

"A lot of people probably have my cell number, Jello. Just because it's on this phone doesn't mean I know the guy."

"You look at the notes?" Jello glanced over. "Push the button with the notebook on it."

Shepherd pushed the button Jello described. The address book disappeared from the little screen and was replaced by a cream-colored background that was apparently supposed to look like a notepad. The page was entirely blank except for three lines at the top.

EK418
Wednesday, 1805
Grand Hotel

"That's your flight number, your arrival time, and the hotel where you're staying, isn't it?" Jello asked.

Shepherd nodded slowly. EK was the international airline code for Emirates Airways and 418 was the number of the flight he had taken to Bangkok. The day and time of his arrival and the name of his hotel were right, too.

"What's going on here, Jello?"

"I was sort of hoping you could tell me. Who knew which flight you were on?"

"Nobody. I booked it myself."

Jello shrugged and inclined his head toward the black Motorola Shepherd was holding. "Try again."

Shepherd thought about it as he looked out the window at the sidewalks of Charoen Krung Road. Even at this hour, street vendors were setting up their carts and stoking their cooking fires. In another hour the sidewalks would be crammed with office workers grabbing a quick bite on the way to work.

"I didn't tell anybody, Jello. But if someone knew I was flying from Dubai to Bangkok yesterday, it wouldn't have been too hard to guess which flight I was on. There aren't that many and this is the one with the best schedule and the private suites in first class."

"You fly first class?"

"Just until they invent something better."

Jello shook his head. They drove another block or two in silence, then Jello turned right on to Sathorn Road.

"How many people in Dubai knew you were flying to Bangkok yesterday?" he asked.

"I don't know. A few. It was no secret."

"General Kitnarok knew?"

"Of course."

"Anybody else?"

"Like I said, a few people. Maybe a lot of people. I just don't know for sure."

"What about the hotel?" Jello asked. "Who knew where you were staying?"

"Nobody really. But I lived at the Grand for several months last year and I haven't stayed anywhere else since. You know that. Anybody who knows me knows that."

"Why are you in Bangkok, Jack?"

Shepherd hesitated. That was a tricky one. He didn't want just to flat out lie to Jello, but he wasn't particularly keen on telling him the truth either.

"Then let's try it this way," Jello said, while Shepherd was still trying to make up his mind what to say. "Who did you come to Bangkok to see?"

Shepherd had just met with a senior executive of Bangkok Bank through whom he had arranged to bribe a deputy governor of the Bank of Thailand to allow him to move hundreds of millions of dollar offshore. Not something he really wanted to share with a high-ranking officer from Special Branch.

"Nobody," he finally said. "Just stopping over for a few days on the way back to Hong Kong."

Jello cut his eyes at Shepherd. It was plain what he thought of that story. Shepherd couldn't blame him. It smelled like horseshit to him, too.

Then the obvious occurred to Shepherd and he wonder why he had been so slow to see it. He had come to Bangkok to meet Tanit and get Charlie's money out of the country. So Tanit knew he was coming to Bangkok, and maybe somebody had given him the flight number and he had somehow guessed the right hotel.

Was he about to meet Woody Allen again, but this time neatly laid out and very dead? If so, he could hardly stick to that ridiculous story he had just told Jello. He would have to tell him something that was a little closer to the truth without telling him everything. That wouldn't be easy.

And if the body really *was* Tanit's, that put another uncomfortable question on the table as well. Who would have wanted to kill Tanit the night after Shepherd had met with him about getting Charlie's money out of Thailand?

Shepherd thought back to Agent Keur's claim that he, not Charlie, had been the real target of the attack in Dubai because somebody was trying to disrupt Charlie's finances. Suddenly that claim didn't sound so ridiculous. Or maybe it still was. He was getting way ahead of himself.

Shepherd looked around. "What are we doing on Sathorn Road, Jello? Where are we going?"

"The Taksin Bridge. That's where the body is."

"Somebody dumped a body on the Taksin Bridge?"

Jello gave him a look, but he didn't say anything else.

The Taksin Bridge is a twin-spanned structure that arches the Chao Phraya River right in the center of Bangkok. Shepherd knew the bridge was gridlocked with traffic pretty much day and night, but he still couldn't believe the snarl of cars and trucks he saw in the westbound lanes just ahead of them. When they hit the backup, Jello calmly bumped the Toyota up over the curb, drove across Sathorn's broad esplanade, and then bumped back down into the deserted eastbound lanes. He continued toward the bridge as if driving on the wrong side of the road was the most natural thing in the world for him to do. Maybe it was.

"The body's on the eastbound side of the bridge," Jello said as they drove in solitary splendor down the middle of the empty roadway. "We've stopped the traffic at the other side of the river."

"Was it just dumped in the roadway?"

"It was hanging under the bridge. Somebody spotted it from a barge going downriver and we pulled it up."

That was interesting, Shepherd thought. Had Tanit been overcome with remorse at his involvement in a bribery scheme and hung himself? Surely not. The only Thai banker likely to commit suicide was one who *hadn't* been offered a bribe.

"Somebody hung himself from the Taksin Bridge?" Shepherd asked.

"The body was roped around the ankles and the rope was tied off on the rail almost exactly in the center of the bridge. Somebody killed this guy and hung him over the side."

"You can't be serious."

Jello glanced at Shepherd, but only for a moment.

"Okay, so you're serious. But that sounds pretty damn weird."

"You think?" Jello glanced over again. "It gets weirder."

"What could be weirder than somebody hanging a dead body by its ankles from the railing of a bridge right in the middle of Bangkok?"

"The body was decapitated," Jello said. "And we can't find the head."

Twenty One

THE BODY WAS on a white sheet somebody had spread out in the roadway at the very center of the eastbound span of the Taksin Bridge. A collection of brown-uniformed police, some civilian hangers-on, and a few of those knuckle-draggers who seemed to appear everywhere at the first sign of death—even in the middle of a bridge at five o'clock in the morning—moved back to give Shepherd and Jello room.

"You know him?" Jello asked Shepherd.

"Not without a head."

The body was that of a male who was slightly built and not very tall. He was wearing black cotton slacks and a black golf shirt with a new-looking pair of Air Jordans and heavy black athletic socks. Without a head, it was hard to tell much else about the man with any certainty, but as far as Shepherd was concerned he could see enough to answer the main question on his mind right at that moment. Tanit was tall. Even with the head missing, it was obvious the corpse wasn't Tanit.

Shepherd had never seen a decapitated body before and, now that he had, he was surprised to discover the experience was oddly bloodless. Nothing about the corpse looked real. The man had bled out, and his skin was now so pale it was almost translucent. Even the open cavity that used to be his neck seemed artificial, like plastic that had been melted and then cooled back into strange-shaped lumps and whorls. Shepherd could have been looking at a headless mannequin some kid had dumped out of a car to give the punters a thrill. Only he wasn't.

His eyes drifted away from the corpse and out over the bridge's railing. He traced the twisting course of the river to the north. Where Shepherd stood everything was in gray-green dimness, but on the eastern bank of the river Bangkok sparkled with an astonishing radiance. Most of the city's towers were brightly lit, etched into the night sky by lights so blindingly white that they seemed to drain the color from everything around them. The rank of luxury hotels standing watch along the riverfront glistened with jolly red, gold, and blue lights, shards of which snaked over the surface of the water and reached out toward them.

A small boat roared by, heading downriver. It was a long tail, one of the narrow, canoe-like vessels powered by salvaged automobile engines that were the usual form of transportation on the rivers and canals of Thailand. The little boat skimmed through the streaks of light like a stone, glancing lightly off the chop and misting the air with dark fans of spray.

"HAVE YOU EVER seen anything like this before?" Shepherd asked.

Jello took his time before he answered.

"There are a lot of decapitations in the south," he said after a moment of silence. "But this is the first one I've heard of in Bangkok."

For decades the Thai military had been fighting a dirty little war in the south of the country. Most of the world didn't seem to know anything about it, or maybe it was just that the rest of the world didn't care. Thailand is an overwhelmingly Buddhist country, but the three provinces in the far south closest to the Malaysian border are mainly Muslim. Over the years, the calls from the Muslims for greater autonomy had increased and the Thai response was mostly brutal repression. For the last half dozen years in particular, shadowy bands of rebels had been fighting back against the Thai military and doing it effectively. Demands were now being heard for the formation of a new Islamic state entirely separate from Thailand.

Machine gun mounted Humvees scour the roadsides for bombs. Thai soldiers sweep through villages suspected of harboring insurgents. And helicopters clatter above an idyllic tropical landscape over which the Thai military has cast a security net more dense than the U.S. Army ever did in Iraq. The provincial towns under siege have names like Pattani, Songkhla, and Narathiwat, but outside of Thailand almost no one has ever heard of any of them.

It was just another dirty little war, fought in places few Westerners could pronounce, between people with funny names. But the bombings and shootings went on day after day. Thousands had been killed on both sides, maybe tens of thousands. And however funny their names might be, the dead left fatherless and motherless children alone in the half-empty villages fending for themselves.

The Muslim rebels had recently turned to terrorizing those who did not wholeheartedly sympathize with them. Probably not by coincidence, their tactics mirrored those used by the Iraqi and Afghan fighters against American troops. Taking captives and beheading them was particularly stylish. Hundreds of men, women, and even children had been killed that way. Maybe thousands.

Shepherd glanced back down at the corpse. Maybe, he thought, Thailand's homegrown terrorists were tired of being ignored.

Jello cut into Shepherd's reverie. "So you don't know who this is?"

"I guess you'll have to be a real detective and figure it out yourself."

"It would help me a lot if you had any idea at all."

"It would help you even more if you had a head."

Jello just nodded and Shepherd didn't say anything else.

"So that's it?" Jello nudged after a moment.

"That's it."

"You don't have any idea why this guy had your phone number and travel details in his phone?"

"No idea at all."

"He didn't have them because you were supposed to meet him here in Bangkok?"

Shepherd shook his head.

Jello knew there was something Shepherd wasn't telling him, of course. Maybe even a lot he wasn't telling him. But he let it pass for the moment. He could see that he wasn't going to bully anything out of Shepherd. At least not right then.

"Do you think this guy was killed by the decapitation," Shepherd asked, "or was he decapitated after he was dead?"

"We don't know yet."

Shepherd tried to imagine what death by decapitation must be like.

"Somebody must have seen something," he said after a moment. "There's traffic up here all the time. You can't stop a car, pull out a dead body, and hang it off this bridge without somebody seeing you."

"Seeing and coming forward to tell the police about it are different things. I'm not holding my breath waiting for volunteers."

Jello squatted down next to the corpse and Shepherd heard his knees crack. "The phone was in his right trouser pocket."

"Anything else?"

"Some money in a plain gold clip. Not a lot. Thai baht and US dollars. In the other pocket he had a handkerchief. White. Unused. Nothing else."

"No wallet?"

Jello shook his head.

"No ID of any kind?"

Jello didn't even bother to respond.

"What did you find on the phone's call list?"

"Empty."

"All his calls were deleted?"

"Not deleted. Empty. We checked the SIM. The phone has never been used. There's nothing on it but the note your saw and those listings in the address book."

"You can trace the numbers, can't you?"

"They're all prepaid SIMs. No registered names. Other than you, of course." Jello gave Shepherd a look. "You're all we've got, Jack."

Shepherd didn't much like the sound of that.

"My guess," Jello went on, "is that he loaded those numbers into a clean phone specifically to use while he was here. Why would he have loaded your number if he didn't intend to call you?"

Shepherd ignored the question and asked one of his own. "How do you know he was a visitor? Maybe he was local."

Jello shook his head. "We've traced the phone. It was part of a batch shipped to Pakistan about a year ago."

"And the SIM card?"

"Registered in Dubai."

Shepherd nodded his head slowly.

It would *have to be Dubai, wouldn't it? Why couldn't the frigging thing have been registered in Cleveland?*

"If I ask you why you were in Dubai, Jack, would I get a straight answer?"

Shepherd shrugged, which was pretty much what Jello expected him to do.

"Were you there when they tried to kill General Kitnarok?"

"Yeah, I was there."

"Anywhere close to him?"

"You could say that."

"Then the guy CNN said was the assistant he dragged to—"

"Right. That was me."

Jello thought about that for a moment.

"Did General Kitnarok really save your life?" he asked.

Shepherd shrugged again. When people asked him questions about Charlie Kitnarok, that was generally his gesture of choice.

"I didn't think so," Jello said. "I'm glad you're okay, but I'm not sure I feel the same way about that guy you work for."

Shepherd considered going into his usual song and dance about the difference between working for someone and having someone for a client. Under the circumstances it seemed like a particularly petty distinction, so he just let it go.

Shepherd walked over to the railing and stood there, looking off toward the horizon. In the rising half-light of dawn, a long train of teak rice barges slipped silently underneath the bridge and wallowed slowly downriver toward the Gulf of Thailand. The air was heavy and breathless, the dim light cold and mauve colored. He leaned there and looked down at the dark, greasy surface of the Chao Phraya River trying to imagine a headless corpse dangling just above it at the end of a rope. It was easier than he expected.

Jello walked over and leaned on the railing next to him.

"What's going on here, Jack?"

"I've got no idea," Shepherd said. "None."

"What would be your guess?"

"That it's some kind of a message."

"Got to be," Jello said. "Why else would anyone do something like this? Killing a guy is one thing. But killing him this way? Then hanging his corpse off a bridge in the middle of the city? Couldn't be anything but a message."

"So who do you think the message is for?'

Jello said nothing. But he turned his head and looked at Shepherd, his face completely empty.

"Yeah," Shepherd nodded, "I was afraid that was what you thought."

"There's one other thing."

"Is this the part of the conversation when you tell me 'Don't leave town'? Because unless you lock me up, that's exactly what I'm about to do. I'm going home today."

"You have a home?"

"Yeah. In Hong Kong."

"That's home now?"

"I guess," Shepherd shrugged. "At least for a while."

They stood quietly together there at the rail for a while just watching the river.

"What time does your plane leave?" Jello asked after a while.

"About ten," Shepherd said. "This morning."

Jello nodded.

"Be on it," he said.

In the east, out beyond the city, the day began to break in earnest and a washed-out moon slipped into hiding back behind the Oriental Hotel. A cold, white spot of light appeared just on the eastern horizon and then spread slowly until it became a broad grey band stretching from one side of the city to the other. It looked thick and metallic, like the blunt edge of a sword.

Part Three

HONG KONG
BANGKOK
DUBAI

Yesterday upon the stair
I met a man who was not there.
He was not there again today.
Oh, how I wish he'd go away.

— William Hughes Mearns,
"*Antigonish*"

Twenty Two

IT WAS JUST after dawn when Jello drove Shepherd back to the Grand Hotel. In less than an hour, Shepherd had showered, packed, and gotten himself a cab to the airport. A few more hours and he was dozing in a business class seat on a Cathay Pacific 777 halfway back to Hong Kong. He felt good to be headed home again, whatever home actually meant for him these days.

Back when he and Anita had been married they lived in one of Bangkok's tonier apartment buildings. They had a large and airy unit, the walls of which were covered with the colorful paintings that had made Anita modestly famous as a painter in European art circles. The apartment was halfway around the world from where either of them had been born, but it still felt like home to Shepherd. When he went to the refrigerator and made himself a ham on rye, he felt like he was making himself a ham on rye at home. And that was a good enough test for him anytime.

Now he lived by himself in a Hong Kong apartment loaned to him by a guy he knew from law school. A few months ago, Freddy had abruptly resigned from his firm, bought a thirty-eight foot ketch, and pointed its bow south toward Bali. He told Shepherd he wasn't coming back until he had all the adventures he had been putting off since he was twelve years old. Shepherd wasn't entirely sure what those adventures actually were but, whatever it was Freddy was looking for out there on the ocean, he hoped Freddy found it. As for him, what he needed was a place to live and a way to earn a living, and that was why he was staying in Freddy's apartment while Freddy sailed his sea of dreams. The problem was that still didn't make it home. When he went to the refrigerator in Freddy's place and made himself a ham on rye, it felt like he was doing it in Freddy's kitchen, which of course he was.

All of Shepherd's recent dislocations had left him feeling pretty fuzzy about the whole concept of home. He wasn't absolutely sure he knew what it meant anymore. From time to time, a line from Robert Frost drifted through his mind. "Home is the place where, when you have to go there, they have to take you in." If that really *was* the definition of home, then Shepherd figured he was pretty much screwed. He was a homeless man. Simple as that. Maybe he should just buy a shopping cart and be done with it.

Still, Shepherd liked living in Hong Kong well enough, and Freddy's apartment was pretty nice. It was in a district called the Mid-levels, not a particularly romantic name for a neighborhood perhaps, but the designation was at least nicely descriptive since the Mid-levels was the area midway up the hillside between Hong Kong's famous harbor and the top of Victoria Peak. Back in the 1990s, in a highly imaginative but ultimately unsuccessful effort to ease Hong Kong's chronic traffic congestion, they built a half-mile long outdoor escalator running down from the Mid-levels, cutting through the center of SoHo and ending at the financial district in Central near the harbor. It wasn't actually a single long escalator, but rather a ladder of about twenty escalators tied together by short, glass-roofed walkways and moving belts. In the mornings, the whole Rube Goldberg contraption ran downhill and then, late in the morning, it reversed and everything ran uphill for the rest of the day.

What Shepherd liked most about Freddy's apartment was that the Mid-levels escalator was just outside its door. He loved to ride on it down the hill into the heart of the city. Instead of jostling through the crowds packed into Hong Kong's steaming streets, he could stand quietly and contemplate his surroundings while he was towed at a comfortable pace straight through the heart of the bedlam. The Mid-levels escalator turned the mayhem of Hong Kong into a Disneyland ride. It was all he could do not to hum *It's a Small, Small, Small, Small World* every time he used it.

Shepherd liked the Mid-levels escalator so much that he rented a small office about halfway down the hill from Freddy's apartment right in the middle of SoHo, which was an acronym for south of Hollywood Road. Hong Kong's SoHo, like its New York namesake, tried hard to be the hippest and most pretentious neighborhood going. In the blocks around Staunton and Elgin Streets, a cool new restaurant or bar either opened or, more likely, closed almost every week.

In spite of the stylishness of the neighborhood, Shepherd's office was pretty utilitarian. It was a single, averaged-sized room on the second floor of an old shophouse just above a noodle shop. It had very little to recommend it, except for one thing really. The Mid-levels escalator ran right to its front door. That was the real attraction of the place for Shepherd. He could commute to work every day by escalator. How cool was that?

WHEN SHEPHERD GOT to Freddy's apartment, he dropped his bag in the entry hall and walked around pulling back drapes and pushing open windows. Then he unlocked the balcony door and walked outside. The view was one he never tired of. Straight downhill over the towers of Central, out to the harbor, and all the way to the mountains of China, wispy and ambiguous in the distance. He could smell Hong Kong down there, too: that peculiar mix of carbon monoxide, raw sewage, duck mess, and burning incense that was like nowhere else in the world. Shepherd didn't care what anybody said about the smell of Hong Kong. He liked it just fine. He even had to admit the whole disgusting stench was beginning to feel a little like home to him.

The rest of the day Shepherd did very little but catch up on his sleep, watch sports on TV, and hang around Freddy's apartment. During the preceding week, he had been shot at by hired assassins, beaten to the ground by an old lady wielding a folding chair, and dragged out of bed in the middle of the night to identify a headless corpse. Even for Shepherd, that amounted to a pretty full week. He figured he deserved a little down time.

By the next morning, of course, he was already bored. He made coffee and toast and ate it standing at the sink, then he packed his briefcase and headed downhill to the office. He wasn't much of a decorator, but he had fixed the office up enough to be comfortable and he liked being there. He also liked the fact that no one else ever came there. He doubted Charlie even knew where it was. His office was *his* place, the only one he really had anymore.

The shophouse was old, as old as anything in Hong Kong was, and the interior walls were brick with some kind of white glaze over them. They had been troweled smooth on some long ago day and even now still glistened like porcelain. On the north side of the room, three tall windows looked down into Gage Street, a narrow roadway just below Hollywood Road that was so overhung with Chinese-language signs suspended from long metal brackets poking out from the shop fronts that Shepherd could barely see the street through the tangle. It seemed like half the buildings on the street were covered in bamboo construction scaffolding, but then buildings were always being torn down and rebuilt in Hong Kong. It was a city in which a building was hardly finished before it was torn down and something bigger built in its place. Shepherd wasn't sure how his little shophouse had survived the onslaught, but he was glad it had.

Perpendicular to the windows he had placed a long library table he had found in a used furniture shop up in the New Territories, and behind it he had put a new Aeron chair he had paid far too much for. He kept the desk largely bare. There was nothing on it at all except for a large leather desk pad, two computers, and a telephone he used so seldom he generally had to look up the number when anybody wanted to call him on it.

The wall behind Shepherd's worktable was lined with three horizontal filing cabinets, each five drawers high. Locking bars had been welded to the fronts of all three of the cabinets and formidable-looking padlocks dangled from the handles of each of the bars. On the wall to his left was a line of tall bookcases. They were half-filled with mostly out-of-date law books and legal journals while the rest of the shelves held the kind of accumulation of items that men seemed to amass when they were left to their own devices. A green gym bag, a broken coffee maker, a coffee maker that worked sometimes, a half dozen ceramic coffee mugs, a large bag of potato chips, some magazines, a burlwood cigar humidor, a couple of ashtrays decorated with beer logos, and stacks of old copies of *The New York Times*, *The Wall Street Journal*, and the *Financial Times*.

The wall in front of Shepherd, the one on which his eyes rested whenever he lifted them from what he was doing at his big table, was bare except for a single large oil painting hung in the exact center that was at least five feet on each side. The painting didn't actually depict any recognizable form, at least no form that was recognizable to Shepherd. Instead, it was a riot of primary colors that swirled and swooped and splashed over the canvas in a way that seem at a glance to be random, but on closer inspection began to look as intricately interwoven as the fabric of an English tweed jacket. It was the only one of Anita's paintings he still had. She had taken all the others, but she had given him this one for his birthday and so it was his and he had kept it when she left. He had brought it with him from Bangkok and hung it in his new office. Almost immediately he decided that had been a very bad idea. But he had never gotten around to moving it and it was still there.

SHEPHERD SPENT HIS first day in the office catching up with the mail and returning a few calls that had been left on his voice mail while he was away. It was all routine stuff, but after recent events he found a certain comfort in routine stuff.

On the second day, reasonably well rested and pretty much caught up, he brewed a large pot of coffee and turned his attention to the new work he had created for himself in Bangkok. First, he sorted through all the wire confirmations that had come in to make certain Charlie's funds had been moved out of Thailand as they were supposed to have been. When he was sure all the wires had gone where they should have, he distributed the proceeds in the receiving accounts to the offshore investment trusts through which he managed Charlie's money.

He bought some short-dated T-bills in London, established new currency positions in Frankfurt, acquired a pile of Australian government bonds, and even placed an order with one of the brokers he used in New York to take a large position in an exchange-traded fund focused on gold futures. Shepherd wasn't very enthusiastic about gold as a long-term investment, but Charlie was Asian so naturally he loved it.

All in all, Shepherd managed Charlie's investment portfolios with a bias to the stodgy side. He would be the first to admit that there was nothing particularly imaginative about his asset allocation strategy, but all of the portfolio holdings were extremely liquid and that suited Charlie just fine. Charlie wasn't the kind of guy who liked to have his money tied up in shopping malls in New Jersey. What he liked were the kind of investments he could turn into cash at a moment's notice: refugee money, Charlie called it. So that's just what Shepherd gave him.

Shepherd worked later than usual trying to sort out the accounts for some of the offshore trusts, but he just couldn't get them to balance. Finally, around 7:00 P.M., he decided he'd had enough and the problem would keep until the next day. He locked up the office and headed to Jimmy's Kitchen for dinner. An old-time Hong Kong expat hangout down at the bottom of Wyndham Street, Jimmy's was one of Shepherd's favorite places to pull up a stool and have dinner alone at the bar.

He was about half a block from Jimmy's when his cell phone rang.

"We found the head," Jello announced without preamble. "You need to look at it."

"You going to FedEx it up here?"

"I was thinking more along the lines of emailing you a picture."

Shepherd was reasonably sure no one had ever called him before on his way to dinner to tell him he was about to receive a photograph of a severed head. Maybe, he thought to himself, it would be better just to have a martini.

"We've cleaned it up," Jello said, "but it was in the water a long time. It isn't in very good shape. The crabs got to it."

Maybe even two martinis.

Twenty Three

JIMMY'S KITCHEN IS all dark wood paneling, wall sconces with red cloth shades, elderly waiters in black with starched white aprons, and booths that are either tufted red leather or pretty good vinyl imitations. It's the kind of a place where you can easily imagine Frank Sinatra sauntering through the door, throwing a two-fingered salute to the bartender, and breaking into a couple of choruses of 'My Way.' And it is unquestionably the last restaurant on earth with both Beef Wellington and Baked Alaska on the menu. Shepherd liked Jimmy's for three reasons. The food was pretty good; the prices were generally reasonable; and he was almost always the youngest person in the place.

He took a stool at the bar and ordered a Hendricks martini, then he pulled out his phone and checked his email. Nothing but an offer from a Canadian drug store to sell him cheap Viagra. Another couple of weeks like the one he'd just had and maybe he would check that out.

It felt a little cool to Shepherd there at the bar, but he couldn't decide if it really was cool or if he just felt that way because he was waiting for a picture of a severed head to show up in his email. Hong Kong was probably the most over-air-conditioned city on earth so the sensation of being cold on a sticky tropical night was anything but unusual. Air-conditioning not having been invented until 1902, every saloon in Hong Kong had been laboring single-mindedly ever since to make up for lost time.

Shepherd laid his phone on the bar and glanced around. At a table across the room, a middle-aged Chinese couple sitting opposite each other were both talking on cell phones, their drinks left untouched in front of them. Shepherd doubted they were talking to each other, but maybe they were. In Hong Kong, anything is possible.

The bartender placed a coaster in front of Shepherd and carefully positioned a large martini glass on it. Even in the dim light of the bar, he could see the rim of the glass sparkling with a necklace of tiny ice crystals. The bartender lifted a silver shaker in both hands and with a half dozen economical snaps of his wrists blended the martini and strained it into Shepherd's glass.

Before Shepherd could take even a single sip, a low-pitched buzz sounded from his phone and it vibrated against the polished bar top. He glanced down and saw the numeral one superimposed over the email icon. Had the picture from Jello arrived, or was this just another junk mail promising to improve his sex life? He reached for his martini first, just in case. He took a long sip, paused a moment to savor it, then he picked up the phone and opened the email. The message contained no text, only an attachment, but it was from Jello so he had no doubt what it was.

Shepherd put the phone down on the bar and went back to his martini. It wasn't just the prospect of looking at a picture of a severed head that had spent several days on the bottom of the Chao Phraya River that gave him pause, although under most circumstances that would have been quite enough. What really bothered him was that the head was quite probably going to belong to someone he knew. Why would anyone have been carrying a cell phone with his number programmed into it and notes about his travel schedule if they weren't planning to get in touch with him in Bangkok? And what were the chances someone would have been planning to contact him in Bangkok if he had no idea who they were?

Shepherd took his time finishing the martini, but eventually he did. That was when he took a deep breath, picked up his telephone, and tapped on the icon attached to Jello's email. There was a pause as the phone located whatever it needed to display the file. Then the picture expanded quickly until it filled the little screen.

The horror of the image was tempered somewhat by the small size of the cell phone's display, but there was still more than enough horror to spare. The head was hardly recognizable as something that had once sat on the shoulders of a living human being. Both eyes had been torn out of their sockets, both cheeks had been eaten away to the bone, and all of the flesh of the nose was gone. Shepherd had no doubt he would see that picture in his mind for the rest of his life. Then and there he vowed never again to eat in another restaurant that served crab.

In spite of the mutilation, Shepherd recognized the man immediately.

Oh crap.

What in God's name had Adnan, Charlie's Lebanese assistant, been doing in Bangkok? And, probably more to the immediate point, why had somebody cut off his head and hung the rest of him under the Taksin Bridge?

SHEPHERD ORDERED ANOTHER martini, but he had pretty much lost his appetite, so that was all he ordered. When he finished the second martini, he left Jimmy's and just aimlessly wandered the streets for a while. More by accident than design, he walked through Lan Kwai Fong, past the Central District Police Station, and ended up on Hollywood Road at the foot of Ladder Street just in front of the Man Mo Temple. There was a small park across the road from the temple, not much more than some pieces of brightly colored children's playground equipment scattered over a few dozen square yards of concrete with a few wooden benches here and there. A night breeze had come up and the din of traffic from Hollywood Road had faded away, so Shepherd took a seat on one of the benches.

An elderly Chinese woman caught his eye as she pushed through a crowd of Western tourists and entered the temple across the road. She was stooped nearly in half and gripped a bundle of incense sticks as though they were cylinders of gold. He watched through the open doors as she lit the sticks and distributed them methodically among the brass pots filled with sand that were scattered throughout the building. When she was done, she stood for a long time before the main alter, her hands pressed together in front of her chest. She could have been praying for health, or long life, or even world peace, Shepherd supposed, but then this was Hong Kong. That made it far more likely she was asking the gods for a couple of winners at Happy Valley.

Maybe he ought to go over and join her, Shepherd thought. A little intervention from the gods wouldn't do him any harm right then either. Perhaps somebody really was stalking the people around Charlie. Perhaps he really was on somebody's target list.

Shepherd took out his cell phone and called Jello in Bangkok. He told him whose head it was in the picture.

"What was this guy doing in Bangkok?" Jello asked.

"I don't know. I had no idea he was there."

"He wasn't in Bangkok to see you?"

"No."

"Then why was your number in his phone?"

"Charlie has my number. It's no big secret. Maybe he gave it to Adnan. How would I know?"

"You didn't give it to him?"

"No, I didn't give it to him."

Jello weighed that up in silence for a moment or two.

"If he wasn't in Bangkok to see you, who else could he have been meeting?"

"I don't know. It could have been anybody."

"It wasn't just anybody. It was somebody who murdered him."

There was a short silence.

"I can't help you," Shepherd said. "I wish I could, but I can't."

"Watch yourself," Jello said. And then he hung up.

Man Mo Temple at night is an intoxicating and otherworldly spectacle. The intense reds and golds of the building's lacquer work glitter in the low light and the eyes of the deities residing within it seem to examine those who come to pay them tribute. Dozens of huge red coils of incense hang suspended from its ceiling and, burning slowly, turning from solid to gas, they author a mystical transubstantiation of everything around them. Bright lights transform into little more than shimmering colors drifting in the haze, and solid objects turn to whirling smoke that disappears into the darkness.

Across the road, Shepherd sat silently for a long time and watched the clouds of smoke and incense drift away into the night sky. It looked to him as if the whole world were on fire.

AT SIX O'CLOCK the next morning the Mid-levels was as close to pleasant as it was ever likely to be. The narrow sidewalks weren't yet choked with pedestrians and the streets were almost empty of vehicles. Using a lamp post for balance, Shepherd did a few quick heel cord stretches. Then he touched his toes a half dozen times to extend his hamstrings, wheeled his arms impatiently, and began a slow jog west along the sidewalk.

Running isn't a popular sport in Hong Kong. The weather is lousy most of the time, the streets are unfriendly all of the time, and the Chinese think the whole idea of unnecessary physical exertion is absolutely laughable. About the only people who run regularly in Hong Kong are Americans, and even then only those Americans who don't mind the Chinese thinking they are completely mad. When Shepherd was in Hong Kong, he ran regularly.

Shepherd wasn't a big fan of running. He often thought that if he could find a better way to avoid turning into a living replica of a bowling ball he would be on it in a flash, but starvation as a lifestyle was even less appealing to him than running. What Shepherd did like about running was that it is uncomplicated. He didn't need anyone's permission to do it. He didn't have to sit in traffic before he could do it. And he didn't have to make any advance arrangements to do it. When the mood took him, he just pulled on shorts and a T-shirt, laced up his shoes, and headed out the door. What he hated about running was everything else.

It was not quite sunrise yet, but it was already warm and the city was suffused with the deep grey half-light of a heavy, humid dawn. The sky was indistinct, the division between earth and sky uncertain, and the air was so thick he could almost hear the moisture draining out of it.

Shepherd jogged along Caine Road, angled off behind the abandoned hulk of Victoria Prison into Chancery Lane, and emerged on Upper Albert Road in front of the Foreign Correspondents Club. Then, turning south across the Botanical Gardens, he made his way toward Hong Kong Park. Parks don't make any money, which is probably why Hong Kong doesn't have many of them. Hong Kong Park is the biggest public space in the central business district, but it is only a single square kilometer that was carved out of the site of the old Victoria Barracks when the British abandoned it a half century or so back. Entering the park from the north, he began circling it on the broad, smooth walkway that marked its boundary.

Shepherd took it easy for the first loop, but he gradually stepped up his pace and the sweat began to flow. A handful of other runners shared the path with him, all Caucasians of course, but he saw no one he recognized and was spared the ritual of exchanging insincere good mornings with people who, like him, were there precisely because they wanted to be alone with their own thoughts for a while. He felt good that morning, although he didn't really see why he should. He had slept badly, the image of Adnan's mutilated head hovering all night in the darkness just in front of his eyes, but by his second loop around the lake his feet were flying, the perspiration was pouring off him in rivulets, and his mind was as placid as a millpond.

The peaceful feeling lasted until he started his third loop. That was when he spotted the man watching him. He was seated on a green bench near a clump of banana trees and making no effort to conceal himself.

Shepherd, of course, recognized him immediately.

Twenty Four

SPECIAL AGENT LEONARD Keur was alone. He was wearing a dark blue golf shirt and khakis and sat with his legs casually crossed. He was sipping from a large Starbucks cup. Shepherd tried to remember if Keur had been sitting on that bench the first couple of times he had run past the grove of banana trees. He didn't think so, but he wasn't completely certain.

They made eye contact and Keur pointed with his free hand to a brown paper bag on the bench next to him. Shepherd slowed to a jog, turned off the path, and walked over. Keur obviously wasn't in Hong Kong Park at 6:30 A.M. by coincidence.

"What are you doing here?"

"Have some coffee," Keur said, picking up the brown bag and holding it out to Shepherd. "Take a rest. Sit with me for a while. Let's talk."

"I asked what you're doing here."

"It's a nice morning. I'm enjoying this lovely park. Go ahead and have some coffee. What can it hurt?"

"Do I have a choice?"

"Sure, Jack. Everybody's got choices. The trick is to make good ones, don't you think?"

Shepherd looked at Keur for a moment. Then he pulled up his shirt, wiped the sweat off his face, and sat down. Keur was still holding the bag out toward him, so he took it. Inside was a large Starbucks cup with a white plastic lid on it.

"How do you know how I like my coffee?" he asked.

"I don't. That's a latte. You like lattes? There ought to be some sugar in there somewhere if you want it."

Shepherd lifted the cup out and dropped the bag on the bench. The cup was hot, which meant that Keur had bought the coffee within the last few minutes.

Keur must have known he was running there in the park when he bought the coffee, but how could that be? Did the FBI have him under surveillance? That was awfully hard to believe. Maybe Keur had only seen him in the park by coincidence and *then* had gone and bought the coffee. Who was he kidding? That was even *harder* to believe.

Peeling the plastic lid off the Starbucks cup, Shepherd took a sip. He had to admit it was pretty good coffee, but it didn't make him feel any better about finding Keur waiting in the park for him.

"Okay, Keur, what are you doing in Hong Kong?"

"I'm just doing my job, Jack."

Shepherd sipped at the coffee and waited, but Keur didn't say anything else.

"There is no investigation," Shepherd said when he got tired of waiting.

Keur didn't say anything. He just sat there, expressionless, and waited for Shepherd to go on.

"There is no FBI investigation underway involving either Robert Darling or Blossom Trading. I checked."

"What makes you so sure?"

"I asked Pete Logan. He says the FBI has no interest in either Darling or Blossom Trading. You lied to me."

Keur chuckled. "You think?"

"I just don't understand why."

Keur stifled a yawn and leaned back on the bench, folding his arms in front of him. "Too bad about old Adnan, huh?" he said. "Man, that's got to be a rough way to go. You figure he was dead before they cut off his head, Jack? Or you think maybe he saw it coming all the way?"

Shepherd drank the coffee and stayed silent. He watched Keur with a neutral expression.

"How well did you know Adnan, Jack?"

"I didn't really know him at all."

"You don't seem too upset about him getting his head cut off. You didn't like him?"

"I just told you. I didn't really know him."

"Ever talk to him?" Keur asked.

"A few times."

"What did you talk about?"

"Football. Religion. The usual stuff."

"Yeah, if there's anything those Lebanese love, it's shooting the shit about football and religion." Keur sighed. "If we're going to get anywhere here, Jack, you've got to be honest with me."

"Why do you think I want to get anywhere here?"

"What was your relationship with Adnan, Jack?"

"He was Charlie Kitnarok's personal assistant. You already know I do some legal and financial work for Charlie. Other than that, I had no relationship with Adnan."

"Then what was Adnan doing in Bangkok?"

"I have no idea."

"He didn't come to see you?"

"No."

"How did he get there then?"

Shepherd shrugged. "I'm just guessing here, but maybe on an airplane?"

"You were a pretty well-thought-of guy in Washington once, Jack. A real whiz kid. You still get paid a lot of money for giving people financial advice. Maybe you were giving Adnan financial advice."

"I knew you were from the IRS."

"You ever give Adnan any financial advice, Jack?"

"Adnan who?"

"Don't bullshit me, Jack." Keur spread his hands, palms up. "I bought you coffee."

Shepherd drained the latte. He picked up the brown paper bag and stuffed the empty cup back into it. Then, taking his time about it, he crossed his legs at the ankle, leaned against the backrest, and laced his fingers together behind his head.

"What do you really want from me, Keur?"

"I already told you. I need to know what General Kitnarok is involved in these days. I need your help to do that."

"No."

"I'd like to find a way to change your mind."

"Is this where we get to the threats?"

"No threats. Let's just talk for a while and I'll bet you'll come around to my point of view."

"Who the fuck *are* you, Keur?"

"I'm exactly who and what I told you I am."

"Bullshit. You're not really FBI. There's no FBI investigation of Robert Darling or Blossom Trading. Who are you? CIA?"

Keur pulled from his back pocket the same leather ID folder that he had showed Shepherd the first time they met. He opened it and held it up.

"I'm not with the CIA. I'm one of the good guys."

In spite of himself, Shepherd chuckled at that. He bent forward and examined Keur's ID closely. The badge on the left side of the leather folder was shaped like a shield. It was bright gold and glittered in the early morning sun. There was a gold eagle perched on the top of the shield and raised lettering all around it that said: *U.S.*

Department of Justice, Federal Bureau of Investigation. The ID card on the right was tucked behind a plastic window that was cracked and foggy and showing its age. The card had a color headshot of Keur about the size of a passport photograph and just about as sunny. It also had four or five lines of printing, but by then Shepherd had lost interest it what they said.

"That looks really good," he said. "Can you get me one just like it?"

"Ask your pal Logan to check me out if you don't believe I'm who I say I am."

"I did."

"And?"

Shepherd hesitated. "He says you're an agent assigned to the Washington field office."

"So there you go." Keur spread his hands, palms up.

"But he also says the FBI isn't conducting an investigation of either Robert Darling or Blossom Trading. So even if you really are an FBI agent, you're just bullshitting me anyway."

Keur sighed, downed the rest of his coffee, and shoved the empty cup into the brown bag with Shepherd's. He exhaled heavily.

"Logan's right," he said.

Shepherd said nothing. He just waited.

"I'm on my own here," Keur went on. "Officially, I'm on medical leave from the Bureau."

"You look okay to me."

"The Bureau killed the case I was building against Darling and I got pissed off. I took a medical leave and now I'm going to put everything together on my own and shove it right down their fucking throats."

"The CIA would probably spin a story exactly like that if they sent out one of their guys to impersonate an FBI agent."

"Look, jerk off," Keur twisted his body toward Shepherd and

leaned forward, resting his hands on his knees. "I'm not CIA. It was those fucks at the CIA who buried my investigation in the first place. I'd bet my life on it. And whether you help me or not, I'm damn well going to prove it and hang this all right around their fat, flabby necks."

Shepherd said nothing.

"About two months ago," Keur went on, "I stumbled over Robert Darling and Blossom Trading in connection with a money laundering case I was working on involving the casinos in Atlantic City. It didn't take much poking around to figure out that Blossom Trading was a major arms trafficker and Darling was laundering the revenue it generated through a number of different casinos. He wasn't even trying very hard to hide it."

Shepherd still said nothing.

"I took what I had to the Special Agent in Charge of the Washington field office and asked him to authorize a full investigation with Blossom Trading and Darling as the targets. He sent it up the line. Less than twenty-four hours later, he called me in and said he'd been instructed to tell me that both Blossom Trading and Darling were off-limits, but he wouldn't tell me where those instructions had come from. He ordered me to terminate my investigation immediately and to destroy whatever notes I had. It flat out stunk."

"So you think somebody is trying to cover up something."

"Of course they are. There's no doubt about it."

"But cover up what? That the CIA is involved somehow?"

"I don't know." Keur looked away. "I'm working on that."

"Exactly how do you plan—"

"Here's the thing, Jack. A doctor I know helped me get a medical leave from the Bureau, and… well, I've got a month now, maybe two. And I'm going to use it to find out what's really going on here."

"That's *it*? That's your plan?"

Keur looked off toward the lake. He didn't say anything else.

Shepherd followed Keur's eyes and saw that traffic around the lake was picking up. Two girls who couldn't have been over twenty-five and who were probably Japanese or Korean jogged by together, both talking on mobile phones as they ran. They were slim and lovely, small-boned and smooth-skinned, and Shepherd had a moment's regret that neither of them was talking to him.

"I need your help," Keur said. "You need my help. That sounds to me like the makings of a deal."

"Why do I need your help?"

"Somebody is closing in on General Kitnarok, Jack. They're after all his key people, including you."

"Who is it?"

"Ask Adnan," Keur said.

Shepherd said nothing.

"You help me, Jack, and I'll help you. Nothing for nothing, man. You keep me in the picture about General Kitnarok and I'll keep you out of trouble."

"Why do you care about Charlie anyway? I thought you said it was Darling and Blossom Trading you were after."

"I want to make certain General Kitnarok isn't part of this. If he is, I'll nail his ass, too."

"That's not a very convincing story, Keur. You want to try again or just give up right here?"

"Ah, go fuck yourself, Jack. Do you want me to watch your sorry ass or don't you?"

"I'm not going to spy on a client for you."

"You'd really be helping to clear him. That's in his best interest."

"No."

"I can't eliminate General Kitnarok as a part of this without your help."

"No."

"Oh, I'm not so sure about that, Jack. In my experience, people tend to be somewhat flexible about their principles when their butt is on the line."

"I'm out of here, pal," Shepherd said as he stood up. "I've had enough of this. You wasted your time coming here."

"It's not that easy, Jack. They're not going to let you just walk away."

"I'm not walking away. I'm *running* away."

Then, before Keur could say anything else, Shepherd turned his back and broke into a jog. The sun was rising among the towers of Hong Kong's financial district, a tight orange ball burning holes in the grey morning mist, and Shepherd picked up his pace, hurling himself straight at the sun until his breath came in ragged jerks and his legs screamed for him to stop. But he didn't stop. He was sure he could hear a voice calling out to him from somewhere to run away from Keur as fast as it was possible for him to run, and that was exactly what he did.

Later, each time he thought back over everything that happened afterward, the same feeling would return to him over and over with a clarity verging on the telepathic. And each time it did, he would shake his head in pure amazement at it all, at the memory of how much he already understood that early morning in Hong Kong Park.

Even though, at the time, he was sure he understood nothing at all.

Twenty Five

KEUR WATCHED SHEPHERD until he crossed Cotton Tree Drive and disappeared behind the ugly white building that housed the American Consulate. Then he stood up and stretched, collected the crumpled bag with the two empty Starbucks cups in it, and walked slowly in the direction of the Bank of China Tower.

Keur had never liked Hong Kong very much. It was the nosiest, rudest, most overcrowded city he had ever been in, and it had been a hell of a long way to come for a ten minute conversation that didn't appear to amount to all that much. Still, he was convinced it had been worth it. He was beginning to get inside Shepherd's guard. He was sure of that now.

At first, using Jack Shepherd to get to Charlie Kitnarok hadn't seemed like much of a plan. Unless a target's lawyer was stupid or corrupt, preferably both, the lawyer was never likely to be the road in, and Jack Shepherd was clearly neither of those things. He had detailed intel on Shepherd and got updates almost every day. He had studied Shepherd's movements. He had read transcripts of his telephone conversations. He was beginning to understand him.

At first, he just hadn't seen it. He hadn't thought this was going to work. He had to admit that. But now he did. He could see that it *was* going to work.

Keur had always viewed recruitments like this as similar to

martial arts matches. You won, not by attacking your opponent's weaknesses, but by turning his strengths against him. Jack Shepherd was a rational guy. He thought like a lawyer. He took in information, examined that information from first one perspective then another, compared it to other information, and reached a measured conclusion as to what it meant. The conclusions he reached were inevitably both intelligent and reasoned. They were never emotional. That was his strength. And that was his weakness.

Control the flow of information to Shepherd and you control Shepherd. Make common cause with him. Build his reliance on you. Make him trust you. And become the one who feeds him information. How was he going to do that? It was the punch line to a very old joke. *All you need is sincerity. And once you learn to fake that, you've really got it made.*

Keur chuckled to himself and walked a little faster. The more he thought about it, the more pumped up he felt. He was like the magician who distracted the audience with his left hand while he picked their pockets with his right. He would keep Shepherd focused on Robert Darling. Then, in another week or two, he would reach out with his other hand and pry Charlie Kitnarok open like a tin can. This was going to work. He could *feel* it now.

SHEPHERD TOOK A quick shower when he got back to Freddy's apartment, then he dressed and rode the Mid-levels escalator down to his office. And the whole time he rode he kept thinking about that hot cup of coffee Keur had waiting for him in Hong Kong Park. Could he really be under surveillance, or was there was a more mundane explanation for it?

All around him the escalator was jammed with other people who looked like they were going to work, too. Or was it possible that some of those people were there to watch him? How the hell was he supposed to tell? Other than what he had read in spy novels, Shepherd knew nothing about surveillance and he doubted he would be able to spot it unless somebody jumped out in front of him and waved.

Of course, if there actually *were* people watching him, it meant the story Keur had told him about being on a one-man crusade was complete horseshit. It took serious manpower and local cooperation to keep someone under surveillance in places like Hong Kong and Dubai. It wasn't a job one guy could do on his own. Not by a long shot.

And that brought Shepherd face to face with a scary question. Where would Keur get manpower like that? Was the FBI really *that* interested in him, or was Keur somebody altogether different from who he claimed to be?

The more Shepherd mulled the matter over, the more he decided he was letting Keur get to him. He was making way too much out of a single hot cup of coffee. Keur could easily have known he ran in the mornings and he could just as easily have found out where he lived. Putting those two things together would almost certainly have pointed him to Hong Kong Park. There really wasn't any other place in central Hong Kong where a runner *could* be. Yeah, Shepherd thought to himself as he stepped off the escalator just below Hollywood Road, that was probably all there was to it. What other sensible explanation could there be? Surely he wasn't important enough to command intensive surveillance in two countries nearly half a world away from each other? Not from the FBI, and not from anybody else.

That was another thing that bothered Shepherd about Keur's sudden appearance that morning, however, something that was probably more important than how Keur came to be in Hong Kong Park in the first place. Keur's whole pitch to him to spy on Charlie for the FBI, or for Keur personally if his story about being on medical leave was actually true, just didn't ring right. Unless Keur was a complete idiot, and Shepherd didn't for a moment think he was, he had to know that wasn't going to happen. No lawyer who wasn't corrupt was going to turn informant on his own client. So why had Keur allowed himself to appear stupid by asking in the first place? He had even done it twice now, not just once. That just didn't make any sense.

Shepherd ducked into the Pacific Coffee Company and grabbed a large coffee and a cinnamon roll. There was a long counter across from the window that looked out into Hollywood Road and he stood leaning on it, watching the traffic while he ate the roll. There was at least one thing about Keur's story that *did* add up, even if Shepherd didn't much like the look of the total he was getting.

Had somebody been trying to kill Charlie in Dubai, or were they really gunning for him as Keur had claimed? As outlandish as that possibility had sounded when Keur first laid it out, the picture Shepherd had on his cell phone of Adnan's severed head with the eyeballs chewed out had given the whole proposition a degree of credence it hadn't had before. Somebody had gone after one of the people who was closest to Charlie. Could that mean that Keur was right after all? Could that mean that he might be next on the list?

Of course, Shepherd told himself, the attack in Dubai and Adnan's murder in Bangkok might not be connected. It might just be a simple coincidence that a headless Adnan had turned up hanging under the Taksin Bridge a couple of days after those two idiots jumped them in Dubai. Shepherd knew if he could convince himself of that, he would feel a hell of a lot better.

But he couldn't.

Shepherd finished his cinnamon roll and dumped the wrapper in the trash. Then he took the rest of his coffee with him and crossed the street to the little shophouse where he had his office.

THE CONCRETE STAIRWELL was musty and dim and it smelled faintly of cat urine. Shepherd climbed the two flights up to his office. He booted up both computers and sipped at his half-cold coffee until they were ready to use. He opened the browser on one and connected to Bloomberg, where he set up a half dozen windows to monitor that morning's financial data. Then he switched to the other computer and downloaded and printed copies of all the new wire transfer notices that had arrived overnight and checked the balances in the investment accounts.

He added the new wires to his running total and saw immediately that all the incoming transfers in the last few days added up to a little less than the full amount he had wired out of Thailand, but he couldn't immediately see how that could be. He counted the wires from Bangkok Bank and the total number was right, so he went back and compared the amounts of the wires one by one with the amounts he had ordered transferred. Every wire was a little short, shorter than they should have been just to cover the payments he had authorized Woody Allen to make to get the transfers approved by the Bank of Thailand.

For a couple of hours Shepherd ran trial balances and checked and double-checked his figures, but no matter how he worked the numbers he kept getting the same result. About seven million dollars of the nearly six hundred million dollars he had wired out of Thailand, give or take, hadn't shown up in any of the investment accounts. About one million of that was accounted for by what he had agreed to pay the deputy governor of the Bank of Thailand, but what happened to the other six million? Had Charlie's pet banker gotten sticky fingers?

When you're dealing with over six hundred million dollars, not being able to account for less than one per cent of it wasn't exactly a show-stopper, so Shepherd decided to set the matter aside to sort out later, and he spent the rest of the morning on the more pressing task of laying out a detailed investment plan for the new funds. He wanted to talk to Charlie before making any final commitments, but it was still a little early to call him. Dubai was four hours behind Hong Kong, so calling just after lunch would catch Charlie near the beginning of his day. That was assuming Charlie was still in Dubai, of course. If he was somewhere else, the hour might be less convenient, but Shepherd figured that was Charlie's problem, not his.

In addition to talking to Charlie about the way he had decided to bed down his funds, Shepherd also want to ask him what he knew about Adnan's dramatic demise. Maybe he could even find out what Adnan had been doing in Bangkok without having to ask Charlie flat out. He knew it was really none of his business what Adnan had been doing there, but under the circumstances, he told himself, his interest was far more than idle curiosity.

A little after 1:00 P.M., he went down to Archie's New York Deli in SoHo and had a quick corned beef on rye with a couple of kosher dill pickles and a Dr. Brown's Cream Soda. That was one thing Shepherd really loved about Hong Kong, the exotic Asian food. Then he went back to the office and settled in behind his desk to call Charlie.

As a rule, Shepherd generally called one of Charlie's office numbers when he needed to talk to him. He didn't much like calling people's cell phones. He had seen too many men answering phones with their mouths full or, worse, while standing at a urinal, and he didn't much care for the picture of Charlie holding his phone with one hand and his penis with the other. But it was early in Dubai, far too early to expect anyone to answer the office lines, so Shepherd set his policy aside and dialed Charlie's private cell number.

The first time he called, the call went straight to voice mail and he hung up without leaving a message. Charlie never listened to his messages anyway so there was no point in leaving one. Shepherd waited about ten minutes and called again. This time Charlie answered almost immediately.

Twenty Six

THE SMALL TALK lasted no more than a few seconds. Small talk was something neither Charlie nor Shepherd did particularly well.

"I need to tell you how I intend to invest the funds I got out of Thailand," Shepherd said, getting right to the point.

Charlie didn't say anything for a moment, and Shepherd wondered if the six hundred million dollars he had bribed a deputy governor of the Bangkok of Thailand to get out of the country for Charlie had temporarily slipped his mind.

"Whatever you want to do is okay with me," Charlie finally said.

"Let me run over—"

"You're not listening to me, Jack. Handle the funds however you like. I don't want the details."

"You're sure?"

"Absolutely sure. Anything else?"

So Shepherd asked Charlie what he thought about Adnan.

"The best assistant I ever had," Charlie answered. "Why are you asking me?"

"No, I meant what do you think about the reason he was killed."

There was a silence over the telephone so complete that for moment Shepherd wondered if the connection had been broken. Then all at once it occurred to him. Charlie had no idea that Adnan was dead.

"I'm sorry," Shepherd said. "That was stupid of me. I just assumed you knew."

"Tell me," Charlie said.

Shepherd told Charlie what he knew and the silence came again. Shepherd waited for Charlie to break it. It seemed the right thing to do.

"You should get back here, Jack," he said when he finally did.

Shepherd didn't know what he had been expecting Charlie to say, but it certainly wasn't that.

"What do you mean?"

"Come back to Dubai until I find out what's going on. You may be in danger, too. You'll be safe here."

"I was just in Dubai, Charlie, and I clearly remember two guys shooting at us one morning while we were walking through the souk. That's what you call safe?"

"Never mind about that. That wasn't serious. This may be."

Shepherd could have told Charlie that hiding behind a pile of bags while two guys pumped bullets at them seemed pretty damned serious to him, but he didn't bother.

"I've got work to do here," he said instead. "And nobody has tried to kill me in Hong Kong recently. I think I'll stay where I am."

"That's not a good idea, Jack. It would make me feel a lot better for you to be in Dubai."

"There's some money missing from the wires, Charlie. I need to find it before I even think about going anywhere."

"What wires?"

"The ones from Bangkok Bank."

"How much is missing?" he asked.

"Somewhere around six million dollars, I think. Net of gratuities."

"Net of what?"

Shepherd tried it another way, without the cleverness this time, which he figured was the way he probably should have tried it in the first place.

"The wires were short by a total of about seven million dollars in all. We paid a million or so to get the money out of Thailand, so that leaves around six million dollars unaccounted for."

"Don't worry about it."

"I'm thinking your banker may have gotten greedy and helped himself."

"No, that didn't happen."

"Look, Charlie, whether you think it happened or not, there's still six million dollars—"

"Would you forget about the lousy six million dollars, Jack, and get your ass back here to Dubai right now? Will you just shut the fuck up and do that for me?"

Charlie wasn't in Dubai for the food. Shepherd understood that. He was there for the discretion, the no-questions-asked anonymity, and the personal security for which Dubai was well known. Money was money and business was business, and they both mattered more in Dubai than politics. If there was a better place on the planet for a billionaire politician on the lam to go to ground, Shepherd didn't know where it was. He just wasn't certain that the same reasoning applied to Mr. Billionaire-Politician-On-The-Lam's lawyer.

If somebody really *was* trying to pick off the people around Charlie, Shepherd didn't see how he would be better off in Dubai than he was in Hong Kong. But Charlie was the client so he pretty much went where Charlie asked him to go, regardless of how good or bad the reasons for making the trip might be. That was the way it worked. Lawyers kept their clients happy. Not the other way around.

They wrangled on for a while after that, although Shepherd's heart really wasn't in it. He didn't want to go back to Dubai, of course, but Charlie was absolutely insistent. Shepherd knew it would be easier just to do it than try to talk him out of the idea. After a bit of ritual back and forth, Shepherd gave in and they agreed he would finish bedding down the new funds and leave Hong Kong the next day. The matter of the missing six million dollars was left to deal with some other time.

Buying and selling hundreds of millions of dollars in bonds and currencies might sound romantic to a lot of people, but mostly Shepherd suspected it sounded that way to people who had never done it. The truth was that it was tedious and boring work. He sent dozens of emails to banks and brokerage houses, confirmed them all with faxes, and sorted out the mistakes that were inevitably made. Then he did it all again. And again. He always imagined people who worked in banks felt the same way about what they did. After a while, all that money they handled stopped being money and turned into nothing but piles of paper they had to haul around. It wasn't wealth, it was just another load of stuff they had to hump.

The whole time Shepherd was busy humping his load of stuff, he was turning everything that had happened over and over in his mind. Tedium was very productive for some people he knew, including himself. There were people who cut the grass while they thought. Others who did the ironing. He even knew one guy who claimed to get all his best ideas while vacuuming his swimming pool. As for Shepherd, the tedium that really cut the mustard was shuffling wire transfers and revising investment accounts.

Somewhere between checking the long euro positions at Deutsche Bank and adding to the short-dated T-bills in the HSBC accounts, an idea abruptly popped into Shepherd's head. Once it did, as was generally the case with almost all of his best ideas, he was dumbfounded he hadn't thought of it sooner.

SHEPHERD HADN'T TALKED to Tommy for nearly a year and he didn't really want to talk to Tommy now, but he knew that was exactly what he had to do. Shepherd had known Tommy almost from the day he had taken up residence in Bangkok to teach at

Chulalongkorn University. Tommy had made it his business to get to know Shepherd back then because getting to know people like Shepherd was what Tommy did for a living.

Tommy's real name was Tommerat something-or-another, but everyone Shepherd knew just called him Tommy. In the face of all provocation, Tommy stuck doggedly to the story that he was deputy spokesman for the Thai Ministry of Foreign Affairs, but if there was anyone in Bangkok who didn't know that Tommy actually worked for the National Intelligence Agency, Shepherd had never met them. The first time he had introduced Tommy to Anita, she had been terribly amused at the idea that there was such a thing as a Thai spy and she had tossed out a couple of pretty snappy one-liners on the subject. Shepherd tried to explain to her later that there was absolutely nothing amusing about Tommy, and certainly nothing to laugh about, but he didn't think Anita really believed him.

Talking to Tommy wouldn't help him very much, Shepherd knew, but talking to Tommy would get him in to see Tommy's boss. And that was a different matter altogether.

He could call Kate directly, at least he thought he could, but approaching her through Tommy seemed a better way to reach her for at least two reasons. First, Kate was the Director General of the Thai National Intelligence Agency, and not exactly the sort of person you rang up and expected to be put through to right away. And second, he and Kate had a history of sorts. The problem was, Shepherd wasn't entirely certain they both saw that history in exactly the same way.

Kate wouldn't necessarily tell him what she knew about why Adnan was murdered just because he asked her to. But then again, she might. Particularly if she thought he might be in danger, too. They had a healthy enough history for that. At least he thought they did.

There were not many Thai women in government, fewer still

in powerful positions, and absolutely none as gorgeous and refined as Kate. Governments rose and fell in Thailand with monotonous regularity, but Kate had remained in control of NIA for four years while three prime ministers had come and gone. Shepherd knew some people wondered why. He guessed it was pretty simple. By now Kate must have gotten enough on the shifting cast of ignorant, corrupt Thai politicians to have the blundering old fools in mortal terror of her. This attractive, elegant, soft-voiced woman, not yet forty years old, was probably the J. Edgar Hoover of Thailand.

After poking around a little online, Shepherd found a four o'clock flight to Bangkok the next afternoon. It arrived around 6:00 P.M. and then there was an overnight flight from Bangkok to Dubai that left at 2:00 A.M. That would give him nearly eight hours between flights. More than enough time to get back and forth from the airport, meet with Kate somewhere, and ask her what he needed to ask. And doing it that way had the additional advantage of letting him keep his promise to Charlie to come back to Dubai as soon as he finished everything he needed to do. He would just skip over mentioning to Charlie that making a stopover in Bangkok to meet with Kate was one of the things he needed to do.

Shepherd booked first class seats for himself on both flights and then took out his phone to call Tommy. Maybe Tommy could even arrange for him to bypass Thai immigration and save him from standing in those long, slowly creeping lines at the Bangkok airport. Of course the little weasel could arrange for him to bypass immigration. He would damn well insist on it.

Twenty Seven

SOMEWHAT TO SHEPHERD'S surprise, everything was arranged in Bangkok exactly the way he had asked. As soon as the aircraft door opened a dark-skinned man wearing gold-rimmed sunglasses and a white shirt with a blue tie slipped inside and scanned the first class cabin. He held a brief, whispered conversation with a stewardess in the forward galley and she turned and pointed at Shepherd. Shepherd fought back the impulse to wave.

The man led Shepherd out into the loading bridge while the flight attendants held the other passengers on the plane. He opened a small door set into one side of the bridge and pointed to a set of metal stairs attached to its exterior. A big black Mercedes was waiting on the parking apron at the bottom of the stairs. The windows were so heavily tinted it was impossible to see who was inside, but Shepherd figured he could guess.

The driver got out as Shepherd came down the stairs and opened the right rear passenger door. He was a serious looking guy, not so much big as barrel-chested and solid. He had a close-cropped military-style haircut and wore a black safari suit. Shepherd nodded at him and slid into the backseat of the car.

"It's been a while," Tommy said. He didn't offer his hand.

"You don't sound too sorry about that," Shepherd said. He didn't offer his hand either.

"Sometimes I am, sometimes I'm not. I like you, Jack, but let's face it. When you lived here, you were a pain in the goddamn ass."

The Mercedes pulled away from the plane and followed a road marked out with yellow lines painted on the tarmac, one that was used primarily for luggage carts and catering vans.

"I checked a bag," Shepherd said. "We need to go by baggage claim."

"Don't worry about it."

"What do you mean, don't worry about it? I don't want to lose my suitcase."

"We've already pulled it from the aircraft. It's in the back."

Shepherd nodded, impressed in spite of himself. They drove parallel with the terminal building until they passed the last loading bridge, then they made a right and after that another right and passed through a sliding chain-link gate. A half dozen soldiers stood to one side and saluted the darkened windows of the car. The soldiers were in full battle dress and had automatic weapons slung across their chests.

"What's with the storm troopers?" Shepherd asked.

Tommy shot him a look. "What's that supposed to mean?"

"You've got heavily armed troops guarding the airport. It looks like somebody is expecting trouble."

"That's exactly what we're expecting. Maybe you should tell your pal that we're ready for him."

"I don't do politics, Tommy. I'm just a lawyer who manages money."

"Yeah, I've heard that shit from you before, Jacko. You can't wipe the mud off that easy. Lie down with dogs, get up with fleas."

"You got anymore clichés you want to toss out while I'm still listening?"

"Yeah, try this one. Go fuck yourself."

"Hey," Shepherd said, spreading his hands, "I thought you said you liked me."

"I lied, asshole."

Within minutes they were out of the airport and speeding down the expressway into Bangkok. The big Mercedes was like the QE2 cutting through a fleet of dinghies, and the hood ornament held the setting sun like a gun sight. Out of the corner of his eye, Shepherd looked Tommy over. He had a soft, almost pink face, and he wore plain, black-rimmed glasses. His dark hair was neatly cut and he was conservatively dressed in a dark suit that was neither snappy nor expensive, a white shirt, and a plain tie with a muted pattern. He looked like he could have been just about anybody which, when Shepherd thought about it, was probably what made him good at what he did. Still, Tommy looked older than the last time Shepherd had seen him, and not the kind of older that comes purely from the passage of time. It was the kind that came from nerves and fear whittling you down, the kind that tugged at the skin under your eyes and etched deep lines into your forehead.

"So how's the spy business these days?" Shepherd asked.

Tommy turned his head very slowly and looked at him without expression.

"How many times do I have to tell you, Jack, I am not a spy. I am merely the deputy spokesman for the Ministry of Foreign Affairs."

"Got it," Shepherd nodded. "But seriously, how's the spy business?"

Tommy smiled in spite of himself.

"I'm keeping pretty busy," he said after a moment. "There's a lot going on."

"Other than the red shirts and the yellow shirts?"

Tommy shrugged. "There's a lot going on," he repeated.

The Mercedes entered the outskirts of Bangkok and Shepherd stared idly out the window as it worked its way into the city. No one would ever claim Bangkok was a beautiful city, but it was twilight and Shepherd thought Bangkok looked a lot better at twilight than it did in the hard light of midday. Some people said there was so much crap in Bangkok's air that it would be easier to walk on it than to breath it, but there was something undeniably magical in how, just after sunset, all that pollution colluded with the last rays of the sun to make the sky glow with a soft, mango-colored haze. For a few minutes at least, the light turned dreamy and otherworldly. Like a blanket of fresh snow, it camouflaged the ugliness. Twilight was as good as Bangkok got.

Shepherd heard the soft crackling sound of static from the front seat and a radio suddenly spat a blast of colloquial Thai spoken so rapidly Shepherd didn't understand a word.

The driver glanced back at Tommy. "*Rod mae kwang thanon Petchburi trong soi Asoke,*" he said. "*Rod ja tit maak krub.*"

"*Pai tang eun dai mai?*" Tommy asked.

"*Long pai soi Ekamai, Laew Pai Tang Sukhumvit. Arj ja dee kwa krub.*"

Tommy pulled a Blackberry out of the inside pocket of his jacket and studied the screen. He punched a speed dial key and lifted it to his ear. Then he turned slightly away, murmured a few words, and listened.

"Yes," he said after a few moments. "Yes, I think so."

"What's going on?" Shepherd asked.

Tommy ignored him and listened some more. Then he looked at his watch.

"Thirty minutes, maybe a little more," Tommy said into the phone.

He returned the Blackberry to his jacket and leaned toward the driver.

"*Pai apartment ti thanon Sathorn,*" he said.

"Are you going to cut me in here?" Shepherd asked.

Tommy leaned back and scratched at his neck.

"We've changed the location for your meeting," he said after a moment.

"Trouble in River City?"

"There's usually trouble in River City."

Shepherd thought back to the riot on Silom Road when he had been attacked by a teenage kid apparently keen to take his head off with an iron bar and eventually beaten to the ground by an old lady wielding a folding chair. Bangkok had been on edge for months and he knew some people were even beginning to whisper the unthinkable. That the whole place might be about to come down around their ears. Shepherd wasn't so sure about that. Thailand had always had a near mystical way of righting itself just before it went over a cliff. But he knew things were getting worse, and that things might even get a lot worse before they got better. That is, assuming they ever did get better.

"What's happening today?" Shepherd asked.

"Your red shirts have stolen some buses and blocked Petchaburi Road."

"They're not my red shirts, Tommy."

Tommy snorted, but he didn't say anything.

"Snort all you want, little man. I have nothing to do with the red shirts."

"Save you breath, Jacko. You may have my boss fooled. But you're not fooling me."

Shepherd let that pass. He was tired of fencing with Tommy. "Why do you care about buses blocking Petchaburi Road anyway?"

"Traffic will be backed up halfway to the Cambodian border. We'll never get across town tonight."

"Where across town are we going?"

"Nowhere now."

"So where across town were we going?"

"You don't need to know that."

"Where are we going now?"

"You'll find out when we get there."

"For fuck's sake, Tommy, you're so full of shit. You think I'm going to run around telling everybody where your shitty little safe houses are, you stupid turd?"

"There we go." Tommy bobbed his head and grinned. "There's the guy we all remember. What was with all the politeness and restraint anyway, Jacko? You used to be all attitude, man. I miss that."

"Ah, fuck you," Shepherd said, and went back to staring out the window.

"Right," Tommy nodded, "Fuck me. I love Americans. Yeah, I really do."

Twenty Eight

THE CAR TURNED into Soi Ekamai, the main thoroughfare through one of the city's most popular residential and commercial districts, and immediately bogged down in traffic. Shepherd knew the Ekamai area pretty well and was surprised to see it so crowded. Although there were generally plenty of people around, Soi Ekamai wasn't exactly Fifth Avenue. He wondered what was going on.

Almost as if he knew exactly what Shepherd was thinking, Tommy pointed out the window. "Take a good look, Jacko. Those are the kind of people you've teamed up with."

Scattered among the street vendors and sidewalk peddlers who crowded the city's sidewalks day and night, Shepherd saw up and down the street loose knots of people dressed in identical red polo shirts. They could have been students and alumni headed to a University of Alabama football game. But of course they weren't.

"I haven't teamed up with anybody, Tommy. I'm just—"

"Yeah, I know. You're just a lawyer. Save it, Jacko. I think you're full of shit."

"Possibly so, little man. But not about that."

The red shirts were mostly male, and young, and none of them were doing very much but hanging around. Some of them were eating, but then Thais were always eating. Most of them were just standing there and quite a few were watching the Mercedes as it crawled by.

"Why are they looking at us?"

"Big car, government plates, darkened windows," Tommy shrugged. "They probably think you're somebody important."

"I am somebody important."

Shepherd reached for the button to open the window, but Tommy lunged across the seat and slapped his hand away.

"What the fuck are you doing?" he snapped.

"I was going to wave."

"Wave? *Wave*? Have you lost your goddamned mind, Jack? These are dangerous people."

"They don't look very dangerous to me."

"You just can't see it, can you, Jack?" Tommy shook his head. "People like you, you can't ever see it."

"People like me? What the hell does that mean?"

"Americans, Brits. You people from countries where nothing has changed in hundreds of years. You think life just goes on the same way forever. You think civilization is like the air you breathe. It's just there and it always will be. Tomorrow your mail will be delivered and the trash will be picked up and you'll drive down to the club and play a little golf with your pals. Out here, my friend, we know it can all be gone in a moment. We've lived it. We've lost it and gotten it back and lost it again. We've done it over and over. You don't know a goddamned thing about that."

"I know that—"

"You know shit, asshole. Ask the people in New Orleans how strong civilization is. The government gave up on them and in twenty-four hours they were ripping each other's hearts out. We're savages, Jacko. We're twenty-four hours from the fucking jungle. Without government and law, we're nothing but animals."

Shepherd looked back out the window at the groups of red shirts gathered along both sides of the street. He understood what Tommy was saying. He even more or less agreed with him. But these particular guys looked pretty benign to him. Mostly it was just hard for Thais to look anything other than benign.

"These are just people with a different idea of Thailand than you have, Tommy. That's called democracy. Thailand is a democracy, isn't it?"

"They're barbarians," Tommy snorted. "They want to destroy everything we've built, everything that gives this country a chance at a real future."

"The barbarians are at the gate, huh?"

Tommy said nothing. He just looked away.

On the sidewalk just outside the window a young boy who appeared to be about seventeen or eighteen was juggling a stubby iron bar in one hand. While Shepherd watched, he flipped the bar back and forth between his hands, but the kid was too young and skinny to be threatening so it didn't particularly bother Shepherd.

"There's going to be a civil war in Thailand, Jacko." Tommy was still looking away, but he spoke in a voice tight with anger. "Your pal General Kitnarok is going to lead that rabble out there into the streets and the rest of us are going to fight back. We're not going to let people like that take over our country. We'll do whatever it takes to stop them. Whatever it takes."

"You're afraid of people like that, aren't you, Tommy?"

"I'm afraid of what they might do to this country."

"The folks on your side aren't exactly candidates for sainthood."

"You haven't any fucking idea what you're—"

A loud noise cut Tommy off, a single metallic bang as if something had fallen from the sky onto the roof of the car.

"What the fuck was that?" Tommy snapped.

Almost immediately there were two more bangs, but this time they had both seen the rocks come arcing in from the sidewalk before they hit the car. Shepherd cut his eyes back to the red-shirted kid with the iron bar just in time to see the kid wind up and fling the bar at the Mercedes. It hit flat against Shepherd's window, the same one he had started to roll down before Tommy stopped him. The glass spidered to the edge of the frame, but it didn't break. Shepherd had never thought much before that about the benefits of bullet resistant glass, but right at that moment it seemed to him to be one of the world's greatest inventions.

The driver wrenched the steering wheel to the left and popped the accelerator. The heavy Mercedes swayed into the opposite traffic lane and jerked as the driver cut between a bus and a delivery van and shot away up a side street.

"You fucks!" Tommy screamed. He twisted around in his seat toward where the red shirts along Soi Ekamai were rapidly disappearing behind them. "You fucking cunts! We'll destroy you, you lousy little shits! We'll kill you all!"

Leaning his head back against the seat, Shepherd closed his eyes. He had no doubt Bangkok was entering a slow slide into chaos. Malice and spite were everywhere. He could even feel it in the dim grayness of the early evening.

Tommy's breathing turned ragged as he struggled to control himself.

"Fucking shits," Tommy muttered, and then he was quiet.

Shepherd said nothing.

A FEW MINUTES later Shepherd opened his eyes and straightened up. They were on Rama IV Road cruising steadily through traffic toward the financial district. He saw no more knots of red shirts on the sidewalks.

When the car reached the concrete pillars of the expressway, the driver turned underneath them and drove along a narrow road with very little traffic. They passed a string of junkyards and construction dumps, then made a right and a left and came to a T-junction in front of a run-down hotel. Shepherd knew roughly where they were, but not exactly. They were somewhere near the center of the city, in a warren of narrow streets just to the north of Sathorn Road. They made a left in front of the hotel and then almost immediately took a right and pulled into a small parking area in front of a nondescript apartment building.

"Let's go," Tommy said as soon as the car stopped.

He got out and Shepherd got out with him.

The air was still and heavy and the city stunk. Shepherd looked up at the building where they had stopped. It was a dozen or so floors high and indistinguishable from the hundreds of other characterless apartment buildings that dotted Bangkok. A few lights were on in the gathering dusk, but the building was mostly dark. He assumed Kate was somewhere up there waiting for him. Maybe she would tell him what was really happening in Thailand, but maybe she wouldn't. After all, he was just a foreigner. Even at the best of times, Thais didn't have much interest in cutting foreigners in on the intrigues that powered their secretive society. And these were a long way from the best of times.

"She doesn't have much time for you, Jacko," Tommy snapped. "So let's get your ass upstairs and get this over with."

"You don't sound very happy about this meeting, Tommy."

"If it was me, you wouldn't be here. But she's the boss and I'm not."

"And you're not likely to be, are you?"

Tommy stepped close to Shepherd and leveled a finger at his chest.

"Watch your mouth, Jacko."

"Step away, little man. Don't push your luck."

Tommy let a second or two go by without moving. Shepherd knew he was just saving face, but saving face was important to Thais, so Shepherd said nothing. After a moment or two, Tommy lowered his finger, turned his back, and walked into the lobby of the apartment building.

Shepherd took a deep breath and followed him.

Twenty Nine

THE APARTMENT TO which Tommy led him was on the second floor. It was completely nondescript. Worn gray carpet, bare walls, and a few generic furnishings that looked like they had been bought at a tent sale after the closing down of a Holiday Inn somewhere in Ohio. Tommy pointed Shepherd toward a chair upholstered in some kind of nubby-brown fabric and took a seat on a couch set at a right angle to it.

On the other side of the room, standing half in and half out of a pool of yellow light cast by a green-shaded floor lamp, Kate was talking on a cell phone. Her back was to them, which gave Shepherd a moment before he had to say anything. He figured that was probably his good luck. Men tend to babble when they talk to beautiful women, and he knew he wasn't any exception. As much as he liked to think of himself as the reincarnation of Humphrey Bogart, most of the time he suspected he sounded more like Joe Biden.

Kate glanced back over her shoulder as Shepherd sat down. She waggled her fingers in a little wave, then went on with her conversation in a low voice. She was wearing a yellow silk suit with a straight skirt that ended just at the tops of her knees. She had on no jewelry other than a single strand of grey pearls and a gold watch with a brown leather strap, a model so exclusive that Shepherd couldn't immediately identify the make. Her legs were smooth and bare and slightly tanned, and she had on a pair of green pumps exactly the color of a '57 MG Shepherd had once owned. He noticed that her shiny black hair was cut much shorter than it had been the last time he had seen her. Instead of a neatly shaped bob that fell to her shoulders, it was now closely cropped all around and hugged her head like a helmet. Shepherd wondered what that meant.

An old girlfriend whose name he had long forgotten once told him that when a woman made a big change in her hairstyle she was actually saying she wanted to change a lot of other things, too. Shepherd assumed then the woman had just been tweaking his male ego, feeding his conceit, that eventually he would piece together enough clues to figure out what the women around him were really thinking. But as the years passed, he suspected more and more that she had been telling him the truth.

So what then was the real story behind Kate's radical chop? Was it a sign she was looking for a change in her life? And if it was, what kind of a change did she have in mind? Shepherd thought he just might have to give that question some careful thought.

KATE CLOSED HER phone and walked over. She sat down on the couch opposite Shepherd, crossed her legs at the knee, and smiled. *What a great smile*, Shepherd thought. But then Kate had always had a great smile so he wasn't going to read anything into it.

"How have you been, Jack?"

"Good," he nodded. "Good."

"You've gone back to practicing law I hear."

"Yeah, more or less."

"And I also hear you have some rather interesting clients."

Shepherd shrugged and said nothing.

"Want something to drink? We've got beer and wine in the fridge, I think."

"A beer would be good."

Kate looked at Tommy and lifted her head slightly. "And a glass of wine for me, please, Tommy."

Tommy scurried off without a word into what Shepherd assumed was the kitchen. He liked the idea of the little turd being sent off to fetch drinks. He liked it a lot. He and Kate sat in silence while they waited for Tommy to return and he liked the comfort of the silence, too.

Shepherd and Kate had trusted each other not long ago when something big and dangerous had come unwound around them. At first, it was because they had to. Later, it was because they wanted to. That was when their moment had come. But then it passed. Maybe their timing was lousy or maybe it was something else altogether. Either way, what did it matter now? Their time had come. And it had passed. Simple as that.

Shepherd had never been one to attempt CPR on the past. Trying to breathe new life into yesterday was a lousy way to deal with tomorrow. Besides, he didn't know anyone who had ever succeeded at it, no matter how much they might have wanted to. Still, Shepherd couldn't help speculating a little as he and Kate sat quietly there together. I could have been a contender, he thought. *Once upon a time, I could have been a contender.*

Tommy came back and set out their drinks.

"I think it would be better if Jack and I talked alone, Tommy," Kate said when he was done. "Could you wait downstairs, please?"

Tommy didn't look particularly happy about that and Shepherd couldn't really blame him. It had to be embarrassing to be dismissed that way, but Tommy covered it reasonably well and just nodded and left the room. Shepherd almost felt sorry for him, but then he quickly came to his senses and the feeling passed.

Kate began.

"It's good to see you, Jack."

"It's good to see you, too," Shepherd said. "I mean it's really good."

Prattling already. He bit his tongue.

If Kate noticed, she gave no sign.

"All the same," she said, "I gather you're not here just to say hello to an old friend."

Shepherd shook his head. "No, I'm not."

"I didn't think so."

Kate's purse was on the floor next to the couch and she reached down and lifted it into her lap. It was the same color as her shoes and looked expensive. Shepherd watched as she felt around inside and then took out a red and gold box of Dunhill Filters and a gold lighter.

"I didn't know you smoked," he said.

"I stopped and then started again. And then I stopped a few more times and started a few more times." Kate shrugged. "You know how it goes."

Shepherd made a noise he hoped sounded sympathetic.

Kate broke the cellophane around the box with her thumbnail and flipped up the top. He watched her fingers extract a cigarette and decided they were without a doubt the most graceful fingers he had ever seen. Long and slim, elegantly shaped, nails neatly trimmed and varnished in deep red. He followed the cigarette with his eyes. She lifted it to her mouth and slid it between her lips. He heard rather than saw the top of her lighter snap back and her thumb spin the wheel. He saw her lips pucker slightly as they shaped themselves around the filter and sucked gently at it.

Watching her, Shepherd thought back a year or so to when he lay in a hospital bed in Phuket recovering from two bullet wounds he had acquired when a ham-fisted hit man had confused him with one of his clients. He had lost a lot of blood and passed out at the side of the road. He might have bled to death if Kate hadn't found him and gotten him to a hospital in time.

Kate had stayed at his bedside all of that first day, and when she left that night she had bent down and brushed his lips with hers. He wanted to tell her right then how that made him feel, but he was so tired he wasn't sure what he had said to her. He had tried, he could remember clearly that he had tried, but he didn't know how much he had been able to put into words before sleep took him. Kate never mentioned it, and he had never figured out a way to ask without sounding like a complete jerk. Whatever he had said, or hadn't said, this obviously wasn't the time to talk about it.

Kate took a long draw on her Dunhill and exhaled slowly, uncrossing her legs and then re-crossing them in the opposite direction. She returned the cigarettes and lighter to her purse and put it back on the floor.

"Okay, Jack," she said. "What's on your mind?"

"I need to know if I've got to watch my ass."

Kate pursed her lips and took another draw on her Dunhill.

"If you're asking me to watch it for you, perhaps we can come to some kind of an arrangement."

Shepherd looked away. One sentence out of his mouth and the conversation was already spinning completely out of control.

"Let me start again," he said. "I'm sure you know all about the attack on Charlie in Dubai."

Kate nodded.

"And you know that a couple of days ago somebody decapitated his personal assistant and hung him under a bridge here in Bangkok."

She nodded again. "You think there's a connection?"

"There has to be. It can't just be a coincidence."

"Do you know what the connection is?"

"I think so. Somebody wants to be certain Charlie gets the message."

"Which is what?"

"Somebody is telling him they have a lot of ways of getting to him and there isn't anything he can do about it."

"And you think they may be planning to send that same message a few more times."

"It's possible," Shepherd said.

"And I gather you also think next time your name may be the one in the subject line."

"That also seems possible."

Kate looked away and smoked quietly, lost in her cigarette. After what felt to Shepherd like about an hour but was probably more like a couple of minutes, Kate stubbed her cigarette out in a heavy glass ashtray. Then she shifted her eyes to his.

"How involved with General Kitnarok are you, Jack?"

"He's a client. I manage money for him. I shuffled corporate papers and talk to banks and accountants. It's not very exciting stuff."

"You moved nearly half a billion dollars out of Thailand three days ago for General Kitnarok. That sounds pretty exciting to me."

Shepherd shrugged, but he didn't say anything.

"Do you know what the general's plans are?" Kate asked after a moment of silence.

"Plans for what?"

"His political plans," Kate said with what sounded to Shepherd like just the slightest touch of impatience. "Do you know what his political plans are?"

"I don't do politics."

"So you're telling me you have nothing to do with what's going on in Thailand now?"

Shepherd thought back to the young faces wearing red shirts he and Tommy had passed on the drive into town. He thought back to the anger in their eyes.

"I'm not only telling you that, Kate, it's true. I really don't have anything to do with Charlie's politics. Nothing."

Kate considered that and let her eyes drift to the wall over

Shepherd's head. It was a while before she spoke again, and when she did, it was in a voice so soft he had to lean forward to hear her.

"Do you like him?" she asked.

"Charlie?"

Kate nodded.

"Yeah," Shepherd said. "I like him."

"How far would you go for him, Jack?"

"He's a client. I respect his confidences. I do the job he pays me to do. Everything else, if there is anything else, is beyond my pay grade. What are you really asking me here?"

"I need to know whose side you're on."

"I'm on my side."

Kate didn't say anything. Shepherd tried to wait her out, but eventually he gave up.

"I'm here to ask for your advice, Kate. I just need to know how much risk I'm taking in representing Charlie. Call it personal advice if you like. This is for me, not for Charlie."

"There's something you're not telling me, Jack. You didn't pull something like this out of thin air."

Shepherd hated playing poker with women. Every time he tried he ended up feeling like he was made out of Plexiglas. He thought about it for a minute and decided he had gone this far and might just as well go all in. So he told Kate about Special Agent Keur. And he told her about Keur's claim that he had been the real target in the Dubai ambush, not Charlie. And he told her how he had shrugged off the whole idea as fanciful until Adnan was murdered. That had made him reconsider Keur's claim in a new light.

"If Keur is right," Shepherd finished, "maybe somebody is trying to cripple Charlie by knocking off the people he relies on. Killing Charlie might even energize the very movement that whoever this is wants to damage. But killing people like Adnan—"

"And you."

"And me," Shepherd nodded. "Killing us would make it harder for Charlie to operate. It might even stop him altogether."

"That's not a bad idea," Kate said. "I wish I'd thought of it."

Shepherd wasn't sure whether he was supposed to laugh at that or not. Before he could decide, Kate stood up and smoothed her skirt down with one hand. Then she picked up her purse.

"Let's take a drive, Jack. Safe houses aren't always that safe. We need to talk."

Thirty

IT WAS DARK and quiet in the forecourt of the apartment building. Off in the distance, Shepherd could hear the city humming with energy and he wondered again what was really going on out there.

Tommy was leaning against the front fender of the black Mercedes, his arms folded and his legs crossed at the ankles. He straightened up as soon as Shepherd and Kate appeared and started walking toward them, but Kate waved him off. Instead, she went over and said a few words to him. Then she turned away, crossed the courtyard, and slid in behind the wheel of a blue BMW 7 Series parked just past the building's main entrance. Tommy shot Shepherd a hard look. Shepherd ignored him and got into the BMW's passenger seat. He wondered where Tommy thought he and Kate were going.

Kate drove out of the courtyard, turned left, and wound her way through the gloom of a series of tiny back streets until they reached the expressway. As soon as she saw the strings of orange lights marking the entrance ramp, she took a deep breath, let it out again, and jammed the accelerator to the floor. The big car jumped, and by the time they hit the top of the ramp they were doing sixty. Kate quickly settled them into a cruise in the inside lane at what Shepherd figured had to be at least a hundred.

Kate looked over at him and smiled. "Alone at last."

Shepherd liked that smile. It really was a wonderful smile.

But right then he would have been a lot happier if Kate had been watching where they were going instead of looking at him, even if she *was* smiling. He pointed his index finger at the road and smiled back.

Kate laughed. "Still a real candy-ass, aren't you, Jack?"

But at least she shifted her eyes back to the road.

The expressway traced the edge of Bangkok's deep-water port on the Chao Phraya River. Dozens of huge container cranes were lined up side by side along the eastern bank, each of them etched against the black sky by strings of tiny yellow lights. They made Shepherd think of a long train of circus elephants tied nose to tail. After two or three miles, they shot through a ramp curling off to the left and joined the Bagna-Trat Road that ran southeast from Bangkok, lifted fifty feet above the barren, swampy coastal plain on a forest of thick concrete pilings. Six lanes, nearly empty, and dead straight for almost thirty miles. Shepherd knew exactly what was coming next.

Sure enough, Kate floored the accelerator and Shepherd could have sworn they went slightly airborne. It felt exactly like they were in a helicopter flying low over the marshy ground.

"This car was swept two hours ago," Kate said. "It's as good a guarantee as you're ever going to get that this conversation is entirely between us."

Shepherd nodded and waited.

"Have you ever heard of a company called Blossom Trading?" Kate asked.

The question blindsided Shepherd and he hesitated.

Kate caught his reaction. "Are you involved with Blossom Trading, Jack?"

"No," he said, "I'm not involved with Blossom Trading."

"But you obviously know something about it."

Shepherd thought about that for a moment and then nodded. "The Kitnarok Foundation operates out of a floor of their building in Dubai. Charlie has some kind of interest in the company, but I don't know what it is."

"Go on," Kate said. "You know more than that."

Shepherd hesitated again. He played back Keur's claims that Blossom Trading was running guns to Iran. He didn't really know whether it was a good idea to tell Kate about that or not, but he told her anyway.

"Keur's right," Kate said. "Your client is an arms dealer. You didn't know?"

"Blossom Trading isn't my client and I don't know any such thing. And I don't know any such thing about Charlie."

"Blossom Trading sells guns all over the world, most of them off the books. Kitnarok owns half of the company. So there you go."

"Who owns the other half?"

"Robert Darling."

Shepherd smelled the rain coming, although he couldn't see it. Lightning rippled like quicksilver across the sky to the east and he saw they were headed directly toward a solid wall of thunderclouds. The wind rose, thrashing at the rice stalks in the fields along both sides of the road, and the first big drops splashed onto the windshield.

Kate switched on the wipers. "How well do you know Darling?"

"He's the other trustee—"

"I know that. Other than as a trustee of the Kitnarok Foundation, how well do you know him?"

"Not very well. Hardly at all, I guess."

"Look out for him, Jack. Robert Darling is a dangerous man. He's connected to people, a lot of people, in ways we don't quite understand."

"Like who?"

Kate shook her head.

Shepherd listened to the swish-swish of the wipers and the hiss of the tires against the wet asphalt. He summoned up a mental image of Robert Darling and examined it carefully. It was difficult for him to think of someone who wore bow ties as a dangerous man.

"There's something else, Jack. It's not something I should tell you, but you need to know."

The big car flew on through the darkness. Shepherd took a deep breath and waited for Kate to go on. Eventually she did.

"Do you know anything about the insurgency in the south?" she asked.

"A little," Shepherd said. Then he thought it over. "Not very much actually."

"Neither does the rest of the world."

That was true enough, Shepherd thought.

"Blossom Trading has been supplying the Muslim separatists with arms and ammunition for the last couple of years," Kate continued. "We think the Muslims were asking Blossom for larger shipments and heavier weapons. We think that's why Adnan was in the country when he was killed. To negotiate a bigger deal with them."

"Are you saying that Adnan was killed by Muslim rebels from the south? That's why he was beheaded? So you would know they were responsible?"

"Either that or somebody was trying to make it look that way," Kate said. "My guess is something went wrong with a deal he was working on. Maybe the separatists wanted more guns than he could deliver. Maybe Adnan had his hand out and got greedy. Maybe it was something else altogether. Whatever it was, Adnan must have pissed off his customers."

"So they beheaded him and hung him under the Taksin Bridge."

"Like you said, it was a message. When your business is selling military weapons to murderers, you need to be careful how you treat your customers."

The rain picked up and Shepherd listened to it pound against the car.

"Did the Muslims organize the hit on Charlie in Dubai?" he asked after a while.

"That would have been quite a stretch for them. They've never operated outside of Thailand before."

"Then who was it?"

"We don't know, but it wasn't them."

The rain was coming down in torrents now. It was an angry bombardment, but Kate didn't slow down. Their headlights disappeared into an uncertain void.

"You're saying you think there's no connection? The attack on Charlie in Dubai and the murder of Adnan in Bangkok were unrelated?"

Kate nodded.

"So there's no plot to kill off Charlie's advisers."

"Not that I know of."

"And I'm in the clear."

"That very much depends on how you look at it, Jack."

Shepherd wasn't sure what that meant, but he let it ride.

"Why would Charlie be in the arms business?" he asked instead. "He's got more money than God. Why would he get involved in something like that?"

"General Kitnarok isn't in it for the money."

"Then why is Charlie peddling guns?"

Kate glanced over again. "I really don't know how much I can say, Jack. I don't know how deep into this you are."

"Oh for God's sake, how many times do I have to tell you? I've got nothing to do with Charlie's businesses."

"But you do. You're involved with them on a daily basis."

"I just shuffle papers. I move money around."

"You make the trains run on time."

"You don't have to make it sound like that," Shepherd said. He watched the water streaming back from the windshield and listened to the slap of the wipers. "Not unless you want to."

"There's going to be a civil war in Thailand, Jack. General Kitnarok is going to make sure of it. That's why he's selling arms to the Muslims in the south."

"Oh, horseshit. Charlie Kitnarok leading a Muslim army into battle against the rest of you? What a load of crap."

"General Kitnarok doesn't care about three provinces in the south. He'll give them an Islamic republic if he thinks it will help him achieve his real goal. What Kitnarok wants to do is stir things up. He thinks he can tie the government down fighting the Muslim separatists, then come at us from a different direction."

"What are you talking about? What other direction?"

Kate glanced over at Shepherd again.

"General Kitnarok is arming the red shirts, too," she said.

"Arming the red shirts? You can't really think—"

"There have been two weapons shipments so far that we know of," Kate interrupted, "both from Blossom Trading and both delivered to an airstrip in the south that is under Muslim control. We missed the first one, but we got the second one when they tried to move it to Bangkok for distribution. Two hundred AK-47s with ten thousand rounds of ammunition. We think the one we missed may also have included some rocket launchers and incendiary devices. We don't know where it is now."

Shepherd said nothing. Kate was wrong about Charlie. He was pretty sure she was. But, he had to admit to himself, he wasn't *absolutely* sure.

"What time is your flight?" Kate asked.

"Not until 2:00 A.M."

"Good. Then there's something I want to show you. It won't take long."

Kate blew past a pickup truck in the inside lane. Shepherd glanced over at her as the truck's lights washed through the BMW, but she was as expressionless as if she were waiting for a bus.

A mile or so further along, a highway interchange appeared out of the darkness, although there didn't appear to be a highway connected to it. There were only entry and exit ramps that went nowhere and an overpass arching high over the Bangna-Trat Road. Shepherd had seen senseless pieces of construction like that scattered all over Thailand, the product of a public works system designed primarily to generate payoffs to politicians rather than to provide anything of value to the country.

Kate swung off on the exit ramp, U-turned across the overpass, and re-entered the elevated roadway heading back the way they had come. She punched on the CD player and adjusted the volume and a moment later one of Bach's Brandenburg concertos filled the car. Shepherd had no idea which one it was, but as they listened to it together Shepherd could see Kate's whole body relax.

The asphalt glistened in the headlights and the lights of Bangkok beckoned in the distance. As suddenly as it had begun, the wind died and the rain stopped. The moon appeared from behind the clouds off in the west. It was as bright and white as a flame.

Thirty One

A LITTLE LESS than an hour later Kate turned into a parking garage next to a hospital. She drove to the top floor, nosed the BMW in against the wall, and cut the engine. She got out, walked behind the car, and opened the trunk. Shepherd got out, too. He looked around at the largely empty parking garage.

"What are we doing here?" he asked.

Kate didn't say anything. Instead, she took a pair of powerful-looking field glasses out of the trunk. She handed them to Shepherd and pointed to the waist-high concrete wall that surrounded the top floor.

"Have a look," she said. "Tell me what you see out there."

Shepherd took the field glasses and walked over to the wall. They were just south of the old Bangkok airport, Don Mueang. It had been shut down when Suvarnabhumi Airport opened a few years before and now, except for the Thai military and an occasional private flight, the field was mostly deserted. The predictable scuffle within the bureaucracy had been rolling on for some time, rival ministers each seeking control over the process of disposing of the land. The bribes generated by selling off hundreds of acres of prime urban land near the center of Bangkok would be a prize cash cow for some politician.

"Look right below us. That building with the flat black roof."

Shepherd focused the glasses and swung them back and forth until he found the building Kate was talking about. It was roughly square, perhaps a hundred feet on each side, and looked to be the equivalent of three or four stories high. It had a mirrored surface that appeared black or dark blue in the fading light. He could see no specific source of illumination and the walls reflected the building's surroundings so perfectly that it was both there and not there at the same time. Neither of the two sides he could see appeared to have any windows or doors, but he supposed they were there and the mirrored surface just made them difficult to pick out.

The building appeared dim and deserted, but Shepherd doubted it was. There was a razor wire fence all around it that separated it from the rest of Don Mueang, and a single gate with a guardhouse. The windows of the guardhouse were made of the same reflective material as the building and it was impossible to tell if there was anyone inside. The gate was closed and inside the fence about thirty parking places were striped out in white against a blacktopped surface. Half of those parking places were occupied, mostly by new looking pick-ups and SUVs.

"It looks like it was built recently," Shepherd said.

"It was."

"Why would anyone build a new hanger at a closed airport?"

"It's not a hanger."

Shepherd lowered the field glasses and looked at Kate. "Why don't you just make this simple and tell me what I'm looking at?"

"Look just to the left of that building," she said instead of answering him. "What do you see there?"

Shepherd gave Kate a long stare, but after a moment he lifted the field glasses again. There was an aircraft parked where she told him to look. It appeared to be a 737, probably a cargo-only conversion since it had no windows. The entire aircraft was painted white and had no logo on its tail or any other visible markings.

"I call it Harvey," Kate said.

Shepherd lowered the glasses again and looked at her. "You give airplanes names?"

"Not all airplanes, just that one. You never saw the movie?"

Shepherd said nothing.

"It was back in the fifties," Kate said. "Jimmy Stewart had this imaginary friend called Harvey. Harvey was a six-foot tall white rabbit that went everywhere with him. Only nobody else could see Harvey."

"You'd think it would be pretty hard to miss a six-foot tall white rabbit."

"You'd think it would be pretty hard to miss a white airplane with no markings, too. But that's exactly what everybody seems to be doing."

Shepherd hadn't seen a registration number anywhere on the aircraft, but it had to have one. Every aircraft flying anywhere in the world carried a registration number. It was often called a tail number since it was usually painted on the aircraft's vertical tail surface, but the 737's tail surface was as white and clean as new snow. He raised the glasses again and examined the airplane carefully.

"Where's the registration number?"

"Look above the forward door."

He shifted the glasses. Sure enough, there it was. In black letters so tiny he had missed it.

"A6-NSU," he read. "Where is that from?"

"The United Arab Emirates. Dubai, to be precise."

Shepherd lowered the glasses again. "You're not going to tell me this plane belongs to Charlie, are you?"

"No."

"Okay, so I give up. Who does Harvey belong to? Some rich Arab who just loves the local massage parlors?"

"Unfortunately, no. The plane is registered in the UAE, but it's chartered to a company called Trippler Aviation. Trippler is based at a private airstrip in central Florida. You ever hear of them?"

"It sounds familiar," Shepherd said, "but right off the top of my head—"

"Trippler Aviation is a CIA proprietary, a front company for the CIA. Trippler got a lot of public attention when they were running guns into Angola for the CIA in the late 1980s and one of their planes crashed."

"This plane belongs to the CIA?"

"It's being operated by one of their front companies. That's more or less the same thing."

"What's it doing here?"

"For the last five or six years, Trippler Aviation has been in the torture taxi business."

Torture taxi was a catchy expression somebody had coined for the CIA's extraordinary rendition program. The program involved the moving of high-value prisoners, mostly Muslim extremists, among so-called black sites to prevent interference with their interrogation.

"You're telling me this airplane I'm looking at right here is used by the CIA to transport secret prisoners to secret prisons?"

"Yes," Kate nodded. "Along with a lot of other things."

"Then what is it doing in Thailand?"

But before Shepherd had finished speaking the question, he figured out the answer on his own.

"The new building?" he asked. "That building belongs to the CIA?"

"That's right," Kate said. "The CIA has very close links with the Thai military. The CIA needed a secure place to put a new interrogation facility and the Thai Air Force was happy to provide it."

"Do you really expect me to believe that the CIA is torturing people right here in the middle of Bangkok?"

"Believe what you like, Jack. All I know for sure is that your Central Intelligence Agency—"

"It's not *my* Central Intelligence Agency."

"—is housing prisoners in that building down there as well as conducting other operations out of it. I have no idea what they do with the prisoners, but I doubt they're teaching them English."

"Even if you're right—"

"Oh, I'm right, Jack. That's what I do around here, remember? I gather intelligence. I may not know what they are doing in the goddamn building, but at least, by God, I know who's going in and out of it."

"Okay, calm down."

"This *is* calm."

"Even if you're right," Shepherd repeated slowly, "why are you showing this to me?"

"Because I want you to understand what you're into."

"I guess I just don't get it. Why does this have anything to do with me?"

Kate rested her palms on the wall and looked out at the 737 parked on the airfield beneath them.

"We know that Harvey sometimes flies into a field close to the Malaysian border that's under the control of the Muslim separatists," she said. "We know that it has flown weapons for the separatists. And we also know that at least twice it has flown weapons into that field that were then moved on to another location. It was after the second flight that we intercepted the cargo of weapons I told you about, the one that was moving north toward Bangkok. The load from the first flight has disappeared."

"I thought you said that the weapons going into the south were from Blossom Trading."

"They are from Blossom Trading. The CIA is transportating them."

Shepherd took a deep breath and thought about that. He turned around and leaned back against the wall.

"This is all a little hard for me to believe, Kate. The CIA isn't normally in the business of arming Muslim separatists."

"Oh no? How about the Taliban in Afghanistan when they were fighting the Russians instead of you? The CIA even gave them shoulder-fired Stinger missiles. Stinger missiles for a bunch of rag-tag fighters bent on dragging their country back into the sixteenth century? Good God, what were you people thinking?"

"I imagine somebody was thinking they could hang a killing defeat on the Soviet Union. They were thinking they were getting something valuable enough to make the risk worth taking."

"And exactly the same thing is happening again right here in Thailand. Your guys think they're getting something pretty valuable this time, too."

"They are *not* my guys."

Kate shook her head and looked away, but she didn't say anything.

"Okay, I'll bite," Shepherd said. "What does the CIA think it's getting by helping Blossom Trading run guns to your Muslim rebels?"

"General Kitnarok is in bed with the Thai military and the Thai military is in bed with the CIA. Kitnarok supplies guns to the rebels through Blossom Trading and uses the profits to pay for weapons to arm his red shirts, which he then brings in through areas in the south controlled by the rebels and ships north. In return for the Thai military permitting the CIA to operate a secret facility here, the CIA provides transportation for the weapons."

"But why would the CIA want to help Charlie start a civil war in Thailand?"

"Because they don't like this government. They'd much rather have Kitnarok and the military running things again. If a strong civil government can endure in Thailand, they're afraid that will be the end of their cozy little deal with the military and they'll get thrown out on their asses."

"Is that possible?"

"Oh, I hope so. I really do hope so."

Far off in the distance, Shepherd heard a siren start up. It was a European siren, one of those with the kind of *whoop-whoop-whoop* sound that always made him think of late night black-and-white movies about Nazis searching for Anne Frank. He listened until it stopped as abruptly as it had started. That was when a question occurred to him that he should have already asked Kate.

"You said Trippler Aviation operates Harvey under a charter deal and that it's registered in the UAE. Do you know who actually owns the plane?"

"Yes, I do. It took a while to find out, but eventually we traced the charter payments Trippler is making. For nearly three years, the CIA has been paying about a million dollars a month through Trippler to charter it."

"That sounds like way too much to me."

"It's maybe ten times what the plane is really worth on the charter market."

Shepherd thought about that while he looked at Harvey sitting next to the black-mirrored building on the empty airfield. "Then I gather what you're really telling me is that the CIA is using the charter arrangement to funnel money to somebody."

"That's exactly what I'm telling you."

"Who?"

"Harvey's legal owner."

"Who is that?"

"A shell company in the Cayman Islands."

"That's a dead end then."

"No, it's not a dead end."

That surprised Shepherd. Obscuring the actual ownership of

Cayman shell companies wasn't particularly hard. He had done it a few times himself. Either somebody got careless, or they just didn't care enough to try very hard.

"Some friends of ours used their sources in the Caymans. We know who really owns the shell company. So we also know who owns Harvey and who's getting the CIA's money."

Shepherd was curious about who those friends might be, of course. It could have been anybody but, if he had to bet on it, he would go with the Chinese. Still, he didn't bother to ask Kate who had cracked the ownership for her. It didn't really matter and she wouldn't have told him anyway. Instead, he asked her about Harvey, which was apparently something she did want to talk about.

"Okay, I give up," he said, spreading his hands. "Who's getting the sweet deal from the spooks? Who owns Harvey?"

"*You* own Harvey, Jack."

"What the hell are you talking about?"

"The Kitnarok Foundation owns Harvey and you're a trustee of the foundation. The CIA's been funneling money to an organization you're presumably supervising."

Thirty Two

KATE DROVE SHEPHERD from Don Mueang to Suvarnabhumi Airport to catch his flight to Dubai. Neither one of them said much during the drive. When they got there, she pulled to the curb at the Emirates Airways entrance.

"Tommy's going to bring your stuff out. He'll see that it gets on the plane."

"After what you've told me, I've got more important things to worry about than my luggage."

"What are you going to do?"

"I don't know," he said. "Let me think about it."

Shepherd opened the door and got out of the car. To his surprise, Kate got out as well. He didn't know what he was expecting. He supposed he thought Kate would just drive away when he closed the door, but she didn't. Instead she walked around the car, put her arms around him, and gave him a hug. Maybe it was a sisterly hug, and maybe it was something else. Standing there in the harsh metallic wash of the airport lights and breathing the carbon monoxide from the idling vehicles all around them, Shepherd couldn't decide.

"Watch yourself," Kate said. "I'm not asking you to do anything about this. I just wanted you to know. It's not your responsibility to fix it. It's mine."

Shepherd said nothing.

Kate broke off the hug, took half a step back, and gave him a look.

"The real truth is that I told you what I did to convince you not to get involved. Not to entice you into it."

Shepherd said nothing.

"They're not going to let you get in their way, Jack. There's too much at stake. You wouldn't have a chance."

"I'm not going to get in their way. I just don't like being lied to. If I was."

Kate hesitated at that. She seemed to think about saying something else, but she didn't. She just nodded, walked back to the driver's side of the BMW, and got in. She bent down and smiled at Shepherd through the window, then straightened up and drove away. Shepherd thought about that hug for a moment, maybe two, and then he turned around and walked into the airport.

THE FLIGHT TO Dubai didn't leave for another couple of hours so after Shepherd checked in he went to the Emirates lounge, got himself a large whiskey, and found a seat by himself off in a half-darkened corner. Airports are bleak places in the middle of the night. They are not great places anytime, of course, but in the hours after midnight airports are particularly desolate. Shepherd didn't know if there was a waiting lounge to catch the ferry over the River Styx, but if there was, he had no doubt it would feel and smell exactly like an airport at one o'clock in the morning. The scotch helped a little, so he swung his feet up onto a low table, stared out the window into the darkness, and thought about what Kate had told him.

Was Blossom Trading really in the arms business? Keur was clearly a man with contacts and he had claimed Blossom Trading was running guns to Iran. Kate, someone who was probably even better informed than Keur, had added that Blossom Trading was supplying arms to both the Muslim rebels in the south of Thailand and to the red shirts in Bangkok. Two people like that, with information like that, were pretty hard to ignore.

Okay, so maybe Blossom Trading was selling arms. And the company was presumably owned in equal shares by Charlie and Robert Darling. So what? It isn't necessarily illegal to sell arms. Arms are legally sold every day, both by private companies and governments. Just because a company sells weapons, that doesn't automatically mean it's involved in criminal activity any more than a pharmaceutical company is automatically involved in criminal activity because it sells drugs.

The question was whether Blossom Trading was breaking any laws with regard to how they did their selling and to whom they did it. But whose laws? Was there any law in Thailand against selling arms to Muslims in the south? And, even if there was, did that law necessarily apply to a company in Dubai that had no office or other place of business in Thailand? And what about the red shirts? Maybe there was no law in Thailand saying ordinary people couldn't buy guns. Surely the issue was what the red shirts did with those arms after they bought them, and how could the seller be responsible for that?

Shepherd took a long pull on his whiskey and thought about the many benefits of a legal education. He could turn pretty much anything upside down, couldn't he? He remembered Charlie had once said he could make chicken salad out of chicken shit. Maybe it was a natural talent. Maybe he hadn't even needed the three years at Georgetown Law to learn how to do it. But he was pretty certain they had helped a whole lot.

Thoroughly disgusted with himself, Shepherd knocked off the rest of his whiskey and went to find his airplane.

THANKS TO THE drink, he slept all the way through the six-hour flight. But it was 5:30 A.M. local time when he arrived in Dubai, and sleep or no sleep, he felt like shit.

Airports aren't any more attractive at 5:30 A.M. than they are at 2:30 A.M. If dawn brings hope and rebirth in most places, airports aren't most places. In airports, dawn brings mobs of dirty people in rumpled clothing dragging various kinds of wheeled containers behind them. It's like being caught up in an army of the homeless suddenly on the move. Which, in a manner of speaking, is exactly what it actually is.

A very large bearded man in round silver-framed glasses was working the immigration counter where Shepherd lined up. He was wearing a *dishdasha* and *ghutra* so white they hurt Shepherd's eyes to look at them. The man peered at Shepherd doubtfully and took his time examining his passport and immigration card. Eventually he stamped the passport and returned it to him. Shepherd followed the crowds through to the baggage hall. To his complete astonishment, his bag was there waiting for him. He wondered briefly if Tommy had examined it before passing it over to Emirates Airways. Of course he had. Shepherd hoped his dirty laundry had smelled awful.

He hauled his bag outside to the taxi line and for a few moments he just stood quietly in the softness of the dawn light letting the warm desert air wash over him. It was dry and pungent, filled with fragrances he could not identify and brimming with hints of enigmatic events occurring somewhere just out of sight. When he made it to the front of the line, he got into the cab while the driver stowed his bag in the trunk. It wasn't until the man got back behind the wheel and asked where he was going that it occurred to Shepherd he didn't have a clue.

He hadn't made a hotel reservation. He was there only because Charlie had demanded he come. He glanced at his watch. Barely

6:00 A.M. To hell with it, he thought, and he told the driver how to get to Charlie's villa.

THERE WAS VERY little traffic at that hour so they made it to Palm Jumeirah in less than thirty minutes. The cab stopped at the security gate in front of Charlie's compound and Shepherd paid off the driver and collected his bag from the trunk. It surprised Shepherd that no one emerged to check him out. Maybe Charlie's security guys weren't very alert that early in the morning.

The taxi drove away and still no one came out. Shepherd walked over to the gate and slapped on it a couple of times with his open hand. The sound of his hand against the metal echoed in the morning quiet. The first thing Shepherd noticed was that the gate was green-painted aluminum rather than iron as he had always assumed. The second thing he noticed was that the gate was unlocked. It drifted open a few inches from the impact of the slaps.

"Hello!" he shouted through the opening.

He got no reply.

Pushing at the gate, he swung it back far enough to stick his head through. He did so very cautiously. He was not wild about the idea of surprising guys who carried guns.

"Hello!" he shouted again.

Still no answer. Where were Charlie's security guys? Shepherd dragged his bag through the narrow opening and glanced around. Everything about the compound looked normal enough, but both the main house and the house that Charlie had converted into an office gave off that particular air that deserted buildings do.

What the hell is going on here?

Even if Charlie had suddenly decamped for somewhere without telling him, there would still have been people in the office. Shepherd walked all the way around the villa where the offices were. Then for good measure he made a circuit of the main house, too. Both were empty and locked up tight. There was no one there. No one at all. He made his way back to the courtyard and stood for a while just opposite the security gate. It was still early morning, but the desert sun was already pitiless. The compound looked small and flat and exposed. It lay there as if stunned by the hard morning light.

"You want a ride somewhere?"

Startled, Shepherd whirled around.

Special Agent Leonard Keur was standing just inside the security gate with a half smile on his face. He was wearing a light blue seersucker suit with a white shirt and a dark tie.

"They cleared out last night," Keur said. "All of them."

Shepherd was too nonplussed to respond. *Where the hell had Keur come from?*

"You look as if you could use some coffee," Keur said. "Come on. I've got a rental car. There's a Starbucks not far away."

Thirty Three

SHEPHERD PEELED THE top off his coffee and looked around the room. They were on the ground floor of a black glass building facing another almost identical black glass building on the other side of a huge but otherwise unremarkable concrete plaza. The plaza was broken here and there with a few palm trees and stone arches of varying sizes that were apparently supposed to make it look warmer and more human-scale, but they didn't. They just made it look bleaker and more desolate.

The Starbucks was exactly the same as every other Starbucks Shepherd had ever been in. The colors were the same; the signs were the same; the wall decorations were the same; the displays were the same; the bags of coffee and overpriced mugs were the same; the furniture was the same. Even the view through the floor-to-ceiling glass windows was pretty much the same. He could have been anywhere in the world.

But he wasn't just anywhere in the world. He was somewhere called Dubai Internet City, a complex of buildings that like most buildings in Dubai were bland, monotonous, and new. About two miles away, out on Palm Jumeirah on the other side of Sheikh Zayed Road, Charlie's compound sat quiet and abandoned. And he was at a table in Starbucks calmly drinking coffee with an FBI agent who was trying to recruit him as an informant. It was one of those moments that would cause almost anybody to look around and ask himself the same question: *How in the hell did I get* here?

"Where's Charlie?" Shepherd asked.

"I don't know. Do you?"

"No idea."

Over Keur's shoulder something about two men just settling themselves down at another table caught Shepherd's eye. Both were middle-aged Caucasians wearing wrinkled shirts and baggy khakis, but their short haircuts and solid-looking builds screamed either military or ex-military private contractors. Shepherd didn't much like the way they kept looking in his direction, but he sipped at his coffee and turned his eyes back to Keur.

"You sure you don't know where the general has gone, Jack?"

Shepherd said nothing. The two men were staring openly toward him now and so he shifted his eyes just enough to keep them in his peripheral vision.

"Why don't I believe you, Jack?"

"Because you're an unhappy and deeply suspicious person?"

One of the two men pushed back his chair and started toward Shepherd.

Maybe Kate was wrong, Shepherd thought. Maybe somebody whose motives weren't yet entirely clear actually was targeting Charlie's advisers. With all the secret facilities, anonymous airplanes, and clandestine arms dealing swirling around, how could he have just accepted at face value Kate's assurances that nobody had any interest in him?

The man was only a half dozen steps away now, and he was picking up speed.

But surely, even if he *was* being targeted by somebody, they wouldn't send people after him right here in the middle of a Starbucks on a sunny morning in Dubai, would they? And, even if they were willing to do that, how the hell did they know where he was? Even he didn't know where Keur was taking him until they got there.

And then all at once it hit him.

How in God's name could he have been so stupid? First Keur turns up out of nowhere, and then he takes him here. Of course! It was Keur! Keur had been setting him up from the beginning!

The man was almost on him. Shepherd half rose from his chair and lifted his hands by reflex, although he had no idea what he was going to do with them. This was obviously a trained military man, someone who knew how to kill, and about the only thing Shepherd could do with his hands was operate a laptop. Somehow he doubted he would be able to email this guy to death.

He was still trying desperately to come up with some kind of plan when the man gave him a peculiar look and passed by. He approached two women sitting at a table a short distance away and launched into what looked like a well practiced chat-up routine. Shepherd sat back down feeling very foolish. He glanced at Keur. Keur was watching him with a puzzled expression.

"I thought I knew that guy," Shepherd said.

Keur looked skeptical, but he nodded slowly.

"Okay," Keur said after a moment or two of silence, "If you don't have any idea where the general went, you don't."

Shepherd just nodded.

"I guess I really can't blame him for going to ground. It's way too hot around here for him right now."

"I thought you said those guys were really gunning for me. So why would Charlie start worrying about the attack now? Doesn't he know I was the target?"

"What the hell are you talking about?" Keur asked.

"You said that those two gunmen who attacked us in the souk—"

"That's not what I'm talking about." Keur waved a hand in dismissal. "Nobody gives a shit about that anymore, not after what happened this morning."

"What are you talking about? What happened this morning?"

"The prime minister was shot. Haven't you heard?"

"The prime minister of Dubai was shot?"

Keur looked at Shepherd carefully trying to decide whether or not he was kidding. "You really haven't heard?"

"Haven't heard *what*, for Christ's sake?"

"Not the prime minster of Dubai," Keur said, "The prime minister of Thailand. Some guy with a long name."

"Somchai Woramaneewongse?" Shepherd asked. "Somebody shot Somchai Woramaneewongse?"

"Yeah, right," Keur said. "Him."

"Is he okay?"

"Not really. He's dead."

Shepherd just stared at Keur, trying to process what he was hearing.

"There were two gunmen on motorcycles. They ambushed his motorcade with automatic weapons early this morning. On some road with a funny name. Suck-something."

"Sukhumvit Road."

"That's it." Keur nodded. "They used a hijacked bus to block off the security car trailing the prime minister. Then they shot up the car he was riding in. They killed him, two security guys, and the driver."

"Have the shooters been caught?"

"Both of them made a clean getaway."

Shepherd was still struggling to get in front of what Keur was telling him. "Are you saying you think Charlie was responsible? That Charlie had the prime minister killed so he could move back in and take power in Thailand?"

"No, I doubt that. But an awful lot of other people are going to blame him. If I were General Kitnarok, I wouldn't be hanging around here like a sitting duck either, just in case some of the folks on the other team get it into their heads to deal out a little revenge. I'm sure that's why he took off."

If that was what happened, Charlie would have called, or at least left a message about what was going on, wouldn't he? Shepherd took out his cell phone and checked for messages, but the screen was dark. He must have forgotten to turn the damned thing back on after getting off the airplane. Maybe that was why he hadn't heard from Charlie. Shepherd pushed the power button and waited for the little beep that would tell him the phone had logged onto a local network.

"Don't bother," Keur said. "I tried both his cell numbers. The telephones are turned off."

Shepherd's phone beeped and he looked at the screen again. Sure enough, no messages. He took a quick glance at his email. Nothing from Charlie there either.

"How did you get Charlie's private cell numbers?" he asked Keur.

"Come on, Jack. Get real. I'm the fucking FBI, remember?"

Shepherd put his phone down on the table and wrapped his hands around his coffee cup. Six hours on an airplane and he had stepped off it into a world entirely different from the one he left. It was like science fiction.

"Thailand is going to fall apart," Shepherd said. "You can't build a real country out of nothing but colored t-shirts."

Then he thought about it some more. Maybe he was looking at everything backward.

"On the other hand, maybe this will work out okay," he said. "With Somchai dead, there's nobody left now but Charlie. Maybe the Thai people will carry Charlie back into office on their shoulders and that will be that."

"I don't think so," Keur said. "I hear the government has already picked a new prime minister. They're digging in for a fight."

Shepherd was bit surprised by that, he had to admit. He didn't think the existing government had anyone with enough stature to take Somchai's place. It seemed unlikely to him that they would be able to come to an agreement on a new prime minister without months of wrangling, not to mention hundreds of palms being crossed with considerable sums of money.

"Are you serious? A new PM? Already?"

Keur nodded.

"Who is he?" Shepherd asked.

"It's not a he," Keur said. "It's a woman."

If Shepherd had been surprised before, now he was downright dumbfounded. The yellow team had chosen a *woman* as prime minister? No woman had ever been prime minister of Thailand. In a nearly feudal society like Thailand, women had little or no political power. In fact, the only woman he had ever heard of who held a genuinely significant government position in Thailand was—

Keur interrupted Shepherd's reverie. "The new prime minister used to be the director of the National Intelligence Agency. Her name is—"

"Kate," Shepherd said. "Her name is Kate."

Thirty Four

"WHERE DO YOU want me to drop you off?" Keur asked when they got back to the car.

Shepherd didn't really know what to tell him. He had come to Dubai to lay low with Charlie only because Charlie had insisted on it. Charlie's abrupt and mysterious departure had not only rendered that idea quaintly naive, it had left Shepherd homeless again. He could always check into a hotel, of course, but what would be the point of that? With Charlie in the wind, there was really no reason at all for him to be in Dubai.

So maybe he ought to just fly back home to Hong Kong. *Okay,* he thought, *and do what after he got there?* Shuffle papers while his client was on the run, perhaps even somewhere plotting to start a civil war? Sit around drumming his fingers while he waited for Charlie to call and tell him what the hell was going on? Watch CNN wondering if Kate would be the next Thai prime minister to be murdered?

Shepherd made a snap decision that didn't really commit him to anything, which he thought under the circumstances the best kind of snap decision to make.

"The airport, please," he told Keur.

He could decide where he was going after they got there.

SHEPHERD LOOKED IDLY through the window as Keur drove out of Internet City and wound his way among dozens of medium-rise office buildings that all looked more or less the same. The grass was impossibly green and the artificial lakes were impossibly blue. Everything looked as if it had been colored with food dye. And for all Shepherd knew, it had. Eventually they emerged from the office park onto a busy road and followed it until it joined a yet even busier road. Then they followed that one too until they came to the massive Sheikh Zayed Road. SZ Road was a concrete arrow that ran dead straight through the desert for thirty miles all the way from the middle of Dubai to the neighboring emirate of Abu Dhabi. Keur eased into the heavy traffic and turned east toward the airport.

Shepherd watched the utterly flat and featureless landscape slide by. In less than a generation this desolate wasteland of sand and scrub had sprouted hundreds of soaring towers filled with offices and apartments, all connected together by massive coils of freeways and a glittering monorail system. At what must have been a staggering cost, vast stretches of desert had been laced with water pipes and carpeted with thousands of acres of deep, rich grass interspersed with full-grown trees flown in and arranged into complete forests.

In spite of all that, there was an unmistakable feeling of fragility to Dubai. Men could bring water to the desert, pave it with concrete, and set down spires of glass and steel that reached hundreds of stories into the heavens, but they still had not figured out how to put down roots in a place like this. Out beyond wherever they stopped building, there was always the sand. The sand simply waited and bided its time. There was too much of it, and it had been there too long. It would never be defeated.

They sped on down SZ Road, the car's tires whirring hypnotically on the smooth concrete. Occasionally, stretches of the roadway dipped below ground level and the wide excavations through which it ran were lined on both sides with blue and white tiles that had been formed into the shape of huge waves. The whole effect was very much like driving at high speed through a giant men's room.

After half an hour they crested the Al Maktoum Bridge high over Dubai Creek and Shepherd saw the airport off in the distance. By then, he had decided exactly what he was going to do.

KEUR PULLED THE car to the curb outside the Emirates Airways terminal.

"Where can I reach you?" Shepherd asked.

"Does that mean that you're going to help me?"

"It means that I might want to call you one of these days."

Keur looked at Shepherd, unsure of what that meant, but he took only a moment to give up trying to decide. He pulled a business card out of his shirt pocket and scribbled something on the back.

"Use this number," he said.

Shepherd took the card, glanced at the number written on it, and turned it over. A blue-and-gold seal was embossed in the upper left-hand corner. Department of Justice, Federal Bureau of Investigation, it said around the shield. Below it was an address in Washington and a telephone number.

"What if I call this number in Washington instead?"

"They'll tell you I'm not there. They may even tell you I'm on medical leave, but maybe not. I'm not really sure what they'll say. When I call myself I generally use the cell number I gave you. You probably ought to do the same thing."

Keur got out and opened the trunk. Shepherd followed him around and retrieved his bag.

"Thanks for the ride."

Keur nodded and tossed off a little salute.

"Don't be a stranger," he said.

INSIDE THE TERMINAL, Shepherd strode straight to the Emirates first class check-in desk… and then walked right past it.

He found a staircase that led to the arrival level of the airport, trotted down the steps, and went back outside. In five minutes he was in a taxi on his way to the Dusit Thani Hotel. If Keur or anyone else who had been following them had parked and come inside to see where he was going, they would be out of luck. And even if they eventually worked out that he hadn't gotten on an airplane at all, a Thai-owned hotel was probably the last place in Dubai anyone would think to look for him.

The Dusit Thani had an executive suite available. Shepherd took it for one night and paid cash. The girl at the check-in desk never batted an eye. If he had tried to pay nine hundred dollars in cash for a hotel room in New York, Shepherd figured the cops would probably have rushed in before he got his wallet back in his pocket, slapped the cuffs on him, and charged him with felony failure to use an American Express card. In Dubai, tossing out a big pile of cash was about as sinister as wearing a Rolex.

After the bellboy left, Shepherd went into the bedroom, got undressed, and took a very long, very hot shower. There were few conditions in life that couldn't be improved with either a hot shower or a drink and, since it wasn't even 10:30 A.M. yet, he chose the shower. Drying off and dressing in a fresh shirt and jeans, he opened the drapes and picked up his cell phone. He settled into a big upholstered chair in front of the windows, swung his feet up on the coffee table, and started dialing for dollars.

MAYBE SHEPHERD HAD caught a plane home to Hong Kong. Or maybe he had caught a plane to wherever General Kitnarok was. But Keur was almost certain he hadn't done either.

Shepherd wasn't a guy likely just to go home and sit around

sucking his thumb until somebody called him. On the other hand, right now Keur was pretty sure Shepherd didn't have any better idea where General Kitnarok was than he did. Keur had watched his face carefully when they talked about the general's abrupt disappearance, and he had looked carefully for any sign that Shepherd was bullshitting him. He had seen none.

No, Shepherd didn't know where Kitnarok was, but he did have ways of finding out. He *would* find him. Keur would make book on that. And he would lay even better odds that *trying* to find out was exactly what Shepherd was doing right at that moment.

Shepherd had doubled back through the airport, gotten in a cab, and checked into a hotel in Dubai. He had probably taken a shower, wrapped himself in the fluffy bathrobe that came with his expensive room, maybe ordered something from room service, and now he was sitting back in a big chair with his feet propped up on a coffee table making telephone calls. That was what Keur would have done, and he didn't have the slightest doubt that was what Shepherd was doing.

That was why Keur was absolutely certain Shepherd would call him within twenty-four hours. Once he found General Kitnarok, what was he going to do? That was when Shepherd would realize that he needed Keur's help and that was when he would call.

After that, he would be in. After that, it would only be a matter of time.

But what if he was wrong? What if that *didn't* happen?

Keur guessed then that he would just have to start over. Maybe with Shepherd again, or maybe with someone else altogether. Either way, he was going to get this done. He had always accomplished what he set out to do and this time wasn't going to be any different. General Kitnarok wasn't going to be the first asshole to slip through his fingers. He just wasn't going to allow that to happen.

Thirty Five

SHEPHERD'S FIRST CALLS were to the numbers where he usually reached Charlie: his cell numbers and the private number at the Palm Jumeirah compound. None of those numbers answered or were even redirected to voice mail. They just rang until Shepherd got bored listening to them and hung up.

Then he called the Kitnarok Foundation, identified himself, and asked if Charlie was in the office. Shepherd knew he wouldn't be, of course, but he wanted to see what they said. They didn't say much. The woman fielding calls was someone whose voice he didn't recognize and she just said Charlie wasn't there and they didn't expect him. Although Shepherd had assumed the foundation would be a dead end, he was still disappointed it was quite as dead an end as it turned out to be.

Shifting tacks, he tried Kate's private cell number in Bangkok. Not surprisingly under the circumstances, his call was diverted directly to voice mail. He hung up without leaving a message. Then he tried calling Tommy. The result was the same: voice mail. He hung up again without leaving a message.

Shepherd really wasn't doing any worse than he expected to do, but he was still a little frustrated. He had been hoping to catch some kind of a lucky break.

Then with his next call, he did. Jello picked up on the first ring.

"It sounds like you were sitting there just waiting for me to call," Shepherd said.

"When shit hits the fan, I'm always waiting for you to call," Jello said. "Where are you?"

"Dubai."

"Figures."

"I need a favor," Shepherd said, getting straight to the point.

"This is not a good time to ask for favors, Jack. You may have heard we're a little busy. Having a prime minister murdered tends to make a real mess out of my day."

"Yeah, well, imagine what it did to his."

"What do you want, Jack?"

"This is a favor for you, too, man. But you're going to have to trust me on that. I can't tell you why right now, but this is connected with the matter that has your full attention today."

Jello didn't say anything.

So Shepherd told him about the white 737 with the UAE tail number parked at Don Mueang. He didn't tell him how he knew about it, and he certainly didn't tell him that Kate called the plane Harvey. Bringing Kate's name into the conversation would have spun it off in directions he really didn't want to go, and telling Jello the airplane had been named after a six-foot rabbit from a fifty-year-old movie would probably have caused him to hang up.

"I need to know if that airplane is still there," Shepherd said. "And if it isn't, I need to know when it left and what kind of a flight plan they filed."

Jello still didn't say anything, but he didn't hang up either.

Shepherd could tell he was thinking it over. "Yes or no?" he prodded. "I promise you that by tomorrow you'll be happy you did this for me."

Jello made a sound on the other end of the phone that Shepherd didn't much like.

"Come on, man," he pleaded, "trust me here."

There was a pause and then Jello sighed heavily. Shepherd knew then that he had him.

"Where do you want me to call you?" Jello asked.

"On my cell."

"Give me fifteen minutes," Jello said.

Then he hung up.

JELLO CALLED BACK in ten minutes.

"Your plane left this morning. It took off at 9:27 A.M."

"Exactly when was Somchai murdered?"

Jello was quiet for a moment as he thought about why Jack was asking him that.

"A little after eight this morning," he answered slowly.

"Your shooters were on that plane."

"Listen, Jack, whatever you know about this—"

"What about the flight plan?"

"They filed for Dubai with a stop in Phuket."

"Dubai," Shepherd muttered. "Fuck me dead. When did you say they took off?"

"9:27 A.M."

Shepherd did the math in his head. An hour and a quarter to Phuket, maybe a half hour to make a quick landing and take off again, then a little over six hours to Dubai, give or take. That would put the plane on the ground in Dubai around 5:30 P.M. Bangkok time, which was 2:30 P.M. Dubai time. He glanced at his watch. It was 11:40 A.M. The plane was still three hours out.

Of course, flight plans got changed for all kinds of reasons. Sometimes pilots even filed flight plans to one destination and then re-filed them to another destination after they were out of the departure airport's control zone. Maybe the plane wasn't coming to Dubai at all.

Who was he kidding?

The CIA didn't use Harvey for weekend jaunts to Las Vegas, did they? Of course the plane was coming to Dubai. Blossom Trading was in Dubai and everything that was happening was somehow tied into Blossom Trading. Even if he wasn't yet sure exactly *how*.

"Did you check when the plane actually left Phuket?"

"Yeah," Jello said. "It didn't."

"You mean it's still there?"

"No, I mean it never left because it never arrived."

"Then where did it go?"

"Beats me."

Maybe Somchai's killers had been onboard the plane when it left Bangkok and maybe they hadn't been. But they most certainly wouldn't be on it when it got to Dubai. The plane had landed somewhere, probably at a private strip in the deep south of Thailand. Filing a flight plan to Phuket would have taken it in exactly the right direction for that. That would have been where the shooters got off, but it didn't really matter to Shepherd where the shooters got off. They were just hired guns and he didn't really give a damn about them.

What he *did* give a damn about was what the plane was going to do after it offloaded the shooters, and his guess was that the plane was coming to Dubai for another cargo of weapons. That those weapons would then be loaded onto it and then it would fly right back to Thailand. Maybe Charlie was even waiting at the airport to get onboard himself and slip quietly back into Thailand without anyone knowing about it. *Unlikely,* Shepherd thought, *but not impossible*.

The ground in Thailand would never be more fertile for Charlie to stage his triumphant return. All his followers needed was some leadership and a little muscle, and the whole country would be theirs for the taking. Charlie was the leadership, of course, and the arms from Blossom Trading were the muscle. He didn't even want to think about where that left Kate and a whole bunch of other decent and honorable people who thought Thailand deserved better than another military dictatorship sponsored by the CIA.

That 737 coming into Dubai was the key. It was the key whether it was there to transport weapons, or Charlie, or both. Shepherd hadn't the slightest doubt about that.

Okay, so what the hell was he going to do about it?

He had plenty of time to get to the airport before the plane turned up since the airport was only about a half hour's drive from the Dusit Thani. But Dubai had an awfully big airport and he had no idea where the 737 would be parked. Then, even if he could find it, what was he going to do after that? Turn himself into Bruce Willis, round up some wisecracking cops, seize control of the airplane, and take it away from the CIA? Not freaking likely. He was going to have to come up with a hell of a lot better plan than that. Fortunately, he had an idea.

"I owe you, big guy," he said to Jello.

"Goddamn it all, Jack, if you—"

Shepherd didn't hear the rest of whatever Jello was trying to say. He had already cut him off and was dialing the number Keur had written on the back of his business card.

Thirty Six

SINCE SHEPHERD AND Keur both knew where it was, they met thirty minutes later at the Fat Burger in the Dubai Mall. Shepherd ordered a chocolate shake, which he thought showed what a cool guy he was. Keur ordered plain black coffee, which Shepherd figured said more about Keur than he really wanted to know.

"Just out of curiosity," Keur said, "did you actually intend to go anywhere when you asked me to drop you off at the airport this morning?"

Shepherd said nothing.

"You still don't trust me, do you?" Keur asked.

"No."

"I didn't think so."

A smiling Filipina girl of indeterminate age brought the shake and the coffee on a red plastic tray and they bagged the snappy repartee until she was gone.

"What is this all about, Jack? Why are we here?"

Shepherd took a slurp on his chocolate milkshake and belched slightly.

"You're going to love this," he said.

Keur just sat and waited.

"I know what's happening," he continued. "Well, some of it at least."

Then Shepherd told Keur the truth, more or less. As a member of the bar in good standing, telling the truth was pretty much the last resort for him most of the time, and he certainly didn't want to get into the habit. But right at that moment, it seemed the way to go.

"I need help," he said. "And you're all I've got."

"Help doing what?"

"Stopping Harvey and then finding Charlie."

"Who the fuck is Harvey?"

"An airplane."

Keur looked at Shepherd carefully.

So Shepherd told him about the mirrored building at Don Mueang Airport in Bangkok. He told him about the 737 with the UAE tail number. And he told him about the weapons shipments into the rebel-held areas in the south of Thailand.

Keur was absolutely expressionless.

So Shepherd told him why the airplane was called Harvey. He figured at least that would get a rise out of Keur. He was right.

"You named this airplane after an invisible white rabbit?" Keur asked.

Shepherd shrugged. "Not me."

"Then who?"

He shrugged again, but he didn't say anything.

Keur sipped at his coffee. Put the cup down, picked it up, and sipped some more.

"Where are you getting all this stuff?" he finally asked.

"I can't tell you that."

"Then I can't help you."

Shepherd didn't want to say anything about Kate, of course, but it was starting to look like he had no choice. He needed Keur's help and he wasn't going to get it without telling him where his information was coming from. He could hardly blame Keur for that. If their situations had been reversed, he would have insisted on knowing, too.

So Shepherd told Keur about Kate. All in all, he pretty much dropped his trousers for Keur.

"So this is really about a woman, is it?"

"Oh, crap," Shepherd snapped. "Will you listen to me, Keur? What I'm trying to tell you is—"

"So after all the moralizing bullshit you gave me before," he interrupted, "you're willing to fuck over General Kitnarok after all. And this is all because now he's squaring off against a woman you want to bang."

"Maybe this is all just too hard for you to understand."

"Then make me understand."

"Charlie Kitnarok is my friend as well as my client. I'm not going to betray him to anyone."

"But you just told me—"

"Kate is also my friend. I care about her. I don't want to see anything happen to her either."

"You can't bat for both sides, Jack. Make up your fucking mind."

"I *can*. I *am* on both sides. I'm going to find a way to shut off the weapons shipments. No guns, no civil war. Then Kate and Charlie can battle out the politics in some way that doesn't kill anybody, least of all either one of them."

"Oh hell, I fucking knew it." Keur pushed back his chair and threw his arms in the air. "You're going to bring peace to the country and earn the everlasting gratitude of the little brown people. Shit, I really don't need all that do-gooder crap right now."

"That's the difference between you and me, Keur."

"What? You're a starry-eyed sap and I'm a realist?"

Shepherd looked away. This wasn't going exactly the way he had hoped it would. He was getting nothing but attitude from Keur. Shepherd took a deep breath and went on anyway.

"Harvey's here," he said. "I want to stop it from taking off, or at least stall it for a while."

For a second Keur looked confused. "You're talking about this plane you named after a rabbit?"

"Kate named it."

"Whatever. But you're saying the plane is here in Dubai?"

"More or less. It should be landing in about an hour and a half. If I'm right, they'll take on a load of arms and fly right back to Thailand."

"Maybe they're picking up General Kitnarok. You ever think of that?"

"Yeah, I thought of that. But I doubt it. Going back to Thailand in a cargo aircraft isn't Charlie's style. He'd want to make a triumphal entry, not sneak in."

Keur looked at Shepherd and looked away. Then he looked back again.

"Just spell it out, Jack. What are you telling me?"

"You want my help nailing Darling. I'm telling you I'll give it to you. I don't give a shit about Darling. You help me stop that plane and I'll help you nail Darling."

"How are you going to do that?"

Shepherd kept quiet. He figured he had said about all he could. If Keur wouldn't go for it, he wouldn't, but anything else he might say now wasn't going to help.

"Look," Keur said after a moment, "even if I were far enough out of my mind to be willing to get involved with this, you don't seriously think I can just—"

"I don't know what you can do. Charlie's apparently got the CIA on his side. All I have is you. So I'm hoping for the best."

There was a pause. Keur looked away and tapped his fingers against his empty coffee cup. After a minute or two he shifted his weight and leaned forward on his forearms.

"I know somebody at the airport here," he said. "Maybe—"

"There you go!" Shepherd shouted. He jumped up from the table and slapped Keur on the shoulder.

The man at the next table slowly turned his head to see what the commotion was all about. He was a large, heavy man with a pointed beard who was dressed in flowing white robes and a white headdress. Shepherd caught his eyes and wished he hadn't. They were dead and unblinking, so black that they seemed bottomless. The man stared hard at Shepherd. He looked as if he was memorizing his appearance, just in case.

"For God's sake," Keur said. "Sit down and lower your voice. If this all goes tits up, I don't want some fucking Arab putting us together."

Shepherd didn't give a damn what anybody put together as long as he could stop that plane. At least stop it until he could find Charlie and convince him to abandon the plan he was apparently hatching to force his way back into power in Thailand.

If he couldn't do that, people were going to die. Maybe a lot of people. Maybe even Charlie and Kate, too.

Thirty Seven

WHEN KEUR SAID he knew somebody at the airport, Shepherd pictured a brawny Arab baggage handler wearing baggy shorts, a wrinkled T-shirt, and floppy socks. What he did not picture was a tall, blue-eyed German woman with long blond hair, a white suit that looked like Armani, and white pumps that looked like Jimmy Choos. And he *really* didn't picture someone with a front porch on which you could park a helicopter.

"Jack Shepherd, meet Rachel Rein," Keur said. "Rachel is Emirates Airlines Group Vice-President of Security."

"Why have you never told me you have such a good-looking friend, Lenny?"

Lenny? Shepherd shot Keur a quick look. He remembered Keur introducing himself as Special Agent Leonard Keur, of course, but somehow ever since he had stopped thinking of Keur as the sort of person who had a first name. And he absolutely didn't seem the sort of person who had a first name like Lenny.

"Are you with the FBI, too, Mr. Shepherd?" Rachel asked.

"Nope," Keur cut in before Shepherd could answer her. "Jack's a bag man for a corrupt Thai politician."

"Ah Jesus," Shepherd muttered.

"A bag man?" Rachel smiled. "How fascinating. I have never met a bag man before."

Shepherd wanted to say something in his own defense, but he wasn't quite certain what it would be. Sadly enough, Keur's characterization of his occupation wasn't completely inaccurate. He settled for doing his best to look indignant and said nothing.

"Look, Rachel," Keur said, completely ignoring Shepherd's display of umbrage, "I'm sorry to drop in on you unannounced like this, but—"

Rachel cut Keur off with a hug and a kiss on the cheek. "Nonsense, Lenny. You know I am always happy to see you. Sit down."

Shepherd had expected to be in a smelly freight shed in some forgotten corner of the airport talking to a baggage handler who smelled more or less like the shed. Instead, here he was in a snazzy office at the headquarters building of Emirates Airways ogling Miss Deutschland of about 1995. He settled back on the butter-soft leather of one of Rachel's very expensive sofas and awaited developments.

"Coffee?" she asked.

Keur and Shepherd both accepted. Rachel called somebody to serve it and while she was on the telephone Shepherd looked around her office. One entire side was floor-to-ceiling glass with a panoramic view of Terminal 1, the building occupied entirely by Emirates Airways. He had always thought the Emirates terminal was an odd-looking structure, long and thin and half round on the top, like a bead of toothpaste that had been squeezed across the field from a giant tube of Crest. Rachel's office looked a lot better: cream-colored leather sofas, thick carpet the shade of a correctly-made cappuccino, and two giant Sony flat panels mounted on the wall opposite her desk. One was showing CNN and the other was showing BBC News, both with their sound muted.

Keur sat down next to Shepherd. Rachel hung up the telephone and smiled at him.

"So what can I do for you, Lenny?"

"I'm calling in that favor you owe me. I need some information, but I can't tell you why I need it."

"Ah," she said, "a mystery. I love a mystery. Are you some kind of a spy, Lenny? You say you are FBI, but I have never really believed you. I have always wondered if you are really a spy."

Keur looked away and cleared his throat.

"What do you think, Mr. Shepherd?" Rachel asked, turning those big blue eyes on him. "Is our friend Lenny here really with the FBI? Or do you think he is some kind of a spy?"

"I certainly hope not."

"Rachel sees spies everywhere," Keur cut in. "She was a deputy director of the BKA before she joined Emirates."

Shepherd had no idea what Keur was talking about and it apparently showed.

"The *Bundeskriminalamt*," Keur explained. "The German Federal Criminal Police."

"The BKA is like the FBI, Mr. Shepherd," Rachel said. "Only much, much smarter."

There was a knock on the door and a chubby, middle-aged woman entered carrying a wooden tray with three cups of coffee. They fell silent until she had served. Then she left again, closing the door behind her.

"Could we get back to the point now?" Keur said after she did.

"Oh, you had a point, Lenny?" Rachel winked at Shepherd. "And what might that have been?"

"There is an aircraft we are interested in that we think will be landing here very soon. Probably at about…"

Keur stopped talking and looked at Shepherd.

"At about two-thirty," Shepherd said, picking up the story from there. "It's a 737. An all-freight configuration. And it will be coming from Thailand, I think."

"Bangkok?" Rachel asked, sipping at her coffee.

"I don't know for sure. The flight originated in Bangkok, but they filed for Phuket first. Then from there to Dubai. But the plane never landed in Phuket. My guess is it landed somewhere else, probably at a private strip not far from Phuket. Wherever it went, I think it will be coming to Dubai from there."

Rachel didn't ask any of the obvious questions. Shepherd assumed that was because she had some kind of a relationship with Keur that made her think she could trust him. He hoped she was right about that.

She just pulled a pad toward her and picked up a pen. "Do you have a tail number?"

"A6-NSU," Shepherd said.

"A UAE registration."

It wasn't a question, so Shepherd said nothing.

She wrote down Harvey's registration number and then glanced back up and held Shepherd's eyes for a moment.

"Whose aircraft is this?" she asked.

"It's being operated on charter by Trippler Aviation."

Rachel tapped the point of her pen against her pad a couple of times, then put the pen down. "Do you know anything about Trippler Aviation?"

"A little," Shepherd said. "Enough probably."

Rachel looked at Keur. "Do you know who actually owns this aircraft, Lenny?"

Keur pointed at Shepherd.

"Well then, Mr. Shepherd," Rachel said, shifting her eyes to his. "Can you tell me who owns this aircraft you're so interested in?"

"No," Shepherd said, "I can't."

"Can't?" Rachel asked, "Or won't."

"Let's just say it would be better if I didn't. Better for you."

Rachel nodded and looked down at her desk. She picked up the pen again and went back to tapping the point against her pad.

"We think the aircraft is coming into Dubai to pick up cargo," Keur said after a minute or two had passed in silence. "All we need is to find a way to delay its departure until we're certain what's on it. And where it's going."

"That's *all*?" Rachel laughed.

Neither Keur nor Shepherd said anything.

"Is this official, Lenny?"

"Depends what you mean by official."

Rachel looked from one to the other and thought about that.

"Is this aircraft bringing cargo into Dubai?" she asked after a moment. "Or just carrying cargo out?"

"We don't know for sure."

"Are we dealing with drugs here?"

"No," Keur said. "Arms and ammunition."

Rachel's face showed no reaction.

"Do you know who's servicing the aircraft in Dubai?"

"No."

"Do you know where on the airport it will be parking?"

"No idea."

"For two reasonably intelligent men, you don't know very much, do you?"

Keur and Shepherd both shifted their eyes away to the windows and said nothing.

Rachel pursed her lips and made little popping sounds. Abruptly she dropped her pen, looked straight at Shepherd, and pointed at him with her index finger.

"What's he got to do with all this, Lenny? Who is he really?"

"I'm his lawyer," Shepherd answered before Keur could say anything.

Rachel actually chuckled at that.

"It's true," Shepherd said. "I really am."

"*Lieber Gott*," Rachel said, shaking her head. "Another spy."

Thirty Eight

SHEPHERD AND KEUR sat without speaking while Rachel tapped at the keyboard on her desk. The flat panel monitor was big and white and it faced away from them so they couldn't see what she was looking at, which left them nothing to do really but to watch Rachel while she watched the screen. Either that or look out the windows at the airport. Shepherd chose to watch Rachel. He hoped Keur was smart enough to make the same choice.

"According to the flight plan, A6-NSU left Phuket at 1136 local time today," Rachel said after a minute or two, reading from her screen. "It is estimated Dubai at 1423."

"I have information the plane was never in Phuket," Shepherd said. "And I trust the source of my information."

Rachel looked up and shrugged. "The pilot didn't file until twenty minutes after take off. He might have taken off from another airport near Phuket instead, I suppose. That is possible."

She studied her screen for another moment or two, and then said, "Here's something that's a little odd."

"What?" Keur asked.

"A6-NSU is scheduled to park at remote bay 211A."

"Why is that odd?"

"Well…" Rachel studied the screen a little longer. Her tongue poked at the inside of her cheek, flicking rhythmically up and down.

"It's not a normal parking bay for a cargo aircraft. It's around the side of the cargo terminal. There's not much there but a government hanger."

Keur and Shepherd exchanged glances.

"Do you have an exact time of arrival yet?" Shepherd asked.

Rachel's eyes flicked across her screen and traveled up to one corner. Then she glanced at her wristwatch as if to confirm what she had seen on the screen.

"You timing is really quite remarkable. It's probably on final right now."

Rachel pointed to the windows.

"You ought to be able to see it land any minute."

Rachel bent down and opened a desk drawer. When she straightened up, she was holding a pair of powerful-looking field glasses. She held them out toward Keur, but he shook his head and pointed to Shepherd.

"Mr. Shepherd then," Rachel said. "I gather you are the officially designated plane spotter for today."

The glasses were Leica 10x52s. Big and tough and expensive. They were exactly the kind of glasses Shepherd would expect Rachel to have. He took the glasses from her and walked over to the windows.

A British Airways 747 was just touching down on the runway closest to them. Its huge undercarriages gave off tiny puffs of smoke when they kissed the concrete, like smoke signals rising from Indian country in some old black-and-white movie. Off on the other side of the terminal, there was another set of parallel runways probably a half mile away. After another minute or two, Shepherd saw the white 737 lining up for a landing over there.

"Harvey's here," he said.

The plane was still too far out to make out any details, but he had no doubt he had the right airplane. He lifted the glasses and nudged the focus wheel until the image was sharp, and then he watched the 737 slip down the glide path onto one of the far parallels like a four-year-old coming down a playground slide. Just above the runway's threshold, the pilot lifted the nose slightly and the plane flared and settled so smoothly onto the concrete that its arrival was entirely smokeless.

Shepherd was watching the airplane and didn't realize Keur and Rachel were standing behind him until Rachel spoke.

"Who's Harvey?" she asked.

"It's what Jack calls the airplane we're looking for," Keur said.

"He has given this airplane a *name*?"

"Yeah. Named it after a big white rabbit."

Rachel fell silent after that. Shepherd could hardly blame her, but he didn't bother to explain.

He lowered the glasses and they all watched as the white airplane rolled about halfway down the runway, slowed, and turned off onto a taxiway.

"Where is this parking spot it's been assigned to?" Shepherd asked.

"Over past the end of the cargo terminal," Rachel said, pointing. "You see that big DHL sign, the yellow one?"

Shepherd's eyes followed her finger until he located the sign.

"Got it."

"Now follow the parking apron to the left, all the way to the end. There's a yellow line pointing toward that hanger with the green roof. That's the marker the pilot follows to dock at 211A."

Shepherd lifted the glasses and studied the area Rachel was indicating. It was isolated, just as she had said it was. That end of the parking apron was recessed slightly behind one end of a long white building that was so huge they might have been building 747s inside it, but he knew it was probably the airport's primary freight facility. Sitting at the edge of the apron, the hanger with the green roof was tiny by comparison, but it was still large enough to swallow a couple of pretty good-sized airplanes and close the doors behind them. Right now the doors were open. There was one small airplane inside that looked like a Gulfstream executive jet, although he wasn't sure since he didn't know all that much about private airplanes. Other than that, the hanger appeared to be empty. Which left plenty of room for a 737.

"Who owns that hanger?" Shepherd asked.

Rachel didn't reply right away so he lowered the glasses and looked at her.

"Officially," she said, "it's a UAE military hanger."

"And unofficially?"

Rachel glanced at Keur, but he was watching Harvey and didn't appear to notice.

"Unofficially," Rachel said when she looked back at Shepherd, "it's used by the American embassy. Some people say it's actually a CIA facility."

Harvey continued to taxi across the field and the three of them watched it in silence. When it reached the freight building, it turned left, followed the apron to the end, then swung around and lined up its nose wheel with the yellow line pointing to the hanger with the green roof. Shepherd raised the glasses again.

A man in white coveralls had appeared from somewhere and was using a pair of red paddles to direct Harvey into its parking position. He was standing on the seat of a little vehicle that looked like a lawn tractor painted yellow. Waiting off to the side was a pickup truck with a metal box on top about the size of a small shipping container. The truck was unmarked, but it looked to Shepherd like one of those aircraft catering vehicles that are common around all airports.

The man with the paddles had his arms extended over his head and was pulling the paddles repeatedly back toward himself, a gesture obviously meant to tell Harvey's pilots to keep coming forward, which they did. Then the man stopped waving and crossed the paddles over his head in the form of an X and Harvey came to an abrupt stop. The man with the paddles jumped down from his little tractor and tossed the paddles inside, then took out a pair of yellow wheel chocks and trotted forward to wedge them under both the front and rear of Harvey's nose wheel.

As soon as the chocks were in place, the pickup started moving toward Harvey. The truck swung around and lined up with the door just behind the cockpit. The door popped open and Shepherd could see a man in khaki pants and a white golf shirt pushing on it with both hands from inside the aircraft. It swung all the way back against the side of the fuselage, the man gave the ground crew a friendly-looking wave, and then he disappeared back inside.

The truck stopped at the aircraft door and the steel box on top of it lifted, scissoring upward on a pair of yellow-painted struts. When it was level with the door, another man dressed similarly to the man who had opened the door of the plane leaned out of the box and pushed a ramp forward until it bumped up against Harvey. Two men immediately emerged from Harvey, walked across the ramp, and disappeared inside the metal box. Then it was lowered back onto the top of the truck.

As Shepherd watched the truck back away from the aircraft and then turn and drive into the hanger with the green roof, he ran the scene he had just witnessed back and forth through his mind. He was not absolutely certain he believed his own eyes. The men had moved quickly out of the aircraft into the catering truck and he had only gotten a glimpse of them as they crossed the short ramp. Perhaps he was mistaken. Perhaps he only thought he recognized them.

Who was he trying to kid? He had recognized both men. He didn't have the slightest doubt about it.

The first man out of Harvey had been Robert Darling. That Darling had been in Thailand and was flying into a CIA facility in

Dubai on an aircraft operated by a CIA front company wasn't that big a surprise to Shepherd. Perhaps it should have been, but it wasn't.

The real bolt from the blue was the second man he had watched emerge from Harvey. His appearance on the scene was so entirely unexpected that it opened up a whole new and deeply nasty can of worms.

The second man Shepherd had seen leaving Harvey right behind Robert Darling was Tommy.

Tommy who was not a Thai spy, but merely the deputy spokesman for the Ministry of Foreign Affairs.

Thirty Nine

"ARE YOU ABSOLUTELY sure, Jack?"

Keur had already asked the same question three or four different ways and Shepherd was tired of answering it. It was Tommy he had seen getting off that plane. He was certain of that. He just wasn't certain what that meant.

"Tommy's a little weasel," Shepherd said. "If he's hooked up with the CIA, he's operating on his own. It can't have anything to do with NIA. And it can't have anything to do with Kate."

"How do you know that?"

"I just do."

Keur just shook his head. "You mean because she's a good-looking woman—"

"Kate's not involved with the CIA," Shepherd interrupted. "Believe it."

"Okay, let's just assume you're right," Keur said. "But if this guy who works for her is, what's his game?"

"I don't know," Shepherd conceded.

There was a silence after that. Keur eventually broke it.

"Why do you even *care* what's going on here, Jack? None of it has anything to do with you."

That was a good question, Shepherd had to admit. And he wasn't sure how to answer it.

That he cared because he had a lot of friends in Thailand and he was growing increasingly concerned about what might happen to them? Yes, of course. That he cared because he had personal attachments to both Kate and Charlie and didn't want to see them square off against each other? Yes, that, too. That he cared because the poor, benighted little country of Thailand might not deserve much, but it did deserve more than to be ripped to pieces and have its bones picked over by faceless men who only cared about lining their own pockets? Sure, that as well.

That was all part of it, of course, but Shepherd knew there was something else, too. Something that had more to do with him than it did with Thailand.

Once upon a time he had been a player, a master of his own corner of the universe. He had held a place in the world that he thought mattered. But for nearly a year now he had done nothing but push papers and shuffle money for Charlie. Shepherd knew he was still up to doing something more important than that. At least he wanted to believe he was.

Stopping a civil war in Thailand wasn't his cause, that was true, but it was a good cause. And right then, he needed a good cause as much as any good cause needed him. Maybe more.

Shepherd didn't have a clue how to explain any of that to Keur, so he didn't even try. Instead, he shifted his eyes to Rachel.

"Can you get me onto the field?"

"Should I ask what for?"

"Probably not."

"You won't be able to get anywhere near that hanger, Jack. And those two men are probably long gone by now."

"What difference does it make anyway?" Keur asked. "What are you going to do even if they're still there. Walk right in, baffle them with bullshit, and then break their little airplane?"

Shepherd let his eyes drift to the big flat panel monitors hanging on the wall and watched the silent images for a moment.

"If you wanted to keep that plane here for a few days," he asked Rachel, "how would you do it?"

"A mechanical problem would ground it, of course," she said. "Anything serious enough for spare parts to have to be flown in would keep it here for a day or two."

That was getting back to the Bruce Willis thing again and Shepherd knew that wasn't going to work. He shook his head.

"And I suppose," Rachel went on, "some kind of law enforcement order might work."

"Law enforcement order?"

"You know, the police could prevent the plane from leaving on some kind of legal grounds."

"Like what?"

"I don't really know," Rachel said. "I was just thinking out loud. Maybe some kind of national security threat?"

"Couldn't they just take off anyway? It's not likely Dubai would scramble jet fighters and shoot it down, is it?"

"They wouldn't have to. There are a lot of moving parts involved in getting a big commercial jet into the air. The process involves way too many people to do it without the necessary approvals. It's not a car. You can't just get into it and drive away."

As Shepherd thought about what Rachel was saying, he could feel the beginnings of an idea stirring in his mind.

"How would an order like that be put into effect?"

"The authorities would inform the airport administration that an order had been issued barring the plane's departure," Rachel said. "Then they would notify air traffic control not to accept any flight plans for the plane or grant any take off clearance. They would also instruct ground handling not to fuel or load the aircraft."

The idea stretched a little and moved up to the front of Shepherd's mind.

"And they couldn't just fly the plane out without clearance?"

"They're not going anywhere without fuel."

The idea rose to its feet and strutted back and forth a few times. Shepherd had to admit he liked the look of it. He would also have liked to reflect on it a little more before introducing it around, but there wasn't enough time for measured reflection.

"I think I can get an order issued to impound the plane."

"Why would the cops do that?" Keur asked. "You got nothing on anybody. Even if you did, once they figure out they're fucking with the CIA, the locals won't do jackshit."

"Not the cops. I mean a civil impoundment order."

"What the fuck are you talking about, Jack?"

"The courts in Dubai are very sensitive to demonstrating to the international business community that the rule of law prevails here," Shepherd said. "What if I seek an emergency order impounding Harvey because the operator hasn't made its payments to the owner under the terms of the aircraft operating lease?"

"How do you know they haven't?" Keur asked.

"I don't have the slightest idea whether they have or not. I'm making this shit up as I go along."

"It might work," Rachel said, nodding slowly. "It would take the operating company a day or two to show that the lease payments had been made, maybe more than that if the real operator of the aircraft actually is the CIA and they want to stay out of the picture. Meanwhile, the plane would be held here under a civil impoundment order. That would get you a couple of days, maybe a little more."

"Good enough."

"Doesn't matter," Keur shook his head. "It's all just academic. The owner of the airplane is the only person with standing to apply for an order like that. You couldn't do it since you're not the owner."

"But I am," Shepherd said, "in a manner of speaking."

Keur and Rachel just looked at him.

"The Kitnarok Foundation is the registered owner of the plane. I'm a trustee of the Kitnarok Foundation. As a trustee, I have the legal authority to act for the foundation."

Keur burst out laughing. "You're going to use the Kitnarok Foundation to stop Harvey from flying back to Thailand to deliver arms to Charlie Kitnarok's troops?"

Shepherd nodded.

"That's beautiful, absolutely beautiful," Keur said. "I love it. I fucking love it."

"I know a local lawyer I could call for you," Rachel said. "Sharp guy, and he'd never bat an eye at doing something like this. He really hates Americans."

Wonderful, Shepherd thought. *I've got to have somebody I can rely on here, somebody whose tact and discretion I can depend on absolutely, and I'm about to trust a big-busted German woman I met an hour ago to put me into the hands of an anti-American Arab laywer.*

That was what he thought, but that wasn't what he said.

"Get the guy on the telephone," he told Rachel.

Forty

RACHEL PLACED THE call and made the introductions, then she put Shepherd on the telephone. Shepherd explained to Rachel's anti-American lawyer pal what he wanted to do. He thought the guy sounded young, smart, and capable, and he seemed to get it immediately. So Shepherd decided not to worry about the lawyer's political views. As long as he delivered on the impoundment order, he could have all the fun he wanted.

The guy didn't seem to think it would be any problem at all to get an order issued. He casually mentioned that he would take it to a judge who was a good friend of his. Shepherd got the idea without making him say it a second time. After all, he had lived in Thailand. He knew how this kind of thing worked in third world countries. The price the lawyer quoted was astronomical, of course. Having a friend who's a judge tends to run up the bill pretty quickly in almost any country. But Shepherd didn't care. The bill was going to the Kitnarok Foundation anyway.

The lawyer asked Shepherd to email him a statement of facts and an affidavit. He said that if Shepherd could do it immediately he would file the petition before the end of the day. Shepherd wrote down the guy's email address on a pad on Rachel's desk. Then he thanked the lawyer and gave the telephone back to Rachel.

While she and Shepherd's new pal were talking about something else, Shepherd pulled out his telephone and drafted an email with the materials the guy had asked for. Since he was making most of it up, it didn't take very long. He added the email address he had written down and hit send. Rachel and the lawyer were still talking when he was done, so he and Keur just sat and stared at the flat panel monitors on the wall on which CNN and BBC continued to flicker in complete silence and waited for her to finish.

THE DEPRESSING MONOTONY with which people all over the planet were laboring to kill each other seemed slightly less horrific when it was reduced to a silent movie, but Shepherd wasn't entirely certain whether that was a good thing or not. Maybe it would actually be better if somebody could find a way to make it more horrific instead. Perhaps that way some of the hideousness of mankind's collective savagery might eventually penetrate people's desensitized minds and shame them into behaving like human beings again.

Shepherd and Keur sat quietly like that for several minutes while Rachel continued to murmur into the telephone. Keur didn't seem anymore interested in conversation than Shepherd was, each of them content to wait silently in the company of their own thoughts, until after a few minutes of sitting like that something on CNN caught Shepherd's eye. It registered immediately as familiar, but it took a moment or two for his brain to catch up with his eyes.

When it did, Shepherd realized that CNN was broadcasting a headshot of Liz Corbin, the Bangkok bureau chief for *The New York Times*. Below Liz's picture was a single line of white type: *On the Telephone from Bangkok*. And across the bottom of the screen was a much larger caption, all in red letters. It read: *TERROR IN THAILAND*.

"I need to hear that," Shepherd said, pointing at the monitor.

Both Keur and Rachel glanced at the screen. Then Rachel took a remote control off her desk and tossed it to Shepherd. He found the mute button, clicked it, and the sound popped on. Shepherd was only vaguely aware of Rachel murmuring hasty goodbyes into the telephone.

"... nothing more about the real seriousness of the situation here in Bangkok until tomorrow morning," a woman's voice Shepherd recognized as Liz Corbin's was saying on CNN.

"Do you know yet exactly how many explosions there were?" a male voice asked.

"The government is saying officially that there were four, Keith, but I am hearing unofficially that it was almost certainly many more than that. Perhaps as many as a dozen. What has caused real panic here, however, is not the number of explosions, but the apparently well-coordinated nature of the blasts. The initial explosion at Government House was followed within ten minutes by those at the Hyatt and the Four Seasons, and then shortly after that by those at other international hotels, two major shopping malls, and of course at the airport. The attacks appear to have been planned to kill and injure as many foreigners as possible and, by doing so, to strike a fatal blow at Thailand's vital tourism infrastructure."

"Is the government providing any casualty figures?" the man prodded.

"No, none at all. At the moment, the government's reaction seems to be to try to keep a lid on everything as long as possible. They are saying very little and they certainly aren't giving out any figures. My sources, however, say that more than a hundred are dead and hundreds more, perhaps thousands, are injured."

"Where are you now, Liz? Can you see any of the damage from your location?"

"Right now I am about two hundred yards north of the Grand Hyatt. The air is heavy with smoke and dust and I cannot see very clearly. But I can tell you that the hotel appears to have collapsed right in the center and is almost wholly demolished. It would not surprise me if the casualty toll from that one bombing alone was many hundreds of people."

"What is the mood there in Bangkok?"

"It's almost impossible to move around the city right now so I have spoken to very few people. The military has appeared in the streets, but they don't seem to be doing much of anything. The Four Seasons Hotel is only a few hundred yards south of here. I'm going to try to make my way to it on foot and see what the level of destruction is there."

"Have there been any claims of responsibility yet, Liz?"

"As you know, Keith, the Thai government is locked in a bitter struggle with the supporters of former strongman General Chalerm Kitnarok, who was forced out of office with a blizzard of corruption charges. At the same time, they are fighting an increasingly violent Muslim insurgency in the south. The assumption here, of course, is that these explosions are a clear attempt to destabilize the government and therefore the most likely culprits would come from one of those two camps, but there is no specific information as yet concerning who actually is to blame."

"Has the new prime minister made a statement yet?"

"Prime Minister Kathleeya Srisophon has been in office for less than a day, having been chosen by the governing coalition immediately after the murder of former prime minister Somchai in an attack on his motorcade yesterday morning. She has made no statements of any kind as yet and reports are that she is in an undisclosed location for security reasons. It is easy to understand why. In a country seemingly poised on the brink of chaos, the murder of a second prime minister would almost certainly send it tumbling over the edge."

The image on the monitor shifted to a studio shot of a blow-dried newscaster who looked to Shepherd more like an actor in an unsuccessful daytime soap opera than a journalist.

"Thank you, Liz," the man said. "That was Elizabeth Corbin of *The New York Times* on the telephone from Bangkok, where an unknown number of apparently well-coordinated explosions shook the city just after five o'clock this afternoon, Bangkok time. Initial reports are that there are many dead and injured, including a large number of foreigners. CNN is urgently trying to gather more information and we will have it for you as soon as we can. Meanwhile, back in Washington, the federal budget crisis shows no sign of ending with…"

Shepherd clicked the mute button on the remote and looked at Keur.

"It's started," he said.

Forty One

SHEPHERD STOOD UP, found the field glasses, and walked back to the window. He scanned the field and found the hanger with the green roof. But he didn't see the plane any longer.

"I think Harvey's gone," he said.

"They couldn't have taken off that quickly," Rachel said. "They would have to fuel after the flight from Thailand. It can't be done that fast."

She walked over and took the glasses from Shepherd, then studied the place where they had seen Harvey park.

"The hanger doors are closed now," she said. "They must have towed the plane inside."

"How do you get off the field from there?" Shepherd asked. "Would the passengers have to go over to the passenger terminal to clear immigration?"

"Theoretically, yes," Rachel said, "but there's an exit gate in the airport boundary right behind the hanger. Since the facility actually belongs to the UAE government, it's accessible from there."

"That means people can come and go from that hanger without any interference at all, right? No customs or immigration?"

"Yes, that's right. That's what it means."

"Is the gate manned?" Shepherd asked.

"No, there's not enough traffic for that. Access is by a security card and a code entered into a keypad. You've got to have both to get through the gate and we change the code weekly."

"Who changes the code?"

"I do." Rachel pointed to the computer sitting on her desk. "From right there."

Shepherd thought about that for a moment.

"I guess you probably have trouble with the gate occasionally," he said.

"Not really."

"I mean with it breaking down and jamming so that people can't open it to get out."

"No, as far as I remember, that gate has never…"

Rachel trailed off into silence and looked at Shepherd.

"If the code were changed," he said, "and nobody knew it, the gate wouldn't open. To anyone who tried to use the old code, it would seem like the gate had broken down, wouldn't it?"

Keur roared with laughter again. "Damn, Jack, I do like your style."

"What would happen if somebody came out of that hanger, tried to operate the gate, and discovered it didn't work?" Shepherd asked.

"They could go across the airport and exit on the other side, or go through the freight facility and get off the field that way," Rachel said. "But they would have to get permission from ground control to move around the field. It would be a bit of a nuisance and it might take a while."

"So the odds are they would just call somebody instead. They would tell them they were waiting there to leave the field and to send somebody to fix the goddamn gate right the hell now."

Rachel nodded slowly. "That would be my guess."

"How interesting," Shepherd said. "And would you be informed if that happened?"

"I might be. Particularly if I had arranged to be informed."

"Who would you send to fix the gate?"

"You have anybody in particular in mind?" Rachel smiled.

"Now that you ask," Shepherd said, "I just might."

Rachel used her computer to change the gate code. Then she called someone and told them to route any complaints about that particular gate directly to her. She also found a light cotton jacket and a blue baseball cap in her closet and gave them to Shepherd. As disguises went, it wasn't much, but it didn't have to be. He wasn't intending to fool anyone for very long.

A few minutes later, Shepherd's phone binged. He checked his email and found a message from his new anti-American lawyer. The guy's pet judge had already signed an emergency order impounding Harvey pending a full hearing on a claim that the lease payments were in default. That hearing had been set for the next day, but the lawyer said he had heard a rumor the judge felt a bout of flu coming on and would probably be forced to postpone it for a day or two. That was about as much as he could do, he said. How sick could one judge actually be before eyebrows were raised?

Shepherd and Keur sat back to wait. They kept an eye on CNN for any further reports about the explosions in Bangkok, but something called World Sport was on instead of the news. As far as Shepherd could tell, World Sport meant extended coverage of any sport not played anywhere in the United States. The planet's twenty-seventh largest city was in flames and all CNN could talk about was Italian league soccer.

Rachel did paperwork at her desk and took several calls during the next half hour. As each call was put through to her she shook her head at Shepherd. Finally, she took a call and didn't shake her head.

"Here we go," she said.

When the call was put through, Rachel murmured apologies for the gate malfunction in a throaty voice with just a trace of an accent. She sounded pretty good to Shepherd. If he heard a voice like that coming down the telephone line, he figured he would accept an apology for World War II. From the look on Rachel's face, however, whomever she was talking to was far less enamored by the sound of her voice than Shepherd was.

When she put down the telephone, she gave Shepherd a long look. "You didn't tell me how charming your Mr. Darling was."

"He called you himself?"

"In person, the asshole. He wants me to send someone to fix the gate. He seems to be in a hurry."

"Well then. Let's not keep the man waiting."

They all trooped downstairs to the garage and got into Rachel's official vehicle. It was a Toyota Land Cruiser with a blue bubble light on the roof and a couple more blue lights behind the front grill. It took only a few minutes for them to cross the main road and enter the airport through a manned security gate right on the other side.

Once on the field, Rachel switched on her blue lights and turned into a perimeter road just inside the fence. The road circled around the runways to the other side of the field where Robert Darling was fuming in front of a gate that wouldn't obey him.

"This is fun," Shepherd said. "Let's switch on the siren, too."

"I don't have a siren."

"Damn."

A big commercial jet passed directly overhead and the thunder of its engines enveloped them like a rainstorm. The plane was so close that Shepherd could pick out the individual rivets peppering its skin. They looked like a bad attack of metallic acne. He knew all the scientific explanations about why airplanes flew, of course, and he believed them. Up to a point. But when he was a couple of hundred feet directly beneath one of those aluminum monsters, watching it hang there in the air without any visible explanation for the apparent miracle of it all, he could only hold his breath and hope that science wasn't just blowing one out its own ass.

When the engine noise had died away, Keur cleared his throat. "I think I should be the one to talk to Darling, Jack."

"Too late," Shepherd said, holding up the jacket and baseball cap. "I got the disguise."

"That's not going to fool anyone."

"It will just long enough for me to walk up to his car."

"And then what are you going to do?"

It was a good question, but a little embarrassing since Shepherd hadn't worked that part out yet.

"Look, Jack, I'm a trained law enforcement officer. I do this kind of thing for a living."

"It's my play, Keur. Don't try to pull rank on me."

"But what do you think you're going to accomplish?"

Damn, another good question.

"Make up your minds, boys," Rachel said. "ETA three minutes."

Shepherd twisted around in his seat and looked at Keur.

"I know Darling," he said. "Even better, I irritate him. I'm going to ambush him and piss him off and see if he screws up."

"Screws up what?"

"Look, Keur, think about what we know here."

"That won't take long."

"Darling owns half of Blossom Trading," Shepherd went on undeterred, "which you say is really an arms dealer. He's just arrived in Dubai from Thailand, which seems to be on the verge of civil war. He arrived on an airplane operated by a CIA front company, which I'm told is being used regularly to run guns into Thailand. Charlie owns the other half of Blossom Trading. He's disappeared. Three days ago, Charlie's assistant turned up in Thailand hanging beneath a bridge with this head cut off. Now what connects all of that?"

"I don't know," Keur said. "You tell me. What connects all of that?"

"I have no goddamned idea either. So I'll ask Darling. Maybe he'll explain it to me."

"There's the car," Rachel interrupted.

A white Mercedes sedan was sitting in a driveway that ended at the airport's perimeter fence in front of a closed gate. Next to the gate was a small grassy area shaded by a half dozen palm trees with a white picnic table and two benches. It looked like the quarantine area for smokers. No one was in sight, so Shepherd assumed Darling had to be inside the Mercedes. The question he really ought to be asking himself, he knew, was who else might also be inside the Mercedes?

But he didn't ask. He already had a matched set of questions he couldn't answer. What use was one more?

"Stop in the blind spot on the driver's side," Shepherd said to Rachel.

He pulled on the jacket and pushed the baseball cap down on his head.

"Block him in against the gate, but don't be too obvious about it."

Rachel glanced at Shepherd. She looked like she might be about to say something, but instead she just nodded.

As soon as the big SUV stopped, Shepherd pushed the door open and jumped out. He tilted his head down so that the bill of the cap hid his face and pretended to study something in his hands as he walked quickly toward the Mercedes.

The driver's door started to open just as Shepherd reached the car, but he shoved it shut and pushed his hip against it. The driver lowered his window and Shepherd bent over to look inside.

Darling was in the driver's seat. And he was alone.

Forty Two

"HELLO, ROBERT."

"Jack?"

Darling appeared completely bewildered.

"What are you doing here?"

"The very question I was going to ask you, Robert. The very question."

Shepherd had never before seen Darling wearing anything but a suit with a bow tie. But now he was wearing a black t-shirt and jeans. It took a little getting used to. Darling tried again to open the car door, but Shepherd kept his hip against it and Darling stayed inside the Mercedes.

"Easy question first, Robert. Where did Tommy go?"

If Darling had begun to recover from his shock at finding Shepherd standing on the airport driveway and pinning him inside his own car, the mention of Tommy took him all the way back downhill again. His eyes shifted first one way and then the other. He seemed to be trying to convince himself that he had misunderstood Shepherd's question.

"Look, Shepherd, I haven't a clue what you're—"

"I saw Tommy with you when you left Harvey."

"What are you talking about? Who in the everlasting fuck is Harvey?"

Shepherd decided it wasn't the best time to start talking about a six-foot tall white rabbit and made a mental note not to use the name Harvey with Darling again.

"I saw Tommy leaving the plane with you. A white 737, all-freight configuration, tail number A6-NSU. The one that's…"

Shepherd turned and pointed at the hanger with the green roof.

"… in there."

Darling remained expressionless, but Shepherd was watching his eyes. He was pleased to see the shock there. Shepherd had hoped to see at least some fear, but he didn't, so he laid out his best card.

"With that impoundment order in place," Shepherd added, "you're not going to be flying that arms delivery back to Thailand for a while. You do know about the order, don't you?"

Darling's face stayed as flat as a dinner plate. He didn't even blink.

"What the hell's going on here, Shepherd?"

"I've arranged for your plane to be impounded. It's not going anywhere."

"How did you manage that?"

"I've got a lot of friends."

Actually, Shepherd figured he probably only had two friends right then. And they were both in the SUV with the stupid-looking light going around on top of it like somebody was about to announce a K-Mart blue light special.

He stepped away from the Mercedes and pulled open Darling's door.

"Come on, Robert. It's come to Jesus time. Let's go sit under that tree over there and have a good old fashioned heart-to-heart."

They left the Mercedes where it was and walked over to the picnic table. Darling sat down on one of the benches. Shepherd took off the baseball hat and jacket and sat on the other.

"All we need is some potato salad and fried chicken," Darling said.

He glanced again at the darkened windows of the Land Cruiser.

"Would your friend like to join us?"

"It's just an airport security man they assigned to drive me. Forget about him."

Darling nodded slowly, but Shepherd saw some uncertainty in it. It wasn't much, but it was something. Maybe it would even help.

"So why is Tommy in Dubai with you?" he asked. "And where is he now?"

"I'm not going to answer that."

"Why not?"

"Because you're a civilian, Shepherd. I don't answer questions from civilians."

Darling pulled a box of Gitanes Brunes out of the right-hand pocket of his jeans and shook out a cigarette.

"Still haven't managed to quit, huh?" Shepherd asked.

Darling threw out another of those Gallic shrugs that Shepherd wished he could do just half as well.

"We've all got to die of something," he said.

In an automatic gesture of courtesy, Darling tilted the box toward Shepherd and raised his eyebrows. Shepherd shook his head. Darling produced a book of matches and, leaning forward, cupped both hands around the tip of his cigarette to shield it from the light breeze and lit up. Darling tossed the book of matches onto the picnic table and exhaled slowly, blowing smoke out through his pursed lips in a steady stream. Then he returned the box to the pocket of his jeans.

"You don't have the slightest idea what you're into here, do you, Shepherd?" he said. "Not the slightest."

"Hey," Shepherd said, leaning back and spreading his hands, "I'm willing to learn."

Darling smoked quietly and seemed to think about that. He looked like a man who had just gotten a low-ball offer for his car and was mulling over whether a counteroffer was even worth the effort.

Darling could just get up and walk away anytime, Shepherd

knew, but he hoped he wouldn't. What could he do about it? Wrestle him to the ground and tickle him until he spilled the beans? But Darling didn't get up and walk away. Darling started to talk. It seemed to Shepherd that Darling looked almost happy to have the opportunity.

"Thailand's fucked, Shepherd. It's going to be in somebody's pocket when this is all said and done, and I want it to be ours."

"Ours?"

"The US of A, my friend, your native-born country. Or now that you're living large in the third world, maybe you've forgotten that you're an American."

"I haven't forgotten."

"Good man, Shepherd. Good man."

Darling fell silent and smoked some more. Shepherd didn't push him. He seemed to be trying to make up his mind about how much to say, so Shepherd just waited.

"I'm only going to say this once, Shepherd. Listen carefully."

Shepherd nearly asked Darling if he wanted him to take notes, but he choked back the words before they slipped out. This probably wasn't the best time to launch into one of his wiseass routines.

"The future is going to come down to America and China," Darling continued after a moment. "Nobody else matters. It's the Chinese and us, and we're going to divide the world."

Shepherd thought that was a lot of garbage, probably, but he nodded encouragingly anyway. At least Darling was talking. He could decide later if he had said anything worthwhile.

"You ever hear of something called the Greater East Asia Co-Prosperity Sphere, Shepherd?"

Shepherd shook his head.

"It was the concept used by the Japanese to justify their aggression in East Asia in the 1930s. They equated it with establishing a new international order for Asian countries in which they would share prosperity and peace, free from Western domination. The Greater East Asia Co-Prosperity Sphere is remembered today as a front for Japanese control of occupied countries during World War II, a period during which puppet governments manipulated local populations and economies for the benefit of Imperial Japan."

"Are you saying that—"

"China is beginning to flex its muscles just like Japan did in the 1930s. But they are more cautious than the Japanese were. They are feeling their way, expanding their influence first just to their immediate neighbors. Hong Kong and Macau are already Chinese. The Europeans gave them back without a struggle. Tibet is firmly under Chinese control, too. Taiwan will come next. After that, it will get more difficult for China."

Shepherd nodded again. Darling kept talking.

"To the west and north, China is sealed in by Russia. There's Mongolia, of course, but who gives a fuck about Mongolia? To the south, they are sealed in by the Himalayan Mountains and, on the other side of them, India. To the east, there's not much but the Pacific Ocean. To the northeast, there's Korea, but who gives a fuck about Korea either? That doesn't leave any direction for China to go but southeast. Burma, Laos, Cambodia—"

"And Thailand."

"Thailand's the prize. It's the most developed country in Southeast Asia and geographically it's at the heart of it. Control Thailand and the rest falls into your hands. First mainland Southeast Asia, then Malaysia and Indonesia. It's China's twenty-first century version of the Greater East Asia Co-Prosperity Sphere."

"You're telling me you believe that the Chinese are about to invade Southeast Asia?"

"Don't pretend to be a simpleton, Shepherd. You understand exactly what I'm saying."

"Spell it out for me. Just in case I don't."

"You don't take countries over by invading them anymore. You take them over by replacing their institutions and culture with your own institutions and culture. Ethnic Chinese already control all of the banks in Southeast Asia and most of the money, and you know where their real loyalties lie. All China needs is for a few governments to be beholden to them, too, and they're home free. Complete domination of the economies of their client states, naval bases on the Gulf of Thailand and the Indian Ocean, the works."

Shepherd nodded some more and tried to look like he agreed with Darling. It wasn't all that difficult. Darling wasn't completely wrong, and Shepherd knew it.

"The political upheaval in Thailand has already tilted it toward China," he finished. "It's the Chinese who are really behind the yellow shirts. All this people-power, love-and-peace stuff you hear from them is a bunch of shit. Those are China's people, Shepherd, and that's why they're taking control of Thailand, to hand effective control to China. We need Charlie back in Thailand. He's ours. He belongs to America. He's bought and paid for."

Darling stubbed out his cigarette. Almost immediately he pulled the box of Gitanes back out of his pocket and lit another one.

Maybe that's the way to solve all this, Shepherd thought to himself. *Just keep Darling talking long enough and he'll die of lung cancer.*

Forty Three

"DO YOU WORK for the CIA, Robert?"

Darling inhaled and blew the smoke out very slowly.

"Everybody in my business either works for the CIA or with the CIA, Shepherd. The little dogs follow the big dogs. If you don't, you get eaten."

That wasn't exactly an answer to his question, of course, but Darling looked like he was still trying to decide how much more to say. Shepherd gave him a little nudge.

"Then let me ask the question this way. What is Robert Darling's involvement in all this?"

"I'm just helping Charlie. I'm his friend."

"Come on, Robert, don't treat me like a dick. There's a lot more to it than that."

"Charlie and I are partners in Blossom Trading. Blossom Trading sells armaments."

"Who do you and Charlie sell arms *to*?"

Darling said nothing. He looked as if he hadn't even heard Shepherd.

"Are you arming the Thais?"

"Not *all* the Thais. We're selling to Charlie's people. And we've sold some stuff to the Muslim separatists. We're not amoral, Shepherd. We only sell to the guys who have the same aims we do."

"And what aims are those exactly?"

Darling smiled. "To restore good government to Thailand."

"Is that what Adnan was doing for you in Thailand that got him killed? Restoring good government?"

"I don't answer to you, Shepherd."

"But you answer to *somebody*. And my guess is that you answered to somebody about Adnan. Did Adnan's head and his body end up in separate places because you fucked up, Robert? Did you fuck up and get Adnan killed?"

"Adnan is—"

"Was."

"Adnan was," Darling corrected himself, "a man who sometimes overplayed his hand."

"With who?"

"Look, the demands from the Muslims were getting out of hand. Adnan seemed to be the right man to explain to the little pricks that there are limits as to how much support we can give them."

Darling took a long pull on his cigarette and exhaled slowly.

"In retrospect… maybe that wasn't the case," he finished.

"So Adnan was decapitated by Muslim separatists?"

"They're melodramatic motherfuckers, aren't they?"

"So you're saying you sent Adnan to tell the Muslim separatists to toe the party line and they killed him?"

Darling shrugged. "Maybe they have a problem with authority figures."

"And who's the authority figure here? You?"

Darling shrugged again. Shepherd was getting really tired of watching him do that no matter how good at it he was.

"Let's just be absolutely clear here," Shepherd said. "What you're telling me is that the CIA is controlling and coordinating the opposition in Thailand to the present government. Both the Muslim separatists and Charlie's red shirts."

Darling held up both hands, palms out. "Hang on, Shepherd. I never said anything like that."

"Yes, you did."

Shepherd pointed over Darling's shoulder to the hanger with the green roof.

"There's an airplane in there that's been carrying your arms shipments into Thailand. You're flying into a strip in the south that's under the control of the Muslim rebels, leaving some of the weapons there, and taking the rest of them north to Bangkok by road."

Darling looked down, took a final puff on his cigarette, and flicked it away. He didn't say anything.

"Your airplane is on charter to a company called Trippler Aviation. Trippler Aviation is well known as a CIA front company."

It might have been a bit of a stretch to say that it was well known. But what the hell, Shepherd thought. He was rolling.

"The registered owner of the airplane is the Kitnarok Foundation. You are a foundation trustee just like I am, Robert, so you should know that. Do you? Do you know that?"

"Where are you getting all this shit, Shepherd?"

"That's really not the important question, is it? The important question is what Charlie knows. Does Charlie know his foundation owns an airplane that's been chartered by the CIA to smuggle arms into Thailand, arms that are being used to start a civil war and overthrow the Thai government?"

Darling stood up so abruptly that Shepherd involuntarily leaned back. Darling reached across the picnic table and poked him in the chest with his index finger.

"You self-righteous, insignificant little piece of shit," he screamed. "Who the *fuck* do you think you are?"

Darling poked harder and Shepherd leaned further back.

"There are rules to this game and there are lines you don't cross, Shepherd. You're nothing. We can crush you like a bug."

Shepherd said nothing. It was hard to sound tough sitting at a picnic table while Darling was standing over him pushing a finger into his chest.

"Get out of our way, Shepherd. If you don't, I'll end your inconsequential little life without a second thought. Do you read me, mister?"

Shepherd slapped Darling's finger aside and slid off the bench. But by the time he had gotten to his feet, Darling had turned his back and was striding angrily toward the hanger.

"Don't go away mad, Robert," Shepherd called after him.

Darling didn't answer or even look back. He just raised his right hand above his shoulder, extended his middle finger, and kept walking.

AFTER DARLING DISAPPEARED into the hanger, Shepherd stood there for a moment and thought about his options. Or he would have thought about them if he'd had any options to think about. As far as he could tell, he was fresh out. The book of matches that Darling had tossed away was on the table right in front of him. He sat back down, picked it up, and twisted it back and forth through his fingers while he replayed in his mind everything Darling had said.

He had rattled Darling's cage. He had no doubt he had at least done that much. But otherwise it looked to Shepherd like he had pretty much blown it. He had heard Darling's justification for what he was doing, but he didn't know anymore about *how* Darling was doing it than he had before. What was Tommy's role? And where the hell was Charlie?

The impound order on Harvey wouldn't hold up for long. Shepherd's guess was that it wouldn't take Darling more than a day or two to get the Agency to come down on the UAE government and have it lifted. That meant in not much over forty-eight hours Harvey would be back on the ground in Thailand and the guns would be flowing.

Thailand was already coming apart. Reds and yellows were in the streets bashing each other with bats and iron bars, and random bombings targeting foreigners were holding Bangkok hostage to terror. Putting automatic weapons into the hands of the red shirts' street fighters would trigger a full-scale slaughter. But what could he do about that in forty-eight hours? Shepherd had absolutely no idea.

He stopped twisting the matchbook in his hand and glanced down at it. Registering the crest on the cover, he raised his eyebrows in surprise. The matchbook was from the Duke of Wellington in Bangkok. Shepherd thought back to his meeting at the Duke with Pete Logan, the FBI's man in Thailand. It was shortly after that Logan had told him the FBI had no interest in either Robert Darling or Blossom Trading.

So what was Darling doing now with a book of matches from the Duke of Wellington? Probably that was no more than a coincidence. Hundreds of people drank and smoked in the Duke every week. Having a book of matches from there only meant that Darling had been in Bangkok at some point, which was hardly surprising.

But what if it *wasn't* a coincidence? Thailand was a very small place and people sometimes turned out to be connected to each other in surprising ways. He needed to keep that in mind.

Shepherd stood up from the picnic table, shoved the book of matches into his pocket, and trudged back to the Land Cruiser.

Forty Four

KEUR AND RACHEL just looked at Shepherd when he told them what Darling had said. He got the impression that the artistry of his interrogation was lost on them both.

"He looked pretty angry when he stomped away," Rachel said. "That's something, I guess."

"At least I'm sure now the Agency is behind everything. I got that much."

"I don't believe him," Keur said. "Darling's the bad guy here, not the US government."

"Come on, Keur. The Agency's been pulling this shit as long as it's been in business. Subverting governments they don't like, installing new ones they do. Of course, they almost always make a mess out of it, but they keep trying. Cuba, Chile, Iran, Greece, Vietnam, even Italy. You want me to go on?"

Keur shook his head, but he said nothing.

"We know the plane delivering the arms shipments is chartered to a CIA front that's paying ten times what the charter is worth," Shepherd continued. "It's obvious Agency money is being laundered through the inflated charter fees to pay Blossom Trading for the weapons they're flying into Thailand."

"Then you've decided that General Kitnarok is fronting for the CIA?" Keur asked. "You think this is really a CIA operation to install a military government in Thailand with General Kitnarok at its head?"

"Yeah," Shepherd said. "That's exactly what I think."

"Then he sure had you fooled up until now."

Shepherd said nothing. He knew he deserved that. He didn't like it, but he deserved it.

Shepherd didn't want to believe that Charlie was working with the CIA to overthrow the elected government in Thailand, but the evidence was piling up. Charlie had a lot of faults, and Shepherd didn't always see the world the same way he did, but he would have bet the old bastard loved his country enough that he wouldn't have been a party to anything like that. It made Shepherd feel a little foolish now to think that Charlie might have been running a game on him the whole time they had been working together. Just stringing him along, day after day.

"What do you want to do now?" Rachel asked after a moment. "I can't keep that gate closed much longer."

"Doesn't matter," Shepherd said. "I've got all I'm going to get out of Darling, and Tommy is probably so shit scared now that he wouldn't leave the hanger if you burned it down. Go ahead and do whatever you need to."

Rachel picked up a microphone clipped to the dashboard of the Land Cruiser. She keyed it and told somebody to re-enter the gate's original code and notify the man who complained that it was working again.

Keur looked at Shepherd. "So what's next, Lone Ranger?"

Shepherd just sat and shook his head.

"I'm damned if I know, Tonto."

RACHEL DROVE THEM back and they retrieved Keur's car. The sun was low in the west and the air had taken on that peculiar luminescence that announces sunset in the desert. All around them, Dubai glowed softly with an otherworldly, golden light. It was an altogether different place from the brassy, hard-edged megalopolis that lived its days in the harsh white glare of the desert sun.

Before they left the garage, Shepherd took out his cell phone again and tried both of the numbers he had for Kate. He needed to warn her that Harvey would be flying back to Thailand with a load of weapons soon. At least he was reasonably certain it would. It would probably be a day or two before the paper barrier he had erected in Dubai would be knocked down, but inevitably it would be. A day or two wasn't much, but it was something. Maybe it would give Kate the time she needed.

Both of Kate's numbers went directly to voice mail and Shepherd hung up without leaving a message. Normally at that point he would have called Tommy and asked to be put in touch with Kate. But with Tommy and Darling holed up together in the hanger where Harvey was parked, that no longer seemed like a particularly good idea.

"They're about to light the fuse, Keur, and I can't even reach Kate to warn her."

Keur just nodded, but he didn't say anything.

"I've got to find Charlie," Shepherd said. "I've got to get to him before everything turns to shit. He can stop it. Maybe he's the only person who can stop it."

"I thought you'd say something like that."

"Charlie is either in Thailand now or he's going to be soon. Either way, there's no point in hanging around Dubai any longer. All roads lead back to Thailand. That's where I need to start looking."

"I think you're right."

Shepherd fell silent. He was fresh out of things to say.

"You want some help?"

"Help with what? I have no idea what I'm going to do."

"Neither do I, but judging on how you've handled yourself so far,

I'll bet it's going to be something that kicks ass. I want to be there for that."

"Then thanks," Shepherd said. "I accept."

"I'm your man, Jack. You can count on me."

Keur stuck out his hand and they shook.

KEUR DROPPED SHEPHERD at the Dusit Thani Hotel where he showered and packed while Keur went off presumably to do the same thing. An hour later, Shepherd took a cab to the airport and just before nine he and Keur met again in front of the Thai Airways check-in counter. Shepherd had already booked first class tickets for both of them on the 10:40 P.M. nonstop to Bangkok, and he brushed off Keur's offer to pay for his own ticket. He had charged the tickets to the Kitnarok Foundation, so what did he care?

Shepherd felt lousy to be back in an airport again. As they walked to the first class lounge, he started thinking about the amount of time he had spent in airports just in the last week. Maybe he ought find a new way to earn a living.

Shepherd and Keur sat in the lounge until the Bangkok flight was called. They were hungry and tired, too tired to look for real food. They made do with some bags of pretzels and a couple of Diet Cokes they scrounged out of the self-service bar. So much for the glamour of international air travel.

Finally, boarding was announced and Shepherd and Keur walked to the gate. They were calling for first class passengers when they got there, so mercifully they walked straight onto the airplane without having to hang around in the gate lounge. Later, Shepherd worked out that the flight had probably taken off right on schedule, but at the time he didn't have a clue it had taken off at all, let alone when. He was fast asleep before the cabin door even closed.

Forty Five

WAKING UP ON an airplane was always a disorienting experience for Shepherd. His muscles ached in strange and novel ways, and the sounds, the smells, and the light all seemed completely alien. He didn't know how it would feel to suddenly realize he was dead, of course, but his best guess was that it would feel exactly like waking up on an airplane.

Shepherd brought his seat upright, reconnected his brain to his lips, and glanced across the aisle at Keur.

"How long before we land?"

Keur looked up from the book he was reading and consulted his watch. "About an hour."

"Don't you sleep?"

"I drink, I eat, I read. But I stay awake just in case the pilot needs my help."

"Nervous flyer, huh?"

"Don't we have anything more important to talk about?"

Shepherd held up his hands, palms toward Keur.

"Coffee first," he said. "Lots and lots of coffee. No conversation without coffee."

Keur nodded and went back to reading his book.

Shepherd searched around for the call button and gave it a push without having much conviction it was actually connected to anything. Much to his surprise, a lovely Thai woman wearing a green and yellow silk sarong materialized almost immediately in the aisle next to him. She had smooth brown skin, a dazzling smile, and didn't look a day over twenty, but with Thai women he had long ago learned you could never really tell for sure. He asked for water and black coffee, and she hit him again with that smile and went off to get them.

He stumbled out of his seat to the bathroom where he emptied his badly overloaded bladder, washed his hands, threw some water in his face, and combed his hair. There was a straw basket of toothbrushes on one side of the washbasin, so he unwrapped one and gave his teeth a few quick swipes as well. Much against the odds, he found he was feeling vaguely human again.

When Shepherd got back to his seat, he found coffee and a glass of ice water waiting for him. The smiling vision in the silk sarong had also covered his table with a starched white cloth and set out a plate of exotic-looking fruit and a basket of muffins. Suddenly he remembered how hungry he was and dug in. Three cups of coffee, a half dozen glasses of ice water, two muffins, and a plate of completely unidentifiable fruit later, he was finally capable of coherent conversation.

"Why are you doing this, Keur?"

Keur put a bookmark at his place and closed the book on his lap. "What do you mean?"

"It's not your fight."

"It's not your fight either."

"I know," Shepherd nodded. "But I've got nothing better to do."

"So there's your answer," Keur shrugged.

"If Darling is working for the Agency, trying to arrest him will be a waste of time for you. What would you charge him with?"

"Maybe... being an asshole? That would be easy enough to prove."

"If we can get proof that Darling is directly connected to these arms shipments, I think Pete Logan would move on it. He's one of the good guys."

Keur bobbed his head, but he didn't say anything.

They sat in silence for a long while after that. Shepherd still didn't understand exactly why Keur cared so much about taking Darling off the board. He knew what Keur had told him, of course, but that hardly seemed enough to account for his single-mindedness. Still, Shepherd could see that Keur didn't really understand what was driving him either. And he could hardly blame Keur for that. He wasn't absolutely sure either.

He had no dog in this fight and yet here he was, about to jump directly between the two biggest dogs in Thailand. On one side was a man he liked, even admired. A friend who was tangled up in ways Shepherd didn't yet understand with the CIA and a cast of characters no one would want to invite to dinner. On the other side was a woman who he probably should have fallen in love with. But he had hesitated, and that had been that.

So what did he hope to accomplish now by getting between Charlie and Kate? To become their mutual hero and earn their eternal gratitude and respect?

That wasn't likely to be the outcome, and he knew it. The man who tries to stop a fight usually becomes the enemy of both combatants. More often than not, he ended up being blamed by both sides, and by everyone else, for the whole uproar. Shepherd knew that full well. And yet here he was, his course still set, no doubts in his mind.

So what the hell was he thinking?

He wanted to believe it was his sense of righteousness, his dedication to justice that was driving him. But maybe he was just kidding himself. Maybe all he was doing was trying to prove he was still a big-time guy, that he still mattered. Maybe he was just showing off for Charlie and Kate. Maybe he was just trying to be one of them again.

Through the window Shepherd looked down at Bangkok. Out there in the grey half-light of dawn, millions of people were facing another day. They were hoping for the best, fearing the worst, and doing what they could to survive and look after the people they loved. Most of them deserved better than they were getting. Certainly they deserved better than they would get if Robert Darling and his pals had their way and pulled the whole country down around them in a misguided effort to keep it from falling under Chinese influence.

The golden spires of what seemed to be a hundred temples gleamed as they reflected the first rays of the rising sun.

Part Four

BANGKOK
PHUKET

Now I'm hiding in Honduras
I'm a desperate man
Send lawyers, guns and money
The shit has hit the fan.

— Warren Zevon,
'*Lawyers, Guns, and Money*'

Forty Six

IN THE EARLY 1970s, the Thai government announced it was building a new, technically advanced international airport for Bangkok. They began purchasing land in the middle of what was locally known as Cobra Swamp, an unpromising area of marshy terrain about twenty miles southeast of the city, and said that construction would begin shortly. However, the new Suvarnabhumi International Airport was not completed for nearly thirty-five years. It eventually opened in 2006.

During the more than three decades it took to build the new airport, the Thais were anything but idle. On the contrary, the project spewed money like a broken fire hydrant and they exuberantly collected every last drop of it. The new airport became a seemingly inexhaustible fount of bribery, extortion, cronyism, nepotism, patronage, graft, and embezzlement. Entire generations of political figures, government bureaucrats, military officers, and their families and friends and acquaintances, saw the new airport as little more than a source of jewelry for their wives, condos for their girlfriends, and Mercedes for themselves. That Suvarnabhumi Airport ended up as a badly-designed, poorly built, thoroughly screwed up mess came as no surprise to anyone in Thailand. Nor did anyone in Thailand seem to care all that much.

As for Shepherd, this was one morning on which he cared a great deal. It was barely 7:30 A.M. He was cranky and sore from the six-hour flight from Dubai, he really needed to pee, and there wasn't a toilet anywhere that he could see.

The nearly mile-long crowded walkways through which he and Keur were forced to elbow their way in order to wedge themselves into a hot, confused, and overcrowded immigration hall reminded him why otherwise normal people became mass murders. He found himself fondly thinking back to his last trip to Thailand when Tommy had picked him up right next to the airplane in a chauffeured Mercedes and they had driven directly off the airport with no stops for any irritating nonsense like clearing immigration and customs.

They were shuffling slowly forward in one of the interminable lines snaking toward some immigration counters off in the far distance when Keur gave Shepherd a nudge.

"How long do you think this is going to take?" he asked.

"Long enough for me to figure out what we're going to do when we get out of this hell hole."

"That long, huh?" Keur mumbled.

SHEPHERD AND KEUR took a taxi to the Grand Hotel. They didn't have reservations, but with the country on the verge of civil war, hotels in Bangkok weren't exactly overflowing and Shepherd was sure Mr. Tang would have no trouble finding a couple of rooms for them. He didn't.

"I've got to get some sleep," Keur said as they dragged their luggage into the elevator and bumped slowly up to the third floor. "I'm dying."

"I think I'll go out for a run," Shepherd said. "I need to clear my head."

"You can't possibly be serious."

"I always run after a long flight. It gets me going again."

Keur just shook his head and they stood in silence until the elevator doors opened.

"Besides," Shepherd added as they got out, "I've still got to figure out where we start looking for Charlie. Running helps me think."

"Then go by all means. I've been waiting to hear the master plan ever since we left Dubai. You've promised one more often than a politician promises to cut taxes, and produced it exactly as often."

Keur found his room, gave a little wave over his shoulder, and closed the door behind him.

Shepherd's room was down at the other end of the corridor. He threw his bag on the bed, pulled out his running gear, and changed. He glanced around and thought about the way somebody had tossed his room the last time he had been at the Grand, but this time there wasn't anything for them to find other than his dirty underwear. If they really wanted to look at that, it was okay with him.

He did a few grudging stretches and quickly got bored, so he shoved his key and cell phone into his pockets and headed out to try his luck on the streets of Bangkok.

THE NEIGHBORHOOD AROUND the Grand is made for running. The streets are quiet and mostly empty of traffic. The sidewalks are dappled with shade from the rows of big-leafed eucalyptus trees that overhang them along both sides. The high walls around crumbling villas capture the warm breezes redolent with smells of charcoal cooking fires and fresh fish. The rest of Bangkok is not made for running.

It was barely 10:00 A.M. when Shepherd got to Silom Road, but it was already choked with traffic. Waves of heat radiated from the pavement and reflected off the trucks, buses, and taxicabs stalled in the gridlock. He dodged a street vendor selling counterfeit DVDs and a tout offering massages from beautiful young girls and settled into a gentle lope along the sidewalk heading eastward toward Lumpini Park.

Most of the shops along Silom were closed and steel gates had been pulled down over their windows. Shepherd saw no obvious evidence of damage anywhere. Apparently this area had been spared bombings like those that had laid waste to the Hyatt and the Four Seasons. Air conditioners hummed and dripped from high overhead. He passed the Duke of Wellington, the only thing around that looked like it was open, and took a shortcut through the parking lot of the Dusit Thani Hotel. Security guards were stopping every car entering the parking lot and checking identification.

Just as he hit the big intersection on Rama IV Road, the traffic light went green and he crossed the road without slowing and jogged through the big iron gates into Lumpini Park. He turned onto a wide sidewalk and looked around. Everything about the park seemed normal enough. No colored-shirted rioters, no sounds of explosions, no tanks grinding into position to fire on local landmarks. Just vendors here and there selling snacks and cold drinks, a few people strolling the walkways, and one guy napping on his back in the grass with a newspaper over his face.

As he circled the park, Shepherd thought about what he was going to do. It took him three circuits to convince himself that the obvious thing to do was also the right thing to do. He had to talk to Kate. He still didn't understand exactly how Tommy and Robert Darling were connected, but he really didn't see how it could be in any good way. Whatever it meant, Kate had to know about it. And she had to know a fresh shipment of arms was almost certainly on its way to Charlie's red shirts in Bangkok.

But how was he supposed to reach Kate? Tommy had always been his contact and that obviously wasn't an option any longer. He could keep ringing the two cell phone numbers he had for Kate, but she hadn't answered either of them recently. Somehow he had difficulty imagining the new prime minister rummaging around in her handbag when her cell phone began to ring. He could always just call the prime minister's office and leave a message for Kate, of course, but he doubted that a call from an unknown foreigner claiming to be a friend of the prime minister would be taken very seriously by anyone.

That just left one possibility that Shepherd could see. He would have to do what everyone else in Bangkok did when they needed to get something done. He would have to call somebody who knew somebody. And the obvious man to call was Jello, since he was not only a high enough ranking policeman to command a lot of respect, he also knew just about everybody in Thailand who was worth knowing.

Shepherd slowed to a trot and headed for the shade of a stand of palm trees just off the sidewalk. He pulled his cell phone out of his pocket and leaned against one of the trees catching his breath and rethinking his plan one more time.

Was there any reason not to tell Jello that he needed to speak to Kate? None that he could think of. Jello would want to know why he needed to speak to her, of course, but Shepherd was sure he would understand and accept that he couldn't tell him. He was equally sure Jello would find a way to help him regardless. After all, they were friends, weren't they? Friends trusted friends. And friends helped friends, too, didn't they?

"YOU WANT ME to do *what*?" Jello bellowed when Shepherd explained to him why he was calling. "What is this all about?"

"Look, Jello, you know I'd like to tell you, but—"

"Never mind," he interrupted. "Don't even start. There is no way you're going to get me involved in whatever you're up to. Do you have any idea what's going on here right now?"

"Yeah, I can see it for myself. I'm in Bangkok."

"Why doesn't that surprise me?"

"Look, you have to trust—"

"I don't fucking have to do anything, Jack. You work for the wrong people."

"I don't work for any—"

"Fuck you don't. And don't try to tell me you just have clients. You're General Kitnarok's man and everyone knows it."

"I'm not anybody's man, Jello. Now are you going to shut the hell up long enough for me to talk?"

Jello cleared his throat. "So talk."

Friends trust friends, Shepherd reminded himself. So what can you do when you need one of your friends to do you a favor and they don't like the idea of doing it? Easy. You tell them a good lie.

"Kate isn't answering either of the cell numbers I have. I need for her to know I'm here. I need her to know that I want to talk to her. That's it. This is personal, Jello. It's got nothing to do with politics."

"Personal? What does that mean?"

"Well, it means…" Shepherd trailed off into a silence that he hoped sounded embarrassed. "You know."

Are you serious, man?"

"Well… you know."

There was a little silence while Jello digested that.

"You dog," he murmured after a moment. "You goddamned hound dog."

"Can you get a message to Kate to call me on this cell number or not?"

"Probably."

"Will you do it?"

"Maybe."

"What the hell does—"

"That's the best you're getting from me right now, pal. The very best. Just live with it."

"Good enough then."

"You're sure this is nothing to do with politics?"

"Nothing, Jello. You have my word on it."

"You goddamned, fucking hound dog."

Close enough for government work.

ALONG SHEPHERD'S ROUTE back to the Grand, he saw more and more signs of the tension that was tightening on Bangkok like the jaws of a vice. The parking lot of the Dusit Thani Hotel was now entirely closed off with metal barriers. Cars were being allowed to leave, but none were being permitted to enter. The traffic on Silom Road had thinned noticeably and the sidewalks were nearly empty. Every shop he saw was now closed, their facades covered with metal grates. Even the Duke had gone dark. And the street vendors and touts had completely disappeared. He didn't think that had ever happened before.

Shepherd speeded up a little, jogging back to the Grand a bit faster than he had been going when he left. He felt silly doing it, but he did it anyway.

Forty Seven

SHEPHERD HEARD NO obvious signs of life coming from behind the door of Keur's hotel room, so he went to his own room and stood under a very hot shower until the water turned tepid. While he was toweling off in the bathroom, the telephone on the bedside table rang, but it stopped ringing before he was dry enough to answer it. Keur must be awake now, Shepherd thought to himself. Since nobody else knew he was at the Grand, who else would be calling?

He pulled on a polo shirt that wasn't too wrinkled and a pair of chinos. The he slipped into some boat shoes and walked down to Keur's room and knocked. When Keur came to the door, he was rubbing sleep from his eyes.

"I thought you were awake," Shepherd said.

"I can't imagine why you'd think that. Real people need sleep, Jack. We're not all vampires like you."

"That wasn't you on the telephone?"

"Did it sound like me?"

"The phone stopped ringing before I could answer it. I just assumed it was you since nobody else knows we're here."

"Well, it wasn't me."

It wasn't entirely true that nobody else knew they were there, of course. Shepherd had told Jello he was in Bangkok, and Jello could have easily guessed where he was. But there was no one else. He was sure of it. He and Keur just stood there in the doorway and looked at each other for a moment.

"Don't get paranoid," Keur said. "Somebody just called the wrong room."

"You're probably right."

And Keur probably *was* right. But there was still something unnerving about a telephone ringing in a hotel room where nobody was supposed to know he was.

"Give me ten minutes," Keur said, "I'll get dressed and come right down."

TO KILL TIME while he was waiting for Keur, Shepherd turned on the television and flipped through the channels. He watched CNBC for a few minutes, but the stock and currency market reports he normally monitored now seemed far-off and inconsequential, like the light from distant stars that had been created thousands of years before. He flipped over to CNN, but World Sport was showing again, and no matter how bored he was he wasn't going to watch replays of Portuguese soccer games.

Keur knocked at the door. Shepherd muted the sound, but he left the TV set on.

"That was fast," he said when he opened the door.

Keur didn't respond immediately and that was when Shepherd registered that Keur's eyes were focused on something over his shoulder. He glanced around and saw that CNN had shifted back to the news.

On the screen now was a city street that looked a lot like Silom Road. It *was* Silom Road. Shepherd grabbed the remote control off the bed and punched the sound back on.

"—from yesterday afternoon," a male voice was saying. "Elizabeth

Corbin of *The New York Times* is in Bangkok and she has the latest developments from there for us."

Keur came in and closed the door behind him and they both stood with their arms folded and watched the screen. Liz appeared holding a microphone above a big, half-empty street. Shepherd thought she must be standing on one of those pedestrian bridges over Sukhumvit Road. He was pretty sure he could see a corner of the Marriott Hotel in the background.

"There have been two important developments in Bangkok today, Keith."

It seemed to Shepherd that Liz looked a little jumpy.

"The first development is that we have just learned that some local fishermen have found a shipping container in the Gulf of Thailand which is filled with what appears to be numerous sets of human remains. The container was found in an area about two miles offshore from a beach resort called Hua Hin that is about fifty miles south of Bangkok."

"Holy shit," Keur said.

"The fishermen refused to be interviewed on camera for fear of reprisals, but one of them told me there could be many more containers and hundreds more bodies in the same area. They also say they think that explains the exceptional catches they have been making in the area recently."

"Christ," Keur murmured, "I'll never eat fish again."

"There is intense speculation in Bangkok that the area was used as a dumping ground by the military for the bodies of hundreds of protesters who disappeared during what has become known as the Yellow Shirt Uprising just before the last election. We have been trying to obtain some comment from an authorized spokesman for the Thai military, but none of our calls have been returned."

"Oh, man," Shepherd said, shifting his eyes from the screen to Keur. "If that turns out to be true, then—"

"What the hell?" Keur interrupted, still staring at the television screen.

When Shepherd glanced back, it took him a moment to process what he was seeing. Even when he *did* process it, it still didn't seem real to him.

There on the television screen, in vivid color, was a photograph of *him*. The picture looked slightly familiar, although he couldn't immediately think where it came from. Maybe CNN had poached it from some web site.

"The second important development today concerns this man," Liz continued. "He is an American resident of Hong Kong whose name is Jonathan William Shepherd."

Shepherd stared open-mouth at the television screen, rooted to the spot.

"Shepherd is the personal lawyer of General Chalerm Kitnarok, the Thai military strongman ousted in the elections last October that brought the present government to power. Sources in the Thai government are saying that Shepherd has slipped quietly into the country. It is widely believed that General Kitnarok is plotting a return to power in Thailand and that he may even be arming bands of his supporters in order to launch a campaign of violent revolt against the present government. We are told that this is the second time in recent weeks that a close associate of General Kitnarok has slipped into the country. The first was a Lebanese associate named Adnan Haddad, who has subsequently disappeared without a trace."

Shepherd knew exactly where Adnan had gone, of course, both parts of him. But, under the circumstances, his superior knowledge gave him very little pleasure.

"These same sources tell me that the authorities here have launched an intense search for Shepherd. They hope that his arrest will shed some light on General Kitnarok's plans and even perhaps what is in store for Thailand in the immediate future. This is

Elizabeth Corbin reporting from Bangkok for CNN."

The scene shifted to a middle-aged male in a studio somewhere. Shepherd was still rooted to the spot, visions of Adnan's severed head dancing in his mind. Keur took the remote control out of his hand and muted the sound again.

"Have you told anyone where we are?" Keur asked.

He could see the answer right there on Shepherd's face.

"Who?"

"Jello isn't responsible for this."

"What the hell kind of a name is Jello?"

Shepherd told Keur who Jello was and about asking his help to reach Kate.

"He's my friend, Keur. He knows I don't have anything to do with Charlie's politics. Jello isn't responsible for this."

"But he's a high ranking policeman."

Shepherd nodded.

"Did you tell him where we're staying?"

"No, but I told him I'm in Bangkok and he'd guess. I always stay here."

"Pack," Keur said. "We're leaving."

"Come on, I don't think—"

"Do it now," Keur interrupted. "Don't argue with me. I'll be back in five minutes."

Before Shepherd could say anything else, Keur was gone.

SHEPHERD SAT DOWN on the edge of the bed and thought about what might be happening. A lot of possibilities came to mind, none of them good. When Keur came back ten minutes later, Shepherd still hadn't moved.

"Goddamn it, Jack, move your ass. We're leaving right now."

"Do you really think—"

"Yes," Keur snapped, "I do. Pack. Now."

Shepherd got up and retrieved his bag. While he rummaged around the room collecting his things, Keur sat in the straight chair at the small desk. His own bags, a common-looking wheeled airline bag made of heavy black fabric and a scratched-up brown leather briefcase, were on the floor at his feet. Something about the picture bothered Shepherd, but he couldn't put his finger on what it was.

"I called a guy I know," Keur said. "I've arranged for us to use a Bureau safe house for a few days until we figure out what this is all about."

Somewhere between stuffing into his bag what little clean underwear he had left and collecting his toilet gear in the bathroom, it occurred to Shepherd what was bothering him about the picture of Keur sitting in front of the desk with his bags at his feet. It was the briefcase. Keur hadn't had a briefcase when they checked into the Grand.

"Where'd that come from?" Shepherd asked, pointing to it.

"I asked the embassy to send some stuff over. That's what it came in."

"Research material?"

"Not exactly."

Shepherd nodded and thought that over.

"So it's not just Jello," he said. "The American embassy knows where we are, too."

"They know where *I* am. I didn't tell them anything about you."

"What's in the briefcase?"

"You don't trust me, Jack?"

Shepherd said nothing.

A half smile spread over Keur's face as he stood up and tossed his briefcase on the bed. He popped the clasps and lifted the top. Shepherd could see what was in it from where he stood. There was a black handgun in a leather holster. There was also a small short-barreled revolver that was silver plated and looked like a Smith & Wesson detective special.

"One for you and one for me?" Shepherd asked.

"Not really," Keur said. "They're both for me."

"Why do you need two guns?"

"I don't like walking around naked," Keur said.

"You didn't seem to have a problem with that in Dubai."

"I felt safe there."

Shepherd chewed his lip while he contemplated the handguns in Keur's briefcase.

"Is that a Glock?"

"No, a SIG-Sauer 9mm."

"I thought you Bureau guys all carried Glock .40s now."

Keur closed the briefcase and took it back to the chair at the desk. He placed it next to the wheeled airline bag and sat down.

"When did you become such an expert on law enforcement handguns, Jack?"

"It's just something I remember from somewhere. I've got a few friends at the Bureau."

"Well, here's your chance to update your knowledge. We have a choice of standard sidearm. Either the Glock or the SIG. Maybe I'm just an old fashioned guy, but I like the SIG."

"What's the little revolver for?"

"Sometimes a SIG is hard to conceal and you need something a bit smaller."

"The Bureau gives this kind of stuff out to agents who're on medical leave, does it?"

"You sound suspicious, Jack."

"Just a little curious. A guy insists I move out of my hotel, wants to take me to some apartment he suddenly came up with from somewhere, and then shows up with a bag full of guns. Wouldn't that make *you* curious?"

"If Adnan had an armed FBI agent with him, he might still be walking around today."

"Where'd the guns really come from?"

"The embassy sent them over, Jack. Just like I told you. You're not the only one who has friends."

"You talked to Pete Logan? He sent them to you?"

"No," Keur said.

"I thought Pete was the only Bureau guy—"

"Logan isn't my contact here."

"I don't understand."

"You don't really need to, Jack. Now, are you going to pack your fucking bag so we can get out of here? Or do I have to do it for you?"

Shepherd looked at Keur and thought about that for a moment or two. Keur had his own agenda here. He understood that. But how did this safe house and the two guns fit into that agenda? It looked like Keur was preparing himself to take somebody down, if he got the chance, and that somebody was obviously Robert Darling. Maybe Keur had information that Darling was in Thailand and he didn't want to share it. Maybe he didn't want to share it in order to make certain that information didn't get back to Pete Logan and the Bureau. Was this really some kind of a private vendetta Keur was playing out? Was he hunting Darling for some reason other than what he had told Shepherd?

If Keur *was* stalking Darling for some other reason, he sure as hell wasn't going to admit it just because Shepherd asked him to. And Shepherd knew he still needed Keur's help to find Charlie. He didn't see how he could pull that off completely on his own. So he needed to keep Keur sweet. Let a few more cards come down on the table. Watch and wait. Stay loose.

Shepherd was good at that. Staying loose. He had been so loose for the last year he was damn near completely untethered. He shrugged, dropped the subject, and finished packing.

Forty Eight

JUST UNDER AN hour later, Shepherd and Keur were in an apartment high up in a large building on Soi Thonglor, a pleasant thoroughfare on the far eastern side of Bangkok. The apartment was large and expensively decorated. If this was a Bureau safe house, Shepherd figured the Bureau's safe house budget ought to be investigated by somebody.

The living room was at least forty feet long. It was anchored by a grand piano at one end and floor-to-ceiling bookshelves at the other. Both the east and west walls were broken by a succession of big windows through which Shepherd could see the office towers of the city in one direction and the distant glimmer of the Chao Phraya River in the other.

They sat facing each other on two sofas upholstered in rich damask patterned linen. Between them was a six-foot long square coffee table that was dotted with stacks of art books.

"Nice apartment," Shepherd said. "When does the butler come in?"

Keur said nothing.

"As much as I appreciate the hospitality, I'm not going to accomplish anything hiding out here," Shepherd went on.

"You're not going to accomplish anything by getting yourself arrested either."

"My guess is somebody doesn't want me find Charlie and that's why the arrest order was issued. They're trying to keep me pinned down. I've got to get that order lifted."

"How are you going to do that?"

"The first step is to find out where the arrest order came from. So I'm going to call Liz and ask her."

Shepherd swung his feet up onto the coffee table and pulled out his phone. But before he could dial, Keur leaped off the other sofa like he had been stabbed in the ass and wrapped his hand around it.

"What the *fuck* you doing?" he snapped.

"What does it look like I'm doing? I'm calling Liz to ask her where she got that story. We're old friends. I'm sure she'll tell me."

Actually, Shepherd wasn't at all sure she *would* tell him. But he had always believed that sounding confident was more than half the battle, particularly when he actually didn't have a clue what the hell was coming next.

Keur just stared at Shepherd for a moment, then put the phone on the table and sat back down.

"Oh, give me a break," Shepherd said. "You're not saying somebody's listening to my cell phone, are you?"

"Probably not. Cell phone signals are hard to isolate unless they already know roughly where you are."

"And nobody but you knows where I am right now."

"Right," Keur nodded. "On the other hand, I'll bet a lot of people know where the *Times* chick is right now."

Shepherd hadn't thought of that, but he wasn't about to admit it to Keur. Instead, he arranged his features in a look of bored disinterest and waited.

"I'll be back in a few minutes," Keur said. "You want something to eat?"

"Where are you going?"

"McDonald's. There's one next door."

McDonald's didn't do much for Shepherd, but he hadn't eaten anything since he got up and all of a sudden he realized how hungry he was.

"Bring me some of whatever you're having," he said.

He had always held the view that it didn't matter what you ordered at McDonald's. Everything they sold tasted more or less the same anyway.

WHEN KEUR WALKED back into the apartment a half hour later, he handed Shepherd two paper bags. One of them contained a Big Mac, a large fries, and an apple pie. The other contained five identical Nokia cell phones, the cheap ones without any of the bells and whistles, and five chargers.

"All prepaid and untraceable," Keur said. "Bought them down the street and loaded each one with five hours of air time. One's for you, one's for me. The batteries are pre-charged so we should be good to go."

"Who are the other three for?"

"For whoever you want to talk to. When you use prepaid numbers for both ends of a conversation, you stay anonymous. At least you do for a while."

"You seem to know quite a lot about this kind of thing, Keur."

Keur didn't say anything. He just handed Shepherd a card on which the shop had written the numbers for the five phones.

Shepherd took the card and turned on three of the phones. After the numbers came up on their screens, he wrote his name by one of the numbers on the card and dropped the phone into his pocket. Then he wrote Keur's name next to another number and handed that phone to him.

Shepherd held up the third phone.

"I need to get this to Liz," he said.

"Do you know where her office is?"

"Yes. Not far."

"Give me the address and I'll go downstairs and hire a motorcycle taxi to deliver it."

Shepherd rummaged in a desk drawer until he found a large envelope. He wrote Liz's address on it, sealed the telephone inside, and gave it to Keur. While Keur took the envelope downstairs, Shepherd turned the television on to pass the time. CNN was running World Sport again. Did they ever broadcast anything else? He muted the sound and sat staring at interminable and interchangeable images of people playing soccer until Keur came back.

"Ten minutes," Keur said. He glanced at the television set. "I didn't know you liked soccer."

"I don't. I loath soccer."

"Me, too," Keur said. Then he sat down on the couch across from Shepherd and focused his attention on the television set.

Fifteen minutes later, World Sport was still broadcasting excerpts from European soccer games and Shepherd and Keur were still staring at the muted television set in silence. *How many soccer games could be played on the planet every day?* Shepherd wondered to himself. But he quickly decided any number greater than one was way too many and lost all interest in trying to work it out.

Shepherd picked up the new Nokia, consulted his list of numbers, and dialed the one for the phone Keur had sent to Liz's office by motorcycle taxi. No answer.

Five more minutes of silent soccer and he tried again. Still no answer.

"Maybe your delivery guy hasn't made it yet," he said to Keur.

"Maybe your pet reporter's not in her office."

Shepherd shrugged and put the Nokia down on the coffee table. Almost immediately it began to play some kind of irritating jingle. He jerked it back up again and answered.

"Who the fuck is this?" a woman's voice bawled in his ear. "And what the fuck is going on?"

"It's Liz," he said to Keur.

"Jack?" Liz's voice dropped to a stage whisper on the telephone. "Is that you, Jack?"

"Yes. It's me."

"Did you send me this phone?"

"Yes."

"And you just called me on it? Twice?"

"Yes."

"What is this number you called me from?"

"It's my temporary phone. Just like the phone you're talking on now is your temporary phone."

There was a little silence while Liz took that in.

"Where are you?" she asked.

"Close."

"Close? You mean you're in Bangkok?"

"Never mind about that now, Liz. I heard your report. Why are they looking for me?"

"You don't know?"

"I wouldn't be asking you if I knew."

"The government thinks you're General Kitnarok's man and that he's about to start a civil war here. They figure you've got something to do with that. Maybe you're even pulling some of the strings."

"I don't do politics, Liz. I thought you knew that."

"This government isn't going to let General Kitnarok take them down. They're going to fight. They think you're involved, Jack, and they're coming after you."

"You mean coming after me the way somebody came after Adnan?"

"What are you talking about? Who the fuck is Adnan?"

It suddenly occurred to Shepherd that Liz didn't know anything about Adnan's headless corpse dangling under the Taksin Bridge. The military must have hushed it up pretty effectively if the press hadn't sniffed out anything about it. That was interesting. If the military had been involved in killing Adnan to scare Charlie's supporters, why would they keep it quiet?

"Why did you send this phone to me?" Liz interrupted Shepherd's reverie before he could decide what to make of that.

"Because it's untraceable."

There was another silence and this time he could almost hear Liz thinking.

"Are you telling me my calls are being monitored?"

"Maybe. We think it's possible."

"We?"

"Later," Shepherd said, glancing at Keur. "What the hell is going on, Liz? That's what matters right now. Who's looking for me?"

"I'm not actually quite sure. The police, I guess."

"I talked to Jello not more than an hour ago. He didn't know anything about it."

"If you say so."

"It was your story, Liz. You even had a photo of me. Where did you get it?"

"We got the picture off the internet. We went to the site for—"

"Not the goddamned picture, Liz. I meant the story that the Thai authorities are looking for me. Where did you get the story from?"

"You know I can't tell you what my source—"

"Bullshit, lady. Somebody is after me and I want to know who it is. Don't give me some academic horseshit about protecting your sources."

Liz said nothing at all for at least half a minute. Shepherd knew he was about to find out how friendly they really were.

"The story came from a guy at NIA," she eventually said. "But that's all I'm going to tell you."

"You got this story about me from the National Intelligence Agency?"

"Yes."

"Who was it? Who gave you the story?"

"Jack, I'd like to help you, I really would, but—"

"*Who the fuck was it, Liz?*"

In the silence, Shepherd could hear Liz breathing on the other end of the phone. Maybe he had gone too far. Maybe begging would have been a better tactic. Sometimes Shepherd despaired at his lousy judgment about how to get women to do what he wanted. He had no problem with men. With men he could be very persuasive. But women? He thought he knew less about dealing with them now than he had when he was about five and the only women in his life were his mother and his kindergarten teacher. And he hadn't known shit about how to deal with them either.

But this time, for once, the cylinders clicked down and the lock popped open.

"His name is Tammarat," Liz said, "Tammarat something-or-another."

"*Tommy?* Tommy is the one who told you that the cops are looking for me?"

"That's right. You know Tommy?"

Oh yeah, Shepherd thought to himself. *I know Tommy all right.*

"Did Tommy tell you *why* the NIA was looking for me?"

"He said you were running things here for General Kitnarok."

"And you believed that?"

"I know you work for Kitnarok, Jack. Everybody knows that. We just don't know for sure what you do for him."

"So you figured that fomenting revolution might be as good a job description as any? Sort of like a Che Guevara on an hourly rate?"

"If it's not true, come on over here and I'll do an interview, Jack. I'll give you a chance to tell your side of the story."

"Right. And have your buddies from NIA waiting for me? Fat chance."

"I wouldn't do that, Jack."

Shepherd knew Liz probably wouldn't, but how could he be sure about something like that anymore? There was a time not very long ago when Shepherd would have said that he and Tommy were friends, too. Or if not friends, at least acquaintances who wouldn't stab each other in the back. But the last time Shepherd had seen Tommy, the little shit was in Dubai slinking off Harvey right behind Robert Darling. And now he was apparently back in Bangkok and planting stories with the press that Shepherd was stirring up a civil war in Thailand.

"Keep that phone handy, Liz. I'll think about it."

But Shepherd wasn't going to think about it very hard. It was time for him to figure out who his friends really were.

And he wasn't about to bet his butt that *The New York Times* was one of them.

Forty Nine

"YOU GET MOST of that?" Shepherd asked Keur he hung up.

"I think so. What are going to do now?"

"Can you find out if Harvey is still on the ground in Dubai?"

Keur glanced at his watch. He nodded. "I can do that."

Shepherd held out his hand. "Give me the other two phones."

"What are you going to do with them?"

"There's not a lot of time left and I've got to get back in the game. The place to start is with Kate. If I can get a phone to her, I can tell her about Tommy and put an end to this horseshit."

"How are you going to do that, Jack? Everybody is jumpy as hell right now. You can't get close to her."

"Want to bet?"

SHEPHERD WAS SITTING at a table in the Marriott hotel drinking a cup of coffee when Jello walked past the big front windows. Jello was on his way to Bully's Pub for lunch just as Shepherd figured he would be. Jello ate at Bully's Pub almost every day. He parked at the Marriott, then walked next door to the pub and had a Bully's Burger and a Diet Coke while he read the paper. Jello was a man of habit.

Shepherd was wearing sunglasses and a baseball cap he had

bought in the hotel shop. The cap was black and had a large red and yellow beaded elephant on the front, and he had tilted the brim down as far as he could without being obvious about it. In other words, he looked pretty much like most of the other dopy Western tourists in Thailand. Just another middle-aged white guy trying to shake off last night's hangover. No one gave him a second look.

The prepaid Nokia rang and the number of the phone Keur was using showed on the screen. Shepherd answered.

"The plane is still in Dubai," Keur said. "But Rachel says an application to lift the impoundment order has been filed."

"How long do I have?"

"You might get another twenty-four hours. But that's probably the most you can hope for. After that, the plane will be able to take off."

"Thanks," Shepherd said and broke the connection.

He dropped some money on the table and walked out onto Sukhumvit Road. A hundred feet to the east, he pushed through the doors into Bully's.

The place was mostly empty. Jello was sitting in a booth by himself all the way in the back. The seats were red Naugahyde doing a lousy job of trying to look like leather and the table was black plastic laminate with aluminum trim. Shepherd walked over and slid into the booth opposite Jello. He took off his sunglasses and hat and put them on the table.

"I got bored waiting for you to call me back," he said.

"What's with the get up?"

"It's a disguise."

"No shit? Pretty lame if you ask me."

"Good enough to fool you," Shepherd said. "I was sitting right in the window of the Marriott when you walked by. You never even glanced at me."

"Should have crossed your legs."

Shepherd mimed a laugh.

"You going to tell me why you need a disguise?" Jello asked.

"It appears that I'm a wanted man."

A half smile appeared on Jello's face. "Not by me," he said.

"I didn't think so."

Then Shepherd told Jello about the CNN report and what Liz had told him about getting the story from Tommy.

"Huh," Jello grunted. "I haven't heard anything about it."

"You haven't?"

Jello shook his head slowly.

"Doesn't that strike you as funny?"

"Yeah," he said. "It does."

"So it's probably not true that the police are looking for me?"

"Probably not."

Then Shepherd told Jello about seeing Tommy in Dubai coming off Harvey.

"So you think Tommy may be playing for the other team?" Jello asked.

"I don't know," Shepherd said. "I'm not even sure I know what the other team is anymore."

Jello nodded and they both sat in silence watching a basketball game flickering silently on a big flat-screen TV above the bar.

"I need to talk to Kate," Shepherd said after the silence had stretched on for a while. "Now you know why."

Jello didn't say anything.

"She needs to know about Tommy. Then I've also got to tell her…"

Shepherd trailed off.

"Yeah?" Jello asked.

"Forget it."

Shepherd didn't want to tell Jello that he suspected a shipment of arms would be coming in on Harvey when it was finally permitted to leave Dubai, arms that would be going to Charlie's red shirts.

It wasn't that he didn't trust Jello, but he needed to tell Kate first. When Kate knew about the arms shipment, she could decide how to deal with it. Shepherd didn't want to preempt any of her options by starting to spread the word himself in advance.

He took one of the Nokias out of his pocket. He laid it on the table, put one finger on it, and pushed it across to Jello.

"This is a clean phone. Can you get it to Kate?"

Jello looked at Shepherd for a long moment, but then he took the phone and dropped it into his shirt pocket.

"When can you get it to her?" Shepherd asked.

"I don't know."

"Today?"

"Maybe."

"Tell her to call me as soon as she has the phone. I have a clean phone as well. The number is already programmed. It's the only number in the directory."

"You going to give me the rest?"

"I can't. Not now. But I will. Or somebody will."

Jello just nodded. He didn't argue.

"It's a real shame," he said, "that you don't have another of those—"

Shepherd pulled out a second Nokia and put it on the table. Jello picked it up and smiled.

"You're still pretty sharp, aren't you, old man," he said.

"Anything else you want to say?"

"Yeah. One thing. I saw you right away when I walked by the Marriott. You looked fucking ridiculous in that hat."

KEUR WENT OUT and bought some chicken and rice and a half dozen bottles of Heineken from a street vendor and they ate in the apartment that night and drank the beers while watching a Celtics game on television. Shepherd didn't have much of an appetite and he didn't much like watching basketball on television, but he ate and watched anyway. It was something to do.

It was hard for Shepherd just to sit there and wait for a phone to ring. Harvey would soon be in the air and on its way back to Thailand. He had little doubt of that now. And that would be the match to light the fuse that would blow this shaky little country apart. Somehow he had to find Charlie before that happened. And he didn't have a damned clue where to start. Worse, before he could even begin looking for Charlie, he had to get that little shit Tommy off his back.

It was the third quarter when the Nokia rang. He looked at the screen, saw the number of the phone he had given Jello, and answered.

"She has the phone."

"When is she going to call?"

"I've got no idea if she will call you at all. That's up to her. She's the prime minister. I'm just the delivery boy."

"Thanks, Jello. I owe you."

"No you don't. If you can stop this, I'll owe you. We all will."

Then he broke the connection without another word.

The fourth quarter came. Somebody scored a lot of points, but Shepherd didn't care enough to register who it was. There was less than a minute left in the game when the Nokia rang again.

What could be more fitting? Shepherd thought.

"Jack?"

"It's me, Kate. How are you?"

"What is this all about?"

No time for small talk. Yes, she was right about that.

"Are the police looking for me?" Shepherd asked.

"Not that I know of. Why would they be?"

"Then I need to see you. Alone. There are people around you who are betraying you."

"What are you talking about?"

More than anything, he wanted to trust Kate. But he knew that might be naive and that was why he didn't want to tell her about Tommy over a telephone. He had to tell her in person. He had to see her eyes at the moment he told her. That was the only way he would know for sure. Was Tommy really acting on his own, or was he just playing a role in a bigger game? One that Shepherd couldn't even begin to imagine. One in which he might be as expendable as Tommy, or Adnan.

"I need to see you," he repeated. "You need to see me."

"Can you find the apartment where we met three days ago?" Kate asked.

Three days ago? Was that really only three days ago?

"Yes," he said. "I can find it."

"There will be two men downstairs in the lobby. Tell them your name is Cary Grant."

"When?"

"An hour," Kate said. And then she hung up.

Shepherd hit the disconnect button on the Nokia and put it back in his pocket.

"You want me to go with you?" Keur asked.

Shepherd shook his head.

"Think about it, Jack. Something very strange is going on here and you're walking right into the middle of it."

"I don't think Kate—"

"Pull your head out of your ass, man. Just because she's a good-looking woman doesn't mean she won't have somebody waiting there to take you down. You know too much."

Shepherd did know a lot. That much was true. But he still couldn't work out what any of it actually meant.

He figured he had only two choices left. He could run away. Or he could trust somebody. He was going to trust Kate. It was just that simple. If he was wrong, he would pay whatever the price for being wrong turned out to be.

"No," he said, shaking his head again, "I'm going alone."

Keur shrugged. "I'll bet that's just what Adnan said."

"I'm going alone," Shepherd repeated.

"Okay. I guess it's your funeral."

That was just an expression, of course. It was a cliché, not a prediction.

At least Shepherd hoped it was.

HE HAD MORE trouble finding the apartment than he thought he would. He located the rundown hotel just north of Sathorn Road easily enough, but when he got out of the cab and looked around, all of the apartment buildings near it looked alike to him.

He walked a short way in one direction and then back in the other, but nothing looked familiar and nothing stood out. Bangkok was a hodgepodge of nondescript architecture, a mass of cheaply built, cookie-cutter, look-alike apartment buildings, and he had never hated them more than he did right at that moment.

Just as he was wondering if he was going to have to walk into the lobby of every building within half a mile and announce "*I'm Cary Grant*" to anyone who happened to be standing there, two pairs of headlights appeared at the top of the narrow lane he had just crossed. Shepherd watched the little convoy from the shadows until it turned into the parking area in front of a building about fifty yards in front of him. When it did, he saw a blue BMW trailed by a black SUV. The blue BMW looked familiar. At least it looked familiar enough.

By the time he got to the building, both vehicles were parked and empty, but he had no doubt by then that he was in the right place. Just inside the lobby door were two hard-cases who couldn't have been anything else but muscle. They were both wearing identical dark-grey safari suits and pointy-toe black shoes, but that was where the resemblance ended. One of them was short and wiry and quivered with nervous energy like a whippet held at heel. The other one looked half asleep, but he was the biggest Thai Shepherd had ever seen in his life. The guy made Jello look like a midget.

Shepherd opened the lobby door. He spoke quickly, not wanting either of these guys to have a chance to get jumpy.

"I'm Cary Grant," he said.

If Keur was right, if this was really a trap, then this was when it would be sprung. And if it was sprung, he guessed he was toast. The bruiser looked like he could take out the entire offensive line of the New York Giants all by himself, and the little guy seemed the sort who could give martial arts lessons to Bruce Lee.

The bruiser looked him over with hooded eyes while the whippet just stood there and quivered. After what felt like a week to Shepherd, but was probably more like a few seconds, the bruiser pointed to the elevator.

Shepherd got in. The bruiser followed. There was barely enough room for both of them.

Fifty

THE BODYGUARD KNOCKED twice on the apartment door and then opened it without waiting for a response. He waved Shepherd inside and closed the door behind him. Kate was sitting on the couch smoking a cigarette. She was alone.

"I don't know whether to be happy to see you or not," she said with a weary smile. "I can't remember the last time you brought me good news."

"I'm sorry to say this isn't going to be one of those times either."

"I've only been prime minister for two days, and already I'm wondering how I got myself into this."

"Thailand is lucky to have you. You're more than it deserves. Why did you take the damn job?"

Kate looked at Shepherd like she had never actually thought about that before.

"I have no idea," she said after a few moments, and laughed.

Shepherd walked over to an old leather chair opposite the couch and sat down.

"That's all the security you've got?" Shepherd tilted his head to indicate where he assumed the bodyguards were waiting outside. "One big guy and one little guy?"

"Mutt and Jeff are the best. Don't underestimate them."

"I don't care how good they are. A hit squad armed with

automatic weapons came after the last person who had your job. And they got him. Don't you think that calls for having more than just a couple of guys around you?"

"If somebody wants to kill me, they will. But I don't think anybody really wants to."

"You don't know that. Don't be so damned Zen about all this."

"Mutt and Jeff will do me fine, Jack," Kate said, closing the subject with the finality she put into her voice. "What have you got to tell me?"

What indeed? A bunch of suspicions, mixed with a few observations, seasoned with several bad feelings? Not much. Maybe not anything.

But Shepherd wanted Kate to pay close attention. So he laid out his very best card first.

"Do you know where Tommy is?" he asked.

"I hope he's home getting some sleep for a change. Why do you ask?"

"Tommy was the source for a story that CNN is running right now. He told Liz Corbin that the Thai government is searching for me. They intend to arrest me because they think I'm in the country to help Charlie start a civil war."

"Are you?"

"No."

"Then why would Tommy put out a story like that?"

"I think he's trying to drive me to ground. Not because I'm trying to start a civil war. But because he knows I'm trying to stop one."

"You're not making any sense, Jack."

Then he told Kate about seeing Tommy in Dubai getting off Harvey alongside Robert Darling.

"In Dubai? You must be mistaken. Tommy hasn't been in Dubai."

"I was there, Kate. I saw him."

"And this is the same Robert Darling who is—"

"Charlie's partner in Blossom Trading."

Kate thought about that for a few moments while Shepherd waited in silence.

"I've known Tommy for twenty years, Jack. You can't expect me to believe that he's really working with General Kitnarok."

"I don't know that he is."

Then Shepherd told Kate about the building at the Dubai airport where he had seen Tommy and Darling disembarking from Harvey.

"It's an Agency facility," he said, "just like the one you showed me here in Bangkok. Tommy wouldn't have been at an Agency facility on an Agency-operated aircraft unless he has some connection with the CIA. Maybe it's recent, maybe it's not. But you have to at least consider the possibility that perhaps Tommy's been an Agency asset all along."

Kate stabbed out her cigarette and immediately lit another one.

"Why is the CIA involved in all this, Jack? What do they want?"

"They want Charlie back in charge in Thailand. He's military and he's reliable. They think he would be an effective counterweight to what they see as spreading Chinese influence."

"And they think that I'm… what? A Chinese stooge?"

"A lot of your supporters do think China would be a better ally for Thailand than the United States. You know that's true."

"So it's necessary for Thailand to sign up for one team or the other, is it?"

"Some people think so."

"Such as the CIA?"

Shepherd said nothing.

"Do you think General Kitnarok had Somchai killed?"

"No," Shepherd said, "Charlie might do a lot of things, but I don't think he would organize an assassination."

"Somebody gave the order to kill Somchai, Jack. If it wasn't General Kitnarok, then who was it?"

Shepherd saw where Kate was going with this, of course, so he kept his mouth shut.

"Do you think the CIA killed Somchai, hoping the government would collapse and General Kitnarok would return to power?"

"I don't know. It's possible. I just don't know."

"They're never going to learn, are they?" Kate shook her head.

Suddenly she stood up and walked to the window, although as far as Shepherd knew there wasn't much outside to see.

"I think they're getting ready to arm the red shirts," he said quietly.

Kate nodded. She didn't seem surprised.

"That could tip us over the edge. If the street mobs get guns…" Kate left the thought unfinished.

"You've got a little time if I'm right that they're using Harvey to bring in the shipment. I managed to get the plane impounded for a few days."

Kate turned from the window and looked at him with a quizzical expression. "You did what?"

He explained, briefly, the ploy with the impound order he had managed to get filed in Dubai.

Kate smiled, the first genuine smile Shepherd had seen from her since he had come into the apartment. He had forgotten how that smile grabbed him. It was really something.

"How long will that work for?" she asked.

"Not long," he said.

He felt a twinge as he watched Kate's smile fade.

"They'll get the order lifted by tomorrow. If Harvey is loaded and ready to go, it will be here by tomorrow night."

Kate turned away from the window and sat back down on the couch.

"When did you last speak to General Kitnarok?" she asked.

"A few days ago. He asked me to come back to Dubai. But when I got there he was gone."

"Gone where?"

"I don't know. His compound was empty. I phoned around, but no one seemed to know anything."

"Do you think General Kitnarok is here in Thailand now?" Kate asked.

"My first thought was that he had just gone into hiding after Somchai was shot. And that's what Keur seemed to think, but—"

"Keur? Who's Keur?"

"An FBI agent who's trying to nail Robert Darling for illegal arms dealing. I sort of got hooked up with him. It's a long story. Nothing to do with Thailand, except maybe…"

Shepherd trailed off. Keur hadn't exactly told him to keep the information confidential, but his lawyer instincts were shouting at him to shut up. He told his instincts to pipe down.

"Keur says his investigation is being stonewalled. He thinks the Agency is protecting Darling. That would tally with the Agency protecting Blossom Trading's activities here in Thailand, too. Harvey in Dubai. Tommy on the plane with Darling. It all fits."

"Do you believe this man Keur?"

"Not all together. But I want him where I can keep an eye on him."

Kate shook another cigarette out of her pack and lit it.

"Too many of those things can kill you," Shepherd said.

"Being Prime Minister of Thailand can kill me."

Kate was right, of course. He didn't mention the cigarettes again.

"If General Kitnarok is determined to arm the red shirts," Kate said, "I don't know that I can stop him."

"I don't think Charlie's your real problem any more. I think it's the Agency."

"Why would you think that?"

"It's got to be the Agency behind the arms shipment. Charlie wouldn't be arming street gangs. I know him. He's my friend."

Kate looked at Shepherd, smiled slightly, and tilted her head to one side.

"I thought I was your friend," she said.

"You are."

"Then, my friend Jack, you are in one hell of a lousy position here."

Shepherd couldn't argue with that.

Abruptly, Kate stood up and headed for the kitchen. "I hope to hell there's something to drink around here someplace."

While Kate was in the kitchen, Shepherd walked over to the window where she had been standing and looked out. Sure enough, the view was pretty prosaic. But there was still something about it that held him.

Everything seemed so peaceful out there, and yet in here he and Kate were talking about weapons to arm street mobs and the assassination of prime ministers. Within a couple of days, if he were standing in this very place again, he wondered if he would be hearing gunfire and watching smoke rise over the city. Shepherd thought back to the riot he had been caught up in a few days ago on Silom Road. He remembered the fierceness and the rage he had seen then in people's faces. If Bangkok were flooded with weapons, it would be a slaughter. There would be no going back.

"The whiskey is probably fake," Kate said from behind him. "The NIA would never spring for decent booze."

Shepherd glanced over his shoulder and watched Kate put a half-full bottle of Black Label on the coffee table along with two glasses.

"I'll take my chances."

Kate poured two generous measures. She handed one to him and took the other one. They tipped their glasses toward each other.

"To your health," she said.

"No, Madam Prime Minister," Shepherd said, "to *yours*."

They sat and drank quietly in silence. It was a companionable silence and the warmth of it did a great deal to ease Shepherd's growing sense of dread.

"Can you find General Kitnarok?" Kate asked after few minutes.

"I'm certainly going to try. At least I will if you'll make sure nobody arrests me while I'm at it."

"Don't worry about that. I'll take care of Tommy."

Shepherd just nodded. Although he did wonder for a moment exactly what Kate meant by that.

"If General Kitnarok really is being used by the Agency," Kate said, "he could help me stop this thing."

"I think he could."

"But you've got to find him first."

"I'll do my best. Keep that Nokia I gave you handy. We don't want to talk about this on any of your usual telephone numbers."

"Do you really think—"

"This is the CIA we're going up against, Kate. Occasionally, they do get something right."

Kate nodded and looked away, thinking.

"I have some people in Dubai," she said. "I'll get them to watch the facility where Harvey is. They'll let me know when it leaves."

"Can you get the flight plan?"

"It won't mean anything. They'll file for some neutral destination and then divert at the last moment to wherever they're really going."

"But you'll see the plane on radar. You'll know where it is."

"It's not as easy as you make it sound. If they change their flight plan at the last moment and alter their transponder code at the same time, it will take a while to figure it out. We'll find them, of course, but by then they could be on the ground somewhere and offloading their cargo."

"So how do we stop the plane?"

Kate smiled at that. "What do you mean *we*, white man?"

"That's a very old joke," Shepherd said. "You probably stole it from me. I hold the copyright on all very old jokes."

Kate didn't laugh and she didn't say anything else for quite a while. She just sat there smoking quietly. When she was done with her cigarette, she stubbed it out, folded her arms, and looked at Shepherd.

"I'm not going to let them win, Jack."

Shepherd just nodded.

He knew she wouldn't.

But he also knew they might win anyway.

Fifty One

WHEN SHEPHERD GOT back to the apartment, Keur was sitting on one of the sofas in the living room with a glass in his hand. The glass was half full of something clear. It could have been water, but Shepherd doubted it.

"You didn't have to wait up for me, Mother."

"Sure I did. If they cut off your head, I wanted to be the first to say 'I told you so'."

Shepherd didn't think that was very funny so he said nothing.

"Did you see her?" Keur asked.

Shepherd nodded.

"And?"

"I'm not the object of any manhunt after all. Tommy gave Liz a phony story."

"Figures. He's trying to take you off the board."

"Yeah, but he has to know that won't work for very long. I was bound to find out what he was up to in a day or two and get somebody to fix it."

"So what? You knew that impound order on their airplane wouldn't work for more than a day or two either, but you did it anyway."

That was a good point, Shepherd knew. He had gone after the impound order because buying a little time was better than buying none at all. And with a little luck, a little time would sometimes solve your problem. He wondered if Tommy was thinking the same way. If he was, that meant that whatever Tommy wanted him out of the way for was going to happen soon.

"Kate didn't know Charlie was in the wind either," Shepherd said. "She thinks he may be here."

"Here? You mean in Bangkok?"

"Not necessarily, but somewhere in Thailand."

"Kitnarok would only be in Thailand now if he was sure the red shirts were going to win."

"Maybe he *is* sure they're going to win. If Harvey is bringing in a load of weapons, the reds will sure as hell have the yellows outgunned."

"So what are you going to do now?" Keur asked.

It was a hell of a good question.

"Kate's got somebody watching Harvey, so she'll know when it takes off," Shepherd said after a moment. "Until it does, there's no way to guess when it's going to land."

"And there may not ever be a way to guess *where*."

"Maybe not, but I don't know what else we can do. Not unless the US government wants to call in a missile strike."

"Unfortunately, Dick Cheney is no longer in the loop."

"So there you go," Shepherd said. "We wait and we watch."

"And that's it. That's your plan?"

"Not entirely. The plane is going wherever it's going, but I figure maybe Charlie is already wherever that is."

"Not a bad thought." Keur mulled over that possibility. "Not bad at all."

"So I'm going to keep trying to track him down. Maybe, if we get lucky, we can roll everything up at once. Charlie, the plane, the load of weapons. What do you think?"

"Works for me."

"Okay, then pour me one of whatever you're having. I've got to make some calls."

Shepherd took out his own cell phone and tried Charlie's two cell numbers again, but they were both still going straight to voice mail. Then he called all the Dubai numbers he had. Three numbers at the house, two at the office, and even the number for the Kitnarok Foundation. No answer anywhere. All in all he had made eight calls and reached exactly nobody. Not much of a start.

Keur came back and handed Shepherd a glass that, like his, was half full of clear liquid. Shepherd sipped cautiously at it. Cold water. He made a mental note never again to say to an FBI agent, *I'll have what you're having.*

Out of desperation he started thumbing through the address book on his cell phone, looking for anybody who might have any idea where Charlie might be. As he watched the names flick by on the little screen, something began to scratch at the outer edge of his consciousness. Was one of the names reminding him of something that might help locate Charlie? The harder he stared at those names and tried to decide what was hanging there just out of reach, the more convinced he was there was *something*. He just couldn't bring it into focus. Eventually, he gave up thinking about it and went back to trying to decide who to call.

Since it was almost 1:00 A.M. in Bangkok, that made the problem a little more complicated. No commercial number in Europe was likely to answer since it was well past normal business hours there. He tried a few numbers anyway. Two bankers, two accountants, and a lawyer, all of whom did work for Charlie. Three of them were in London, one in Paris, and one in Zurich. He knew it was ridiculous to hope that any European might be in his office after 5:00 P.M., but he called the numbers anyway. Sure enough, none of them answered. Shepherd had made thirteen calls and still hadn't spoken a word to anyone. He was beginning to detect a pattern.

Shepherd went back to his address book and almost immediately saw a listing he had missed the first time around: Sally Kitnarok. He couldn't remember why he had a number for Charlie's wife, but he crossed his fingers that it was a private cell phone and dialed. After two rings somebody picked up, then immediately cut the connection. When he dialed back, the number went straight to voice mail. Somebody had shut the phone off when his call came in. It was the kind of thing most people automatically did when a cell phone they had forgotten to turn off rang when they were asleep.

Shepherd looked at his watch again and did the math. If Sally was in Europe or even the Middle East, it was unlikely she would be asleep yet. But if she were in Thailand...

He didn't want to jump to any conclusions. Maybe Sally wasn't even with Charlie, wherever he was. Maybe she just didn't want to be disturbed by a call right then. But if that was the case, she would see his cell number when she looked at her missed calls and call him back in an hour or so. If she didn't call back, then that would make it more likely she was in Thailand. And that she didn't want to talk to him.

It wasn't much, Shepherd knew. It might not be anything. But it was all he had after more than a dozen phone calls.

His eyes drifted back to the address book and he found himself looking at another name he had passed over before: Tanit Chaiya, Charlie's man at Bangkok Bank.

Then all at once Shepherd realized exactly what had been scratching at him before. And he realized how he just might be able to find Charlie after all.

Keur had been sitting silently on the other couch, watching Shepherd make his phone calls. He stood up, stifled a yawn, and stretched.

"Okay, now what?" he asked. "Got any other ideas?"

"Yeah," Shepherd said. "I sure do."

WHEN CHARLIE INSISTED that Shepherd drop what he was doing in Hong Kong and come straight back to Dubai, Shepherd had been trying to find out what had happened to some of the money he had wired out of Charlie's Thai bank accounts.

The fact that a little money was missing wasn't all that alarming by itself. It wasn't uncommon for international wires to be misrouted, and only five or six million dollars out of a total transfer of nearly six hundred million dollars was unaccounted for. Five or six million dollars was a lot of money when it represented a beach-front house in Maui with a couple of mind-blowing cars in the garage and a steady flow of hot women, but in the world of international capital flows of the magnitude that Shepherd routinely dealt with for Charlie, it was little more than spillage.

Shepherd hadn't thought any more about that missing money since he left Hong Kong. But now, sitting there looking at the name of Tanit Chaiya in his address book, he started thinking about it again.

Why had Charlie brushed him off when he said he wanted to follow up and figure out what had happened to that money? If Charlie wanted to launder some money, he had picked a hell of an effective way to do it. He had even managed to hide it from his personal laundry man.

Maybe part of Charlie's plan all along had been to make that six million dollars disappear when Shepherd moved the rest of the Thai funds to safety. Maybe that was why Charlie hadn't wanted Shepherd to get too curious about what happened to it. Maybe Charlie had a use for that money he didn't want to tell Shepherd about.

All at once Shepherd felt things starting to come together. And, as it was when good ideas occurred to most people, he wondered why it had taken him so long to think of it.

If he could find out where that money had gone, he could find Charlie, too. He would bet his last dollar they were both in exactly the same place.

When Shepherd told Keur what he was thinking, Keur looked unimpressed.

"Why would General Kitnarok do something like that? He'd just be stealing from himself."

"You're missing the point. The idea was to make the money untraceable. Charlie was creating a hidden slush fund that nobody knew he had."

"What does he need a slush fund for? He has more money than God."

Keur scratched at his neck and thought about it some more.

"Wouldn't it be easy enough to trace the wires from General Kitnarok's accounts, regardless of where they ended up?" he asked.

"Yeah, it would. But if the missing money was never wired in the first place, you wouldn't find it, would you?"

"I'm not following you."

"If the six million was drawn in cash instead of being wired, put in a couple of suitcases and moved to wherever Charlie wanted it to go, there would be no way to trace it."

"How would he get suitcases of cash out of Thailand?"

"That would be difficult, so my guess is he didn't try. He must need the money here."

"Six million dollars in cash? Here in Thailand? What in God's name for?"

"You really don't understand how politics works in Thailand, do you, Keur?"

"You're saying Kitnarok needed the money to bribe someone?"

"No, not for a bribe. Bribes are an ordinary business expense here. They're paid by check or wire transfer just like other business expenses. Nobody even bothers to cover them up."

"Then what would he need cash for?"

"For the red shirts, Keur. Think about it. Five hundred baht a day is the going rate for a demonstrator, a little over fifteen dollars. Pay the going rate and you can turn out as many people as you need. A hundred thousand people would cost Charlie a million and a half dollars a day. With the six million that went missing, he could fill Bangkok's streets and shut the city down for four days."

"Then what? A few days of people in the streets wouldn't do him any good. He needs the whole country to take a huge hit. That won't do it."

"It would if Harvey is full of AK-47s, rocket launchers, plastic explosives, and grenades. And if those weapons are distributed to a small group who move into the city under cover of the demonstrators," Shepherd said. "They fire at the troops trying to contain the demonstration; the troops fire back; hundreds if not thousands are killed on both sides; and there's your civil war."

Keur took that in and chewed it over.

"You think General Kitnarok is really that cynical?" he asked after a while.

"Maybe Charlie doesn't know it's going to happen," Shepherd said. "Maybe Charlie really does think he's just buying a political demonstration."

"Then who's pulling the strings?"

Shepherd said nothing.

"The CIA?"

Shepherd said nothing.

Keur smiled. Then he leaned back on the sofa and laced his fingers together behind his head.

"Even if you're right," he said, "what difference does it make? You have no way of finding out where that money went."

"Maybe I do," Shepherd said. "But it's the middle of the night. No matter how much I might want to, I can't do it right now. I'll tackle it first thing in the morning."

"What are you going to do in the morning?"

"Not just me, Keur. You, too. We're going to drop in on somebody unannounced."

"Who?"

Shepherd waved the question aside.

"Be ready to go at eight," he said. "And have that cute little FBI badge of yours all polished up. You can be the bad cop and I'll be the good cop. That's typecasting, I know, but what the hell."

Shepherd left Keur thinking about that, went into his bedroom, and closed the door behind him. He barely managed to get his clothes off before he dropped into bed and slid almost immediately into a deep and dreamless sleep, the kind some people call the sleep of the dead.

That was just an expression, of course, one he had heard a hundred times before. But Shepherd's last conscious thought before sleep took him was that he really wished it were called something else.

Fifty Two

SHEPHERD AND KEUR were in a taxi on the way to Bangkok Bank when Shepherd's cell phone rang. He took it out and answered it, but it kept ringing anyway.

"Not that one," Keur prompted. "It's the Nokia."

"Right," Shepherd nodded. "I need more coffee."

He fished out the Nokia and pressed the answer button.

"Jack, it's Kate. Can you talk?"

Shepherd's eyes flicked involuntarily to Keur. They were trapped in traffic on Rajadamri Road right in front of what was left of the Four Seasons Hotel. It would probably take them another fifteen minutes or more to fight their way through the gridlock and cover the remaining five hundred yards to the Bangkok Bank Building. He didn't see what choice he had.

"Go ahead."

"Harvey left Dubai about forty minutes ago. They filed a flight plan for Bangkok. It says they're landing at Don Mueang."

Shepherd thought back to when they had stood on the top floor of that parking garage and Kate had pointed out Harvey parked outside what she said was a CIA facility at the old Don Mueang airport. Would the Agency really ship a planeload of arms into Bangkok and distribute them right out of their own facility? That seemed wildly unlikely. Not even the Agency was that arrogant.

He glanced at his watch: 8:15 A.M. It was a six-and-a-half hour flight to Thailand from Dubai. That meant the plane would arrive in Thailand somewhere around 2:00 P.M., local time, depending on whether they actually intended to land at Don Mueang or not. Just because they filed a flight plan for Don Mueang didn't mean the plane was going there. And he would bet they weren't. But wherever the plane was going, one thing at least was now absolutely clear. The clock had started.

He had less than six hours.

WHEN THEY GOT to Bangkok Bank, Keur flashed his badge at the security desk in the lobby and they took the elevator straight up to Tanit Chaiya's office without being announced. Shepherd liked their chances a lot better that way.

"Don't laugh," he told Keur in the elevator, "but this guy looks just like Woody Allen."

They brushed past Tanit's secretary and pushed straight into his office. Tanit half rose from his desk, his heavy black glasses sagged to one side, and his mouth dropped open.

Keur looked at Shepherd and laughed out loud. "Goddamn," he said, "the little shit really does look like Woody Allen."

They took the two chairs facing Tanit's desk without being asked to sit down. They didn't say a word until Tanit sat back down, too. Then Keur took out his badge wallet, flipped it open, and held it up for Tanit to see.

"I am Special Agent Leonard Keur of the FBI," he announced in his best television voice. "I have some questions for you."

Shepherd thought Tanit looked less impressed than he had expected him to be.

"You have no authority here," Tanit said.

"Where's the rest of the money?" Shepherd asked, hoping to

get Tanit's full attention before the issue of authority took over the conversation.

"What money are you—"

"Cut the shit," Keur snapped. "A little over six million dollars is missing from a series of wire transfers you arranged on Mr. Shepherd's instructions. If you tell us what you did with it and where it is now, we're out of your life and no one else needs to know about this. If you don't, I am personally going to fuck you up, you worthless piece of crap."

Tanit's eyes opened wide and he looked at Shepherd. Time for the good cop to take the stage.

"I know you didn't take the money, Tanit."

Tanit quickly began shaking his head.

"But unless you tell us what happened to it, I'm not going to be able to convince him," Shepherd went on, inclining his head toward Keur. "And he's the one you have to convince."

Tanit licked his lips anxiously. "You must understand that—"

"I must understand shit, you little turd," Keur snapped. "Where's the fucking money?"

Being the bad cop looked to Shepherd like a lot more fun than being the good cop. Especially the way Keur was playing it. Either he was a whiz at method acting or he had a lot of experience in the role.

"You have to understand," Tanit said, his eyes shifting to Shepherd, "that I…"

"You what?" Shepherd prompted.

"I was just following my instructions."

"I gave you your instructions. I didn't tell you to—"

"Not my instructions from you," Tanit said. "My instructions from General Kitnarok."

Shepherd glanced at Keur, who smiled.

"What were those instructions?" he asked.

"To send six million United States dollars from the accounts to our Phuket branch before transferring the rest according to your instructions."

"Whose account did it go into?"

"No one's. It was to be converted into cash. Then we packed it into two suitcases and held it for collection."

"Who collected it?"

Tanit hesitated, his eyes flicking rapidly back and forth from Keur to Shepherd.

"I don't think—"

"Damn right you don't think, you little shit," Keur exploded. "If you don't tell me—"

Shepherd waved Keur into silence.

"Who was it, Tanit?"

Tanit sighed and looked away.

"It was the wife," he said after a moment. "It was General Kitnarok's wife."

"Sally Kitnarok?" Shepherd asked. "Are you sure?"

"I am sure of nothing," Tanit shrugged. "I was told to send six million US dollars to our Phuket branch and that General Kitnarok's wife would collect the money in cash when she wanted it."

"US dollars?" Shepherd interrupted. "He wanted the cash in US dollars?"

"No," Tanit said. "He wanted the cash in Thai baht."

"Did Sally collect it? Personally?"

"So I am told."

"Then Sally Kitnarok is in Phuket?"

"I have no idea where she is. I was informed she appeared at our Phuket branch and collected the money. That is all I know."

"When did she collect it?"

"Two days ago."

Tanit sighed heavily again and slumped in his chair.

Shepherd sighed, too.

Phuket, he thought to himself. *Fucking Phuket.*

He should have known that, in the end, it would all come down to fucking Phuket.

IT WAS MONTE Carlo that Somerset Maugham described as a sunny place for shady people, but he could just as easily have been talking about Phuket. An island resort off the southwest coast of Thailand about five hundred miles to the south of Bangkok, Phuket is set in the turquoise splendor of the Andaman Sea and soaked by sunshine nearly year-round. It is a glamorous, alluring vacation hideaway that has become justly famous among sailors, golfers, scuba divers, and social glitterati all over the world.

But Phuket has also attained a certain measure of fame among quite a different group: international criminals on the lam. The weather is good, the living is easy, the food is terrific, and the women are… well, Thai. Best of all, if the local police notice them at all, rascals on the run are generally offered the option of making a modest contribution to the local authorities to renew their invisibility. A lot of people seemed to think of Thailand as not much more than an asylum for the morally impaired anyway—it's the cuisine and the sex, the theory goes—so what better place could there be for a scoundrel to lie low?

Every now and then a small piece would appear in the *Bangkok Post* about a German bank robber or an American con artist who had been discovered living quietly in Phuket and bundled off home for trial. These intermittent demonstrations of Thai cooperation with international law enforcement were very impressive, and it was doubtless a coincidence that they usually occurred just after the fugitive had exhausted the booty from his misdemeanors. Regardless, the total population of villains hiding out in Phuket never seemed to be significantly diminished by an occasional extradition in the name of international cooperation.

Speaking personally, Shepherd had a lousy history with Phuket. A couple of years back a former law partner from Washington had come to Shepherd and begged for his help. The fellow had been framed for embezzling tens of millions of dollars from a Philippine bank he thought he had been running but eventually discovered was merely a front for a worldwide network of crooks and criminals. He ended up hiding out in Phuket. Shepherd followed him there and found the missing money for the fellow easily enough. But it led to absolutely nothing good for either one of them.

Then, a year or so after that, an immensely wealthy and wildly infamous American who was on the lam from a variety of charges in the US also took refuge in Phuket. His name was Plato Karsarkis and the press dubbed him the world's most famous fugitive. It was clear that Karsarkis had crossed the wrong people and the political smell from the charges against him was unmistakable. Plato wanted a presidential pardon and he thought Shepherd was just the man to get it for him. Reluctantly, Shepherd took on the case, but before it was resolved that one turned sour on him as well.

Two prominent clients in Phuket. Two prominent clients who, it has to be said, ended up somewhat less than fully satisfied with his services. Not a hell of a good track record for Jack Shepherd where Phuket was concerned.

KEUR STAYED SILENT until they were well outside the Bangkok Bank Building, but the minute they hit the sidewalk he blurted out the one question he wanted Shepherd to answer.

"Does that mean General Kitnarok is in Phuket, too?"

Shepherd thought about Sally and Charlie and how he had always admired the closeness of their partnership.

"If Sally's there, Charlie is, too."

"Any idea where?"

Shepherd wanted to tell Keur that Phuket was a big island and he had no idea at all where the Kitnaroks could be. But he *did* know. He knew exactly where they were.

Charlie had bought a house in Phuket about a year before. Of course, Charlie owned a lot of houses in a lot of places, some of which he had probably even forgotten he owned, which was why the significance of this particular house hadn't occurred to Shepherd before. The legal owner of the Phuket house was a shell company in the British Virgin Islands. As far as Shepherd knew, nobody realized the house actually belonged to Charlie. Nobody, that is, except for him. He knew because he had handled the purchase for Charlie and he had set up the British Virgin Islands company that held the title.

It was an extraordinary house on a rise overlooking the Andaman Sea just south of Nai Thon Beach, a relatively isolated area on the northeast coast of the island only a few minutes from Phuket International Airport. Charlie had never spent a single night in the place as far as Shepherd knew, but there was a staff there that kept it ready for his use at a moment's notice.

Shepherd knew a lot about that house because, as it happened, he also knew the seller. That had made the transaction easy for both sides, although it was not easy for him. He had hoped he would never have to think about that damned house again because it had belonged to his former client, Plato Karsarkis, the guy who wanted Shepherd to use his influence in Washington to score him a presidential pardon.

Now Charlie owned Plato's former residence in Phuket.

And Shepherd had not the slightest doubt that Charlie was there right then.

Charlie was there. Sally was there. Six million dollars in cash converted into Thai baht was there. And within the next four hours,

Shepherd would bet a white 737 would be unloading a cargo of arms and ammunition about ten minutes from there.

It all added up. He just didn't like what it added up to.

"Come on, Jack," Keur prompted. "We don't have time for all this. Do you know where General Kitnarok is or don't you?"

Shepherd took a deep breath and let it out again.

"Yeah," he nodded. "I know where he is."

Fifty Three

SHEPHERD DIALED THE number of the Nokia he had given Kate.

"The plane is going to Phuket," Shepherd said when she answered. "That's where they're unloading the weapons."

"How do you know?"

"Trust me. I know. They're going to Phuket."

He hoped to Christ he was right.

"Okay," Kate said. "We'll let them land and then take the plane and whoever is meeting it there on the ground."

Shepherd said nothing.

Kate read his silence correctly. "You think General Kitnarok is in Phuket, too, don't you? You think he'll be there to meet the plane."

Shepherd hesitated. The whole idea had been to keep Charlie and Kate from destroying each other, not to feed Charlie to his enemies.

"I just want to talk to him, Jack. If General Kitnarok and I can talk, maybe we can stop all this from happening."

"There are people on your side who probably have other ideas, Kate. I don't feel good about setting Charlie up for them."

"You have my word that nothing will happen to him."

Shepherd trusted Kate, of course, but he wasn't sure she was making a promise she could keep. He ought to be there with Charlie. Then he could be sure she kept it.

That was a problem, of course. By the time he made it out to the airport, got himself on a flight to Phuket, and landed at the airport there, everything would probably be over. Harvey would already be on the ground and Kate's people would have the cargo under their control. If Charlie was there, too, they would have him as well.

But maybe Charlie wouldn't be there. Maybe he would keep his distance from the shipment. If he did, what would he do when he found out Kate had seized the guns? According to Kate, there was a shipment of guns already in the country and nobody knew where it was. Did Charlie know? Would he decide that was all he was going to get, that the yellow shirts were getting too close, and push the button? Would Kate grabbing the new shipment cause him to turn the red shirts loose to do their worst?

Shepherd knew he had to get to Charlie before Kate's people took Harvey down. He had to be there before Charlie even started thinking about pushing that button.

"Can you get me a helicopter?" he asked. "Something fast."

When Plato Karsarkis built a pair of tennis courts alongside his house in Phuket, some people wondered why he needed two courts. But Shepherd knew. They had been re-enforced to double as a landing pad for helicopters. The tennis courts hadn't actually been used for that purpose very often, almost certainly not at all since Charlie had owned the property, but surely they were still there. Charlie didn't play tennis, but he would have had no reason to rip out the courts either.

By helicopter, he could get to Charlie's house from Bangkok in about two hours. That was more time than a commercial jet would take to get to Phuket but, door-to-door, a hell of a lot less time than organizing ground transportation and shuffling in and out of two commercial airports. Of course, showing up in the middle of Charlie's compound in a government helicopter might not be such a hot idea if his red shirts had automatic weapons, but what was life without a little risk?

"I'll have the rotors turning on a Blackhawk at Don Mueang in thirty minutes," Kate said. "Go to the military VIP terminal. I'll leave word to let you in."

"Make it twenty minutes."

"Fine. I'll see you there."

"Wait a minute," Shepherd said. "What are you talking about?"

"I'm coming to Phuket with you. I told you that I want to talk to Charlie."

"No, you're not coming with me. That's stupid, Kate. Anything could happen when we get there. They might start shooting."

"Don't argue with me, Jack. It's my goddamned helicopter."

She had him there.

"Okay," Shepherd said, "but just you."

"I can't leave Mutt and Jeff," Kate said. "They wouldn't let me go without them."

"This is turning into a goddamned mob scene."

"We're not negotiating here, Jack."

Shepherd took a deep breath and let it out again.

"Okay," he said. "You and Mutt and Jeff. That's it?"

"Right. That's it."

"See you at Don Mueang. In twenty minutes."

He clicked off the phone and shoved it in his pocket. Keur put a hand on his arm.

"I'm going, too," he said.

Shepherd threw his hands in the air.

"Sure. Why the hell not? The more the merrier. Let's take some cold chicken and a bottle of wine and make a fucking picnic out of it."

THEY FOUND A taxi driver who led a secret life as a NASCAR driver, handed him a hundred dollar bill, and exactly twenty minutes later they completed the one hour drive by screeching up to the military's VIP terminal on the east side of Don Mueang. One of the two guards at the door phoned somebody for instructions while the other watched them carefully, his finger twitching nervously around the trigger of the M-16 held across his chest.

Shepherd glanced over at the parking garage from which he and Kate had watched Harvey four days earlier. Had that really been only four days ago? It seemed to him like at least a couple of lifetimes. The guard hung up the telephone, snapped off a crisp salute, and slammed his boot heels together with a resounding bang. Then he opened the terminal door and held it for them.

Inside, Shepherd looked out through a glass wall onto the field where the rotors were turning very slowly on a helicopter painted matt black from nose to tail. Before he could ask anybody if that was the Blackhawk that Kate had promised, the door behind them burst open and Mutt and Jeff pushed into the terminal with Kate right behind them. She headed straight for Shepherd.

"If you're wrong about where that plane is going to land, we're not going to get another chance," she said.

Shepherd said nothing.

"I just hope you're right."

Shepherd hoped so, too.

"Who is this?" Kate asked, pointing at Keur.

"This is the FBI agent I told you about. Special Agent Leonard Keur from Washington."

Keur and Kate shook hands and sized each other up. Kate didn't introduce Keur to Mutt and Jeff. They weren't really the introduction types.

"What has the FBI got to do—" she started to ask Keur, but Shepherd interrupted.

"It's not official," he said. "Keur has been helping me for his own reasons. He wants to go and that seems only fair to me. I couldn't have gotten this far without him."

Kate thought that over for a moment, then nodded. "Where do I tell the pilots to go?"

"Tell them to fly to a point three miles south of the Phuket airport. I'll direct them from there."

Kate nodded again and without another word headed for the Blackhawk. Mutt and Jeff stuck close behind her.

Shepherd caught Keur's eye, gave him a little shrug, and they followed.

Fifty Four

A LITTLE OVER an hour later the mangrove swamps beneath the Blackhawk gave way to the azure waters of Phangnga Bay. To the right, the twin spans of the Sarasin Bridge formed the only connection between the island of Phuket and the mainland. And dead ahead was Phuket Airport's only runway.

Shepherd glanced at his watch. He figured they were probably an hour ahead of Harvey, maybe two. Unless of course he was completely full of shit and Harvey really *was* going to Don Mueang exactly as its flight plan said it was. In which case he guessed it didn't really matter what time it was. They were screwed.

Unbuckling his shoulder harness, he moved forward and leaned into the cockpit. Getting the pilots' attention, Shepherd pointed in the direction of Charlie's house since it was too noisy to do anything else. The Blackhawk swayed slightly as the pilots adjusted their course to the south. Shepherd went back to his seat and buckled in again.

They rattled on across Phuket for another few minutes and Shepherd's eyes searched for familiar landmarks. He scanned the island's west coast, counting off the deep coves rimmed with sandy beaches that bit into the island from the Andaman Sea. Charlie's house was above Nai Thon Beach, which was the second cove to the south. Or maybe it was the third. Now that he was looking at the island from the air, he wasn't absolutely certain anymore.

That would really be a pisser, he thought, *if after all this I can't find the damned house.*

Whichever cove it was on, he did remember clearly what the house looked like. It was a U-shaped structure of glass and steel with white-washed walls that hurt your eyes to look at in the tropical sun. The house was at the very peak of the headland just south of the beach, right at the center of a walled compound with a scattering of satellite buildings, a swimming pool, and the two tennis courts where they were going to land. The house stood out spectacularly from everything else, like a giant flying saucer that had landed at the edge of the jungle. Surely he couldn't miss *that*, could he?

He missed it.

The Blackhawk passed over the west coast and headed into the Andaman Sea. One of the pilots twisted around and looked at Shepherd. There was nothing ahead of them now but India and it was a thousand miles away over open water. The guy clearly wondered if Shepherd had any idea where they were going. Shepherd found that entirely understandable. He was wondering exactly the same thing.

Raising his forefinger and rolling it in a circling motion, since he had no idea what else to do, Shepherd felt the Blackhawk swing into a bank. He watched as the earth outside his window rotated and the beaches along the west coast came back into view. Then he unstrapped himself and moved forward again, leaning into the cockpit between the pilots. As soon as he looked east through the Blackhawk's windshield, he saw the house. It was dead on their nose.

He pointed to it and the pilot nodded. Shepherd felt the Blackhawk begin to tilt down, but he put his hand on the pilot's arm and shook his head. Pointing to the house again, he drew a rectangle in the air and made a lifting gesture with his open palm. He wanted the pilot to fly a pattern around the house at a high enough altitude and not be conspicuous while he looked the place over. The pilot seemed to understand immediately.

The co-pilot obviously got the idea, too. Without a word, he bent down, produced a pair of field glasses from somewhere, and handed them to Shepherd. Shepherd nodded his thanks, took the glasses, and went back to his seat.

THE HOUSE WAS just as Shepherd remembered it. Huge, sprawling, and spectacular.

To the west, a sheer rock cliff plunged a hundred feet into the Andaman Sea, and to the east a thick jungle of banana, palm, and rubber trees closed in. Only a single narrow asphalt road twisted through the two or three miles from the highway up to the house. It passed a security gate and a guardhouse, then crested a rise and dead-ended in a gravel courtyard with a fountain in its center that was directly in front of the main house.

Shepherd scanned the property through the field glasses, but he couldn't make out very much. The heat rising from the jungle was intense and it bounced the Blackhawk around. He struggled to hold the glasses steady. He needed some indication of how many people were in the compound.

There were a half dozen or so vehicles in the courtyard in front of the house. Most of them looked like pickup trucks, but most of the vehicles in Thailand were pickup trucks so that was hardly surprising. He saw people there, too, not in huge numbers, but a dozen or so in small groups scattered around the compound. Just at the edge of the jungle there was a clump of what looked like tents, but he couldn't be sure. Perhaps they was just tarpaulins covering some kind of construction work. Of course, no matter how many people and vehicles he spotted from the air, there could easily be a lot more of both. Vehicles were often garaged, and it was so damned hot that he doubted many people would be crazy enough to be standing around outside either.

There were no obvious signs of heavy security. He could see no dogs or foot patrols around the compound's fences. The two green-tinted tennis courts looked exactly as he remembered them.

Shepherd knew it was possible he had simply been wrong about the weapons being bound for Phuket and Charlie using his compound as a staging area. Maybe, right at that very moment, Harvey was on approach to Don Mueang and Charlie's people were lining up there to collect their new weapons and march on the yellow shirts right in the middle of downtown Bangkok.

It was far late to worry about that now, of course. They had found Charlie's compound and there were people and vehicles down there. But what were they doing there? Shepherd simply had no way of knowing for sure.

But he also knew his bet was already on the table and the big wheel was spinning around and around. It was time to find out whether he was a winner or a loser.

Shepherd moved up to the cockpit again. He leaned in between the pilots and handed the field glasses back to the co-pilot. The pilot twisted around and looked at Shepherd, his raised eyebrows posing the obvious question.

Shepherd nodded and pointed his index finger straight down.

Fifty Five

SHEPHERD HAD NO idea what to expect when they landed. But what actually happened wouldn't have made it onto any list of possibilities he might have drawn up.

Nothing at all happened.

The moment the Blackhawk's skids hit the tennis court the co-pilot jumped into the cabin and jerked open the big sliding door. It rolled back with a metallic grinding sound and slid along its tracks until it banged to a stop against the fuselage. Then the last of the noise from the Blackhawk's engines died away and the silence that followed was almost total.

A half dozen local men dressed in shorts and T-shirts lounged on the grass about fifty yards away from where they had put down. If the men had weapons, Shepherd couldn't see them.

"What do you think?" Kate asked.

Shepherd shook his head. "I don't know."

Some of the men glanced at them, but none even bothered to stand up. They looked as if they saw helicopters coming and going all the time and the arrival of yet another one was only a mild distraction from the important business of the day: napping, eating, and talking to their friends in the shade of a grove of palm trees.

Mutt and Jeff unbuckled and jumped to the ground. They split apart, moved about twenty feet away in different directions, and took up defensive positions that allowed them to cover the open ground between the Blackhawk and the main house. Whatever weapons they had, they kept concealed. A few of the men lying underneath the palm trees looked in their direction, but didn't really seem all that interested one way or the other.

"Either Charlie is here or he's not," Kate said. "I guess there's only one way to find out."

Kate unsnapped her shoulder harness and swung around until her feet dangled out the door. She gave the back of the seat a push with her right hand and slid to the ground.

Shepherd looked at Keur and shrugged. Then he opened his harness and jumped down right behind her. Keur followed.

After all of them were outside the Blackhawk, Shepherd saw they had the full attention of the men under the palm trees. He wondered what it was that surprised those men more. To see the prime minister of Thailand standing fifty feet away? Or to see her accompanied by two white guys?

A young fellow with a white scarf wrapped around his head and wearing dirty tan pants and a red golf shirt immediately jumped up and trotted toward the main house. Shepherd gathered they were about to be announced. The reactions of the other men varied. While a couple looked less than thrilled to see them, the overall response was anything other than hostile. Several men jumped to their feet and offered *wais*, a graceful Thai gesture of greeting in which the palms are pressed together in front of the face in deference and respect. One man, a young fellow wearing a New York Giants jersey and jeans, even stood at attention with his arms at his side and bowed slightly.

Kate didn't seem to notice how the men were reacting, or perhaps she just didn't care. Still, Shepherd was wary regardless of how benign everything seemed. They had dropped straight into the red team's clubhouse without an invitation. Somebody had killed the last prime minister of Thailand, quite possibly some of these very guys or some of their pals, and it wasn't that much of a stretch to assume at least a few of them would be happy to see Kate follow Somchai off the planet. Shepherd was responsible for bringing Kate here, and he was responsible for getting her out again. It was just that simple. He had a soft spot for tough-minded women, that was true enough, but only if they were alive.

He was about to remind Kate of all that, but she struck out for the entrance to the main house before he could say anything. Mutt and Jeff moved slightly ahead of her, one on one side and one on the other. They were covering her as well as they could, but there was only so much two men could do. Shepherd looked at Keur to see what he thought, but he was already following Kate.

Shepherd knew this whole show had been his idea. It had seemed, as they say, like a good idea at the time, but now that they were here, he wasn't so sure anymore. He felt like everything was only a beat from spinning completely out of control.

What if Charlie just grabbed Kate and locked her up? Or worse, what if somebody killed her? That would leave the field completely open for Charlie. He could declare victory for the reds and take over the country without firing another shot.

But Charlie was a decent and honorable man, Shepherd reminded himself. He wouldn't do anything like that.

Who was he kidding? Charlie was getting ready to start a civil war and Shepherd didn't think Charlie would be willing to sweep his opponent off the board with a single stroke?

But the truth was he really *didn't* believe that. He had worked with the man for two years. He trusted Shepherd and Shepherd trusted him. Charlie might want power—a lot of people wanted power—but Shepherd was sure that wouldn't turn him into a killer. At least he was pretty sure it wouldn't, sure enough to place a wager on it.

And, come to think of it, he supposed that was exactly what he was doing. He was betting Kate's life that he was right.

THE MAIN ENTRY to the house was up a short flight of black granite steps directly across the courtyard from where they had landed. At the top of the steps, a pair of glass doors was set into a glass corridor that connected the two main wings of the house. The effect of all that glass was undeniably spectacular, since it provided a view all the way through the house and out to a swimming pool set at the very center of the U-shaped structure. The water in the pool was so blue it looked as if it had been dyed, but no one was taking a swim or lounging in any of the teak chairs scattered around it.

Sally Kitnarok opened one of the glass doors and walked outside. She was wearing jeans and a man's white shirt with a pair of red, low-heeled sandals. Shepherd thought that was encouraging. At least she wasn't dolled up in Fidel Castro chic. Who fought a civil war in jeans, a white shirt, and red sandals anyway? On the other hand, he also thought Sally looked a little nervous. That couldn't be a good sign no matter what she had on her feet.

"This is a pleasant surprise," Sally said when they reached the top of the steps. "You should have told us you were coming, Jack. I would have made some arrangements."

Almost as soon as she spoke the words, Sally realized the unintended irony of what she had said.

"I guess that was a poor choice of words," she quickly added. "What I meant was—"

"It's not important, Mrs. Kitnarok," Kate interrupted. "We've come to see the general. Is he here?"

Sally cut her eyes to Shepherd, almost as if she was asking him to give her the right answer to that question. He nodded slightly, although he really had no idea what that was supposed to mean. Sally seemed satisfied.

"Yes," she said, "he is. Please come in."

They mounted the steps and followed Sally down the glass

corridor. The last time Shepherd had walked down that corridor it had been lined with small, terracotta sculptures on tall pedestals that looked to him to be museum quality pre-Columbians, and a long, obviously custom-made Persian runner covered the floor. Now the corridor was empty and it echoed slightly from their footsteps. He wondered briefly what had become of the sculptures and the Persian runner since he had last been there, which caused him to start thinking about what had become of him since he had last been there, too.

Sally led them into the living room at the end of the corridor. The three of them took seats on three off-white couches arranged in a U-shape facing the interior courtyard. They each selected a separate couch and Shepherd smiled at the unintended symbolism. Mutt and Jeff split apart. One moved to a spot along the wall behind them from which he could watch the corridor running back to the front door, and the other took up a position on the front wall so that his field of view covered the opposite direction.

Sally remained in the doorway. She was clearly nervous and stood rubbing her hands together in a cartoonish-looking gesture.

"Well," she said eventually, "let me get Charlie. He's upstairs."

NOBODY SAID ANYTHING while Sally was gone. The only sound in the room was the ticking of a clock from somewhere. Shepherd looked around and didn't see a clock, which made him begin to hope that the ticking he could hear actually *was* a clock.

He glanced at Kate and she returned his glance without expression. He was clueless as to what she was thinking. Keur stared off toward the swimming pool and didn't look at either one of them.

If something unpleasant were going to happen, it would happen now.

Mutt and Jeff seemed to sense the same thing. Shepherd could hear them shifting around slightly, presumably improving their defensive positions.

But nothing happened. Shepherd just kept listening to that damned ticking and wondering where the clock was.

After only a few minutes, probably less than five, Sally returned.

"Jack," she said, "Charlie would like to see you alone first."

Shepherd glanced at Kate, but she gave no sign she had even heard. Her face was so still that she might have been sitting there entirely alone.

"He's upstairs in his study," Sally prompted.

When no one else reacted or said anything, Shepherd nodded slowly and stood up.

"This way," Sally said, and he followed her out of the living room.

Fifty Six

CHARLIE WAS DIRECTLY across from the doorway when Shepherd walked in. He was wearing a green golf shirt and jeans and sitting in one of a matched pair of red leather chairs that flanked a Chinese chest set on a red and blue Persian carpet. The whole arrangement was positioned in front of a wall of glass that offered an unobstructed panorama of the Andaman Sea.

Shepherd walked over and sat down in the vacant chair.

"Hello, Charlie."

Very slowly, Charlie turned his head away from the windows. Shepherd thought he looked a lot older than the last time he had seen him. He appeared drawn and weary, like a man recovering from an unpleasant illness.

"What the fuck is going on?"

"That's funny," Shepherd said. "I was going to ask you the very same question."

"I don't answer to you."

"That's true. You don't."

"You show up unannounced at my house, and you bring that woman here without warning me. I thought you were my friend."

"I am your friend, Charlie. If I weren't your friend, I wouldn't be here."

Charlie grunted and waved one hand dismissively.

"Kate is my friend, too, Charlie. You have to understand that."

Charlie grunted again and looked away. Then abruptly he stood up. "You want a cigar, Jack?"

Shepherd didn't want a cigar, but saying no didn't seem the thing to do so he nodded. "Yeah, a cigar would be nice."

Charlie went over to the floor-to-ceiling bookshelves lining the two sides of the room that weren't glass and pulled on a thick, bronze handle mounted at chest height. A cupboard built into the bookshelves opened and Shepherd could see that it was filled with boxes of cigars. When Charlie came back he was carrying two Cohiba Espléndidos, each one the size of a child's arm. Shepherd had heard somewhere that Cohiba Espléndidos were Fidel Castro's favorite cigar. He hoped that wasn't a bad sign.

A cutter and a box of cedar Davidoff cigar matches lay on the Chinese chest between their chairs next to a big glass ashtray. Charlie handed one of the cigars to Shepherd and then sat back down. He carefully sliced the end off his cigar, inspected the cut like a pathologist faced with a particularly nasty autopsy, then lit a match and puffed his cigar methodically into life. When he was satisfied, he handed the cutter and the matches to Shepherd and smoked quietly while Shepherd cut and lit his own cigar.

Shepherd took several puffs, stared out the window, and waited for Charlie to break the silence. The sky looked hard. It was a shade of blue so steely it seemed almost belligerent. A single cloud, thin and elongated like the remnants of a smoke signal sent from somewhere very far away, lay just above the horizon.

"You shouldn't have brought her here, Jack. No good can come of it."

"Yes, it can. For you as much as for anybody."

"What are you talking about?"

"The two of you working together can stop this, Charlie. You're the only ones who can. That's why Kate is here."

"Stop what? The government is going to fall, Jack. My people are going to fill the streets until this country stops functioning. Then the government will have to call a new election and I'll win it. It's just that simple. There's nothing to stop."

"How much does it cost to fill the streets these days, Charlie? That's what the money Sally picked up was for, wasn't it? So you could pay for your mob?"

Charlie shrugged and took a long draw on his cigar.

"Is that your best shot, Jack? Because, if it is, you might as well leave now. That's the way politics works in Thailand. People expect to be paid to demonstrate. Whether they love you or hate you, they still expect to be paid." He shrugged again. "I don't mind. I've got a lot of money and these people don't have any. It seems fair enough to me."

"And what about the AK-47s and the grenades and the plastic explosives you're giving them? Does that seem fair enough to you, too?"

Charlie chuckled and shook his head. "Get out of here, Jack. Nobody's giving any of these people weapons. Why would I do that? They'd start a fucking civil war or something."

"I know about the plane, Charlie. We all know about it. It will be on the ground in about another hour and so that's all the time we have to shut this thing down. Once they start passing those guns around, it will be too late. Like they say, you can't put toothpaste back in the tube."

"What plane? What the fuck you talking about, Jack?"

Shepherd shook his head and looked out the window. If Charlie was just going to sit there and deny everything, they weren't going to get anywhere. And somewhere downstairs that damned clock was ticking.

"I know all about Blossom Trading. I know about the shipments of weapons you've been trying to get into the country. I know about the 737 that will be landing at Phuket in about an hour with one more load. You're going to kill a lot of innocent people and become the very incarnation of the devil for a lot more. And you're doing it all to regain power in a country where you'd be elected in a landslide anyway, if you would just let it happen."

Charlie took the cigar out of his mouth. "I have no fucking idea what you are talking about."

"Charlie, for God's sake," Shepherd snapped at him. "This is me you're talking to. I sell bullshit. I don't buy it."

Charlie began to puff furiously on his cigar.

"You little shit," he roared. "Who the fuck do you think you are?"

"I am your friend and I—"

"You come into my house and accuse me of smuggling guns into Thailand. You tell me I'm going to start a war here. What kind of man do you think I am?"

"I think you're a man who wants to rule this country again."

"I am that, you motherfucker, but this country wants me, too. I don't need to kill anyone to become prime minister again."

"What about Somchai? Didn't your people assassinate him?"

"I had nothing to do with that," he said. "Nothing."

"Come on, Charlie. Don't try to jerk me off here. You think the government's people tried to kill us in Dubai, so you—"

Charlie started to laugh.

"Give me a fucking break," he said. "Haven't you figured that out yet? I thought you were supposed to be a smart guy, Jack. Maybe you're not. Maybe I've been paying you way too much."

Shepherd looked at Charlie and said nothing.

"That was just a stunt," Charlie said, shaking his head. "Adnan organized it. We thought it might play well with the media. You know, make me look like a hero and make the government look bad. Like they were trying to assassinate me."

"Three people were killed, Charlie."

"I don't know what went wrong." Charlie refused to meet Shepherd's eyes. "Adnan told me everybody was going to use dummy loads, like in the movies. I don't know anything about that shit. I guess the security guys didn't understand or something. They had real bullets."

"So you killed three people for a *stunt*."

"I didn't kill anybody, Jack. My bodyguards killed three people. It was an accident. You know how it is. There's always somebody who doesn't get the word."

"So you're saying you didn't order the hit on Somchai in retaliation for the hit on you?"

"I just told you, Jack, there *was* no hit on me."

"Then who killed Somchai?"

"I have no idea. None."

Shepherd had the feeling there was something Charlie wasn't telling him.

"How about Adnan? What happened to him?" he asked.

"I have no idea about that either."

"I don't believe you, Charlie."

Charlie chewed on his cigar.

Fifteen seconds went by.

Then thirty.

"Okay," he finally said, "I don't know what actually happened to Adnan. I just know what *didn't* happen. Somebody killed him and then beheaded him to make it look like the Muslims did it, but I know it wasn't them. I've got a lot of friends down south. There are some good men there and they tell me the Muslim separatists had nothing to do with killing Adnan. I believe them. I just don't know who did it."

"So when I talked to you and told you Adnan was dead—"

"I thought it might be somebody trying to get to me through the people around me. That's why I insisted you come back to Dubai. I thought you might be next."

From somewhere outside, Shepherd heard what sounded like several car doors slam. Then an engine started, ran roughly for a moment or two, and caught. The vehicle drove away and Shepherd listened until the sound of its engine died away in the distance. He looked at Charlie.

"Some of my people are here," Charlie said. "They're organizing the demonstrations. We want to keep tight control. Make sure nothing gets out of hand."

"So why are you bringing in arms for your people?"

"I'm not bringing in *anything*. I swear to God, Jack, I'm not. Somebody has been feeding you a load of crap."

"Did Sally tell you who came here with me today?"

"Yeah. Kate, her bodyguards, and some other white guy."

"That white guy is an FBI agent named Keur. He's been investigating Robert Darling and Blossom Trading."

"The FBI?" The look on Charlie's face was one of complete incomprehension. "Why would the FBI care about either one of them?"

"Because Blossom Trading is running guns to Iran as well as Thailand. Darling is an American citizen. When an American citizen is involved in illegal arms dealing, it gets the FBI's attention."

"Come off it, Jack. Blossom Trading is just a crappy little company that sells washing machines and automobile tires. It's not an arms dealer, for God's sake. If there were any guns around there, somebody would just end up shooting themselves in the ass."

"Charlie, we're getting nowhere here. Keur knows all about Blossom Trading. He knows all about Darling. He even knows that the CIA has been running a delivery service for you. For God's sake, I saw the plane myself. First in Bangkok, then in Dubai. I even saw Darling and Tommy walk off it."

"Who's Tommy?"

"Tommerat something-or-another. He works—"

"That guy at NIA?"

Shepherd nodded. "He and Darling are both Agency."

"Robert doesn't have anything to do with the CIA," Charlie said. "That's stupid."

"Talk to Keur yourself if you don't believe me. He's right downstairs."

Charlie sat looking out the window for a long time after that, smoking his cigar, saying nothing. Eventually he took a last puff and dumped the remains in the ashtray.

"Okay, get him up here," he said.

"Don't you think it would be better to talk to Kate first about—"

"I want to talk to this FBI guy. What's his name?"

"Keur."

"Yeah, okay. Keur. Get him up here."

So Shepherd nodded and went downstairs to get Special Agent Leonard Keur of the FBI.

HE WAS DISAPPOINTED he hadn't been able to convince Charlie that the jig was up. He really thought he could do it. He had hoped Charlie thought enough of him to come clean when he laid out what they already knew. Apparently Charlie didn't.

Shepherd was happy to hand the ball to Keur and let him take a crack at convincing Charlie it was all over. Maybe his bad cop would get the job done where Shepherd's good cop had fallen flat on its face.

And, if Keur *could* convince Charlie that the jig was up, maybe they would still have a chance to stop this thing.

Fifty Seven

WHEN SHEPHERD RETURNED to the study, Keur was with him. Charlie had moved to a big table at the opposite end of the room and was sitting behind it with his arms folded over his chest. The table was long and narrow and made of rough, dark-stained planks. It looked like an expensive French country antique and probably was.

Shepherd and Keur sat opposite each other on two cream-colored leather love seats positioned perpendicular to Charlie's table. They had to twist to the side in order to make eye contact with Charlie while Charlie lounged in a high-backed chair looking straight ahead at both of them. It was an uncomfortable way for a visitor to have to sit, but Shepherd gathered that was probably the whole idea.

"This is Special Agent Leonard Keur of the FBI," Shepherd said. "If you don't want to listen to me, listen to him."

Charlie studied Keur expressionlessly. Keur looked right back at him and said nothing.

"So, Mr. FBI man," Charlie said when he had lost interest in sizing Keur up, "what's all this shit you've been telling Jack?"

"That doesn't matter anymore," Keur said.

"It sure as hell matters to *me*."

"I'm here with a message for you, General. That's the only thing that's important now."

Charlie obviously had no idea what Keur was talking about. Shepherd knew how he felt.

"Look, Keur," Shepherd said, "I don't know what this—"

"A message from who?" Charlie interrupted.

"It's time for a word from your sponsor, General."

Charlie's head rocked back as if Keur had slapped him. Shepherd looked from Charlie to Keur and then back again, but he still couldn't work out what was going on.

"Who the fuck are you?" Charlie snapped.

"I'm with the Central Intelligence Agency," Keur said.

Oh shit, Shepherd thought. *Shit, shit, shit.*

"I had no idea, Charlie," Shepherd said. "He said he was FBI and I confirmed it with the Bureau guy in Bangkok. He checked out. He really did."

Charlie just grunted.

"Ah crap," Shepherd muttered. "Maybe I should have—"

"Don't blame yourself, Jack," Keur interrupted. "My ID is fully backstopped. No matter who you called, they'd just confirm what I told you."

"I don't get it," Shepherd said. "Why did you go to so much trouble to—"

"Forget it, Jack," Charlie interrupted.

Shepherd glanced over at Charlie. He was leaning forward on his forearms, watching Keur intently.

"Whoever the fuck you really are, CIA errand boy, what's this message you say you have for me?"

"The message is this, General. The party's over. I'm here to pack up the tents and tell the band to go home."

"What party?" Shepherd asked, looking back and forth from Keur to Charlie.

"Your pal here hasn't exactly told you the whole story, Jack," Keur said. "You see, General Kitnarok is our man in these parts."

Shepherd looked at Charlie. "You're working for the CIA?"

Charlie didn't meet his eyes.

"I asked you a question, Charlie, and I think I'm entitled to an answer."

Charlie cleared his throat and stared down at his hands. "We're more like partners."

"Burma, Laos, and Cambodia are basket cases, so Thailand's all we've got to block China's expansion through Southeast Asia," Keur said. "We needed a friendly, reliable government in Thailand and the general here seemed to be the right horse to ride. So we backed him."

Shepherd was still looking at Charlie. "Then you knew all along that Darling and Tommy were Agency," he said.

Charlie said nothing, but his chair squeaked as he shifted his weight.

"No," Keur answered for him, "he didn't know. We used people we already had in place to make sure everything played the way we wanted it to. We thought a civil war in Thailand would burn China's supporters here for quite some time, so Darling and Tommy were supposed to see that both the red shirts and the Muslims got what they needed to turn up the heat."

"You mean guns."

"Light arms, ammunition, explosives," Keur shrugged. "Just enough to stir things up. We weren't exactly going to share nuclear technology with a bunch of fucking farmers, Jack."

"And what was Charlie's part in that?"

"None. He had no part. He just didn't have the stomach for it. Which, I have to tell you, worried us a bit. That's why I cozied up to you, Jack. We were starting to think our boy here didn't have the balls he needed and we had to make sure he didn't go completely tits up on us. I figured sticking close to you was a good way to stick close to him."

Shepherd shifted his eyes back to Charlie. "What the fuck were you thinking?"

"I was thinking you take you friends where you can find them, Jack. That's what I was thinking."

"We figured that when Somchai was out of the way—" Keur began.

"The CIA killed Somchai?" Shepherd interrupted.

"Of course not, Jack," Keur chuckled. "Haven't you heard? The Agency doesn't go in for that sort of thing anymore."

"But I'll bet you still do stunts," Shepherd said. "Fake assassinations? Stuff like that?"

Keur's mouth stretched into something that may or may not have been a smile.

"Charlie told me Adnan arranged the Dubai thing."

Keur said nothing.

"But it wasn't Adnan, was it? It was the Agency."

"Charlie thought that a bit of a show in Dubai would make him look good. We figured it was a dumb idea, but what the hell? It was no big deal."

"Maybe not for you. But it was a pretty big deal for the two dead shooters and the CNN producer who took a bullet in the chest."

"Accidents happen," Keur shrugged.

"The producer may have been an accident, but my guess is you killed the two shooters to keep them from telling anybody that the assassination was a fake staged by the CIA to get publicity for Charlie."

"You don't really think those guys had any idea the Agency was involved, do you?" Keur smiled again and shook his head. "Sometimes we just fuck up, Jack. I hate to admit it, but that's the truth of it."

"I've come too far to walk away," Charlie said, pushing himself to his feet. "Why are you doing this?"

"Jack and his girlfriend have gotten too close. They've figured out too much. It looks like our little project is going to turn to shit and we don't want to be embarrassed by all this."

"I'd think you'd be used to being embarrassed by now," Charlie snapped. "You've sure as hell had plenty of practice."

"We've decided it's better to cut our losses and move on," Keur said, speaking to Shepherd as if Charlie wasn't even in the room. "We're washing our hands off the general."

"What does that mean?"

"It means we're cutting off the general's support. This is the end of the money, the intelligence, the influence, the arms supplies, everything."

"I didn't ask you for any money," Charlie said. "And I damn well didn't ask you for any weapons."

"No, that's right, you didn't. That part was our idea. We thought this might work better if we stirred the pot a little more vigorously than you had the balls to."

Charlie pushed himself away from the table and walked over to the windows. He stared silently out into the compound while Shepherd stayed where he was and tried to get his mind around what he was hearing. Keur sat quietly and said nothing at all.

"Then I guess I'm on my own now," Charlie said after a while.

Keur shook his head. "You're not hearing me, General. It's all over. We've changed our mind. It's as simple as that. We're willing to take our chances with the government Thailand has now. It's time for you to go back to Dubai and play golf."

"I don't answer to you," Charlie snapped.

"Actually," Keur smiled, "you do. We say this is over. So it's over."

"You don't want me for an enemy," Charlie said. "I can do a lot of damage. I know a lot. Don't treat me like some Third World yokel you can send back to the farm when you're tired of him."

"Look, General," Keur said, "you're right about one thing. We don't want you for an enemy. We just want you to walk away. Tell me what you need from us to do that and I'll make it happen."

"I'm not walking away," Charlie said. "I intend to lead Thailand again. I'll do it with or without your help."

Keur shook his head again and sighed heavily. He pushed himself up and walked over to the windows where Charlie was staring down into the compound. He laid one hand gently on Charlie's shoulder.

"Is there *anything* I can do to make this right?" he asked. "Anything I can say to convince you not to fight us on this?"

"You can fulfill your commitment and support me until I'm prime minister of Thailand again."

"That's not going to happen."

"Then I guess there isn't anything you can do. We will be enemies, Mr. CIA errand boy. And there is nothing you can do about it."

"I can think of one thing," Keur said.

LATER, EVERY TIME Shepherd thought back on what happened after that, he felt as if he were watching a movie from which big chunks had been snipped out. There was so much he couldn't remember at all.

For instance, he couldn't remember seeing Keur draw the gun.

One minute Keur was standing at the windows next to Charlie, one hand resting familiarly on Charlie's shoulder. The next minute he had a tiny silver revolver in his left hand.

And the muzzle was pressed against Charlie's temple.

Fifty Eight

"*WHOA, WHOA, WHOA!*" Shepherd shouted.

He jumped to his feet, his hands palms out in the universal gesture of placation.

"What the *fuck* are you doing, Keur?"

Charlie didn't look frightened to Shepherd. He didn't even look all that surprised.

Keur slid his right hand under his shirt and produced the black SIG-Sauer Shepherd had seen back at the apartment in Bangkok. That was when he remembered he had also seen the short-barreled silver revolver in Keur's bag then, too. Keur leveled the SIG at Shepherd without taking the revolver away from Charlie's head.

"Stay where you are, Jack. I'm not your enemy. I'm just a working stiff doing his job."

"You'll never get away with killing me," Charlie said in a voice far calmer than Shepherd thought he could have mustered under the circumstances.

"I'm not going to kill you, General. Jack is. At least that's the way it's going to look."

"That's stupid, Keur. All I have to do is tell them—"

"What makes you think I'm going to leave you around to tell anyone anything, Jack?"

Shepherd was getting angry now and Keur's threat rolled off

him without making any impact. This man had used him to get to Charlie and now he was pointing guns at both of them. He had such a self-satisfied look on his face that Shepherd would have taken a bullet or two just to get close enough to smash the bastard right in the nose.

"You'd kill two people just to cover all this up?" Shepherd asked.

"Heck, we'd be willing to go a lot higher than two," Keur said. "I figure two is a bargain."

"And then you think you're just going to walk out of here?"

"I know I am. I'm a federal agent engaged in the performance of his duty. I have it on good authority that both the Thai police and the FBI will clear me of any wrongdoing in shooting you after you kill Charlie."

"None of this will stand up."

"It probably wouldn't if anybody looked at it too closely, but nobody is. You can count on that."

Keur's attention was entirely focused on Shepherd now. He was enjoying explaining everything to him, telling him exactly how he had brought them all to this moment and what was going to happen next.

Charlie saw his chance. And he didn't hesitate.

Instead of trying to push away the gun Keur had at his temple, Charlie did something much smarter. He dropped straight down and drove the top of his head into Keur's midsection. Keur didn't fire the revolver, realizing he had reacted too slowly to get off an accurate shot. Instead, he swung the SIG that was in his other hand like a hammer. It looped through a half circle and the barrel slammed up into Charlie's head. Shepherd heard the crunch of bones breaking and saw blood spray.

He was no hero, but Shepherd knew their only chance was for him to move right then and he did. Lunging forward before Keur could lift the SIG again, Shepherd grabbed Keur's left wrist with one hand and his right wrist with the other. He pushed Keur's arms up and apart and tried to drive his knee into Keur's groin. But Charlie was in the way. He was on his hands and knees between them, dripping blood from where Keur had clubbed him in the face with the SIG.

They stayed that way for several seconds. Charlie on the floor at Keur's feet; Shepherd holding Keur's wrists and trying to push them upward; Keur trying to pull his arms down. They must have looked like three guys doing a Polish folk dance.

But Shepherd knew the dance was almost over. Keur was stronger than he was, and he could feel Keur slowly gaining the upper hand. So instead of continuing to push against Keur's superior strength, Shepherd suddenly stepped back and pulled.

Keur's arms came down, his knees caught Charlie's back, and he lost his balance. Keur tumbled forward and instinctively reached out with his right hand to break his fall. His fingers opened and the SIG fell from his grasp.

Shepherd snatched the SIG up by the barrel and swung the butt at Keur's face. Keur jerked his head toward it instead of away and Shepherd's wrist hit his ear. The butt of the gun caught nothing but the air.

Charlie was trying to get out of the way, but he was pinned to the ground beneath Keur's lower body. Shepherd shuffled forward and tried to get his knees into Keur's back.

And that was when everything really went bad.

Shepherd was pushing Keur toward the floor with his knees, but he slipped in Charlie's blood and lost his balance. That was the opening Keur needed. He rolled to one side and jerked on Shepherd's legs. Now all three of them were on the floor.

Keur pounded Shepherd in the face with his right fist. At the same time he extended his left arm, the one in which he still held the little silver revolver, until the muzzle was six inches away from Charlie's head. He pulled the trigger twice in quick succession, the double tap of the professional hitman. The shots from the little gun were no louder than the sound of a couple of books hitting the floor.

Charlie made a soft grunting sound, coughed, and died.

Still holding the SIG by the barrel, Shepherd clubbed with the butt toward Keur's face. He heard the satisfying crunch of bone and figured he had gotten lucky, but it didn't seem to faze Keur.

Shepherd could feel Keur's weight coming off him and he knew that Keur was rising up to turn the revolver on him. He fumbled to reverse the SIG in his hand, but he almost dropped it.

He didn't drop it.

Somehow he got the SIG pointed in Keur's general direction, curled his finger around the trigger, and tried to fire. But the trigger pull took more force than he expected and his finger, wet with Charlie's blood, slipped off.

Shepherd heard two more sounds like books dropping, but he felt nothing so he gathered that Keur had fired again and missed. Somehow he got his finger back on the SIG's trigger and jerked desperately at it in exactly the way every gun instructor tells people never to do.

The SIG was right next to Shepherd's ear when he started firing and the sound of the shots were thunderous. He kept jerking the trigger until the slide locked open and he felt, rather than heard, the dry click of the hammer hitting the firing pin. He didn't know how many shots he fired, but it must have been enough. Keur fell back on top of him and Shepherd felt Keur's body jerking as the life poured out of it.

Shepherd dropped the empty SIG and pushed Keur off him. The little silver revolver slipped from Keur's fingers, and he grabbed it up.

IT WAS PROBABLY no more than a few seconds after that before Mutt and Jeff crashed through the door with their guns thrust out in front of them screaming at Shepherd in Thai. But to Shepherd it felt like a couple of weeks.

He had pushed himself up to his knees by then, and he was kneeling there, looking into Charlie's face. He would have checked his pulse, but there was no need. He had no doubt Charlie was dead. No doubt at all.

"Put the gun down, Jack."

It was a woman's voice and it sounded very far away. Shepherd could barely hear it at all over the roar of the SIG still echoing in his ears. But the voice sounded familiar so he twisted his head around to see who it was. Kate was standing in the doorway. Shepherd just stared dumbly at her.

"Put the gun on the floor, Jack."

He was tired, so tired he couldn't keep his eyes from closing. He opened his hand and the silver revolver slid out of his fingers. Then he let his body go, too, and he settled onto his stomach on Charlie's Persian carpet. He thought right after that he heard Kate's voice saying something else, but he couldn't make out what it was.

Shepherd's nose filled with the sugary, cloying odor of blood and he felt consciousness slipping away. The last thing he remembered was looking at Charlie's magnificent Persian carpet. He wondered why he had never noticed before what a vivid shade of red it was.

Fifty Nine

"I'M SORRY, JACK," Pete Logan said. "Really, I am. But I have to place you under arrest."

Pete had shown up in Shepherd's hospital room accompanied by an entire troop of elaborately uniformed Thais, some of them police and some of them military. Shepherd's room looked like the backstage holding area for a rehearsal of the Metropolitan Opera.

"Who are all these guys?" he asked.

"Fucked if I know," Pete shrugged. "I think they're just here to get into the photographs."

"There're going to be photographs?"

"Nope, none." Pete smiled, but only slightly. "That'll fix the little pricks."

Shepherd had only woken a couple of hours before and some guy he assumed was a doctor had told him that he had two bullet wounds. A through-and-through in the lower abdomen and a graze on his right shoulder. Keur had apparently placed the two shots he got off more effectively than Shepherd had realized at the time. He had heard that stress could so load people up with adrenalin that they didn't notice they had been hit by a bullet unless it did some kind of major damage. He had never really believed that before, but he did now.

It was the second time Shepherd had been shot, and the first time hadn't been any fun either. Come to think of it, the other time he had taken a bullet had been in Phuket, too, hadn't it?

Fucking Phuket.

Shepherd made a mental note to kick the crap out of the next person who even mentioned Phuket to him again.

"The FBI is taking jurisdiction over you," Pete said. "We're going to fly you up to Bangkok tomorrow. You'll be held at the embassy while we sort all this out. That's something."

It was indeed something, Shepherd thought. *It was a lot.*

He didn't even want to think what might happen to him in a Thai jail after being found next to Charlie's body holding the gun that killed him. Charlie had quite a few friends and admirers, and not a few of them were in jail.

"How did you manage that?" Shepherd asked.

"I didn't do much. To tell you the truth, I just answered the telephone. The Ministry of Justice called and told me that they were turning you over to us."

"Why would they do that?"

"I hear you're pretty well connected. That probably has something to do with it."

Shepherd just nodded. Kate would have fixed it, of course.

Pete began shooing the troop of Thais out of the room. Since there weren't any photographers around, they left without a fuss. He closed the door behind them and then he pulled a chair over next to Shepherd's bed and sat down.

"Look, Jack, I'm really sorry, but I have to play this straight. I'm going to have to put a couple of guys outside your room tonight and you'll be cuffed for the flight up to Bangkok tomorrow."

"Oh, come on, Pete. You don't really think I had anything—"

"You shot an FBI agent, Jack."

"Keur's dead?"

Pete nodded.

Shepherd didn't ask about Charlie. He didn't have to. He would never forget looking into Charlie's eyes just before he lost consciousness. He already knew Charlie was dead, too.

"Keur wasn't an FBI agent," Shepherd said. "He was CIA."

"That's not true. You asked me to check out Leonard Keur and I did, remember? Keur was an FBI agent attached to the Washington field office. There's no doubt about that."

"Keur was CIA, Pete. The FBI stuff was just a cover."

"That sounds pretty wild to me, Jack. What kind of meds are they feeding you in here?"

"Keur was a clean-up guy for the CIA. He used me to keep him close to Charlie so he could kill him if he had to."

"Why would the CIA want to kill General Kitnarok?"

"Charlie was their front man. The Agency was running an operation to put him in control of Thailand, which would put *them* in control of Thailand. The whole thing was coming apart and they saw themselves going down with the ship. Getting rid of Charlie was the best way to clean up everything. He had become inconvenient."

Pete looked away and rubbed at his eyes, but he didn't say anything.

"What happened to Harvey?" Shepherd asked him.

"Who's Harvey?"

"The plane."

"What the fuck are you talking about, Jack?"

"The 737 loaded with weapons that was landing in Phuket. Kate called it Harvey. It was an Agency aircraft and we think it was bringing a cargo of guns into Phuket to arm the red shirts."

"I don't know anything about that."

"Robert Darling was on it."

"Robert Darling is in Paris. I have a surveillance report on my desk. He's been there for a while."

"That's impossible. I saw him a few days ago in Dubai. He

admitted to me Blossom Trading was a CIA front and that they were flying a load of arms into Thailand for Charlie's people. Tommy was with him."

"Tommy who?"

"Tommerat something-or-another. You know him, don't you? He tells everyone that he's just a deputy spokesman for the Ministry of Foreign Affairs, but he really works for NIA. He's somehow connected with the CIA, too."

Pete looked at Shepherd and cleared his throat. "I'm kind of tired, Jack," he said. "Can we save all this for later?"

"You don't even care what's really going on here, do you, Pete?"

"My instructions are to place you under arrest, then bring you back to Bangkok and secure you at the embassy. And that's what I'm going to do."

"Instructions from who?"

Pete didn't answer him, of course, but Shepherd hadn't really expected him to.

"Charlie died," Shepherd said instead. "He died because I didn't do anything to save him."

"Some people think you may have been the one who shot him."

"Do you?"

"I'm just following my instructions here, Jack."

"To arrest me for shooting Charlie?"

"No, to arrest you for shooting an FBI agent."

"So if I didn't shoot Charlie, who did?"

"I'm just following my instructions," Pete said again.

"I should have saved him, Pete. I was there and I should have saved him."

"What could you have done?"

"I don't know. Something. What good are people if they can't do something for their friends at a time like that?"

"I don't know how to answer that."

"Neither do I."

Charlie was murdered, Shepherd thought, *and I didn't do a damn thing to save him.*

Now Pete was giving him the bureaucratic runaround and it didn't look like he could do a damn thing about that, either.

"Fuck you, Pete. Keur was CIA. He'd been told to kill Charlie if Charlie didn't take a dive for them. I tried to stop him and so he tried to kill me, too. I shot him in self defense with his own gun."

"Then it sounds to me like you have nothing to worry about."

"But you're going to arrest me anyway."

"Yeah, I am. Those are my instructions and that's my job."

Shepherd gave up arguing with Pete. He knew he was wasting his breath.

Sixty

SHEPHERD WAS A little surprised that the facilities at the embassy were so good. It made him wonder how often they did this kind of thing. Somebody had even gotten a few clothes and toiletries together for him.

His room reminded him of a small-town motel somewhere in the Midwest, right down to the orange and brown plaid bedspread and the plastic drinking gasses wrapped up in little cellophane bags. Then there were the two young marines standing guard outside the door with sidearms on their hips who told him he was not to leave the room. That part did not remind him of a small-town motel in the Midwest.

At least he had cable TV so he watched an NBA game on the American Forces Network while he waited for somebody to tell him what was going to happen next. He didn't really mind all that much lying around for a while watching sports on TV. He wasn't all that used to getting shot and he needed the rest.

It was the middle of the second quarter and the Knicks were already down by eighteen when one of the marines opened the door and gave Shepherd a stack of newspapers, a couple of Diet Cokes, and a cardboard bucket of ice. Shepherd told the marine he was kind of hungry, too, and asked him to send up the room service menu, but the kid acted as if he hadn't heard.

The papers were the two English-language Bangkok dailies as well as the *International Herald Tribune* and the *Asian Wall Street Journal*. Shepherd went through all of them carefully but he didn't find a word about Charlie being killed. He wondered if the story had already come and gone while he was in the hospital. He hadn't been in the hospital that long, had he?

He had no trouble coming up with great questions. He just didn't have many great answers. None at all, to tell the truth.

For instance, who the devil was Leonard Keur? Was he really a CIA agent? He had told Shepherd and Charlie he was CIA, but then he had also told Shepherd and a lot of other people that he was FBI. Were either of those things true? Maybe Leonard Keur was really somebody else altogether.

And where did Robert Darling and Tommy fit into everything? Were they Agency, too, or was there somebody else pulling the strings? Somebody else he had never seen a trace of?

Shepherd was absolutely sure of at least one thing. Somebody wanted Charlie dead for refusing to stick to the script. And Keur had used him to set up Charlie.

He had set out to save his friend from a life of notoriety as the man who had started a civil war in Thailand. Instead, he had gotten him killed.

However else he might look at everything, he kept coming back to that.

THE KNICKS WERE down by more than thirty in the fourth quarter when someone knocked politely on the door. Shepherd opened it and an average-looking middle-aged man he had never seen before was standing there. The man identified himself as an FBI agent and handed Shepherd a plastic badge on a chain and told him to wear it around his neck. The badge was a laminated card with a red 'V' on both sides, which Shepherd knew stood for visitor. He took that as a good sign. He supposed it could have been a 'P' for prisoner.

The man escorted Shepherd to the end of the corridor. They made a right and went all the way to the end of another corridor, through a grey steel door, and up two flights of stairs to the second floor. Right at the top there was an unmarked brown laminate door that looked just like most of the other doors in the building. The man opened it without knocking and gestured Shepherd inside. Then he closed the door behind him.

Pete Logan was sitting by himself at a grey metal desk that had nothing on top of it. The room was windowless and the walls were bare other than for a slightly yellowed travel poster bearing a large picture of the Statue of Liberty overprinted with the command, *VISIT NEW YORK!* Right then, that sounded to Shepherd like a really terrific idea.

The only furniture other than the desk and the chair on which Peter Logan sat was a single straight chair, also grey metal, with a black plastic seat. Shepherd gathered that was for him so he sat down on it.

"You hungry?" Pete asked.

"Not really."

"Anything else I can get you?"

"How about a Hendricks martini? Very dry. Shaken, not stirred."

Pete just looked at him.

"You asked if there was anything you could get for me," Shepherd shrugged.

"The doctors say no alcohol for forty-eight hours. Not until the pain killers wear off."

"The pain killers are going to wear off? Oh, shit."

Pete looked away and studied the travel poster with more care than Shepherd thought it merited. After a minute or so of silence,

Peter cleared his throat and shifted his eyes back to Shepherd.

"What the hell is this really all about, Jack?"

So Shepherd told him.

All of it.

Right from the beginning.

Shepherd thought he was a reasonably engaging storyteller, and he figured he had a pretty good story to tell, but he couldn't help but notice that Pete didn't seem all that interested. He just sat there with his arms folded and nodded every now and then, possibly to show he hadn't fallen asleep. It was easy to tell Pete was just going through the motions. It was a lot harder to figure out why.

"That it?" Peter asked when Shepherd finished.

Shepherd nodded.

"Nothing else you want to add?"

He shook his head.

"Okay," Pete said. "Sit tight. I'll be back in a minute."

PETE WAS GONE for no more than five minutes. When he came back into the room, he resumed his seat behind the metal desk and folded his arms.

"I'm sorry to have to do this," he said, "but I've got to read you your rights. Then I'll get somebody to take you back to your room."

"Wait just a goddamned minute, Pete. You ask me to tell you what happened, but you clearly don't give a shit. There's nothing in the papers about Charlie. There's nothing on TV. What the fuck is going on here?"

Pete said nothing.

"Charlie was executed in cold blood. And now you're telling me nothing is going to be done about it?"

"We're doing something. We're arresting you."

"Very fucking funny."

"There were three guys in that room and the other two are now dead. So what do you think I ought to do? Arrest the dead guys?"

"So that's it, is it? I'm the only survivor and somebody's got to take the fall."

"No, Jack. That's *not* it."

Pete made a face like he was smelling week-old fish. But he didn't say anything else.

"Who sent Keur to kill Charlie?" Shepherd asked. "You *know* who sent him, don't you?"

"I'm not going to talk to you about this, Jack."

"You talk to me all the time about things you're not supposed to talk to me about."

"Not things this big."

"So how big *is* thing?"

"The size of a motherfucker."

"You're telling me somebody in the United States government ordered a federal agent to kill a foreign national who had suddenly become inconvenient?"

"I didn't say that."

"The United States government murdered my client because they were afraid he wouldn't keep his mouth shut and we're all supposed to shrug and just forget it?"

"Maybe not everybody, Jack, but *you* are. That's sure as hell what *you're* supposed to do."

"And you think I'm going to do that?"

"I don't know. But I hope so. For my sake, for *your* sake, I hope so."

There was a silence in which they each studied opposite corners of the room for a while.

"What happens now?" Shepherd asked.

"I wish I could tell you."

"So tell me."

"I can't."

"Can't or won't."

"Can't. I really don't know what happens now."

"Still waiting for your bosses to tell you, huh?"

Pete said nothing.

"Good dog," Shepherd said. "Roll over. Can you play dead, too?"

Pete cleared his throat. "Like I said before, I've got to read you your rights. You ready?"

Shepherd started to say something else, but he knew he would be wasting his breath. So he just nodded and Pete Logan started reading him his rights.

They sounded to Shepherd exactly the way they do on television.

Epilogue

FOR THE FIRST couple of days, my detention followed the same unvarying routine. I read the papers. I watched television. And I waited for somebody to come in and tell me what was going to happen to me.

The only breaks in the monotony were my meals in the embassy cafeteria. The evening after my session with Pete, the same FBI agent who had escorted me to Pete's office came back and took me to the cafeteria for dinner. We sat off to one side by ourselves at a big round table that could have accommodated eight people. I tried engaging the man in conversation, but he ignored me. He didn't even eat. He just sat there. Eventually I gave up trying to make conversation and finished my meal in silence while watching CNN on one of the television monitors mounted high up on the wall.

For the next two days we repeated the identical procedure for every meal. At breakfast, at lunch, and at dinner my escort took me to the embassy cafeteria. We sat silently at a big table that was empty other than for us, I had my meal while watching CNN, and my escort took me back to the room when I was done. I wasn't taken to see Pete again, and Pete didn't come to see me.

The third day, however, was different. A lot different.

I was at lunch with my escort. I was eating a cheeseburger and paying very little attention to CNN since I was sick to death of it. They were showing film of some buildings burning somewhere in the world that hadn't even registered with me.

Then all at once it did register with me.

I was looking at Charlie's compound in Phuket. I was watching Charlie's house burn on CNN.

I jumped up from the table and walked over and stood under the monitor so I could hear the sound that went with the pictures. I couldn't hear all of it, but I could hear enough.

"... started from unknown causes around four this morning," an announcer was saying. "General Kitnarok has owned the house for several years and there had been speculation recently that he might be in seclusion there preparing to lead his followers in an uprising against the present Thai government. There is no direct indication at this time whether General Kitnarok was actually in the house when it caught fire, but sources in the American Embassy in Bangkok tell CNN that at least two badly burned bodies have been recovered from the wreckage. Neither of those bodies has yet been identified, but US government forensic specialists are assisting the Thais in their efforts to do so as quickly as possible."

With all that helpful assistance from the United States government, I had no doubt at all that the two bodies would indeed be identified very soon. One of the bodies would turn out to be Charlie, of course. That was easy enough to guess. But who would the other one be? Jack Shepherd perhaps? That would tidy everything up rather neatly, wouldn't it?

It might be neat, but I couldn't believe an ending like that was actually in the cards. Pete Logan might be a loyal bureaucrat, but he was also a good FBI agent. He wasn't the kind of man to stand around doing nothing while somebody killed and buried his old friend Jack in order to cover this whole mess up.

At least I didn't think he was.

WHEN I GOT back to the table, my escort had disappeared and in his place, Pete sat picking at the French fries I had left on my plate. It looked like I was going to find out soon enough what kind of man Pete Logan was.

"These are terrible, Jack."

Pete slathered a French fry in catsup and swallowed it.

"How can you eat shit like this? It'll kill you."

I just looked at Pete.

"Okay, bad choice of words," he said. "Sorry about that."

"You here for any reason other than to eat my French fries?"

"I have a message for you."

I didn't much like the sound of that. The last time I had heard that phrase it had been closely followed by two guys I knew pretty well getting shot.

"From who?" I asked anyway.

"The Prime Minister."

"Which prime minister?"

"The Prime Minister of Thailand, you shit head. You know any others?"

"A few."

Pete ignored me, as well he might have.

"She wonders if you could do her a little favor."

"What kind of a favor?"

"I really don't know. She just said she hopes you might be willing to look into something for her. She asked me to tell you to call her. She said that you have her number. Do you? Have her number, I mean?"

I didn't take the bait.

"It's going to be a little hard for me to do much for Kate while I'm enjoying the hospitality of the embassy, Pete. I wasn't aware you had a work furlough program or I would have already applied."

"Oh, didn't I tell you?" Pete said. "You're free to go. You can leave anytime you want."

"I'm not under arrest anymore?"

"Under arrest? Good Lord, Jack, why would anyone want to arrest you?"

"I see."

Pete said nothing. He even managed to keep his face straight.

"Does my sudden release have anything to do with that?" I pointed to the television monitor on which I had just seen the pictures of Charlie's house in flames and heard about the two bodies the US was trying so hard to help the Thais identify.

"I've got no idea what you're talking about, man."

Pete pushed his chair back and stood up.

"Stay in touch," he said. "Don't be a stranger."

Then he just gave me a little wave and walked away.

WITH MY ESCORT gone, I was left to find my way back to my room on my own. But then it occurred to me there really wasn't any reason to go back there so I just walked straight out to the embassy's front entrance and right up to the marine guard post in the lobby. The young marine on duty collected the visitor's badge from around my neck, tapped briefly at a computer keyboard, and then tossed off a snappy salute. I walked through the main doors, crossed the lawn between the embassy building and the high concrete wall surrounding the compound, and pushed out through the revolving security gate to the street.

It wasn't until I was standing at the curb on Wireless Road that it occurred to me that I had no idea where I was going. I was still trying to make up my mind when a taxi pulled to a stop and the driver leaned over and rolled down his window.

"Taxi, boss?"

I looked at the man, but I didn't say anything.

"Where you want go?" the driver persisted.

Having no better idea, I opened the back door and got into the taxi.

"Where to, boss?"

Animal and man share the same instinct. Hide when you're hurt. Go to ground. Find a place where you'll be safe until your wounds heal.

"You know the Grand Hotel?" I asked.

"Sure thing, boss."

The driver floored the accelerator and shot into traffic.

I SLUNK OFF to the Grand to recover from my wounds when Anita left. I had lived there for nearly six months back then and found it to be a pretty good place for mending. I had a different kind of mending to do this time, of course. Maybe it would be harder. But then again, maybe it would be easier.

I was still wearing the clothes the embassy had given me and now that I was out on the street again I wasn't certain I looked my best in an oversized Hawaiian shirt, jeans, and black Nikes. The last place I had seen the suitcase with my own clothes in it had been at Keur's apartment on Soi Thonglor.

Fuck it. Just one more lost bag in a lifetime of traveling.

First, I'd find a place to buy some clothes. Then after that, maybe I would try to reach Kate. I wanted to thank her for keeping me out of a Thai jail. And naturally I was curious about the message Pete had given me.

Of course, I had no intention of getting involved in whatever Kate wanted me to do. None at all. I'd had enough of Thailand to last several lifetimes. There was no way in the world I was going to let Kate talk me into having any more to do with this screwed up little country, even if she was the prime minster now.

What I had to do was to get serious about looking after myself for a change. My only client was dead and what kind of a lawyer doesn't have any clients? Maybe it was time to go home and think about doing something new.

But where was home? I no longer had a wife. And I didn't have a girlfriend. Or a dog or a goldfish or even a house plant. Come to think of it, I didn't have a house plant because I didn't have a house. I was a middle-aged man living in a borrowed apartment with absolutely nowhere to go and nothing to do.

It was time for me to figure out what I was going to do with the rest of my life. That was what was important now. Not chasing around Thailand after some nonsense for Kate. Even if I did owe her a favor.

Still, I knew I really ought at least to give Kate a call before I left Thailand. That was only simple courtesy to an old friend, wasn't it? And, to be absolutely honest, I really was a little curious about what it was she wanted me to look into for her. Even if there was no way in hell I was going to get involved. Absolutely no way.

Honestly, I was just curious.

THE END

About the Author

JAKE NEEDHAM is an American screen and television writer who began writing crime novels when he realized he really didn't like movies and television very much.

Mr. Needham has lived and worked in Hong Kong, Singapore, and Thailand for over twenty years. He is a lawyer by education and has held a number of significant positions in both the public and private sectors where he participated in a lengthy list of international operations he has no intention of telling you about. He, his wife, and their two sons now divide their time between homes in Thailand and the United States.

Please visit Jake Needham's website at www.JakeNeedham.com for excerpts from his other books or to join his mailing list and keep up to date on his new novels. Read his 'Letters from Asia' at www.JakeNeedham.com/blog for more about the places, the people, and the things that make up Jack Shepherd's world.

OTHER BOOKS IN THE JACK SHEPHERD SERIES

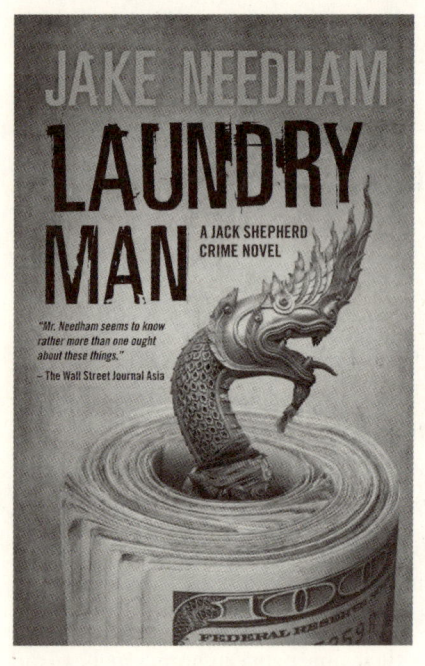

LAUNDRY MAN
ISBN: 978 981 4361 27 9

Once a high-flying international lawyer, part of the inner circle of government power, Jack Shepherd has abandoned the savage politics of Washington for the quiet backwater of Bangkok. Now he is just an unremarkable professor at an unimportant university in an insignificant city. Or is he?

A secretive Asian bank collapses under dubious circumstances. A former law partner Shepherd thought was murdered reveals himself as the force behind the disgraced bank and coerces Shepherd into tracking the money that disappeared in the collapse. A twisting trail of deceit leads Shepherd from Bangkok to Hong Kong and eventually to an isolated villa on the island of Phuket where Shepherd confronts the evil at the heart of a monstrous game of international treachery.

A lawyer among people who laugh at the law, a friend in a land where today's allies are tomorrow's fugitives, Jack Shepherd battles a global tide of corruption, extortion and murder that threatens to engulf both him and the new life he has worked so hard to build.

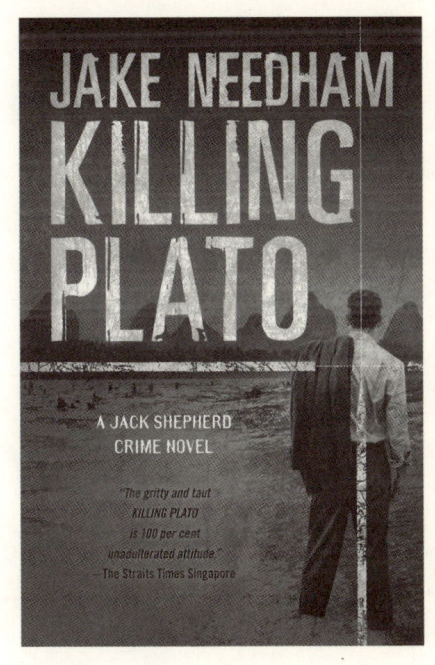

KILLING PLATO
ISBN: 978 981 4361 26 2

Jack Shepherd was a lawyer with friends in high places until he abandoned the fierce intrigues of Washington for the quiet life in Thailand. Plato Karsarkis was a famous financier, a master of the universe, until a New York grand jury indicted him for racketeering, money laundering, and murdering a woman to cover it up.

Now Karsarkis is on the run with the international press in hot pursuit. One day Shepherd walks into a bar on the jet-set island of Phuket and finds the world's most famous fugitive waiting for him.

Karsarkis wants to hire Shepherd to seek a presidential pardon. But the United States Marshals are in Phuket, too, and they want Shepherd to help them arrest Karsarkis. Then Shepherd makes a terrifying discovery that plunges him into a violent spiral of friendship and betrayal and threatens the safety of his personal refuge in Thailand.

The Marshals aren't really in Phuket to arrest Plato Karsarkis at all. They're there to kill him.